Flying Into Limbo

Flying Into Limbo

MARIFRAN DIRKES

To order additional copies of this book, contact:
Xlibris Corporation
1-888-795-4274
www.Xlibris.com
Orders@Xlibris.com

16856-DIRK

This book is dedicated with love and appreciation to Bill, who found me paper and a pencil, and told me to put the words on the page. Thank you, dearest soul mate, for the encouragement to leap, and for the sacrifices you've made along the way. Your faith in me is my safety net, and I am forever grateful.

And to my children, Bill, Jenny, and Annie, who tolerated many "Mommy minutes," and offered me the confidence to call myself a writer. Thank you, dear family, for your gifts from the heart during the seven-year gestation of this book.

Acknowledgements

This book was conceived seven years ago on Mullet Lake, at the home of Aunt Virginia and Uncle John Morris. I am grateful for the privilege of a family vacation in that inspiring setting.

As well, I thank Kym Kuenning and Michelle Young, who slogged through the earlier drafts at the mid-point of this gestation, and offered encouragement and gentle, precise, useful criticism that served as a rudder and a compass.

Diane Shank, whom I knew a lifetime ago, before either of us knew we wanted to write, re-entered my life via a serendipitous and synchronistic encounter at a dinner dance. We shared more than a year of support, friendship, and fun as we formed a very small writing "circle" of two. Diane taught me to analyze and edit to the bone—or to the heart of this story.

David Prem, Hamilton County Assistant Prosecutor, provided crucial legal details, as well as an opportunity to witness the criminal justice system in action. Without David's consultation, the courtroom scenes would have amounted to science fiction or fantasy. Any errors in procedure or process are entirely mine, and may be chalked up to literary license.

Rufus McCall, Administrative Assistant of the Hamilton County Justice Center, provided a first rate, five-star tour of the building that houses local prisoners. Caroline Prem, brave friend and Bunco Babe, accompanied me on the tour, for I wouldn't have dared go alone. Sheriff Simon Leis and his Justice Center Deputies deserve praise for creating an orderly, disciplined milieu, which inspired my awe and ease throughout the tour.

Regina Zimmerman of the Cincinnati Police Department's

Pharmaceutical Diversion Unit offered an early consultation on the first draft of this novel about six years ago. Because of her insightful comments, this book bears little resemblance to what it first appeared to be, and for that I am grateful. Many thanks, as well, to Jim Bertram of the Cincinnati Police Department's Street Corner Unit, who advised me about street slang and related issues.

The late Captain Bill Minturn, beloved friend and United Airlines pilot, provided me with a view of airline life, and important details related to flying a jumbo jet. His wife, Anita Minturn, dearest soul sister and former flight attendant, provided additional information about flight crew staffing processes, as well as Real Life wisdom and encouragement to stay the path of this writing pregnancy.

Joe Rhodenbaugh is the genius who aptly titled this book after hearing a synopsis of the plot—thanks, Joe. I *knew* I'd know the title when I heard it!

Thanks are due to Mike and Rosemary Keiser, who provided the free office space and moral support in which to craft the end of the story. Without a room of my own in which to write, I might have quit the book entirely.

Ms. Sheila Pettersen was the first teacher who ever told me that I could write. Thank you for assigning us themes, and for your encouragement of creative writing.

Miss Virginia Harrod and Ms. Jan Gibson were responsible for disciplining my writing in high school. I pray that I haven't disappointed you. These three tachers influenced me greatly, and I might have pursued a degree in English or Literature, had others not dissuaded me because, "You'll have to get a Master's Degree to get a job, and you'll never make any money." (As if I did not encounter the same, for choosing a career in clinical social work!)

Terri Maue, University of Cincinnati Literature Professor, reviewed this manuscript with a thorough hand and gently worded criticism. I am grateful for the depth to which Terri examined this story, the challenging questions she posed, and the gift she offered by requiring me to "own" the work by answering those questions myself.

Pam Squires reviewed this story for grammar, spelling, punctuation, and overall correctness. Her incisive editing confirms for me that a well-educated, eagle-eyed human tops the computer software every time.

Mark and Kym Kuenning collaborated with my husband, Bill, to create the cover. It required hours of time, expensive equipment, and both technical expertise and an eye for the dramatic. Thank you does not begin to express my gratitude at the eleventh hour efforts to get this out, STAT.

Equal praise is due to the team that proofed galley pages, STAT, turning the work around within three days to expedite the release date of this book: Jane Cohen, Kelly Conway, Jeanette Hutton, David Kohl, Fran Kohl, Kim Kuenning, Barb Luchette, Terry McKay, Anita Minturn, Kathy Raithel, Wease Rhodenbaugh, Kim Bailey Schilling, Kris Schulte, and Diane Shank. Thank you, dear friends, for dropping everything and lending your eagle eyes to create the final product of this book.

This book could not have been produced without the guidance of the Xlibris professionals. Special thanks to Devin D'Andrea, Kim Vangel, Jen Foulk, Jonah Goodman, and Kristina Oberle for their generous recommendations, courtesy, and rapid response in getting this book to print.

Jeanette Hutton is my hearth and home angel who ran errands and tended the house so that I could write in the peaceful fog of the other life I led, watching this story unfold.

Kathy Dobson kept the house from being buried within forests of paper, filing it away such that tax papers were located, prepared, and sent on time.

My parents, Frank and Angie Cassady, my sisters, Kathy Cassady Posdal and Elizabeth Cavanaugh, and my sister-in-law Allison Pick Cassady, read the chapter drafts, and encouraged me to send them *more*, fueling my desire to persevere, and answering tough, fearful questions that shaped the book.

My husband, Bill, prepared dinners and cleaned them up,

and offered computer assistance at critical points. As an anes-thesiologist and twin-engine/instrument rated recreational pi-lot, he also provided medical and avionic consultation (especially regarding flight training, the physics of flying, and the mechan-ics of aircraft response), lending authenticity to the story. Again, any errors within this story are mine, although I have endeavored to present an accurate portrayal of all things medical and avi-onic.

My children, Bill, Jenny, and Annie, called me a writer long before I had the confidence to do so. They tolerated my fugue states, upon emerging from long writing sessions, when I was still "living" within the lives of these characters.

Thank you, dear family, for your loving and generous sacri-fices in the birth of this book.

Prologue

The woman paused to wipe her brow, gazing overhead to locate the source of the whining drone that now sputtered and coughed. Perhaps it was a small aircraft from the nearby field, a student pilot at the controls. She frowned in concern, waiting for the resumption of the engine's steady hum. Would this sacred, peaceful, resting place she so carefully tended become scarred by the high velocity impact of metal and fuel?

"You worry too much," the woman heard, a man's voice.

She breathed deeply with relief as the plane roared back to full throttle, finally emerging over the crest of the hillside, well above the tree line. "You're right," the woman answered. "But you know that's the least of my worries, right now."

"Yes."

She jammed the spade into a box filled with a mixture of potting soil, peat, and manure, scooping a generous portion and dumping it onto the freshly turned dirt. She repeated this twice, and then took a claw-like implement to rake the fibrous loam into the drier, butterscotch clay earth. Odd, she considered, how something so malodorous, so coarse in appearance, nurtured beauty within the flora and fauna of this garden spot.

"*The circle of life . . .*" the other voice hummed. "The grandkids taught me."

The woman laughed gaily, momentarily distracted from her worries. "I'm glad you're paying attention!"

"Oh, I'm doing that," he assured. Moments passed, wordless. Then, he said, "Looks like I'll need to have a talk with our daughter."

The woman was silent, but the man knew her thoughts. That's the way it worked on this side of the gate. She could not read his thoughts. She could not even see him. It was only when he spoke, and only when she was acutely receptive, that the woman heard him. "We had our share of troubles, too," he said softly. "What makes you think they won't come through?"

He studied this woman he had known so many years, reading her thoughts patiently, but flinching as he watched her recall how she'd once thought about quitting their marriage.

Back then, circumstances had sent her spiraling into a dark hole that she'd called hell on earth. Only her anger—and her children's neediness—had kept her alive, fueling her drive to punish the perpetrator of what had seemed a crime against the family.

"I'm sorry," the man said contritely, humbly.

The man believed it important to speak those words of contrition again, although he knew she had long-since forgiven him, and with as much affection as she'd had rage, until their reconciliation.

"It was a long time ago," the woman murmured. She recalled the gift that had accompanied forgiveness was mostly hers, in the form of healing. She had surrendered the control strategies, at that point, opting for faith instead. *Isn't that what we're all supposed to be doing*, the woman wondered?

That leap of faith, so frightening to contemplate because of the control one must cede, had sent her flying into limbo. The journey had been a struggle, and there had been no easy way out. They had faltered, off and on, along the way. Still, when the two had emerged on the other side of that fearsome place, it was with redemption in hand.

"They haven't had the courage to take that leap," the man explained. "And they haven't been tested, until now. It's their choice, whether or not they face their fears, take the plane to the critical angle of attack, and hold on tight to the yoke. They may stall out and end it all in a death spin. Or, like that fella' in the little Cessna over there, they might just grip that yoke, keep the wing pitch vertical, and ride out the fear."

The woman paused from amending the soil to wipe her brow against her shirtsleeve. Squinting into the late autumn sun, she tried to sight the plane again. The noisy aircraft passed the slope, a dark silhouette against the dove gray sky, banking sharply before descending, and then disappearing toward the airstrip on the other side of the ridge. Peeling off her garden gloves, she strolled to the stone ledge for a sip of lime green sports juice. Leaning over the ledge, she spotted one corner of the airstrip below, the small plane barely audible as it floated gracefully onto the asphalt. She lifted the bottle to salute the single-engine Cessna, offering a silent prayer of thanksgiving. The would-be bird was safely landed. Tranquility reigned within this garden of eternal rest, at least for today.

She knew not what tomorrow would bring. Her decision was made, and she might be too ill to plant the spring bulbs by the weekend. *They'll be lovely next March,* she thought, regarding the paper on which she'd sketched a Celtic design in purple, yellow, and white crocuses, ringed with miniature daffodils—the type with bright orange centers.

Will I be here to see them bloom?

"Surrender the details," the man said gently. "What we might initially curse as bad fortune may ultimately be a blessing in disguise."

Blessings, she pondered. *Where were the blessings in any of this?* It was nearly Thanksgiving. Could she talk their daughter into reconciling her marriage before Thanksgiving dinner? *Ah, Jim,* the woman thought, returning to kneel before the freshly amended soil. *It's so good to talk things over with you.* She reached for her gloves, spade, and the bags of bulbs, each clearly labeled. With rapid strokes, she drew out the curves of the Celtic design, forming parallel trenches: one for the crocuses, the other for the daffodils. *Perhaps if I can reconstruct how we got to this point, you'll be able to help me know what to do. I know so little of the details of their story . . .*

Clearly, she hadn't heard his invocation to surrender the details.

. . . but I think it all began last spring . . . .

Chapter One

DRUG DIVERSION

Tuesday, April 2
4:30 PM

The alarm blared from across the bed, shattering the man's otherwise dreamless sleep. John Williams reached from the depths of tousled flannel sheets and sharply slapped the snooze button, the most accessible on his alarm clock. Shaking his head to clear the fog of sleep emergence, he silently wished for a pathologist's schedule, or better yet, a radiologist's schedule—and income.

He reluctantly crawled from the cocoon of covers, rubbing his eyes and temples, and swaying slightly as his body adjusted to the rapid shift in equilibrium, slowly transitioning from horizontal to vertical position. He then navigated eighteen steps across a dense rug covering the plank floor and entered the bathroom. Cool marble tiles awakened his feet, and he blinked in response to the temperature change, more alert now. Five strides to the left placed him before the sink. The hand-painted porcelain fixture was set in a nineteenth-century mahogany sideboard, the latter an estate sale treasure he had discovered in a barn.

At discovery, antique green paint covered the sideboard, and John had lovingly stripped off the paint and refinished the mahogany to its original luster. With the pursuit of this project came relaxation, the final product ultimately a source of immense satisfaction for John. For years, until he stumbled upon an immaculate eighteenth-century William and Mary dining suite, the mahogany sideboard had reigned with honor, a focal point in the combined living and dining room of his med school and residency-era apartment. Once established in medical practice, he and Nancy bought the old stone farmhouse, and the William and Mary dining suite finally had a room befitting its stature. And the beloved sideboard became home to an artist-signed sink bowl and baroque brass fixtures.

Nancy had teased him regarding what she might infer about John's personality, that he would labor over an antique, enshrine it with honor for a number of years, and then desecrate it by gouging a hole in its center and relegating it to the bathroom. In John's opinion, it said nothing about his personality, other than that he was flexible enough to allow for artistic expression in every room of their house.

Tapping on the intricate brass hot lever and swirling shave gel across his jaw, he considered his plans for the remainder of his post-call day off. An anesthesiologist, John was part of a large practice in which each physician was responsible for overnight call once a fortnight. The shift began at 11:30 AM on the "Call" day, and ended at 7:00 the next morning. The on-call doc was then relieved for the day, which sometimes meant that John could visit his favorite antique haunts, or finish a household fix-it project.

Today, however, had been lost to sleep, an effort to recover from a hellacious on-call night. After completing pre-operative assessments for inpatients scheduled for surgery the next day, John and the on-call nurse anesthetist had provided anesthesia for six deliveries, a pair of kidney transplants, and an emergency D & C. In between, John responded to a request for inserting a central line, as well as medication adjustments for three post-op pain patients. Such were his call nights, lately, and the partners deemed John the heir apparent of a legendary black cloud that had previously followed Zac Lyons. A year ago, Dr. Lyons had retired to a life of eight hours nightly sleep and sixteen hours daily leisure: golf, diving, or woodworking.

Today, John would be lucky to accomplish anything. He decided to call the airport and ask if Nancy wanted to fly to Vince's Steakhouse for dinner, only an hour away by plane. Given the sunny April afternoon and the extended daylight of spring, John opted to seize the opportunity for a great meal, with the benefit of adding two hours of flight time to his pilot's log book.

Flying was a newly acquired hobby. While not as mindless or meditative as antiquing or furniture refinishing, flying provided the nearly sacred thrill of ascending from the ground in a burst of power, and then soaring above the rivers, fields, and miniature houses, well beyond the noise of humanity, as if granted the gift of God's perspective. If asked, John would have struggled to label the experience either more a *spiritual* or a *sensual* thrill. Which, he acknowledged, might not speak to his personality, but was perhaps a reflection of his spiritual evolution.

Nancy comprehended as only the air-minded can, having introduced John to the pilot's seat two years ago, his first lesson in a four-seat Piper Archer a gift to celebrate his thirty-fourth birthday. Immediately hooked, John committed the next several months to training in the aircraft whenever he was not at the hospital, weather permitting. His flight instructor, Bob Burke, was a decorated, veteran military pilot who had experienced battle flights in Korea and Vietnam, an eternally youthful man graced with nerves of steel and the patience of Job. John had earned his private pilot license the previous year, and was now training for his instrument rating.

The phone rang, interrupting John's thoughts of dinner and flying. Reluctantly, he shut off the water, snatched Nancy's towel—it was the closest—and toweled off his face and hands briskly before picking up the receiver.

"John, it's Mac. We've got a drug-loss situation that you need to know about."

Mackenzie Franklin was one of John's partners in the fifteen-physician anesthesia practice. She was also a med school classmate and trusted confidante regarding intra-group power battles. She had always been "Mac," at least since medical school. In a rare moment of self-disclosure, she had admitted that abbreviating the family name represented an effort to arm herself in the tough, mostly male medical community.

Yet, Mac was tough enough without the nickname. Gifted with both keen intelligence and dexterous technique, Mac had graduated summa cum laude from Northwestern University. She had finished in the top five percent of her medical school class at the University of Virginia, where she had completed residency and served as a faculty anesthesiologist for two years. Following a marriage proposal by her college beau, who had grown up in the Queen City, Mac had come to Cincinnati in search of practice opportunities.

By then, John Williams had been a member of the group for two years. He had pushed Mac's name to the top of the list of applicants for a position within the practice. The good old boys of the group were reluctant to invite a newly engaged—as in ready-to-make-babies—female physician into their professional family. There had been grumbles about the challenges of a "mommy-track-doc," and allusions to the risk of "raging hormones" within the all-male practice. Yet, Mac's competent presence topped her credentials, and in the end, the anesthesiologists unanimously agreed to invite her to join their practice at St. Catherine's Hospital. That had been five years ago.

"What happened?" John asked. As Anesthesia Department Chairman, Williams was responsible for interfacing with hospital administrators and other medical department directors on a range of issues. Drug diversion was one of them.

"Housekeeping found two syringes, probably narcotic, beneath the phone in the call room. They've made reports with Pharmacy and Security. The VP here knows about it and wants the Drug Diversion cops involved. You should know," Mac added tentatively, "Your name came up. You were on call last night. They're idiots to even suspect you, but . . . ."

"Shit, if I'd had time to even think about going to the call room last night, I wouldn't have wasted today sleeping!" John roared. He ran his hand through his dark, sleep-ruffled hair, then sighed heavily, apologetically.

"Mac, I'm sorry. I know you're just the bearer of bad news."

"Yeah. Well, they took a look at the anesthesia records for last night and figured you probably wouldn't have had time to get to the call room. Someone from the Drug Diversion Unit will want to talk with you, though. Since you're the usual liaison, they may want someone else to investigate on our end. Just be prepared for their questions. Gotta' go get the twins at my mother-in-law's. Call me later, okay?"

"Right," John agreed, as he set down the phone. He realized suddenly that the mental fog was gone, thanks to the adrenaline surge that still had his heart racing. It did not seem possible that one of the docs in his group would steal narcotics. Yet, Fentanyl thefts—if it *was* Fentanyl—were not uncommon in hospitals and outpatient surgical centers.

Fentanyl was an inexpensive, frequently used anesthetic agent, a narcotic that had a rapid onset and short duration. Consequently, patients experienced pain-relief quickly, without the hangover-effect that accompanied longer-acting anesthetics. Fentanyl was extremely addictive, popular among drug-addicted medical professionals because of its quick high. In addition, the short duration of the drug permitted the addict to function without appearing impaired—until the addiction progressed to the point at which drug-craving desperation superseded rational behavior. It was at that critical juncture that most addicts were identified.

But, *was* it Fentanyl in the syringes? John Williams would have to wait for confirmation, but as he contemplated the essentials, he concluded that the thief had to be a doc. The nurse anesthetists had their own call room. A transient paranoid thought crossed his mind. Was someone trying to set him up? Should he contact his lawyer? The consequences of being accused were substantial, even terrifying. He could be suspended from practice during an investigation. Physicians who stole drugs, or those who used any drug recreationally, often lost the license to practice medicine, *in addition* to any punishment doled out by the jurisprudence system.

John felt confident that he could account for every minute

of his time, and that his innocence would become obvious to all who were in a position to threaten his hard-earned license. He had done nothing wrong. Now, it was important to focus on finding who *was* responsible—criminally responsible.

He folded Nancy's towel, still deep in thought, returning it to the rack and then snagging his burgundy robe from a nearby hook. As he slid his arms into the sleeves and tied the belt in a perfect square knot, he wondered, *Who needs to know about this?* Or more importantly, *Should any others know about this, if they don't already?* The culprit might have been tipped off today, if Security and Pharmacy Directors were conferring in the Anesthesia offices.

John quickly lifted the phone receiver and dialed Mac's cellular phone.

"Dr. Franklin," Mac barked.

"Mac, I need to know who is up to speed on this issue—careful what you say on your phone. If Security and Pharmacy were conferring in our offices, they may have tipped off the thief, presuming that it's someone in our group. We need to keep this quiet, especially within the group, if one of us is a suspect." John paced the length of the bedroom as his thoughts raced ahead faster than he could speak. "Do you understand my concern, Mac?" he asked earnestly, pointedly.

"Yes," she answered bluntly. "Call me at home. I'll be there in fifteen minutes, max."

Mac was all business, and John knew that she would not discuss it with anyone else. He guessed that, given the time of day, she was pressed for time, and had to pick up the twins at Grandma's house. The drug diversion query must wait.

John quickly grabbed a change of clothes from his Georgian highboy and retraced the eighteen steps to the bathroom. He flipped on the exhaust fan and walked to the corner of the room, where a beveled glass shower enclosure took up sixteen square feet of the room. Once again grabbing Nancy's bath towel from the nearest bar, a bad habit he'd promised to break, John turned the brass shower lever to HOT, dropped the robe, and let the steam engulf him. He sighed, gulping the steam in deep breaths. Still, the question circled.

Who the hell was pirating narcotics?

5:00 PM

Marilyn and a man named Mr. Stewart had just arrived. Drew Martin watched in silence as they ministered to his wife, Kathy. Mr. Stewart said little as he started the intravenous line, and then injected a small amount of medication into the tube's portal. He instructed Marilyn regarding the dosage, and advised Drew that Kathy would probably sleep most of the next day, about twelve to fourteen hours, as she had the last time.

Drew nodded, and then admitted that he had not been aware of the treatment shift. Mr. Stewart looked sharply at Marilyn, who simply nodded at Kathy. A look of fear replaced the worried furrow, as Drew noticed the odd exchange.

Mr. Stewart noted Drew's distress, and offered a reassuring smile with the promise to return the next evening to discuss the treatment in depth. "You recall how rapidly your wife responded last time," Mr. Stewart reminded Drew. "This medicine can only help her."

5:10 PM

John Williams emerged from the shower to the cacophony of the snooze alarm and what was probably Mac's return phone call. He took care to tap the proper shut-off button on the alarm just as the answering machine was picking up. It was Nancy, not Mac.

"Hi, Captain," he greeted his wife. Nancy, a First Officer rather than an airline Captain, was the third generation of aviators in her family. At the age of sixteen, she had earned her private pilot license, and following graduation from Purdue University's Aviation program, she'd begun flying for Wright International Airlines. She had been flying the Cincinnati to London route until she and John were married seven years ago. She then bid for Eastern domestic routes to lend a margin of sanity to their over-scheduled professional lives. On days that she was off but John was on call, Nancy liked to hang out at Blue Ash Airport, a small airfield which housed two hangars, a couple of small air businesses, and several dozen privately owned single- and twin-engine aircraft. Formerly a single-engine flight instructor, Nancy now bartered Wright International Airline's travel coupons for the use of a small airplane.

"So, how about getting some hours in your logbook?" she teased.

"You read my mind," John countered.

An edge lingered in his voice, which Nancy noted without comment.

"I'm waiting for a call from work," he continued. "I'll tell you about it later. If I can reach Mac now, I'll be at Blue Ash in half an hour, say by 6:00?"

"Let's make it Montgomery Inn if it'll be any later. Tomorrow's an early work day for you, Doc."

"Yes, Mom," John agreed in a pseudo-exasperated tone.

John clicked the off button and dialed Mac's home number. She answered on the fourth ring, more relaxed than earlier.

"Sorry to rush off the phone earlier. My mother-in-law has the kids until our nanny gets back from her annual vacation. Thank goodness tomorrow is Friday—for both of us!" Mac chuckled softly, and clucked a word of warning to Abby and Josh, her two-year-old twins, who were prepared to dive into a bag of Oreo cookies before supper.

John interrupted apologetically, "Mac, I know your kids are starved and you're trying to make dinner. I won't keep you long, but I'm wondering who in our group is aware of the diversion. I don't want to tip off whoever is taking this stuff."

"No problem, John," Mac assured him briskly. "I know only because I was in the office getting pager batteries. The Director of Pharmacy was there with the Chief of Security and Stu. The secretary was at lunch, so she probably hasn't heard. The only people in the group who know about it are you, Stu Adler, and me."

Adler was the group's Board President. In his early sixties, he was the elder statesman of the anesthesia docs, personable and diplomatic by nature, and a gentleman in all encounters. Without an arrogant bone in his body, Stu was widely admired throughout the hospital community for both his professional skill and personal warmth.

"Any idea who's involved?" John asked.

"Not a clue," Mac replied. "It doesn't seem possible that *any* of our docs would be using narcotics. And if someone else put those syringes in the call room to cast suspicion on one of us, there'll be hell to pay."

"I'm more concerned about how this may have affected patients," John interjected. "Have the drug kits been checked?"

Everyone in the operating room knew the routine for handling drug kits. The Pharmacy Department was responsible for putting together drug kits that varied only because one surgical procedure might require different medications than another. Each time an OR was set up, the specific drug kit would include every pharmaceutical that would be needed for the case. However, a commonality among the drug kits was the inclusion of Fentanyl and Limbotryl, narcotics used in nearly every surgery. These kits were labeled with the names of the patient, surgeon, and anesthetist assigned to the case. The anesthetist was responsible for noting the dosage of each medication used, and the anesthesia record represented the primary document for tracking controlled substances. After surgery, the remnants of each drug in the kit and a copy of the anesthesia record were returned to the Pharmacy. There, two pharmacy technicians verified that the anesthesia record corresponded with the full, partial, or empty vials returned. Typically, the accounts matched, and any unused narcotics were then poured down the drain, each technician a witness for the other.

If, however, there were discrepancies between the anesthesia record and the drug kit, the Director of Pharmacy would be notified, and an interdepartmental investigation would ensue to determine if there had been a diversion, or merely inexcusably sloppy documentation. Both scenarios were considered to be se-rious and, in the past, had resulted in either legal charges or job termination for nurse anesthetists and anesthesiologists.

The system was considered fairly effective. Just the previous year, a nurse anesthetist had been caught stealing Fentanyl two weeks into her employment. St. Catherine's Security Director had contacted the Cincinnati Police Department's Pharmaceuti-cal Diversion Unit, which handles several hospital-based drug-loss cases each month. Within twenty-four hours, CPD-PDU had obtained a confession, and immediately arrested the nurse at work. The members of this large anesthesia group, fifteen docs and thirty nurse anesthetists, breathed a collective sigh of relief and prayed that the news would not make the evening paper. It did not, and the deity that protects the reputation of St. Catherine's Hospital was dutifully praised by all who stood to lose.

"Of course the drug kits were checked," said Mac, clearly irritated by John's question. "There's no reason to think that pa-tients didn't get the meds they were supposed to. There weren't any reports about patients complaining of extraordinary pain or being awake during surgery."

John closed his eyes. Mac, his trusted confidante, did not understand his concern. Or how personally he experienced the threat of accusation that *he* was responsible for the syringes found in the call room. "Okay, the kits were checked. But what about testing some of the kits from yesterday?"

"The kits from yesterday's surgeries weren't retrievable, and Pharmacy wants a meeting to discuss random checks," replied Mac, who was obviously relenting about the Oreos with her hun-gry pre-schoolers. A backwards dinner, dessert first, never killed anyone. "What I suspect is that whoever is taking the drug, and I'll bet it's Fentanyl, is using partial doses, then adding saline to make the syringe appear full. It's more likely that some patients were given diluted Fentanyl than any other scenario. We would have seen patients with other problems if saline had replaced the entire syringe of either Limbotryl or Fentanyl."

John considered this briefly. Mac was right, of course. A patient undergoing surgery requires about five carefully titrated drugs to induce anesthesia, and that just gets the patient off to sleep. The narcotic is an essential player in anesthesia: it keeps the patient from experiencing pain during surgery. Too little narcotic and the patient's vital signs indicate distress. An increased heart rate is just one indicator. Sometimes, the patient may actually stir during surgery, another indication to deepen the anesthesia. Had a patient failed to respond when dosed, a red flag would have been launched.

"Let's keep this to ourselves, Mac, and keep our eyes open. Whoever it is will make a mistake sooner or later."

"What about the Board of Directors? Will you let them know?" queried Mac, aware that doing so meant risking tipping whoever was lifting the narcotic—IF it were a doc.

John exhaled deeply, pondering the same issues as Mac. The cast of the Board included Stu Adler, the group's President; Dean Philips, Secretary; Marty Devereaux, Treasurer; John Williams as the Anesthesia Medical Director, and Ron Albers, whose board-officer-at-large position was designed to function as a tie-breaker in close votes. None of them seemed a likely suspect, in John's estimate, and keeping this type of information from the tightly knit group on the Board would be viewed as a statement of suspicion, and a dereliction of the partnership trust. "Yeah, the full Board should be advised. I'll call the Director of Pharmacy and the Director of Security and see what we can do to track the narcotics that aren't used during a case. And, I guess I'll be talking with the PDU cops about this."

"Keep me posted," Mac said. "My guess is that it's not one of us, but I can't explain how the syringes wound up in the call room."

"Let's hope you're right," John replied.

He replaced the phone gently in the cradle. The calls to Security and Pharmacy could wait until tomorrow. He would also track down an OR nursing schedule to determine who was working yesterday, all shifts. The syringes were found in the anesthesia call room, and only anesthesia personnel had keys to the office, which housed the pair of call rooms. The nurse anesthetist who had been on call with John had been just as busy last night, and neither of them had been granted time for a few winks in either the nurses' call room or the docs'. *So who managed to get in,* John wondered?

It was nearing six o'clock, and John quickly pulled on a pair of Dockers and a button-down oxford cloth shirt. He then dashed back into the bathroom to comb down his damp, dark, wavy hair, silently counting one hundred seconds as he ran a toothbrush across his gums.

He tripped lightly down the front staircase, stopping to grab his black flack jacket and flight bag from the foyer closet. Although essentially a neat person, John would never be considered compulsive, and his flight bag proved it. A tangle of cords sat atop several flight maps, his logbook, and a reference book of U.S. airports.

"Everything's here," John muttered, taking quick inventory of the bag's contents, and then slinging it over his shoulder, still unzipped and bursting with paper and gadgets. He walked briskly from the front hallway, through the great room, and into the kitchen, barely breaking his stride as he swung open the door to the fridge, yanked a can of diet cola from its plastic noose, punched the alarm code into the keypad, and exited to the garage, its heavy door opening at the a tap of the button.

The evening light slanted into the garage, a band that widened as the door rose with a grinding complaint. Thus illuminated, John's red BMW convertible looked less sporty than usual, with mud splatters that stretched from the tire walls to the lower third of the side windows. He mentally added a trip to the carwash to his to do list for tomorrow.

In a fluid motion, he swung open the car door, and flung the flight bag onto the front passenger seat. With a flick of the wrist, the engine purred to life. John backed the car without looking, snapping open the tab on the pop can and gulping a generous swallow before checking the rearview mirror. Shifting smoothly into first gear, he noted the newly blossomed crabapple trees that lined the lane, a white floral canopy that stretched from the house to the street. Spring had finally arrived.

It reminded him that he and Nancy were due for another trek through the miles of walking trails at Redbird Hollow, the local nature treasure. They hadn't had a chance to welcome the spring flora and fauna that sprouted there, having last hiked several weeks ago when it was snow-covered, and the proverbial winter wonderland. Maybe they would get in a hike this weekend, John mused.

By 6:20 PM, John was pulling into a parking space at Blue Ash Airport. He grabbed his flight bag, and jogged across the lot to the tidy, pale brick aviation building. Inside, an unmanned counter to the left offered flight maps, books, and enticements to learn to fly. Danny, the jack-of-all-trades who scheduled flight lessons, sold aviation maps and equipment, and fueled or towed planes to the tie-down area, was probably outside.

To the right was a seating area, furnished in cracked-but-comfy vintage vinyl. Against the back wall stretched a map of the United States, an elastic cord anchored on Cincinnati, Ohio. A pilot could determine distances by stretching the cord to the destination of choice, and then to a ruler of sorts that indicated distance in nautical and linear miles. A steel desk was backed against the far right wall, bearing only a phone, complimentary scratch pads from sales reps, and a cup of pens. Here, pilots would file flight plans and call for weather briefings.

From the open waiting room, the building telescoped narrowly to an anteroom, also furnished in vintage vinyl and steel. Broad windows offered sweeping views of the landing strip and taxiways. To the left was a doorway that led to the tarmac, the actual door propped open to let in the breeze on this unusually warm spring day. To the right were the newer leather-look furnishings. Nancy uncurled herself from the sofa, and grinned in greeting as she met her husband.

Of Irish descent, Nancy Cavanaugh Williams was a dark haired, blue-eyed, fair-skinned beauty, lean as a marathoner, although gardening or skiing represented her workouts of choice. "I was just bragging about how you're going to fly me tonight," Nancy said with a wicked grin, enjoying the double entendre as she wrapped her husband in a bear hug and pecked him briskly on the lips.

John returned the grin. "Hold that thought, Captain. Is there time enough to go to Vince's?"

"Sure," agreed Nancy, patting his backside playfully. "Sunset is around 8:30, so you can even practice a nighttime landing on the return flight."

"I'll get the 'Four' and file the flight plan. We'll be out of here in fifteen minutes." John dropped off the flight bag and exited to the tarmac. Danny was towing a sleek King Air 350 into the hangar adjoining the aviation building. John waved a greeting. "We're taking the 'Four' tonight, Danny. Is it fueled?"

"Yeah," assured Danny. "Nancy bugged me to have it ready when Bob Burke came in from a lesson. You oughta' take off Wednesdays like normal doctors. Fly a little. You'll be retired before you have enough hours for your IFR rating, at the rate you're going."

John waved him off with a good-natured smile. The guys who worked or hung out here lived to fly. They worked second jobs to finance their expensive sport, and none of them understood why this doctor, with his reasonable work schedule and financial resources, did not spend every spare moment in the air. Danny, in particular, persistently ribbed John about how long it was taking to earn his instrument flying rating, abbreviated by fliers as IFR.

John crossed the tarmac to the tie-down area where small aircraft were covered and harnessed to the ground. The 'Four,' so designated because of the number it seated, was a single-engine Piper Archer owned by the Aerophiles, a local flying club that had a membership of about thirty pilots. John had joined the club when he made the commitment to learn to fly, and the 'Four' was the plane in which much of his instruction had taken place.

After removing the cover and releasing the harness clips, John proceeded to complete the visual walk around inspection. He lifted the flaps on each wing, checked the rudder at the back of the plane, the propeller at the front, and the pitot static tube—which must be unobstructed to measure altitude—located beneath the left wing. With the inspections completed, he filed the flight plan, and returned to the aircraft with Nancy to prepare for take-off.

He forced himself to remain focused on pre-flight details. Once they were airborne, there would be plenty of time to tell Nancy about the drug diversion. Headset plugged in, John briskly snapped the GPS cord into the electrical supply, mentally anticipating the cross-country excursion. He tapped in the data which would allow him to know exactly where he was at any moment during the flight, and flipped open the plastic-coated, spiral-bound checklist, the required "to do" list before takeoff. John reviewed each item precisely, very much the way he would review his anesthesia equipment and medications before surgery. This type of detail was familiar. Check, check, check, and check. They were ready to roll.

Pushing the throttle forward, John inched the 'Four' onto the access road leading to runway two-four. He applied the brake and stopped short of the runway to complete the final run up.

"Flaps up ten degrees, fuel pump on," he murmured, ticking off several other required pre-flight checks. Done. They were ready to fly. "Blue Ash traffic, this is November seven-seven-seven Alpha-Zulu ready to take the active on two-four."

John thus identified his aircraft by tail number, notified other pilots in the area that he was ready to taxi and take off, and that others would have to yield to him for use of runway two-four, the number indicating its directional heading of two hundred forty degrees. It was not a perfect system of communication, yet it worked fairly well for a small airport that had no control tower.

John released the brake, and again nudged the throttle forward, rolling onto the runway, and turning right to center the plane on the black ribbon of runway. Thus aligned, he steadily pushed the throttle forward, watching both the speed and oil pressure gauges. He allowed the plane to race forward, and when the speed indicator reached sixty-two knots, John pulled back firmly on the yoke. In a heartbeat, the plane lifted its nose, and then its body, the ensuing weightlessness delivering a visceral pleasure to both pilot and passenger.

At five hundred feet, John clicked off the fuel pump button and banked west toward Indiana. The sun beamed well above the cloudless horizon, still bright at the supper hour. While it was easier to fly with the sun at one's back, providing the advantage of a clear view without the blinding dazzle, John willingly squinted into the glare as he enjoyed the sharp contrast between land and sky, a break from the usual haze that obscured the patchwork crazy quilt of farmland a state away.

As the small plane hummed toward its cruising altitude of eight thousand feet, John broached the topic that had rumbled within his thoughts since the first phone call.

"Mac called this afternoon," he said to Nancy. "There were two syringes of narcotic found in the call room last night—not that *I* ever got to the call room with everything that went on."

Nancy stared hard at her husband. "How'd they get there?" she inquired, clearly caught off-guard, although she had picked up the tension in John's voice when they'd talked on the phone earlier.

"Don't know yet," John responded, "But Security and Pharmacy toyed with the idea that *I* did it until they looked at the anesthesia log and realized that I didn't even have time to pee, much less go to the call room last night."

"How do you think the syringes got there?" Nancy asked, on the alert. "The nurse anesthetist?"

"Doubt it," he replied hesitantly. "The call nurse was Brad Klein, and he is as straight an arrow as there is, and he's almost anal about the way he manages his drug kits. Besides, he was up running around all night, too."

"What's going to happen?" Nancy asked, hoping for a clean bottom line, aware that she was wishing for the moon. She shivered involuntarily, recalling the angst of last year's drug incident, which culminated in the arrest, and subsequent firing of one of the other nurse anesthetists in John's group. The days preceding the arrest had been as tense as flying the 'Four' in a thunderstorm. Just as the single-engine plane was not designed to fly in severe weather, John Williams was not cut out for the subterfuge arranged by hospital security, in cooperation with the Cincinnati Police Department's Pharmaceutical Diversion Unit. The strategy had included placing undercover cops in the OR, telling a series of white lies that allowed the nurse anesthetist's thefts to be "discovered," and essentially walking a fine line between fact and fiction. It had all been completely legal, although the shades of gray had nipped at John—and Nancy—Williams' consciences.

Thankfully, the anesthetist had been hired only a week before the first drug loss was discovered. Days later she had been arrested. None of the patients she'd anesthetized had suffered adversely, and both the hospital and John's group were spared public humiliation by the media.

Still, the situation had taken a serious toll on the couple's sleep and appetites. They'd both suffered. John wasn't an actor, Nancy knew, and he preferred the clear-cut black and white of life to its complex shades of gray. For Nancy, the possibility that this scenario might be replayed created gastric instability; much the way turbulence affects the uninitiated flier.

John interrupted Nancy's unpleasant reverie. "What's next is that I'll be on the phone first thing tomorrow with the Director of Security and the Director of Pharmacy, probably the hospital VP, too, since he's been advised of the situation." John glanced over at his wife, reading the fear clearly telegraphed via her expressive face. "Hopefully I won't be the one pulled into the game this time. Stu Adler knows about the situation, and he'll handle it as much as possible. Stu is both diplomat and thespian. If the Drug Diversion team needs to create some fiction, they'll work through Stu. He'll be better at it than I am." John reached to squeeze Nancy's knee. He grinned as he assured, "I can talk Stu into handling it, and he'll be the one losing sleep this time, Captain. Besides, our personnel isn't involved—at least that's what Mac and I think—so this'll be someone else's headache."

Nancy smiled faintly in response to her husband's reassurance, not at all certain that John would be spared. "Will you call the police drug unit? And do they really suspect *you*?" Nancy asked. Her eyes flashed with indignation. At once, Nancy's eyes were her best feature, and her quickest betrayer; luminous glints of sapphire, aquamarine, and emerald.

Flashing crystals met with earnest intensity, as their eyes made contact. "I'll be in touch with the PDU cops, but you know, Nancy," John stated confidently, "Anyone who knows me, also knows that I didn't hide two syringes in the call room. Remember the PDU investigator I worked with last year, Barbara Westover? She'd laugh at anyone who seriously suspected me. We don't need to call in the lawyers."

Nancy nodded briskly, and then broke eye contact as she pointed to the Loran distance indicator on the instrument panel. "Almost dinner time." They were thirty miles from Muncie Airport, home of one of the premier airport-based restaurants. Vince's Restaurant prepared steaks that were the rave of tri-state pilots, and John and Nancy Williams had been almost weekly customers while John was earning his private pilot license. Of course, they would save the red wine until post-flight, at home. It was a small sacrifice to enjoy the freedom of the sky.

The couple remained silent for the last part of the flight, each preoccupied in thought. John surveyed the residential landscape below them, relieved to have shared the news. Still, the question streamed through his consciousness, like a turbulent river at full crest. *Who is stealing narcotics?*

Chapter Two

INVESTIGATION

Wednesday, April 3
7:45 AM

"Dave Johnson," barked the voice at the other end of the line.

"Good morning, Dave. I heard about the diversion and wanted to call you first thing this morning." John Williams was speaking with the Director of Security for St. Catherine's Hospital. They had collaborated the year before, and had a good working relationship.

"When can you stop in, John? I'd rather not talk about this on the phone." Dave Johnson was a cautious man and liked the opportunity to read people as he spoke with them.

"I've arranged coverage so I'll be free for the next half hour. How about now?" John inquired.

"See you in a few minutes," Dave agreed.

Clicking off the cellular phone, John snatched the scrub cap from his head and jammed it into his pocket. He punched the button to call the elevator, and was rewarded when the door opened instantly.

The Security Office was located on the third floor of the hospital, a bit of a hike from the OR area. John hoped that a half hour would be enough time to make the round-trip, and fill in the blanks, or at least have some of his own questions answered.

He'd need to return to the OR area to relieve the nurse anesthetists for breaks.

The day was unfolding briskly. He'd arrived at 6:15 AM, with plenty of time to change into the medium blue scrub wear that both defined and limited OR fashion. At 6:30, he'd met with the group's Board of Directors, who had already been briefed about the drug diversion by Stu Adler. Stu had instructed them to keep the information private, to avoid alerting the perpetrator, and to be vigilant in the OR. Clearly shaken, all present had adopted a low-level paranoia, determined to safeguard their drug kits, and to notice the slightest irregularity.

John had then checked the surgery schedule for the day, noting both his room assignments and the nurse anesthetists he'd be working with. Next, he had completed the three pre-operative evaluations on newly arrived patients having same-day surgery: a hernia repair in OR3, a local-stand-by breast biopsy in OR4, and a knee-replacement in OR8. He wrote pre-operative orders, and discussed all three cases with the anesthetists assigned to manage their respective patients, following induction.

It was the policy of John's group to have the physicians present during anesthesia induction, brief but critical moments when things can go wrong. Today's patients were reasonably healthy, and the surgeries were essentially straightforward. Once the patients had been induced, John had arranged for another doc to cover the rooms while he met with the Director of Security. Having a group of fifteen docs afforded this flexibility.

Arriving at Dave's office door, John knocked to announce his presence.

"Right here, John," called Dave from down the corridor. He had a cup of coffee and a banana muffin from the hospital cafe. "Got here too early to eat breakfast until now," he explained, lifting the coffee for a quick sip. "Heard you had a busy night."

John was direct. "I never got to the call room that night, and I am as ready as you are to find out who's responsible. It's not me."

Dave nodded, slowly chewing his muffin. His eyes took in John

Williams' countenance, appearance, and gestures. Dave's invisible antennae sensed John's emotional state, as well as intangible aspects of personality that more fully represented the individual across the table. A twenty-year veteran of the Alcohol, Tobacco, and Firearms Bureau, Dave Johnson had retired from this branch of the Treasury Department with a federal pension and the opportunity to use his abilities in a less lethal environment.

He had served as Director of Security for ten years, and intended to put in another five before retiring, at age sixty, to his condo in Vero Beach, Florida. Dave didn't *really* suspect John Williams of secreting narcotics, if that's what the syringe held; the test results weren't back yet. Still, over the course of many years, Dave refused to overlook any possibility. He had completed the human experience course entitled 'Burned Once, Twice Suspicious.'

"Any ideas about how it got there?" Dave asked, still nodding.

"No." John sustained eye contact, not blinking. He waited, holding his position, tolerating the pause that lengthened to the point of challenge.

"Housekeeping has a key to the Anesthesia Department offices," Dave said, his steady gaze unyielding. "Anybody else outside of your people?"

"Only the anesthesia techs," replied John. The anesthesia techs were hospital employees, hired, paid, and directly supervised by St. Catherine's Operating Room nurses, not by the anesthesia group. Their function was to keep the operating room stocked with equipment such as endotracheal tubes, syringes, and bags of intravenous fluids.

"The syringe could have been left the day before you were on call, even the day before that," Dave postulated. He licked his fingers after popping the last piece of muffin into his mouth. "We have no way of being sure when it was left."

"What about fingerprints?" John asked.

"Not a chance. Too many people have handled it. Doug Howard has it now," Dave stated, referring to the Director of Pharmacy. "Any ideas about who we might check out?"

John shook his head. "I can't imagine anyone in this group who'd be using drugs, or anyone who'd be careless enough to leave a narcotic-filled syringe in the call room."

"Let's consider that possibility," pounced Dave. "When someone finishes a case, is it possible that he might put something into the pocket of his lab coat? Maybe during a distracted moment?"

"It happens," acknowledged John. "What I'd like to do is check over the drug kits later this evening—I'll be here late since I was post-call yesterday. No one will be around, so I can do it quietly. I guess we'd both prefer to keep this quiet."

Dave was quick to agree. "Give a man enough rope, he'll hang himself."

John smiled, with the reminder, "It could just as easily be a woman."

Dave nodded in silent agreement. "You've been working with the people in your group for several years now. Who do you think we could take a look at, at least in terms of tracking their drug kits?"

John leaned forward to make his message clear. "Dave, I don't think *anyone* in this anesthesia group uses narcotics recreationally. I also can't imagine any one of our people being sloppy enough to leave a narcotic-filled syringe in the call room."

Dave Johnson sipped his now-lukewarm coffee, pondering how much to tell about what had been discovered.

John seemed to read Dave's mind. "The thing that bugs me is that whoever did this wasn't just sloppy. Mac told me that the syringes were found beneath the phone in the physician call room. It sounds like someone wanted to get rid of them quickly, so they wouldn't be caught with them. Or maybe to cast the group in bad light, but that seems like a stretch."

Dave opened his palms in a helpful gesture. "I'll join you to check out the kits later this evening. Let's see what we find. If this is more than a case of someone accidentally leaving the OR with a syringe in his—or her—pocket, we can think about calling in the Pharmaceutical Diversion Unit. They handled that problem last year in a first-class manner. They may also be able to help us narrow the field, whether we look within your group or broader. There are a lot of people in the OR. And we still need the report on what was actually in the syringes. Maybe it's not narcotic."

John stood up to leave. "Right. I'd appreciate the help tonight. There are a lot of kits to go through—reminds me of how much we need the automated record-keeping system."

Dave barked a laugh of consensus. "That would help. But I know plenty of places that have one in place. It doesn't prevent drug diversion, but makes it harder for addicts to hide."

"Well, I'll page you when I finish up," John stated.

"Good enough," Dave assented.

John walked back to the elevator, checking his watch to affirm that he was on time for break relief. It would be a full day for him. The post-call docs, who were either off or early-out yesterday to recover from being on-call, stayed late today. They would not leave until the on-call doc and second-call doc could manage the OR cases still going. This meant that John would not leave the hospital until 6:00 or 7:00 PM—or later. He and Dave Johnson would have plenty of opportunity to check the drug kits that had been used today, collected for review by the Pharmacy Department.

Pharmacy. John reminded himself to call Doug Howard. Reaching into his lab coat pocket, which he wore over his scrubs whenever leaving the OR area, John lifted his cellular phone and asked for Doug's direct line.

"Doug, this is John Williams. I was wondering if you would have time tomorrow afternoon to meet with me. I thought we might take a look at reviewing certain drug kits, and look for any problems that would help identify whoever left that 'present' in the call room."

"I was thinking the same thing," replied Doug Howard. "How about 2:00?"

"That works," agreed John. "Also, Dave Johnson and I would like to check today's drug kits this evening. I'd like to see if there's any pattern of unusual narcotic use within our group, or anything that might help us identify someone specifically. Is that a problem?"

"No problem," Doug replied tentatively, "But that's a lot of records to check. You and Dave are going to go through each case?"

"If there's some other way to do it, I'd like to know."

"If we had the computerized system in place, we could just print out the data," Doug complained. "If wishes were horses . . ." he trailed off without completing the thought. "Anyway, there's no problem with checking. I'll let the satellite pharmacy supervisor know, or you can get a key from the OR supervisor if you'll be doing it after 4:30."

"Yeah, we'll be doing this late, just to keep this quiet," John added.

"Absolutely. I'd offer to help you," Doug stated sincerely, "But I have a meeting this evening. Do you want me to pull one of the pharmacy techs to help?"

"No, thanks anyway. Dave and I can manage. I'll fill you in tomorrow," offered John, clicking off the phone. The ball was in motion, and there was nothing more that he could do until later this evening. It would be a very long day.

4:30 PM

Kathy Martin had awakened around noon, immediately asking for food. She had expressed her surprise at the speed of relief, and even Drew seemed impressed with the quick results.

Marilyn and Mr. Stewart had just arrived, and they gathered now around Kathy's bed. "What we offer," Mr. Stewart stated, "is a medication that puts your wife into a deep sleep. It's called Limbotryl, and it's an anesthesia medicine. This drug isn't used in any other way, such as to treat pain."

Mr. Stewart paused, looking at Drew, waiting for what is typically the next question: Then why give Limbotryl to people with intractable pain?

Drew remained silent.

The Magi continued, "By extending that portion of time within the sleep cycle when endorphins are released—those are the body's natural healing agents—we can generate what appears to be remission. In this instance, Kathy experiences relief from pain. She's more flexible, and because of the pain relief, she's more mobile. Make sense?"

Drew nodded, frowning.

"You may wonder why we don't just write a prescription for the drug and give it to everyone who could benefit," Mr. Stewart said. "This drug is approved for anesthesia, and nothing else. It is administered by injection, through an intravenous line, and that doesn't lend itself to outpatient use. I give it to a fairly small group of people in our area because it's safe and effective, and it gives them *life*. I have the means to help people reclaim their lives, and I do so. Questions?"

Drew shook his head, no questions.

"How about you, Kathy? Anything else you would like to ask?"

"No," she replied softly. "You explained it perfectly. I'm proof of this medication's benefits."

With all his self-discipline mobilized, Drew remained quiet, not voicing his concerns until after the Magi and Marilyn left. He'd struggled with himself throughout the consultation, and now with Kathy, about whether or not the Magi should return. Drew was dumbfounded that Kathy would permit someone she didn't know to inject her with an unknown substance.

Kathy defended her human right to protect, or at least to soothe, her own body. "Are you telling me that I *shouldn't*, or that I *can't*, use the only means we both know will allow me to function?" she shrieked at Drew, never imagining that he would take this tack when faced with the ugly alternative of her misery.

"It sounds illegal," Drew said firmly.

"It is illegal," Kathy retorted. "What you need to realize is that I need this treatment to survive, to function."

"As if it's that simple!" Drew spewed the words. "You forget that you have a family to think of. You are so wrapped up in your own misery that you can't even see what might happen to me, or the kids, if you get caught."

"What a shitty thing to say, Drew! I *do* think of you and the children, and I can consider your needs a hell of a lot better when I'm not strangled by pain. I want this medication so that I *can* be a mother, so that I *can* be a wife. It's not an option without the medicine! What kind of a wake-up call do you need?"

"*Strangled by pain,* Kath? Your flair for the dramatic is exceeded only by your selfish disregard for what might happen if this drug-dealer Magi, as you call him, gets us all in trouble. It's what you and all the other room moms teach the kids at school—it's called drug abuse, and if *you're* in jail for using controlled substances, and if *I'm* in jail as an accessory, who's going to take care of our children?"

"You talk about a moral obligation to follow the law, but what about my obligation to take care of our children!"

"That's *exactly* what I'm talking about!" Drew shouted back, closing the gap between them until he was in her face like a drill sergeant. "You can't do that very well from jail!"

Kathy felt the heat and dampness of his vituperative blast, and angrily shoved him away, bursting into tears. Striding to the kitchen table, she swept her arm across the surface, ceramic plates and silverware clattering to the floor. Refusing to look at Drew, who stood mute with shock, Kathy sobbed noisily as she left the room, stomped up the stairs to the guest bedroom, slammed the door, and locked herself inside.

She collapsed on the bed, cathartically relieved, having wielded her body as a tool of destruction, rather than simply residing within its harbor of pain. Still, shame that her children might have been witnesses inspired gratitude that they were elsewhere, enjoying soccer practice and Brownie Scouts with their friends.

A while later, Drew knocked at the door of the guest bedroom. Kathy huddled beneath the covers and feigned sleep.

"I know you're awake, Kath," Drew said softly, a hint of apology in his voice. "If you don't want to talk now, we'll have to talk later." He paused, as if searching for words. "I'm worried that you're going to get in over your head with this, Kath. I don't want anything to happen to you, or to our family. I like the results, yes. But there are too many unknowns to do this again. Let's just see how long this will last. Today was pretty good for you, pain-wise. Maybe it'll last a week."

Kathy waited, still silent. She eyed the Nyquil cold medicine on the bedside table, which would put her out for the night, if she took a swig or two.

"Kath? I don't want these people coming back tomorrow. I want you to feel better, but we have to be careful about people we don't know, who are peddling something your own doctor won't give you. I'm not trying to be a dick."

Another pause, and then a tap on the door: "Kathy? Can I come in?"

Squeezing her eyes tightly, Kathy Martin rolled over and pulled the covers over her head, praying for sleep. It came quickly, as bid, and lasted until the next morning.

7:30 PM

John Williams was beat. He'd been working for nearly thirteen hours. Now relieved by the second-call doc, John was free to go home. But instead, he and Dave Johnson would check the drug kits. He called home and left a message for Nancy that he'd be leaving in an hour or so.

Then, after arranging to meet Dave at the satellite pharmacy, John snatched his lab coat from the locker hook, shrugged his shoulders into it, and grabbed the paper cap from his head, crumpling it before making a two-point shot into the trash can next to the elevator. He then stopped the OR Supervisor to borrow her key to the satellite pharmacy, which was always locked. As usual, Doug Howard had covered all the bases, and the supervisor was ready with the key, having been briefed that John and the Security Director would be reviewing the OR records and drug kits.

The satellite pharmacy was located near the OR area for convenience, an unstaffed area with a camera patrolling the room in one hundred eighty degree sweeps. The drug kits used in surgery today were housed here for the night. They would be disassembled in the morning. Each vial and syringe used during the previous day's surgeries was accounted for in either the patient's drug record, or in the unused residuals remaining in the drug kit. A red flag would be triggered if the record indicated that the entire drug had not been used, and if the vial or syringe were empty.

It was not a perfect system. An anesthetist, doc or nurse, could draw up a syringe of narcotic medication, record having administered all of it, and return the empty ampule to the drug kit, pocketing the syringe of narcotic for future pleasure. The patient's drug record would return to the pharmacy, where two pharmacy technicians would examine the contents of the drug kit against the drug record for the surgery. As long as there was a match, no one would be the wiser.

For months, John had advocated purchasing an automated record keeper for tracking anesthesia drugs. This computerized system tracked the same information, as the drug record sheet, but with the advantage of retrieving reports easily. Such reports elucidated which anesthetists requested additional—or unusually large amounts of—narcotics for their cases.

The advantage to performing such narcotics reconciliation *now* was that the idiosyncrasies of the anesthetist could be informative. Because John provided anesthesia himself, he was capable of reading cues that a pharmacy tech would miss. Anyone could reconcile a drug record, but John was looking for something that might point to a diversion suspect.

Footsteps from the elevator alcove alerted John that Dave Johnson was on the way. The men exchanged brisk greetings as John inserted the key to the satellite pharmacy door. The key entered stiffly, and John had to jiggle it several times before it sprang the lock.

"Sometimes the duplicates are a little stiff," Dave explained. "I thought that problem was resolved when we re-keyed the entire OR area."

Entering the room and flipping on the lights, the men studied the illuminated shelves of boxes, the drug kits. The nearest shelf contained drug kits from surgeries ending late today. John selected that as his starting point, working systematically to the right, one kit at a time. Dave positioned himself across the room and worked parallel to John, from left to right. There were easily a hundred boxes, one for each surgery that day, and the two men began the laborious process of checking every narcotic filled syringe in all one hundred boxes, silent in their pursuit of clues.

Opening the first box, John unpacked a kit containing a jumble of vials and capped syringes. He then lifted a syringe to the fluorescent light in the ceiling. The barrel of the syringe was labeled: Fentanyl. Half of it was used. Referring to the attached drug record, John noted the amount used during that particular surgery. Verified: 2.5 milliliters had been dispensed. The same was true of the other narcotics in that kit. Methodically, both Dave Johnson and John Williams examined each of the drug kits, finding no discrepancies. The process of checking each kit took longer than either man had anticipated, and it was 9:30 PM when the last boxes were closed.

There would be neither clues nor answers tonight.

Typically, John was reading in bed at this hour. He heard his stomach growl before he felt the gnawing sensation of hunger, so intently had he pursued the task at hand. He flipped off the light and closed the door to the satellite pharmacy, cranking the knob and leaning against the door to ensure that the latch was secure. He then returned the key to the OR Nursing Supervisor, exchanged a few words with Dave Johnson, and changed from scrubs to street clothes, grabbing a package of cheese on cheese crackers from a shelf in his locker to quiet his stomach. In twenty minutes, he would be home. There, he could gobble a turkey and Swiss cheese sandwich before heading to bed. Nancy would not have prepared supper. Their agreement was to trade off cooking, but only on nights when both of them would be home by 6:00 PM. Otherwise, they settled for a sandwich or a frozen dinner.

Shrugging on his jacket, John flipped his pager to "off," shut his locker door, and latched the lock in place. Whistling softly, aware that he wasn't really *tired* so much as muscle-fatigued, John trekked to the parking lot, his thoughts racing along a path of intrigue. Stopping mid-whistle to chomp on the cheesy cracker, John argued with himself about how the drug-loss might or might not have been perpetrated by one of his colleagues.

He knew the people he worked with, some both professionally and socially. He had selected this group as his first choice for practice, aware that finding capable, trustworthy, and fair-minded colleagues required the same careful evaluation as selecting a spouse. The level of commitment and loyalty expected by partners represented a marriage, of sorts. After all, he would work with *these* people—*be with* these people—for more hours of the day than anyone else, even a spouse. They would collaboratively determine how the group would earn and disperse revenues, who would be included in their tightly-knit circle, and how each person would be expected to back up the other. That required a high level of trust. When John had interviewed for a partnership track position, Stuart Adler had explicitly referenced this nearly sacred trust. A trust that may have been violated—again.

The nurse who'd been arrested the year before had been a newcomer to the group when she committed the unpardonable sin. Although this nurse had not attained the rank of "family" within the group, the physicians and nurses alike had experienced a sick feeling of betrayal when the arrest was made. Each questioned his or her ability to accurately judge a person's character, and wondered if someone else within the practice would mar the trust. For a while, at least, the members of the group pulled on armor and withdrew in cautious, guarded vigilance against such threats to their family.

There were no recently hired personnel whom John could suspect now. How much easier it was, he mused silently, to suspect a person who was less well known, or someone dissimilar. The homogenous physician group comprised fifteen men and one woman, all married and most with children, each with a vested interest in the group's success. It was far easier to let his thoughts and suspicions drift to the more heterogeneous pool of nursing staff, both those employed by the group as anesthetists and those employed by the hospital. The latter would include the OR nurses and techs, all of whom had access to the drug kits during and after surgery.

So lost was he in thought, John steered through the light traffic on I-71 without noticing the newly erected column of orange barrels, which announced more construction for the northbound lanes. He arrived at the Kenwood Road exit without any recollection of navigating the interstate. He hadn't even called to let Nancy know he was on the way home, a natural part of his routine. He hit the auto-dial on his car phone, and cringed when Nancy's sleepy voice picked up at the other end.

"What happened today?"

"I'll tell you about it when I get home. No news, though," he admitted.

"See you when you get here."

Click. John yawned broadly, not actually tired enough to sleep, but every muscle groaning with exhaustion. Day two, after a killer night on-call, was when the fatigue typically caught up with him. Tomorrow would be here too soon. At least it would be a shorter workday, the compensation offered to those scheduled to work late. Another yawn generated a pop in his jaw as he inhaled, while contemplating the remainder of the week. Nancy flew out tomorrow and would be gone until Friday evening. The weekend would be well earned.

John palmed the steering wheel into the driveway a few minutes later, the headlights softly illuminating the arch of white crabapple blossoms overhead. He punched the garage door opener and rolled into his spot on the left side of the three-car garage.

Nancy appeared at the door leading from the garage into the kitchen. She waved in greeting, shivering in the cool, spring night breeze, wearing only the oversized t-shirt that she called pajamas. Her eyes were alert; she was ready for a recap. Nancy tapped the garage door button as John rounded her red Honda Prelude. She propped open the storm door, one hip askance, her arms spread wide. "Tell me everything," she said eagerly. "I've got a dinner heating in the microwave."

John tossed his jacket over one of the antique maple Windsor chairs that surrounded their kitchen table. "I talked with Dave Johnson in Security. He knows I didn't have anything to do with that syringe in the call room, and he's itching to find whoever did. He'd like to think it's someone in the group."

"Well, it's a relief that he doesn't suspect you." Nancy grinned as she crossed herself, the gesture less prayerful than playfully reminiscent of her Catholic upbringing. "Did you have a chance to look over some of the drug kits?"

"Yeah, it took a couple of hours to go through all of them. We had at least a hundred surgeries today, and I lost track of time while I was going through the kits." John paused and sheepishly added, "Sorry I didn't call earlier."

"Don't worry about it, Doc," Nancy replied, and in mock scolding added, "but don't do it again." After pecking her husband briskly on the lips, Nancy turned her attention to the beep of the microwave, which announced that the frozen dinner was ready. "I'll get this onto a plate—you can sit down and fill me in." She flicked the cellophane covering the dinner into the trash compactor, scooped the chicken and pasta onto a plain white plate, and lifted a fork from the silverware drawer, fluid as a dancer.

"So, you were in the Pharmacy all this time?" she asked, placing the plate and fork in front of her husband.

"Actually, the drug kits are still in the satellite pharmacy," he answered. "They'll be taken to the main Pharmacy for inventory first thing tomorrow, but I wanted to check them out tonight to see if anything looked screwy." He took a bite of the bland pasta, and then rose to get grated Romano cheese from the refrigerator. "I checked what was in each kit against the drug records, and everything seemed to be right. But I was hoping there'd be some little quirk that a pharmacy tech might not notice—if he's just accustomed to checking the records against what's actually left in the drug kits—maybe something that only anesthesia folks would notice."

"As in something that would cue you that tracks were being covered?" Nancy asked, settling into the chair next to John, and pouring Diet Rite cola into a pair of frosted beer mugs.

John nodded, his mouth full.

"What if someone substituted something to make their kit *appear* to check out?" Nancy asked, "How would that be discovered?"

"It might *not* be discovered," John answered, giving this idea further consideration. "I've been thinking of this from the standpoint that someone who has access to the call room—like someone in our group—left the syringe in the call room. I'd like to think it was accidental, but hiding a syringe or two beneath the phone requires deliberate, evasive action."

Nancy sipped her soft drink pensively. "So, if it's not accidental, then perhaps it's happened before, and maybe whoever left the syringe in the call room wasn't able to cover his or her tracks, for some reason."

"It may *have* happened before," John agreed. "The drug record isn't a perfect accounting system, and that's why I've been pushing for an automated recordkeeping system."

"That won't deter someone who wants to steal narcotics," Nancy noted skeptically. "Especially when they could cover their tracks by drawing up saline or something else to make the kit look good. Isn't that possible?"

John paused mid-bite. "That's the same thing Mac suggested. It's certainly possible," he acknowledged, as he considered how to pursue this avenue without alerting the entire group. "It presumes that the person stealing drugs would have a window of opportunity to actually *use* the drug, and then come back and draw up saline to cover the difference. It would look like the patient received the drug, such as Fentanyl, and whatever was in the syringe would appear to be the remainder. No one would be suspicious." John stopped to take another bite, then washed it down with a gulp of cola. "Then again, maybe they would draw it up in a separate syringe—not from hospital supply—so no syringes would be missing. That way, they could use the drug at their convenience. I could ask the Director of Pharmacy to test some of the syringes in the drug kits from today, just to see if any come up as something we weren't expecting. Like saline instead of Fentanyl."

Nancy nodded, and then frowned as she introduced an unseemly possibility. "I've been trying to think of *who*, of anyone in your group, would be likely to use Fentanyl, or whatever it is, recreationally. Who was on call the night before you?"

"Ron Albers, and there's no way he's using Fentanyl recreationally." John was adamant. Ron was a very bright, talented anesthesiologist, the one John would choose to provide the anesthesia if he or Nancy needed surgery. Albers was also particular about the way drugs were handled for his cases. So insistently, meticulously detail-oriented was Dr. Albers, he irritated most of the nurse anesthetists he supervised. John knew Ron Albers better than almost anyone in the group, except for Mac, and it was inconceivable that Ron could be using drugs, or could be so sloppy as to hide a syringe beneath the call room phone.

"Which of the nurses was on call with Ron?" Nancy asked pointedly.

"I'd have to check on that," John answered, reluctant to proceed from the suspicion that someone in the anesthesia group was responsible. "There are so many people who have access to drugs in the OR that limiting this to the anesthesia group would be shortsighted."

"Yes, but you have to admit that an anesthetist, possibly even a doc within the group, is the most likely. Face it, John. The syringe was in your department's physician call room. How many people who work in the OR have keys to the Anesthesia Offices?"

John pushed away the empty plate and rubbed his eyes vigorously. His only response to Nancy's common sense was a hippo-sized, jaw-popping yawn. He was too tired to think clearly, yet the thoughts streamed unchecked, persistent but lacking order. He needed sleep. "I'm heading up. Coming with me?"

"I'll tuck us both in," Nancy replied, taking his hand and lacing her fingers through his.

Hand in hand, they walked silently upstairs. Within minutes of cuddling beneath the covers, they were asleep.

John dreamed vividly. It was a familiar dream, typically recurring when he was stressed or having difficulty making a decision. His mother and one of his former schoolteachers, a nun, appeared separately. Now, the nun was telling John, at age twelve, that his mother needed medicine. For inexplicable reasons, John Williams—the boy—felt it was dangerous to permit his mother to have the medicine. Yet, at the same time, it was somehow his responsibility to ensure that his mother *received* the medicine. This time, the nun held the medication in a capped syringe. She assured John that the medicine would help his mother, and God would spare her life.

However, by the time he ran back to his house—always in slow motion, as if twenty-pound weights were attached to his feet—his mother was already dead. He had failed to bring the medicine in time. It was all his fault!

In the morning, John awakened with the sense that he had failed an important test. Depressed by the reawakened grief he knew at age twelve, he fought a lethargy that lingered throughout the day.

Chapter Three

PLAYING DETECTIVE

Thursday, April 4
9:00 AM

The day dawned hesitantly, clouds and fog obscuring rays of sunlight that might have enticed a reluctant riser from beneath the shroud of sheets and blankets. Kathy Martin rolled over, noting the late morning time on the Roman numeral face of her childhood alarm clock. She felt only a bit stiff. There was pressure, but no pain. Ah, the relief she had felt yesterday had been so sweet! It was as if she needed to feel desperately bad, in order to appreciate the depth of wholeness, aliveness, that came with the reprieve from pain.

She had a decision to make. Drew said that he didn't want the Magi to return. Should she take the treatment anyway? Perhaps while Drew was at work? She would have to take the treatment for several days in a row, if any benefit was to be sustained. Once she was significantly better, the treatments could be spaced as a maintenance dose, possibly one every two to three weeks.

Slowly folding back the covers, Kathy rolled her legs over the side of the bed, allowing their weight to provide the necessary momentum to stand. Her limbs were definitely stiff compared to yesterday. Had the fight with Drew diminished the effect of yesterday's treatment?

Kathy forced herself to bear weight and shuffled to the guest bedroom door, turning the bolt to unlock and open it, intending to go to the bathroom. Given the time, Kathy expected to be alone in the house for the day, a perfect opportunity to request another treatment. By now, the children were at school and Drew was at the office.

But he was not.

Kathy inhaled sharply as she opened the door, revealing Drew sitting on the floor across the hall. He noticed her stiff movements, the shuffling gait indicative of his wife's discomfort.

Neither spoke for several seconds. Then, Kathy scuffed along to the bathroom. When she exited, Drew assumed the lead.

"You want the treatment today, don't you?" he asked, without judgment in his tone or posture.

"Yes," Kathy answered, her response void of inflection.

Drew sighed. She simply didn't understand the risks she was taking. Moreover, she didn't comprehend the risk to which she exposed their family. How could she be so selfish? It wasn't Kathy's nature to be selfish, and Drew closed his eyes as if to shut out this image of his wife. Last night, he had felt angry and irritated by her shortsighted righteousness. Today, he was too tired to replay the arguments.

The fatigue had as much to do with the battle waging within his mind and heart, as it did with sleep deprivation. Although he didn't appreciate being required, once again, to serve as crisis manager, he no longer felt angry. Rather, he felt sadly resigned. He despaired of any way to reconcile this issue with Kathy.

Kathy, in turn, stared down at the man crouched in the hallway, knowing in her mind that he was her husband, but sensing in her heart that he was a stranger. He lacked empathy, or surely he would comprehend that taking the treatments was her best option, despite the risks. Indeed, the Magi endured greater risks than she did, and greater risks than they as a family. Only the Magi offered salvation. Why couldn't Drew see that?

Taking a medically prescribed, FDA-sanctioned, ineffective treatment was as wrong, to Kathy's way of thinking, as taking the pharmaceutical gifts of the Magi. She had tried the path of conventional wisdom offered by the medical professionals. It had not worked. She'd been unable to care for her children, or even attend to her own needs.

As the hallway confrontation continued, Kathy begged for the Magi to return, and Drew begged her to pull herself together, " . . . *for the family's sake.*"

Kathy turned away, helpless, hopeless, and took a double shot of the Nyquil cold medicine, seeking unconscious bliss. Yet, her effort to rest was fitful, like that of someone delirious with fever.

1:00 PM

John Williams had wrapped up his cases an hour earlier, relieved by Mac, who was second call that day. Finding an hour to burn before his meeting with the Director of Pharmacy, John decided to launch his own investigation. He asked the secretary, Shelly, to photocopy the nurse anesthetists' schedule for the past three months. Later, he'd check out Nancy's query about which nurse was on call with Ron Albers the night preceding John's overnight duty. The schedule might be useful if any future drug loss occurred, if only to identify a pattern. At this point, John would not concede that one of his colleagues had hidden the drug beneath the phone in the physician call room. But he would have to confront the reality that it was the most likely of possibilities.

Picking up the mail in his box, John glanced at the two call room doors that flanked the wall of cubbies. Both were closed, automatically locking when the latch clicked. At this time of the day, no one would be in either call room, and he could quietly check out each, while Shelly made photocopies on the machine around the corner.

John extracted a jangle of keys from his lab coat pocket, quickly inserting one into the door to the left, the physician call room. Flipping the switch, he blinked twice as the room brightened. He scanned from left to right: a twin bed dominated the room, with sheets tightly hugging the mattress, a folded cotton blanket set at the foot of the bed, and two pillows at the head. To the side of the bed was a table, offering a reading lamp, telephone, and notepad topped with a black pen. The door into the full bath was ajar, but an overhead fluorescent partially illuminated the area, permitting a view of the toilet behind the door, the sink, towels and washcloths on either side of the countertop, and a mirrored medicine chest above.

He entered the call room, the door closing with a heavy click behind him. He crossed to the bathroom, pausing at the sink to open the cabinet. Bottles of mouthwash, shampoo, and talcum powder stood in a tidy row. Next to that was a collection of hotel soaps, a lone can of aerosol deodorant in the corner. Closing the cabinet door quietly, John retraced his steps, glancing beneath the bed to the empty floor, noting that the phone was set squarely on the bedside table. Everything was in order, nothing out of place; certainly, nothing was beneath the telephone today.

John flicked off the light, allowing the door to shut behind him, and made his way around the tower of mailboxes to the nurses' call room. Inserting the same key into that lock, turning his wrist counterclockwise, he pushed the door open. The room was a mirror opposite of the one he had just surveyed, and the only difference was the clutter of hair spray, brushes, and sundry toiletries that various nurses had left, offering all manner of creature comforts: shaving cream, lotion, deodorant, blow-dryer, hair gel, hair spray, hairbrushes, combs, back-scratcher, curling iron, antacid, mouthwash, rubbing alcohol, cotton balls, cotton swabs, and tea tree oil.

Who has time to use all this stuff? John marveled. He snapped open the mirrored door of the medicine cabinet. Rows of prescription vials crammed the shelves, each labeled to identify its nurse-owner. Myriad brands of vitamins, Echinacea, Ginko Biloba, antacids with and without extra calcium, and assorted pain relievers—not a single type unrepresented—were stacked two and three high. The manufacturers would be pleased with this group of nurse-consumers. On the bottom shelf, standing in the corner of the cabinet, was a partially rolled up tube of mint-gel toothpaste. There was nothing here that wouldn't appear in anyone's medicine chest at home, he determined.

Leaving the bathroom, John scanned the rest of the room, noting the same features as in the one next-door, albeit more cluttered. A stack of magazines rested beneath the phone on the bedside table. Above the table, a dry-erase board was fastened to the wall, a red marker dangling to the side. Squatting on his haunches, John glanced beneath the bed, clutter-free save for yesterday's newspaper, which meant that Housekeeping had not been in to clean the call room yet, and it was now 1:15 PM. He added this to a list of stray details that he hoped would ultimately offer a clearer picture of how the syringe had arrived in the physicians' call room.

The scratch of a key entering the call room door sent a surge of adrenalin through John's veins. He grabbed the knob and quickly opened the door, startling the Housekeeping attendant, who jumped back a step, her hand at her heart.

"I didn't think anybody'd be in here now," she exclaimed. "You mighta had a Code Blue! Go and scare the daylights outta me like that!" she scolded.

It was Edna Walters, who had worked in Housekeeping at St. Catherine's for the past ten years.

"Sorry, Edna," John said with an apologetic smile. "You okay?"

"Yes, Dr. Williams," Edna replied, her voice a couple of octaves lower as she recovered her composure. "You lookin' 'round for somethin' specific?"

John shook his head pensively. *Had Edna been the one to find the syringe beneath the phone?* He hadn't asked Mac to specify *who* had retrieved the drug, and he realized that Edna could be helpful.

Edna discerned a lot from the trash she emptied each day, and not only about the anesthesia folks. She also cleaned the surgical residents' call rooms, the OR Nurses' locker room, and several other staff-only areas. Edna knew who read the newspaper and who read tabloids. She knew who ate take out from the hospital's cafe and who had pizza delivered. She knew who entertained girlfriends—or boyfriends—in the call rooms, and who among them practiced safe sex. Not that she cared. If asked, she would have shrugged and said, "That's them's business, not mine."

John Williams understood, most importantly, that Edna might know who left a trail of their misdeeds: perhaps a narcotic or alcohol or cigarette vice.

He remained in the doorway of the call room, weighing the risks and the potential benefits. Before he'd completed the calculations, Edna spoke up boldly. "I found somethin' in the other call room the other day. Never seen nothin' like it." Edna's voice clearly stated her indignation. "I know *you* didn't do it, Dr. Williams," she added briskly. "You're one of the neat doctors. Can't say the same 'bout all of 'em." Edna proceeded to the bathroom, where she set her cleaning caddy on the Formica countertop. Pulling on a pair of latex gloves, Edna proceeded to spray industrial strength disinfectant into the sink.

John took a gamble, banking on Edna's goodwill toward him, her reputation for verbal reticence, and her common sense. "Edna, I'd appreciate it if you'd let me know if you see anything that looks unusual. Anytime at all."

Edna glanced briefly up from wiping the basin and countertop. "I'll do that," she agreed.

Stepping back into the outer office area, John allowed the door to close and lock automatically with a thud and a click. He turned to retrieve the photocopied schedule from Shelly's desk, and exited to the maze of subterranean hallways that connected the hospital buildings. Although John's innate sense of direction operated almost like an internal compass, most of the people who initially traversed these arteries had no perception as to where they were in relation to the rest of the hospital. With his gift for navigation, John quickly learned the short cuts. In only five minutes, he crossed the threshold of the Pharmacy Offices.

Doug Howard stood at the secretary's desk, fanning a set of eight pink phone messages like a hand of cards. He looked up as John entered, waving him into the private office on the left.

"The kits from yesterday check out, as you probably know," Doug said briskly as he preceded John into the room.

"Yeah, Dave and I examined the kits and drug records last night, but I was really looking for some quirky indicator that would help focus the investigation," John explained. "If someone is diverting drugs, it may not show up on the drug record."

"What do you mean, 'if' someone is diverting?" Doug asked, his face indicating that he'd raised his guard as quick as a sailor's salute.

"Look, I'm not trying to overlook the possibility that someone in Anesthesia is responsible. But, I'd like to check the contents of remainder narcotic vials," John said tersely. "If someone in the Anesthesia Department is diverting drugs, I want to take care of it now—like last year. It's possible that the records match what's being returned to the satellite pharmacy because whoever is taking the drugs may be replacing it with saline. Can you check it out?"

"Yeah," Doug replied, doubtfully, "But that's a lot of ampules to check. I can't check every narcotic that gets returned on a daily basis. It would help if we could narrow the field. Even if we knew which narcotic was being diverted, I couldn't have every vial checked. It would be possible to look at the kits used by specific people, but unless you can give me some idea about who that would be, the best I can do is a random sweep."

John nodded, appreciating the amount of work that even a random sweep would create for the Pharmacy Director, as well as the Laboratory personnel. "I can't narrow the field for you, other than to eliminate the anesthesia personnel who were off or on vacation. That would eliminate four or five people. I'm not sure that makes the numbers any more doable."

Doug nodded in agreement. "This is a more serious problem if we've got someone substituting saline to cover the diversion."

"This may have been going on for while, too," John added. "I'm not sure someone is actually substituting saline, and it certainly doesn't explain why the syringes were hidden in the call room. Short of placing a hidden camera in the call room, I can't think of any other way to approach this."

"What's Security say about it?"

"They're willing to help us, but we all wish we had more to work with."

"Let's start with random samples. I'll call the Lab and set it up. It may take us a few days to get things up and running. I'll get back with you if anything shows up."

"And I'll be checking the anesthesia drug records each day for narcotics usage and unusual requests," John added. "If we had an automated drug recordkeeping system, it would be a breeze to track who might be using a lot more narcotics than usual. That would help narrow the field."

Doug Howard nodded sympathetically. "It's been on my wish-list for about five years, and the VP of Perioperative Services is on a mission to get it into the capital budget for next year. Won't help now, though, and it's a lot of paperwork for you."

John rubbed his forehead in anticipation of the headache that awaited him each day. "If you can think of something else, let me know. It's the best I can think of to get a handle on this quickly."

"Good luck," Doug said sincerely.

Leaving the office, John clicked off his pager and walked back through the maze to the locker room. Changing from his lab coat and scrubs into slacks and a long-sleeved cotton knit pull-over, he contemplated his computer software's capacity: could it really assist with the monumental task of tracking narcotic use by every physician and nurse in the anesthesia group? He could create a basic spreadsheet, but that would require a lot of data entry for limited information. It was probably better than nothing, and he would set up his database this afternoon. He would tap in data well into the evening, as Nancy would not return until Friday night.

John kicked off the running shoes he wore in the OR and slipped on a pair of soft leather Cole-Haans, which felt comparatively cool to his throbbing, fatigued toes. He snagged his jacket from the hook and slammed the locker door shut. With a plan in mind, John left the hospital to continue his investigative work at home. It was not to be a leisurely "early-out."

3:45 PM

The final cases of the day were wrapping up. This was prime time for opportunity. The tanned blond nurse pulled off the paper hat that resembled a shower cap, fluffing her layered locks nervously. She patted the pocket of her OR scrub pants, comforted by the jingle that assured the presence of keys that opened her gate to heaven, the satellite pharmacy.

She was finished for the day, but remained in scrubs to blend with the environment, her camouflage. A quick glance around reassured her that the other nurses were too busy to note her activity. They were focused on completing the work: sending the patients to Recovery or back to the floors, and finalizing chart documentation. It would be another hour before anyone trucked the surgical drugs back to the satellite pharmacy. She was safe to excavate for her elixirs.

Clamping the keys together so that they made no sound, she withdrew them from her pocket. The largest one opened the door, and it slid in smoothly, the lock retreating with ease. Closing the door behind her, she flipped on the light and looked up at the camera across the room. She smiled, confident that no one would be the wiser; the film was never reviewed unless Pharmacy detected a discrepancy with the narcotics count. Her system was foolproof, she believed.

She dropped the keys into her pocket, again feeling wonder at the ease with which she'd duplicated the key to this haven. She congratulated herself on the decision to keep the original key, which navigated the latch more smoothly than the duplicate, now clinking on the ring buried deep in the pocket of the OR supervisor's scrub coat.

She opened the first drug kit, a treasure trove containing syringes of Fentanyl, Limbotryl, and Demerol. Each syringe contained generous amounts of medication, indicating that this might have been intended for a stand-by case. She paired an empty vial of Fentanyl with a similarly marked syringe. Beginning with this pair, she re-injected the contents of the labeled syringe into its original vial. Then, she fingered a vial of saline, held it to the light, and inserted the empty syringe. Pushing the plunger to clear air from the chamber, she then drew up the same amount of saline, as there had been narcotic. Now, the numbers would match. The next step was to draw up the contents of the vial into a syringe she'd purchased at a discount healthcare supplies store. Then, she'd hide the goody syringe in her lab coat pocket. Last, she'd return the empty vial and the saline-filled, Fentanyl-marked syringe to the drug kit. There, just as she'd found them! The girl wrinkled her nose and grinned with glee at her perfectly planned fait accompli.

There were several more "preferred" drug kits to check, these being assigned to two particular anesthesiologists, who marked their syringes thoroughly, abetting her identification of goodies to exchange: saline for Fentanyl, or Demerol, or Limbotryl. She preferred Fentanyl, day-to-day. Demerol was always a second choice. But Limbotryl was great for weekends. She could zone out for twenty hours, and feel ready to run a marathon when she woke up. What a great drug! And getting it was almost too easy.

Today was a good day. She'd had enough Fentanyl on board to feel high, without compromising her performance. The drug engendered supreme confidence. She was at her peak, and there wasn't a trace of tremor in her nimble fingers as she calmly completed the exchange. Mission accomplished. Almost.

The trickiest part was exiting the room without attracting attention. She'd learned to leave the light on, flipping it off at the last moment so that the bright lights in the hallway wouldn't stun her. Initially, it had seemed easier to turn out the lights and listen for voices and footsteps that would announce the presence of staff. Her hearing was more acute in the darkness. But it compromised her vision, when she entered the hallway, her eyes stinging from the harsh glare of fluorescent lighting.

By now, she had rounded that bend in the learning curve. Sporting a smile of satisfaction, the young woman stepped out of the room and shut the door quietly, barely a click registering in the silence of the hallway.

Twenty minutes later, a second visitor arrived at the satellite pharmacy. He wore OR scrubs, a knee-length lab coat, and a paper cap which obscured his hair and forehead. Moving briskly, familiarly, the visitor located the drug kits labeled with his name, as well as the ones for Dr. Mackenzie Franklin. He had discovered that her system of marking syringes made it easier to select what he needed—what his *other patients* needed, to be precise. With his kits, it was just as easy. He had taken a cue from his partner by marking his own syringes as meticulously as she did, and easily retrieved what he was looking for, substituting a harmless clear liquid for the elixir.

The visitor did not know he had competition, or that what he now possessed was an innocuous solution that would neither heal, nor harm. The first visitor had the elixir. The second had none. His *other patients* would feel the difference.

6:00 PM

John Williams stretched his back, arching in the chair before his personal computer. He had set up the database, separately creating a list of details and random pieces of information. Sliding the mouse to the printer icon on the screen, John clicked his command for a copy of the three-page report. He would look at it later, after a beer and some dinner. Perhaps an inspiration would be forthcoming. Nancy would be calling between eight and nine o'clock, their ritual when either of them was out of town. The worst of his day was over, and it was quitting time now.

He pushed back from the antique mahogany desk, leaned forward to catch the sheets emerging from the printer, and then rose to his feet with an audible yet painless click in his knees. It was yet another reminder that he had reached the point at which the human body, while completely healthy, had peaked in terms of its performance. John decided to skip the beer for now, and to hit the Ski Track after a frozen dinner. He felt nearly as hungry to feel the burn of glycolic acid in his muscles, as he felt thirsty for an ice-cold beer. The latter would reward his virtue for exercising first.

Strolling toward the kitchen, John studied the sheets in front of him. He could not resist the magnetic pull of the documents, despite his intention to take a break.

He glanced at the list of people in the group who had been working the day that the syringes were found: thirty-one nurse anesthetists and thirteen physicians. Next was a list detailing who was assigned to each of the twenty ORs on the lower level of the hospital. Additionally, there were OR suites on the upper level of the hospital, exclusively designated for women's health. However, the pharmaceuticals for that area were dispensed and collected for post-surgical inventory at another satellite of the Pharmacy Department. Unless something cued him otherwise, John decided to investigate only the lower-level ORs for now.

At the kitchen table, John set down the papers and opened the freezer door. He and Nancy had a library of frozen dinners, organized vertically across the shelf, like books. Chicken Francesca, Vegetable Lasagna, Macaroni and Cheese, New England Pot Roast, Santa Fe Beans and Rice, Lemon Pepper Fish, Chicken and Pasta Carbonara . . . . There was something for nearly every craving, although anything would work tonight. He removed a volume entitled "Yankee Pot Roast," featuring side dishes of new potatoes and green beans. While that was heating in the microwave, John removed one of the frosted beer mugs from the freezer, and poured himself a tall serving of diet pop.

Although no one would mistake John and Nancy Williams for gourmands, eating was definitely a pleasurable recreation. Their food interests ranged from the institutional to the sublime, whether macaroni and cheese at the hospital cafeteria or lobster bisque at Cincinnati's only five-star restaurant, the Maisonette.

The beep of the microwave alerted John that dinner was served. He grabbed a fork from the silverware drawer and liberated the meal from its package. He wondered why anyone would choose to eat at a fast food restaurant, given the many delicious frozen meals that one could enjoy in the comfort of home. Perhaps for the company of strangers, he decided.

Comfortable with his own company, John enjoyed the intermittent solitude when Nancy was out-of-town. Although, he preferred to have Nancy home, he accomplished zillions of tasks while she was gone, and they shared more leisure when she returned. Nancy operated similarly, tending tasks whenever John was on call. However, at mealtime, Nancy was more inclined to meet her sister and mother for dinner than to opt for a "volume" from the freezer.

Satisfied with his bachelor-style dinner, John glanced through the mail and perused a catalog that featured Big Boy Toys, resting from his investigative project. Not a morsel of pot roast or accompaniments remained on the plate, by the time he reached page thirty-five.

John admired the catalog's gadgets, as well as the automated-this-and-that's, featured in vivid, glossy color. Page after page tempted him to circle several items for his wish list—Nancy always asked for birthday and Christmas gift-giving ideas, both for her own reference and for family members who were often stumped as to what to get her "man who had everything."

The phone rang as he opened a package of Pepperidge Farm Milano cookies, and John noted the time on the microwave: 6:23 PM. It was Nancy.

They exchanged tidbits about their respective days, and wrapped up the call with "I love yous" and good wishes for the next day. Nancy would fly back from Washington, DC, earlier than originally scheduled. They agreed to have dinner at Funky's Blackstone Grille, and to spend the weekend working in the yard.

John did not mention that he'd need to devote a number of hours to data entry, punching in who was working in which OR, and who dispensed what narcotic—and how much of it—during each surgical case. That bit of bad news could wait.

The phone rang again as John loaded the fork and mug into the dishwasher. It was Mac, and the tone of her voice signaled breaking news.

"John, I'm in the office, not on my cell phone. No one else is in here so I think it's safe to talk."

"What's up?" he asked, munching on a cookie.

"I always mark my syringes with a permanent marker," Mac explained, "You know that. I had just marked a kit for a late case, this afternoon, when I got called to help in one of the other ORs. When I got back to my room, the syringes with my markings were gone. There were syringes there, all with labels, but the markings weren't mine. I've called Pharmacy, and they have the syringes now. I checked with the nurses who were setting up the room, and they said that the only person who was anywhere near the room was Ron Albers, and he didn't even come in."

"What nurse were you working with?" John asked, his heart rate quickening.

"I was setting up for Evvie Smith while she was at dinner," Mac replied. "She was back when I returned to the room, but she got there just ahead of me. I doubt she would have had the time to switch the syringes, and it's hard for me to believe that she's responsible for it."

"Any ideas who is?" John asked. "Who else was in that room?"

"Just the other OR nurses and the OR tech. They said that no one else came in while they were setting up the room."

"Mac, page Dave Johnson. Remember seeing him in the office the other day, when you were replacing your pager batteries?" John opted for that reference, rather than to speak about the diversion directly. "I've met with him about this situation. Tell him what happened, and see if he thinks any prints can be raised from the syringes that you found. Johnson can get them from Pharmacy, if he thinks it's worth a shot. I'll call Doug Howard from Pharmacy. I met with him today, and I want him to hear about this from one of us, not his staff."

"Right. How do I page Johnson at this hour?" Mac inquired.

"Through the hospital operator. He'll call you right back if he's available. If not, leave my number here at home and ask the operator to keep paging, until she hears from me that we've been in touch."

"Got it. I'll talk with you later."

"Thanks for the call, Mac. Maybe this is the break Security and Pharmacy need." John clicked off and tapped into his Palm

Pilot address book for Doug Howard's home phone number. They had exchanged home numbers the year before, when the last drug diversions had occurred. John knew that Doug would not mind the interruption, especially if it offered the prospect of resolution.

"Doug, I just got a call at home from one of my partners. Someone tampered with her syringes while she was called to another OR, and she noticed it right away."

"Where are the syringes now?" Doug asked.

"One of your people picked them up. I wanted you to know what happened, in case you want them handled in a specific way. I asked Dr. Franklin to page Dave Johnson in Security. I'm hoping that he'll tell us that the police lab can raise prints."

"Don't bet on it," Doug responded. "Dave told me it's hard to raise prints on a syringe, or any cylindrical object for that matter. I asked him about that already."

"Damn," muttered John. "At least we're able to narrow the field based on staffing today. Just wanted to let you know what was going on, Doug."

"Thanks for the call. I'll be in touch with Dave Johnson." Click.

John punched in Mackenzie Franklin's cell phone number, wishing for one fleeting, ironic moment that he were the one on second call. He wanted to know who was working anywhere near the OR, something that Dave Johnson would probably know before John arrived at work the next morning. His adrenaline pumped furiously. Whoever had picked up Mac's syringes, and substituted the others, was probably still in the hospital.

"Dr. Franklin," Mac answered.

"Mac, has Dave Johnson answered the page?"

"Yeah, he's coming in," Mac answered. "Whoever made the switch might still be here."

"Right. When things quiet down, could you get a list of who was working today, even the OR techs and OR nurses? See if Dave will let us have a complete list. I'd like to compare who's working now with who worked the night I was on call."

"I'll ask him," Mac agreed, "But I've already started my own list. It's not complete, but it seems more likely that someone out-side our group is responsible. Dave Johnson will probably start with the OR nurses and OR techs who were setting up my room. I'll hang around here until I've talked with him, and I'll call you at home if there's any news. Otherwise, I'm out of here."

"Who are you on call with?"

"Dean and Evvie, and both know about the switch. Dave Johnson will talk with both of them when he gets here, but he asked me not to mention what happened a couple nights ago. Does Dean know yet?"

"Absolutely. The entire Board was briefed yesterday. Who else knows about what happened this evening?"

"The OR nurses who set up the room and the OR tech who was in there earlier, the OR nursing supervisor, and Tom O'Brien from Pharmacy." O'Brien was the Assistant Director of Pharmacy, and he would ensure that adequate precautions were taken with the syringes, whether or not fingerprints could be lifted.

"Okay," John murmured quietly, contemplating the possible suspects. "Ask Dave to call me tonight, even if there's no news, okay?"

"Sure. I'll see you in the morning." Mac hung up, and John replaced the phone receiver in its base on the kitchen wall.

He glanced down at the three pages he had printed earlier, noting that Evvie Smith and Dean Phillips had both worked the day that John had been on call, as well as the day after. So had a couple dozen other people, John knew, and it would take ages to narrow the field this way.

He hoped that Dave Johnson's investigative skills would pick up the pace. It was hard to be patient. Nervous energy pricked at every cell of his body. He decided to get on the cross-country ski machine to kill time, and burn off the nervous energy while he waited for Dave Johnson to call.

9:15 PM

John emerged from the cloud of steam within the shower, grabbing his own towel, instead of Nancy's, and securing it around his waist on the way to answer the phone. Was it his imagination, or did the phone ring with greater urgency when he anticipated an important call?

Dave Johnson skipped any greeting, his update a rapid-fire report. "I've had a chance to talk with the people working tonight. It looks like the switch took place around 5:10, right after Evvie Smith left for dinner break. Whoever did it was fast. Dr. Franklin relieved Evvie Smith around 4:50, and started setting up the drugs for the surgery. She was called out to help with an intubation about ten minutes later, give or take a few, and when she returned to the room at about 5:15, she noticed the switch. The OR nurses saw no one else enter the room, although Dr. Albers apparently poked his head in the doorway looking for Evvie Smith after Dr. Franklin left."

"What about the OR nurses?" John interjected impatiently. "One of them could have made the switch."

"Not likely," Dave responded. "I've talked to each of them separately, as well as everyone else who was working in that OR, and I've verified that they were not alone in that OR at any time. Short of them collaborating, which I doubt, it isn't one of them. They were so worried about being suspected, they practically begged the nursing supervisor to let me inspect their lockers. They were clean."

"Who else was around?" John queried, certain that the guilty party was still there, irritated that Dave had not identified who that was.

"One person from housekeeping, not a factor, though; she never got into the OR. She didn't see anyone else go in either. There was a pharmacy technician who delivered some meds to another OR; also didn't see anyone. John, there were a lot of people down there at around 5:00, and I've talked with all the ones who are still here. A few people left at 7:00 PM, but those folks were nowhere near OR 6. Whoever did this was fast, but he, *or she,* isn't invisible. We missed this time, but they've been spotted twice this week, assuming that the same person is responsible for both incidents. I'll guarantee they'll make another mistake within a few days. Desperate addicts do."

"The problem is that we're going into the weekend," John said urgently. "There will be a lot more opportunity for someone to steal drugs." John ran a hand through his nearly dry waves, a futile gesture of grooming, pensively considering this information. Surely, someone or something had been overlooked. *Shit,* he wished he were there. Not that his presence would alter the circumstances. He was simply succumbing to the illusion that being there would somehow resolve things, or at least diminish the helplessness he felt. John silently acknowledged Dave Johnson's capability, and reminded himself that cases like this were not solved in a couple of days.

As if reading John's mind, Dave interjected, "The case from last year was more clear cut from the beginning. Not all of them are. I'll be calling the PDU people in the morning and we'll try to meet in the afternoon. Are you available?"

"I'll arrange for coverage. Just let me know when it is. The earlier the better, if we're going to do anything to prepare for the weekend."

"You also wanted a list of the people working down here today. What did you have in mind?"

John paused before answering, cradling the phone against his jawbone, and adjusting the towel, which hung loosely about his hips. "I'm just tracking which of the Anesthesia staff are on duty when an incident occurs. I'd like to track the OR nursing staff, too, but you're probably doing that already. It seems like whoever is doing this is right under our noses, so we should be able to find a pattern that narrows the field of suspects."

The anticlimax of this failure to catch the thief hit John squarely, the sensation of loss and fatigue that flowing viscously through his veins. "I really thought this would be resolved tonight," John admitted, sighing with resignation and disappointment.

"It won't be tonight," Dave assured, "But I've never had a case get away from me. Not on my watch."

John felt a twinge of guilt, realizing that his own disappointment may have seemed like a criticism to Dave. "Right. I guess I'll have to be patient with this one. I'll talk with you in the morning."

He returned the phone to its cradle gently, as if to compensate for the implication of his tone during the conversation. It was not that he lacked confidence in Dave's investigative abilities. Rather, this seemingly critical irritability sprung from being out of the loop—at home rather than at the hospital, the scene of the crime.

After notifying the hospital operator that he had contacted the Director of Security, John returned to the bathroom and re-folded his towel, having air-dried while on the phone. He stepped into a pair of cotton knit shorts, pulled on a t-shirt, ran a toothbrush across his teeth, and crawled into bed. He skimmed a glossy wine magazine to settle his thoughts, turning out the light at ten o'clock.

Once again this week, sleep eluded John until well past midnight. He could not stop rehashing the myriad, seemingly unrelated pieces of information. He would awaken the next morning feeling as if he had worked all night.

Chapter Four

CODE BLUE

Friday, April 5
7:45 AM

The front door banged shut as two children raced out to catch the bus, nearly missing it, again. If only she could move from beneath the cocoon-like covers to orchestrate the school day preparations. But it hurt too much, and the drugs that were supposed to stem the pain served only to fog her brain, leaden her limbs, and confine her to this prison of a bed. It didn't have to be a life sentence, but Drew had sent Marilyn and the Magi away. Why did he do that, she wondered, when he knew the power of the Magi's gift?

Perhaps that wasn't the right question. She wondered if she should be asking herself why she wasn't taking the lead, insisting on the treatments, resisting her husband at every turn, defying his righteous authority. He wasn't her parent! She was an adult. Why didn't she take charge of her health? Was that the right question?

Kathy Martin despaired of any answer today, or any day soon. She had made her life what it was.

If viewed only from the outside, she knew she'd be envied as one who had it all. She and Drew had dated throughout high school and college, following a fairly predictable trajectory toward marriage, careers, and family life. Drew, the breadwinner since the birth of their first child, had earned a fairly senior position at a big-eight firm, and lived for his work. They lived in one of the largest homes on the main boulevard in Mariemont, and employed a service to help clean it every other week. Kathy drove a late model minivan, the children attended a private school and had the toy-du-jour, and the family enjoyed annual trips to Snow Mass and Hilton Head Island. How many women could afford to exercise the option to stay home with their children, volunteer at church and school, and *still* enjoy such a high standard of living?

She should be grateful. For so long, she'd considered Drew her soul mate. Together, they'd speculated with wonder at how well they worked as a team, how neatly they'd balanced their talents, and how well-matched they were, as partners in marriage. For years, they'd held their relationship, family life, and career success in the highest esteem, certain that God had blessed them with this life because they'd *earned it.* And now, were they being tested?

At least she wasn't juggling a teaching career with parenthood, community work, and health problems. It might be easier to live with an illness that had a name, but this puzzle of symptoms defied diagnosis: insomnia, fatigue, abdominal and muscular pain, generalized weakness, and susceptibility to infection.

After months of inconclusive tests, she had become involved in a support group for people with chronic conditions such as fibromyalgia, rheumatoid arthritis, Crohn's Disease, Multiple Sclerosis, and Chronic Fatigue Syndrome. She had longed to latch onto one of these names, to claim it as her own if only to affirm that her symptoms weren't all in her head: she wasn't crazy. Yet, in the fellowship of this quiet circle of people who understood her suffering and validated her reality—even in the absence of a clear diagnosis—Kathy had found comfort for her soul, if not her body. It had been there, she recalled, that she'd met Marilyn.

"Can you tell me more about it?" Kathy inquired.

"There are several people within the group who take the treatment, but it's outside of what you'd call mainstream medicine," Marilyn cautioned.

"Right," Kathy said, her tone thick with irony. "As if yoga, herbal remedies, and support groups are part of mainstream medicine. That's what puzzled doctors prescribe for patients like me when they run out of other ideas."

"It's actually something that is offered to only a small number of people here. But I understand what you mean when you say that you want your old life back. You want to feel well enough to participate in life, as a wife and mother, a school volunteer, a Sunday school teacher, a Girl Scout leader."

"Exactly! What do I need to do to get some help: take an overdose of pain meds? Do I need to get so desperate that I schedule an appointment with Dr. Kevorkian?"

Marilyn blanched at the mention of the man's name, and Kathy felt compelled to explain. "Don't get me wrong, Marilyn. I'm not suicidal. But I want some help. My doctors have done little more than prescribe a narcotic cocktail that leaves me feeling like a brain-numbed piece of furniture. I want my life back, whole."

"It's very confidential," Marilyn whispered. "You would be asked to listen to a group of people who have benefited by the treatment, but none of us can tell you what the treatment is. You'd have to experience it first. You'd have to swear to keep the secret . . . and just so you know, there are some people who find it too demanding. And Kathy, I don't want you to misunderstand my reaction when you mentioned Dr. Kevorkian. He's been a friend to people who found help nowhere else. If I looked surprised when you said his name, it's only because I didn't think you were at that point."

Kathy stepped back, erecting her guard against whatever dark, mysterious, witchcraft Marilyn was suggesting. "I'm not at that point. I don't want to die, and I don't want to sneak around taking some secret, shady treatment."

She stalked away, to the extent that her muscles allowed, indignant at Marilyn's suggestion. Surely, she was either one banana short of a bunch, or worse than that, a drug dealer. Kathy wanted nothing, absolutely nothing, to do with Marilyn and her mysterious treatment.

How long ago that seemed, Kathy thought. How far she'd gone, and what ground she'd covered, over months, and months, and months. Too long.

Forcing her arm to push back the comforter, squinting in the glare of the April sunshine that now spilled from the broad windows, Kathy grasped the uncapped bottle of liquid cold medicine, and then lifted it to her lips, swallowing three gulps. She paused to take a breath, and then dashed another swig into her mouth, the medicine burning her gums before she could force her throat to swallow. She set the bottle back on the bedside table, wishing she had the strength to get out of bed and close the blinds and curtains against the glaring sun. Instead, she raised the comforter over her head, groaning as her muscles twitched in complaint, as if bearing tremendous weight. The pain lived on, wave after wave; but soon, she'd be semi-conscious, suspended in that limbo-like state that defied definition. It was not living. And it was not death. *Perhaps,* she thought, *it's dying.*

1:30 PM

Dave Johnson convened the meeting exactly on time, as was his style. Latecomers would have to catch up as well as they could. The conference room featured white on white wallpaper, burgundy carpeting, and a faux-wood-grained Formica-topped table, encircled with stainless steel frame chairs with upholstered seats and backs. A coffee carafe stood in the center of the table. Surrounding the carafe was a collection of mugs, the St. Catherine Hospital logo in gold, as well as congratulatory words, "Celebrating 75 years of Medical Excellence."

There were no coffee-takers but Dave, who tallied seven cups so far today. He hadn't left the hospital until well past midnight, and had returned by 6:30 AM. Caffeine was his friend today.

"Let's get started," Dave announced brusquely. "Some of us know one another, but for the benefit of the rest, we'll begin with introductions. To my left is Barbara Westover of the Cincinnati Police Department's Pharmaceutical Diversion Unit. Next is Richard Ostrader, also with the PDU. Barbara and Richard, I'd like you to meet Dr. Franklin from Anesthesia, Tom O'Brien, the

Assistant Director of Pharmacy, and Hannah Gilbert, the Perioperative Nursing Supervisor who was on duty last night. You already know Dr. Williams. And this is Evvie Smith, one of the CRNAs in the anesthesia group. Doug Howard from Pharmacy will be here momentarily, I'm sure.

"We'll start by recreating a timeline of events. Barbara and Richard may wish to ask questions. I spoke with most of you last night, and this may seem repetitive. Let's just do it once again, rather than rely on my fairly vivid recollection of the details." Dave smiled faintly, aware of the irony of his words, given his prodigious memory. His capacity to recall names, faces, conversations, document contents, and assorted hospital minutia rendered him a near legend, in hospital folklore.

"Let's start with you, Mrs. Smith. You were assigned to . . . ." Dave trailed off, expecting the nurse anesthetist to continue the story. Prior to the meeting, Dave Johnson had reassured the woman that she was not a suspect, although technically everybody was a suspect at this point. Perhaps she sensed that, because she appeared nervous.

Evvie Smith responded hesitantly. "Yes, well, I was assigned to OR 6 with Dr. Franklin. However, I was relieved to take my dinner break a little before 5:00, maybe ten minutes to five, and so I left. Dr. Franklin said that she'd set up the anesthesia drugs for the surgery, and that she'd do the induction if the patient and surgeon were ready before I finished my half-hour break."

Mackenzie Franklin nodded silent encouragement and support of the nurse's statements.

Her confidence bolstered, Evvie went on. "When I got back, Dr. Franklin was talking to the Nursing Supervisor about a problem with the syringes she'd been setting up. I got another kit and started setting up as quickly as possible because the surgeon was in a hurry to do the case and leave for the day—it was his last case, and he was a little upset about the delay."

Dave interrupted, "Dr. Franklin, do you know what time it was when you relieved Mrs. Smith for dinner break?"

"Yes," Mac answered forcefully. "It was 4:50 PM according to the clock in OR 6. I checked it so that I would know when to expect Evvie back from dinner."

"And what happened next?" Dave inquired, fully cognizant of the details Mac would share.

"I took the drug kit that was in the room and started setting up my syringes for the surgery."

"And can you explain for the benefit of the PDU people what that entailed, and offer an estimate as to the time?"

"Yes. It takes about fifteen minutes to set up all the medications that are used for this surgery. I opened the drug kit and drew up seven syringes, each a separate drug. When I set up syringes, I label them two ways. First, I mark the name of the drug on the syringe—everyone has to do that, and no one would use an unlabeled syringe. The second thing I do is mark the concentration of the drug. Not everyone does it, but it's what I do since different concentrations of the same drug are sometimes used during a single case. Marking the syringes with the concentration streamlines my job, making it easier to find what I need quickly."

"And then?" Dave prompted.

"At about 5:00, I was called to help one of the other CRNAs, with a difficult intubation in OR 9, down the hall."

"So, your syringes were set out in OR 6," Dave reviewed briskly. "Who was in the room while you were setting up?"

"Just the OR nurses. Possibly a tech was there for a few minutes, but I remember only the nurses when I was first setting up."

"And how long were you in OR 9?" Dave asked.

"Less than fifteen minutes. The clock on the wall opposite the door into the OR is one of the first things I notice," Mackenzie explained. "I'm very aware of time, especially when we're a bit short-staffed during dinner breaks. Dr. Markham had the case in OR 6, his last for the day, and I knew he would want to wrap it up quickly. So, when I went back into OR 6, I looked at the clock to see how much time I had lost. The clock read 5:15 PM."

Mac was an investigator's delight, conscious of time and details, even a bit compulsive in her approach to work. Such fastidiousness made it a breeze to reconstruct the events of the previous night, for which Dave Johnson was grateful. "And is that when you noticed the syringes on the tray were different?"

"Yes. I could tell right away that they weren't mine. They were labeled with the drug name, but the marker was thicker tipped, the handwriting wasn't mine and, obviously the drug concentrations were missing."

"And what did you do at that point?"

"I decided not to touch the other syringes, in case fingerprints could be lifted from them, and I asked the two OR nurses and the OR tech who were in the room if they had seen anyone touch the anesthesia tray. They said that they hadn't touched it, and that they hadn't seen anyone come into the room while they were there. They asked what was wrong, and I just mumbled something about my labels being screwed up. I don't think they knew that the syringes had been replaced until later, when all the questions were asked."

"So, what did you do then?"

"I got a plastic bag and tapped the syringes into the bag, using a pen to push them from the tray into the bag—I touched only the one syringe—and I left the OR to call Pharmacy to pick up the syringes. After I handed the syringes to the Tom O'Brien personally, I spoke with Hannah about the problem. Then, Evvie returned from dinner break, and I asked her to hurry and get another drug kit and to get set up. I explained that someone had disturbed the syringes I had set up, and that we would have to start from scratch. Evvie took care of it from there."

"And did you return to OR 6 after that?"

"Yes," Mac stated, "To be available during induction. It's our group's policy to have an anesthesiologist present during that phase of the anesthesia. After the induction was complete, I called Dr. Williams."

Dave turned to the nurse anesthetist. "Is there anything else you would like to add, Mrs. Smith?"

"No, I can't add anything," she assured, smiling nervously at the Security Director and the police investigators with PDU.

Her face belied sheer relief, as Dave dismissed her for the remainder of the meeting. Evvie Smith was discerned to be a loyal employee, one who had received nothing less than average marks on her performance reviews, and merely a witness to the timeline of events that had occurred the evening before.

Dave Johnson and John Williams had agreed that no one but the PDU officers would be informed about the syringes discovered in the physician's call room earlier in the week. Dave would share that information later, after the OR Supervisor had been debriefed and dismissed. He waited until the door closed behind Evvie Smith before turning his attention to Hannah Gilbert, the OR Supervisor.

"Ms. Gilbert, who was scheduled in OR 6 yesterday?"

"There were three shifts of staff working OR 6, and I have a copy of the names of those persons." Well organized and efficient, Hannah Gilbert was a striking brunette who had worked as a model for local department stores in her younger days, a sideline to her nursing career. At forty-three-years old, she looked easily ten years younger.

Passing the sheets to Dave and the PDU investigators, Hannah proceeded to articulate a precise description of each nurse's activities during the shift worked, concluding with the two who had worked the afternoon shift. Both nurses were completely trustworthy in their supervisor's opinion. Based on the interviews and search of the nurses' lockers, there was no reason to suspect either of making the substitution. The two nurses had begun setting up the OR at 4:40 PM, and they were joined by an OR tech at about 4:55.

According to Hannah, the OR tech was new, less well known, but she had not been alone in the OR. The OR nurses confirmed that the tech had not approached the anesthesia drug tray. Aware that any question of her integrity would result in swift termination, the tech had insisted that her locker be searched, and of course it was clean. Hannah Gilbert had no evidence that any of her employees, including personnel working in the ORs flanking room six, were responsible for substituting the syringes.

Barbara Westover, one of the PDU officers, stirred for the first time during the meeting, addressing the Perioperative Nursing Supervisor directly. "Ms. Gilbert, what were the nurses and the tech doing closer to 5:10, when you suspect the syringes were switched?"

"At that point, the nurses were getting the patient from the prep area. The OR tech was responsible for helping gown the surgeon who was doing the case, so she was in the scrub area adjacent to the OR. The nurses brought in the patient just as Dr. Markham and the tech finished the scrub. Dr. Franklin walked in at that point, about 5:15 PM. We had no OR staff in the room between about 5:00 to 5:15. Dr. Franklin spoke with me almost immediately, while Mrs. Smith was sent to get another drug kit. I spent the next forty-five minutes searching the OR area, every drawer, nook, and cranny. I found lost ID badges, paperback novels, a sweater, about a dozen pens, and a few other non-essentials. But I did not find any syringe. Believe me, I turned the area upside down."

"So, the person who switched the syringes had a fifteen minute window of opportunity," Barbara Westover reiterated, wordlessly communicating the notion that leaving an OR unattended, but set up with narcotics for the next case, was sloppy procedure. "Whoever did this must have been waiting in the wings. Who was in the OR area without being assigned to a room?"

Hannah Gilbert placed her hands flat on the table, a gesture that matched her terse words. "I didn't see anyone who didn't have business in the OR." Hannah leaned over the table, sustaining eye contact with the female officer. "You may think that an unattended OR is an accident waiting to happen, or a diversion waiting to happen. However, the OR area is typically very busy, staffed by professionals who don't steal narcotics. There are people entering and leaving the OR all the time, and we don't have the luxury of paranoia. We do about a hundred cases a day . . ."

"Wait," Barbara Westover commanded, holding up a hand, "I was thinking aloud. I don't want to criticize you personally or any of your staff. Let's see if we can figure out what we can do to narrow the field. I think we can rule out the OR nurses and the OR tech, as well as Evvie Smith. Dr. Franklin, did you see anyone from your department who was not assigned to the OR area?"

Mac shook her head, "No, the only person who may have been around was Dean Philips. Dean was on call last night. But he was tied up with three other rooms at 5:00 yesterday afternoon. There's no way that Dean is involved in this."

"What about Dr. Albers?" Hannah inquired cautiously. "I don't want to cast suspicion, but he did poke his head into OR 6— never mind," she reconsidered. "Dr. Albers has nothing to do with this any more than one of my nurses did." She looked directly at John Williams and Mackenzie Franklin. "I'm sorry."

Dave Johnson resumed control of the meeting, secretly relieved that the participants were voicing his own suspicions, allowing him feedback from the respected colleagues without having to risk his role or position as investigative facilitator. "We aren't going to come up with any one suspect now," he stated emphatically, "And the purpose of this meeting is to reconstruct the events with input from everyone involved. Having said that, I expect to have an analysis of the syringes that Dr. Franklin sent to Pharmacy for safekeeping. We probably won't be able to discern who labeled them, and lifting prints is out of the question. But we'll know if the drug matches the label, or if something was substituted. Let's shift gears now. What can we do to catch whoever is responsible? Richard? Barbara? Ideas?"

Richard Ostrader spoke up first, recommending that the Nursing Supervisor and the Anesthesia Department collaborate on an interim measure to ensure that each OR was staffed at all times, if only to make it more difficult for the thief to strike again. Additionally, Ostrader suggested that the PDU could put one or two undercover police officers into the operating rooms, which had been done in the past.

Mac and John shared glances with Hannah, aware that the former recommendation would be useful, but impossible to enforce during peak OR time. The latter recommendation was unsettling to everyone, and the OR generally ran smoothly because of the level of trust that existed among the physicians, nurses, and techs. An undercover police officer in the OR would introduce an element of mistrust—as if an element of serious mistrust wasn't already operative.

Dave wrapped up the meeting, leaving the others with an unanswered question—what was the plan? "Give a person the chance, and he or she will screw up again," he said. "For now, we will not discuss this problem with the OR staff, nurses, techs, docs, anybody. If we start mandating that an OR be staffed once a case is set up, we may lose the opportunity to identify whoever interfered with the anesthetics. We already know they operate quickly and quietly. Let's not send them further underground. Let them think we don't have a clue. Maybe we can look at OR 6 as possibly a prime target because of its proximity to exits. Perhaps we can set up a concealed camera in that OR, or maybe in the workroom where the drug kits and supplies are kept. I'll be in touch with you, John, and you, Hannah, when I have a report on the syringes. Any idea when that report will be ready, Tom?"

"Next week, hopefully early," advised the Assistant Pharmacy Director.

Dave stood, signaling the end of the meeting. Of all who attended, he was the sole participant who would call the session productive. He had formulated a plan prior to the meeting, and was not willing to share it in the event that one of the people in the room was his man—or woman, he reminded himself.

✦

The medical professionals understood that they had been dismissed. John asked if he could borrow an OR staffing schedule from Hannah. "I'm tracking some data. It may be a long shot, but if there is a pattern to pick up on, I'd like to do it before we have more problems."

Hannah paused to calculate the implications of refusing. She had no reason to mistrust Dr. Williams, and she actually respected his clinical abilities, as well as his willingness to defuse nasty encounters between temperamental anesthesiologists and the OR staff.

"I suppose I can share that with you," she answered guardedly, adding, "I'm not sure why I feel hesitant about this, I certainly want to resolve the problem."

Dave Johnson interrupted, "Hannah, it's information that *I will* need. We talked about this last night. But, John, how are you planning to use the information?"

"I've set up a spreadsheet to track personnel within the Anesthesia Department, OR room assignments, narcotic dosing, that type of thing. It will take a while for a pattern to develop, but in the absence of a computerized record-keeping system, it's the only way I know of to collect information that might help us. I'd be happy to share it with you, Hannah," John offered, conveying surprise at her resistance.

"All right, John. I'll get a copy to you, and yours is right here, Dave," Hannah said, extending a sealed manila envelope to the Director of Hospital Security. She then turned toward John Williams. "I'd like to see what you pull together, and maybe I can help analyze the data. I just don't want to be left out of the loop on this. Surprises don't agree with me, and if there's someone on my staff who is stealing narcotics, I want to know about it and take care of it myself, in accordance with nursing policy."

"No problem," John assured her. "I'll give you a copy of what I have, say a week at a time? That will give both of us the weekend to see if we spot anything. It'll take me at least a week to collect any worthwhile information, so how about if I get something to you a week from today?"

It was agreed.

The group dispersed, and John Williams and Mackenzie Franklin headed back to the OR area. "I'm going home," Mac announced, glad to finally enjoy her early out, which had been delayed by the meeting. "I'll see you on Monday—good luck with your project!"

"Thanks, Mac," John said with a rueful grin. "I have the double pleasure of spring yard work and data entry this weekend."

Parting at the locker room, John re-entered the workroom to check the progress of the afternoon OR schedule. He glanced at Hugh Lockhart, who was engrossed in The Wall Street Journal, the lone professional loafer within the group.

"How's business?" John commented dryly.

Dr. Lockhart harrumphed in reply, not even looking up from the newspaper.

John glanced at the board that listed each case, and noted the rooms he was assigned to cover. Throughout the recent meeting, Ron Albers had covered the ORs on John's behalf, rooms six, four, and two.

John brushed past Hugh Lockhart swiftly, air currents rattling the man's newspaper, and returned to the OR corridor to resume anesthesia responsibilities.

"I'm back, Ron," John called.

Before Dr. Albers could respond, someone shouted, "Code Blue! Recovery Room C!"

"You go," Ron told John. "I've got the ORs covered."

John darted down the hallway. When a Code Blue was called in the Recovery area, at least one of the anesthesiologists was expected to initiate resuscitation. It was not unheard of to have a patient "Code"—stop breathing—post-surgically, particularly if the patient was elderly, diabetic, or a smoker. In addition, heart disease, hypertension, or a history of stroke increased the risk of post-surgical respiratory distress. The patient who awaited resuscitation was not of that genre. The thirty-two-year-old female, with no known allergies and in good health, just finished having her knee ligaments reconstructed, the injury sustained while playing women's soccer.

"Dr. Williams," called Gina Barrett, the Recovery Area Supervisor. "I don't know what we're dealing with here. She's not breathing; pulse is seventy-two. She was doing just fine, talking a bit but not completely awake, until she got the dose of Demerol that was ordered."

John took charge, calling for an Ambu bag and mask. "How much was she given?" he barked.

"Twenty-five milligrams," the supervisor replied tersely.

"I want to see that syringe," John demanded.

"I checked it," Gina said defensively, "It's labeled. This patient got what was ordered."

The patient was slow to respond, and John reiterated his demand. "Where is it—now!"

Startled, the supervisor patted her smock pocket. "I've got it in here," she answered.

"Good," John said, sliding a laryngoscope into the patient's airway. In a few smooth motions, the endotracheal tube was placed, and the apparatus allowed John to breathe for the patient: a firm, brisk squeeze of the Ambu bag would send air through the endotracheal tube and into the patient's lungs, one puff every five seconds.

"Pulse?" he asked.

"Sixty-eight."

John observed the patient for any indication that she was returning to consciousness. There was none yet. He glanced quickly at Gina Barrett, lowering his voice.

"Once we get this taken care of, I'll take that syringe to Pharmacy for testing. Maybe the label wasn't correct. I'll need you to keep track of it for me in the meantime."

"Done," assured the supervisor.

Suddenly, the patient's arms and legs began to twitch, and then flopped spastically. John frowned in concern. "She's either got a pseudocholinesterase deficiency, or she's got something else on board besides Demerol."

"Oh, shit," breathed Gina Barrett.

"Come on, Laura," another nurse urged the now semi-conscious woman.

A frightening thought lingered in John Williams' mind: *What if someone had substituted a drug that would induce respiratory arrest?*

It wasn't as crazy as it sounded, for healthy thirty-two-year-old women do not arrest or code after fairly simple surgery. But what would a paralytic drug be doing in the Recovery Area? Or, perhaps this wasn't induced by a paralytic, but by a pseudocholinesterase deficiency. Such a condition rendered patients more sensitive to paralytics used prior to anesthesia induction. A simple blood test would rule it in or out. John called for the test to be run, stat.

The patient was now fully conscious, beginning to fight the endotracheal tube, and the team murmured words of reassurance to the woman, whose terror at the inability to breathe was as much a part of the emergency as the arrest itself.

"I'll breathe for you, Laura," John reassured. "I know that you're weak, and this is scary, but I'll make sure you get the air you need." He compressed the Ambu bag rhythmically, sustaining eye contact with the patient, and repeating the assurance. This repetitive reassurance was crucial to managing the care of a patient in such a state of terror, one of waking without the ability to breathe.

For her part, the patient lay wide-eyed, horrified to feel a tube crowding her throat and trachea, terrified that she could neither speak, nor inhale even a puff of breath. She could not make her body move or turn; her arms and legs rendered her little more than a floppy fish, incapable of controlled motion. She knew that she was still partially paralyzed, yet could not voice her questions or fears because of the endotracheal tube.

Before her blood could be drawn, Laura started to breathe on her own. At first, it felt like a hiccup, and grew to a breath, almost as if the machinery of her body had been switched back on.

"That a girl!" cheered one of the nurses. "We'll be able to get that tube out, now."

"Let's give it a couple minutes," John ordered mildly, wanting to ensure that Laura could sustain independent breathing.

Several minutes later, the patient was stabilized and the endotracheal tube was removed. After speaking with the woman and her husband about the possibility of a pseudocholinesterase deficiency, John arranged for the blood test to be run. He doubted that the woman had the congenital deficiency, given that such a condition might have rendered the woman paralyzed for hours, rather than minutes. Still, the test was necessary. In the presence of this condition, the woman would require alternative anesthesia for future surgeries, particularly if intubation was needed.

A damp tickle of sweat trickled down John's back. He exhaled loudly, releasing the tension that had collected within every neuron of his body. He had not experienced stress in the heat of the moment. It was only afterward that John wondered if *he* had breathed during the resuscitation. Since the patient had not responded quickly, the Code seemed to have taken hours. Yet, John also noted the paradoxical sense that, because events had transpired so quickly, only a few seconds had passed. Such was the nature of a medical crisis. It was past, and John now glided flexibly to his next task. Such was the nature of the skilled medical professional.

After detailing the averted crisis in the young woman's medical record, John picked up the syringe from Gina Barrett, and called Doug Howard. After briefing the Pharmacy Director, John requested to have the syringe contents tested, either to confirm that it was Demerol, or to determine what it *was* that sent a healthy patient into cardiac arrest. He then called Dave Johnson, repeating the story unemotionally, allowing the Security Director to draw his own conclusions.

Dave reviewed the list of personnel who had worked in the Recovery Area the week before. "Who's down there now?" he asked.

"Gina Barrett is the Recovery Area Supervisor. She ran the code with me. The other nurses I'm not sure about. I probably should have paid attention, but I can check that out now."

"I'll touch base with Hannah Gilbert, if Gina hasn't already, and I'll get with Doug about whatever is in the syringe. If it comes back positive for something other than Demerol, which is what it should be, Hannah or Gina can give me a staff accounting."

"I'd rather know who was around just before the patient coded, whether or not they are Gina's staff," John stated. "If we wait for the lab results, which may be days, we lose the chance to ask questions while people's memories are fresh. If someone who didn't belong there was seen, it might get overlooked by the time we get lab results back."

Dave Johnson remained quiet on his end of the phone. John Williams' urgency irritated Dave for many reasons, not the least of which was that Dr. Williams was asking him to alter his investigation. The order and pace of an investigation, as well as its observable existence, was determined by a matrix of factors. Physicians had no training in the process, and lacked the seasoned perspective of investigators. Often, the most productive investigations were invisibly conducted and patiently executed.

The matrix of factors impinging on the Security Director's decision to proceed accordingly included the fact that he had no evidence that any staff had acted to harm a patient. In addition, the only known diversions had been discovered in the physician's call room and OR 6, not the Recovery Area. And there were so many unknowns about who might be involved that it was risky to launch a visible investigation, which would alert whomever was involved.

"I'm not trying to tell you how to do your job, Dave," John explained. "It just seems like a good opportunity."

"Look, John, we have no evidence that this Code Blue is related to the other diversions. The fact that this patient coded right after we met about last night's diversion might be making all of us sensitive. But we don't know that there's any connection. Let me get back with you. I'll take care of checking on staffing, but I'll do it quietly."

"All right, but Gina Barrett knows that I think someone tampered with the syringe, and I'll bet she's already talked to her staff about it. I'm taking the syringe to Doug Howard now."

"Then he'll let both of us know what the lab comes up with," Dave stated firmly. "And we'll go from there."

✦

John Williams clicked off his cell phone and made his way back through the labyrinth of underground corridors that led to the Pharmacy Department. His legs felt leaden, and he registered a sense of defeat at Dave Johnson's response.

The Security Director was not afraid to take swift and decisive action, John knew, based on the lightning speed with which the CRNA had been apprehended last year. Dave was anything but a bureaucrat, but John had expected Dave to respond proactively to *this* incident.

Yet, Dave had done nothing more than draw a line in the sand, his initial silence communicating to John that he had come close to crossing a boundary. *Maybe Dave likes to work at these things alone,* John considered. Last year, Dave had presented himself as a team player, but his current penchant for secrecy—especially when several people *knew* that something had happened—and the investigation's plodding pace irritated John. He wondered fleetingly if Dave Johnson was investigating proactively, but not showing his cards—or sharing his information—because of suspicions about *him.*

As John entered the hallway that led to Doug Howard's office, he made a commitment to get the information he wanted on his own. He could do that quietly enough, just by looking at the nursing assignment board in the Recovery Area. He would note who was working this shift, and enter it in the database he had constructed. It would be a narrow accounting of the personnel who may have been in the area. It would not include transporters, IV techs, housekeeping, or maintenance staff. But it was a start. It was something he could *do.*

He arrived at the Pharmacy Department feeling unsettled, but purposeful. The secretary was wearing a headset that connected to the dictation recorder. She lifted her right hand, waving John into Doug Howard's office while typing rapidly with her opposite hand.

"Doug, I have the syringe for you."

"I'll send it out with a RUSH request, but don't expect any information back until the middle or end of next week."

"Why so long?" John queried. It seemed as if everything was taking an inordinately long time: first Dave Johnson's investigation; now the lab.

"I don't have the equipment here to analyze this stuff as accurately as a private lab. It just takes time, but with the rush order we should know by Wednesday. I'll let you know as soon as I hear."

"Is there any other lab that can turn around the results quicker?"

"There are a couple labs out-of-state, but we'd still be looking at Wednesday just because it's Friday afternoon, the syringe wouldn't get there by FedEx until tomorrow afternoon, and the testing wouldn't get done until Monday at the earliest, and getting the results might take a couple more days," Doug explained.

"I don't know that the syringe has anything but Demerol in it. Dave doesn't seem as concerned about it as I am. But if there's something in this syringe that caused a healthy, young woman to code, we've got a big problem."

As John Williams made this comment, several syringes filled with narcotic were lifted from the anesthesia tray in one of the Women's Health ORs. Later in the day, while the last of the cases were being wrapped up in the main OR area, additional syringes would be secreted deep in a lab coat pocket. Although the man who pocketed the syringes had only honorable intentions, they were the variety that paved the road to hell.

4:42 PM

Each time the Magi trekked to an appointment, he followed the same ritual, deviating from the process only when his wife was present. Although she was a teammate in this risky venture, his ritual was personal, private, and nearly sacred.

There was a measure of comfort that accompanied the acute sense of risk, the former born of the knowledge that he was making a difference. For people who were unable to experience the fullness of life, whose chronic, debilitating diseases robbed them of dignity and humanity, the Magi's treatment provided renewal. And for those whose illness was terminal, the Magi's elixir offered a higher quality of life.

He did not crunch the numbers or create a control group to research the impact of this drug. Yet, anecdotally, he knew that the medicine offered not only better symptom and pain relief than most narcotics; but, as well, there seemed to be a reciprocal or reverberatory effect that actually extended their lives. It was as if by living *well,* his patients were able to generate the energy to live *longer and better,* despite the disease.

Remembering this was all part of the ritual that preceded giving a treatment. But there was a deeper significance, as well. Beyond the reminder of the benefits of this treatment, the ritual itself invoked a self-inflicted penance, a reminder of the painful time when the Magi had refused to take such a risk with his life and his livelihood: what he had once considered offering his daughter—and refused to do—he now offered to strangers. He felt the burning shame of such a choice, one that his daughter had begged him to make days before she died.

Thus, it was part of the ritual, conducted in his car, that the man unfolded his wallet, thoughtfully glancing through the series of seven photos, back-to-back, the fourth clear plastic sleeve holding both a photograph of a young woman, and an obituary announcing her death.

His wife considered it morbid to carry the photos and obituary of their daughter. Yet, she granted her husband the privacy of his own grief, so grateful was she that they could collaborate to help others—if only to ensure that other mothers and fathers would not have to lose a child unnecessarily.

And it *was* unnecessary for their daughter to die. Whether or not she had died by her own will, he and his wife shouldered a burden of guilt as if they had delivered their daughter to the angel of death themselves. It was their selfish fears, they decided, that had kept them from doing what was necessary to spare the little girl in the pink tutu.

But that was the second photograph. The first was a birth photo, a black and white shot of joyous, prideful parents, cuddling the newborn girl.

The Magi always winced when he looked at these first two photographs. He wondered how he could have been permitted such a delight when, ultimately, he would squander it in fear: specifically, the fear of losing the chance to practice his profession; fear of losing the trust of loved ones and colleagues, fear of breaking the law. Perhaps more than anything, fear of imprisonment and loss of his freedom.

Ironic, he thought on many occasions. This guilt and grief *is* imprisonment, a life sentence for failing to do what he *could have done* with the gifts he'd been given. If he had to serve a sentence, why hadn't he just taken a chance and offered the elixir to his daughter? A prison constructed of concrete, metal bars, and barbed wire fences would be better than living with a damaged soul that would not accept forgiveness. He and his wife agreed about *that*. Their choice, years back, was unforgivable.

They had never asked for forgiveness. That was never an option. They had sacrificed their Joy selfishly. Better to have offered her the elixir, to have spread the word quietly so that others could receive it, than to have sacrificed Joy on the altar of late-twentieth century laws and social mores. Now, they knew: there were other professionals who would have helped them, who considered such a violation of laws and oaths a worthy part of familial trust and compassionate medical practice.

Too late, now.

That was the next part of the ritual. Remembering that, while it was too late for Joy, it was not too late for others. And perhaps, somewhere down the line, there would be redemption for this damaged soul, this broken heart, this shattered life.

So, the Magi spoke to God in somber tones, confessing his sin, thanking the heavens for the gifts he'd been given to help others, but *never* asking for forgiveness of the unforgivable.

As he completed the ritual of remembrance, thanksgiving, and prayer, the Magi looked carefully at each of the memories within those four clear plastic sleeves. The new family, the child in the stiff, pink tutu, the little girl with the missing front tooth, the shy adolescent glancing uncertainly at the camera, the girl with the hair to her waist, the girl sporting a cheerleader's uniform and a short bob, the young woman in a college graduate's cap and gown, and lastly, the young woman staring—unsmiling—from the obituary notice.

It wasn't their favorite photograph of Joy, but it had been the most current at the time of her death. Illness had robbed her face of expression. The photograph seemed a fitting indictment of her parents' abandonment of her needs to their self-protection, and the young woman's parents had known immediately that it would be the most suitable for announcing her death.

For which they were responsible.

If they were to be caught now, it would be a relief, of sort. They could simply own up to what they considered themselves to be: guilty. Everyone would know them as the imperfect parents they were. They did not deserve Joy, and so she was taken from them—first by *their* choice, then by her own. Perhaps she would have reconsidered life, had they done what they could to make it bearable for her.

There, the ritual was completed. It was painful, yet it offered both a release and a focus for the next step. And that was to offer healing.

Chapter Five

SHIFTING SEASONS

Monday, April 8
7:30 AM

"What I have amounts to a week of film," Dave Johnson explained. "Typically, we recycle tapes, so I can't show you anything that predates last week. I've hung onto these because of the recent diversions."

He glanced from the television monitor to the group assembled around the Board Room conference table. "As I fast forward through the tape, you may stop me at any point. I will need you to identify your personnel, and confirm that each person on tape had a justifiable reason for entering the satellite pharmacy. Unless we install an access system that's activated by swiping an ID badge, or hire someone to monitor the room, there's no other *secure* way to log who is entering this area."

John Williams, Hannah Gilbert, and Doug Howard had been assembled to review the tapes. Each had arrived with staffing records for the previous eight days, and anyone captured on tape would be identified and confirmed for authorized entry to the satellite pharmacy. Although most of those assembled were skeptical about the value of this exercise, none of them could suggest an alternative. With the latest incident, in which a healthy patient nearly died, it became imperative to ascertain if the safety precautions in place were adequate.

"We'll begin with last Monday," Dave stated, tapping the fast-forward button on the video-player. Initially, only Hannah and her assistant were seen on the tape. At the bottom of the monitor, the date and time flickered in fast-forward mode. At the end of the tape, Stu Adler—president of the anesthesia group—entered the room. John glanced down at the physician call schedule. Stu had been on-call that day, so he might have had a reason to enter the satellite pharmacy.

Dave looked over at John, whose nod indicated that this was acceptable.

The next day again featured Hannah and her assistant, as well as a brief view of a nurse who merely opened the door and closed it once again. Hannah checked her nursing schedule and nodded that Casey Blanchard would have been scheduled on that day, and might have been assigned to take care of something in the satellite pharmacy, borrowing Hannah's key.

John Williams stifled a yawn as the next day's tape progressed in fast-forward. Boredom began to cloud his attention, his mind drifting to names and faces that might be suspects in the diversion. Truly, he could not fathom any of his colleagues doing such a thing. The sixth day of tape was racing along, a Saturday. Stu Adler and Ron Albers were both featured, Albers early in the day, Adler in the early evening. The similar names generated a moment of confusion, quickly clarified by John. Such mix-ups in the two physician's names occurred frequently, especially when records were being reviewed or phone messages delivered. Several months ago, the group had remedied the problem by instituting the practice of signing one's full name, not merely initialing, requests for drug kits or anesthesia equipment.

John snapped to attention, quickly scanning the call schedule for that weekend. Ron Albers had been second-call, and may have had reason to enter the satellite pharmacy. But why would Stu Adler be in there? He wore scrubs, as if he were working. John rechecked the schedule and confirmed that the senior partner had not been scheduled to work that weekend. Although he could not vouch for Stu, John held back from flagging his colleague's presence.

Dave had noticed John's shift to attention and paused the tape. "What?" he inquired. Hannah and Doug shifted their attention from the monitor to John.

"Nothing. I don't think it's anything." John stated, considering his response. He was expected to participate by sharing information with this group. "I need to check the log book to see if Dr. Adler was covering for Dr. Ford. He has been selling his weekend call days. I'll get back with you." John chided himself for failing to bring the logbook to this meeting. Each party had been asked to bring complete records, and the log represented full accounting of days traded or on-call days sold. He should have at least consulted it before this meeting.

Dave restarted the tape. It was now Sunday, and no one entered the room. The screen turned blue, indicating the end of the film. Dave snapped off the monitor and rewound the tape. "That's it for now," he announced. "John, if you have any information from the logbook, I'd like it as soon as possible."

John nodded agreement, feeling the need to add, "I really don't think it's anything. But I'll let you know."

Dave flipped a page in his planner. "I'd like to meet again a week from today. In the absence of any other plan, I'd like to continue meeting to review the tapes in fast-forward, if only to identify anyone who may not belong in the satellite pharmacy. Will this time and day work for you?"

He'd addressed the entire audience. Nods and murmurs of reluctant agreement confirmed the plan. It would be a tedious way to identify a suspect, and one not wholeheartedly endorsed by the people convened.

Still, amidst the doubts, evidence was being created. The videotape recording at that moment would reveal a substantial clue about *one* of the perpetrators.

4:20 PM

The dark-suited figure entered the bedroom of Nathan Warden. A Winnie-the-Pooh nightlight, generally reserved for his granddaughter's visits, illuminated the far corner of the room. Although there were still hours of daylight remaining, the room-darkening blinds effectively turned day to darkness. The nightlight's pale yellow glow allowed adequate light to check the dosage of medication in the syringe, as well as to insert it into the intravenous line that snaked from Warden's slender, bruised arm.

He had battled a tenacious lung infection, and was finally responding to the antibiotics, which dripped steadily into his veins. While he slept deeply now, Nate had been agitated and veering close to belligerence with his wife earlier. He wanted the medicine that made him feel young and healthy, even if it was only a brief respite from his diseased and failing body. "I just want a vacation from my body!" he had shouted shrilly at Mae, his wife of forty-six years.

Their youngest child, the only daughter, was being married in less than a week. Nate wanted to be well enough to play father of the bride, and to enjoy the grand party of a reception that Mae and their daughter, Lisa, had planned. Their sons were coming back to Cincinnati from Tucson, Raleigh, and London. Maybe even the son from San Francisco would condescend to attend. It would be a family reunion, maybe his last, and Nathan Warden intended to be in top form for the event. But he needed that medicine.

"Curse the doctors!" he had told his wife. They hadn't done squat for him, compared to what his medicine man provided. The first round, more than a year ago, had allowed him to travel to his third son's doctoral graduation at Oxford University in England. The last few days of the trip had been rough, but the medicine man fixed him up again, upon returning stateside. What had permitted the trip to England last year, would allow his full participation in Lisa's marriage ceremony, and the festivities that would follow.

"Listen, my daughter's wedding is coming up. All I need is the potion so I can fight this infection," Nate had said to his friend, the medicine man, whom others called the Magi. Thus, Nate's medicine man had arrived with the healing elixir in a pocket of his tailored suit.

Now, lifting the strand of IV tubing, the shaman found the portal through which the potion would make its way into Nate's bloodstream. He uncapped the syringe, unveiling the sharp needle. Then, he raised the barrel to catch the glow of the nightlight, careful to check for air bubbles that might create a lethal embolus. There were none.

The medicine man slipped the needle into the portal and plunged the potion into the tubing. Nate Warden needed larger doses of the medicine now, and would need them more frequently to gain the necessary rejuvenation. Only that would allow Nate to host his daughter's wedding.

Having completed the injection, the medicine man removed the spent needle from the portal and recapped it tightly. He then placed the syringe in his jacket pocket, whispering "Good Luck" to the man in bed. Leaving as quietly as he had entered, nodding farewell to the patient's wife, the medicine man offered a silent prayer that he could access enough of this elixir to grant the Warden family's wishes.

5:00 PM

Rain splattered the jalousie windows, liquid darts that tapped insistently against the panes. Nancy Williams grimaced as she wound the stiff crank, the hinged glass creaking partway open with seasonal complaint. A damp, blossom-scented breeze swirled through the porch, while the slanted jalousies kept the rain out. Nancy crumpled several sheets of the weekend newspaper, and arranged them in the stone fireplace that straddled the porch and the family room.

Stretching to reach the box of long wooden matches from the shelf above the fireplace, she reconsidered her evening plans.

She and John had intended to mulch the front yard flowerbeds, hoping to do so before the predicted rains began. Another day, Nancy decided. Or, perhaps it was time to call back the gardener they'd used a few years ago.

The chance to finish spring yard work had eluded them the previous weekend. John had spent hours in front of the computer, tapping in names, dates, shifts, more names, drug dosages, additional dates, ad nauseam data. Typically, Nancy was able to distract her husband. But his determined pursuit of a pattern, gleaned from drug records and schedules, rendered Nancy a computer widow for all of last Saturday.

While her husband keyed data, Nancy cleared the last of the late-fallen leaves and trimmed some bushes. On Sunday, John left the computer long enough to lend a hand spreading several yards of aromatic mulch into the boxwood beds. The tulips were just blooming, tardy as spring this year, so the flowerbeds in front would wait.

So much to do, so little time. *How do people with children get everything done?* Nancy mused.

She scratched the match briskly against the hearth, immediately rewarded with a yellow-orange flame. Bending close, Nancy touched the match to crumpled newspaper that surrounded dry logs in the grate. The paper crackled and writhed, and the log soon surrendered to the flame as well.

Dinner, what's for dinner? Nancy considered briefly. There were the last pair of Omaha steaks that her mother had given to John at Christmas, and he was on kitchen duty this evening. Her husband had come into marriage well prepared to do his share of the cooking, cleaning, ironing. For this, Nancy was eternally grateful to John's mother—or perhaps his aunt, who raised John after his mother died.

Far more than just doing his share, John Williams was an adventurer in the kitchen—*if* he was cooking for an audience of at least the two of them. Frozen dinners were fine for solitary dining, but tonight, he was likely to be preparing the dinner accompaniments from a dog-eared copy of *Bon Appetit* or

Gourmet magazine. If time permitted, he would even create a dessert.

Nancy was more of an "entree-only" chef, happy to leave the execution of an intricate menu to John. What one brought to the table was sustenance, the other artistry. It was this balance, or complementarity, that characterized their marriage, and Nancy could not conceive of a force that might disturb that happy, satisfying equilibrium.

She'd once thought that children might create that sort of upheaval, and friends who had two and three children assured Nancy and John of that truth. Nancy preferred the freedom—which felt like eternal youth—that she and John had enjoyed throughout years of marriage, and guarded the guiltily kept secret that she had no physical or emotional urge to have a child. So why was the notion creeping into her consciousness today?

Watching the fire lap across the log, Nancy contemplated the call from her mother that seemed to precipitate a morbid contemplation of her life. And what she would leave in the end, when life was finished. She mentally listed a couple dozen good reasons why a couple might not have children, then challenged herself to call forth a single good, unselfish reason *for* having children. None were forthcoming.

"My mother may have cancer," Nancy spoke to the fire, testing the words as well as her own response to the freshly articulated possibility. "My mother may die, therefore I want to have a child?" She shook her head irritably, utterly at a loss to comprehend her thought processes.

In complete honesty, Nancy admitted that the notion hadn't simply bitten into her mind with the phone call. Rather, this feeling that something had been left "undone" had nagged at her subconscious the past several months. Elusive of name, this sensation featured restlessness, which Nancy had called everything from winter blues to wanderlust. Efforts to curb the feeling—ranging from videotaping their household possessions for insurance purposes, to clearing out boxes of stuff that she and John never used to make room for an exercise room in the basement—failed to quell the urgency. There was something that she should be doing; she could feel it. Yet it was all done. She and John had done it all. Well, almost.

Before they married, John and Nancy had discussed having a family. Nancy risked judgment by admitting that she had never felt comfortable with babies, and that while children were sweet, she didn't particularly want to have to make tough decisions about balancing her love of flying with the needs of dependents. Dependency of any sort was anathema to Nancy, although she'd recently started to think of herself as emotionally dependent on John as a partner in life's adventures. It was a scary possibility, dependency.

Although John respected Nancy's point of view, he'd always envisioned a more traditional marriage, including children after a few years. Despite the absence of little ones, their lives had become settled, predictable, suburban-without-children, and provincial, within the category of double-income-no-kids.

Was it *that*, a steady-state sort of humming through life that precipitated this evolving notion that there was more to be had, to be done, or to be enjoyed? Or was it actually *static?*

God, don't take my mother from me. Nancy heard the words echo in her mind, nearly a prayer, words she repeated silently, as if reciting a litany. The heat from the flames inside the hearth did not thaw the chill of fear anchored in her soul.

6:00 PM

"My mother called today," Nancy called to John in the other room. "She's going in for a breast biopsy tomorrow."

Nancy slipped a couple of brass rings around the floral cotton napkins and placed each at the kitchen table. John reappeared in the kitchen, a bottle of Cabernet Sauvignon in hand.

"That's not good. When did this come up?" he asked.

"Don't know, maybe just another false alarm. Maybe something else." Nancy avoided eye contact with her husband, sensing his concern without looking at him. She would melt into tears if she allowed herself to look at him, to accept his concern. For now, for reasons that she didn't understand, she would take greater comfort in keeping the discussion clinical—at a distance from emotion.

"Is Schmidt doing the biopsy?"

"Not after Mom's last round with him."

Nancy's mother had endured a few breast cancer scares within the past decade, the most recent about five years ago, coinciding with the discovery that Nancy's father had metastatic lung cancer. It had been a black period for the family, and the highly skilled but less than compassionate Dr. Schmidt had burned a bridge with Nancy's mother.

Following surgery, the doctor had refused to give Nancy's father additional pain medicine, claiming that it would create an intestinal blockage that could be fatal. "It could even stop his breathing," Dr. Schmidt had said. "I'm giving him the upper limits of narcotics. Anything more and I'd be practicing euthanasia." The unremitting pain rendered "Iron Ace" Jim Cavanaugh as pathetic as a whimpering puppy.

Never one to go quietly, Diane Cavanaugh, Nancy's mother, had contacted several local organizations that provided hospice and home health services for terminally ill people. She had learned that, while many physicians were reluctant to prescribe enough narcotic, there *were* internists and oncologists who would prescribe generously, cognizant that the patient wouldn't survive long enough for addiction or intestinal blockages to become an issue, and compassionate enough to work within the gray area of medical ethics concerning dosage effects on patient breathing.

"Will you ask Ron to do Mom's anesthesia?" Nancy asked, grateful for John's professional "in," well aware that her mother would receive red carpet treatment during the outpatient procedure. A good friend as well, Ron Albers was Nancy's favorite anesthesiologist in the group. Ron offered tremendous clinical skill, and a gentle, non-patronizing bedside manner. "Mom says that it'll be a local/stand-by procedure, but I'd feel better if Ron were there, in case she has to have general."

"Sure," agreed John. It was fortunate that Nancy's mother had the option of local anesthesia with sedation. It typically meant that patients were able to tolerate the procedure comfortably, without the risk and added recovery time of general anesthesia. For simple procedures, whether biopsies or cardiac catheterization, local/stand-by represented a safe, convenient option for patients. "I'll call Ron tonight and make sure it's on the schedule. I can meet you up there if you page me when you get in— you're driving your mom, aren't you?"

"Yeah. Can you believe she didn't even let me know about this until today? It was scheduled a week ago, and Mom never said anything to me or to Sandy."

Nancy and her sister, Sandy, shared a close relationship with their mother. As the only two siblings in Cincinnati, they frequently enjoyed a girls' night out when John was on call. Whether antique-hunting in Lebanon or sharing a good cry at the theater over "Little Women" or "Remains of the Day," they protected and treasured the time to giggle or weep, to dream or share secrets, and to offer the brand of moral support that comes only from family females who love and accept one another.

Nancy plopped heavily into a Windsor chair, aware that she was treading close to the edge of emotion.

"It's not like your mom, keeping something like that to herself." John shook his head silently as he stirred the shallot-cognac-cream sauce for the steak au poivre dinner. He was unsure how to respond: Should he reassure Nancy that her mother didn't call about the biopsy earlier because *she* wasn't worried about it, and didn't want Nancy to worry about it? Or, would it be better to sympathize with Nancy's sense that her mother must be concerned about this biopsy, and for that reason did not want to share the information until the last possible moment?

John rested the spoon on the counter and took the middle road, wrapping Nancy in a bear hug from behind. "I want her to be fine, too."

Pulling John's arms tightly around her, a warm shroud of comfort, Nancy rapidly blinked back the threatening tears, now ready to be consoled. "I keep thinking about Dad," she said unsteadily. "I know that this isn't necessarily fatal, or even cancerous. Mom's secrecy just isn't like her, and I wonder if this is more of a problem than she's let on."

"Your mother usually tells you and Sandy everything," John agreed, sustaining the hug, the soft warmth of Nancy's skin against his own a touchstone of comfort. He could not take away the pain of her anxious concern, but somehow skin-to-skin contact seemed to absorb the more toxic aspects of anxiety, and Nancy's voice was firm and modulated when she spoke again.

"I'm glad I'm here to take her. My schedule is more hectic next week, and with Sandy traveling so much . . . ."

"Sandy will go nuts when she finds out," John said, grinning at the idea of what his mother-in-law would go through when her Irish-tempered daughter learned that she had been left out of the loop about such a crisis.

Nancy whooped with laughter at the thought. "It'll be worse than surgery!"

Rising from her chair, Nancy unfolded the cloak of John's arms and turned to deliver a gentle, prolonged kiss. John sighed in relief that he had hit the mark.

"Thanks," Nancy whispered quietly. It was all that needed to be said, for now.

8:15 PM

Kathy Martin collapsed against the wall of the guest bathroom, her right arm curled around the bowl of the toilet. She closed her eyes, but the stars and sparkles that signaled faintness remained. It was the fifth time in three hours that she'd vomited, having risked snacking on soda crackers and applesauce. Her gums, esophagus, and diaphragm burned from the acid assault and physical force of each heave. Her legs and fingers twitched mercilessly. Yet, she could not bear to smell, much less taste, the liquid cold medicine that would zonk her into spasm-free unconsciousness. Perhaps she could swallow an allergy-relief pill—

over-the-counter, of course—with a sip of water. But, how long would it stay down?

"Mommy? Are you in there, Mommy?"

Dear God, I can't take this, Kathy thought. *Where is Drew? Why isn't he getting the children to bed?*

"Mommy, are you okay? It's me, Mommy. Let me in!"

"Leave Mom alone. She's sick," the older child whispered. "Don't worry, Mom, we're gonna have a snack and go to bed. I think Dad will be home soon, but we did our homework."

"That's good, kiddos," she forced herself to call, albeit weakly. "You're great kids." *Damn that Drew! He thinks more about his damned clients last-ditch tax shelters than his own children!*

"Goodnight, Mommy!" called the girl.

"Shhhh!" hushed the older brother. "Come on!"

It would be over soon, tax season. Drew would help, then. *God, get me through until then.*

10:00 PM

"Hmmmmmm," John purred playfully, draping his arm across Nancy's belly.

The Williamses cuddled warm and breathless beneath the cotton sheets, enveloped in exhilarated fatigue. Nancy traced the outline of her husband's eyes, nose, lips, and ears as she considered her next words.

"I'd like another set just like them around here, one of these days," Nancy said softly, stroking the outer curve of John's ear. "In miniature," she added.

His eyes shot open. "Well, that's a change of heart," he murmured. "When did you decide that?"

They hadn't even broached this subject since before they were married, save for a single conversation some years ago, shortly after Nancy's father became sick. Nancy had felt torn between wanting to create another generation for her father to enjoy, and sustaining the freedom to fly, the exclusiveness of her husband's attention, and the pleasurable pursuit of leisure—with consideration for no one but herself and John. In the end, she'd admitted to John that the parcel called parenthood, concomitantly a gift and a responsibility, was not the package she was ready for, then. John had felt disappointed, Nancy knew, and she'd felt guilty for her selfish reasons not to have children. Still, he had agreed that if and when they were *both* ready, that would be time enough.

It appeared that the hour had arrived.

"I've been thinking about it for a while. Just trying to figure out if I want it for the right reasons."

"And . . . ."

"And," Nancy replied with certainty, "I want us to be parents. For us, not for anyone else. It's time."

"So what is the right reason?"

"I'm not sure there *is* a right reason. It's simply the right time," Nancy repeated, reaching for her husband once more.

Had he anticipated this turn of events, John Williams might have insisted on a clear articulation of Nancy's position. He recognized his wish to simply believe the determined certainty in Nancy's voice. Maybe there are plenty of wrong reasons, and no single, genuine, *right* reason to have a child. Some things are more a manifestation of instinct or intuition, and they defy logical explanation.

Perhaps Nancy was right; quite simply, it was time.

Chapter Six

CANDID CAMERA

Tuesday, April 9
8:00 AM

Although Diane Cavanaugh's biopsy was scheduled to be done under only local anesthesia with sedation, the possibility that general anesthesia might be needed to give adequate pain-relief precluded breakfast that morning. Diane's fingers struggled with the strings at the back of her gown, refusing to function without the usual dose of caffeinated coffee.

"Let me tie that for you, Mom," Nancy offered briskly, taking the back panels of the flimsy hospital gown in hand, and quickly tying bows at the neck and waist of the garment. The surgery wasn't scheduled for another hour, and Nancy had declined breakfast in a useless but symbolic gesture of support.

They had agreed that, unless Diane needed general anesthesia—which would extend her recovery and kill her appetite—dinner would be early that day: at Spazzi's, above the Waterfront Restaurant. Nancy and her mother shared mutual cravings for the seafood minestrone soup. Meanwhile, Nancy preferred the shared suffering of hunger, and ignored her mother's scolding that she should get something to eat.

"I'm not even hungry," Diane insisted, "Just clumsy. Why don't you run to the cafeteria and eat something while I give the nurses, doctors, and the rest of the press corps my life history."

"Mom, why did you have children?" Nancy blurted, without prelude. "I mean, did you actually *decide* that you would have children? Was it a conscious choice? Or did you just have children because it was part of the marital package?"

Stunned, Diane Cavanaugh untied the upper bow of her patient gown and slowly, thoughtfully, retied the strings. "Nancy, I made a choice to have children, but not at all the way people choose these days. I knew when I was young that I wanted children of my own. Children were an important part of the family culture I was raised in. What makes you ask?"

Nancy raised her eyes to the speckled acoustic ceiling tile, fluffing her bangs as she gathered her thoughts. "I've always known that there are very good reasons *not* to have a child. And I've used a bunch of those reasons to defend the choice John and I have made. It does seem to be a position that requires defense, at least in this family that cherishes children so greatly."

It was a baited reference, related to incessant queries by the wives of Nancy's two brothers, regarding children. Sandy was single, so it wasn't an issue for her. Nancy, however, had felt beleaguered by the inquiries.

Diane returned her daughter's direct gaze, eyes bright in anticipation, but remained silent, insistent that Nancy must sustain the lead here.

An irritated expression crossed Nancy's face as her mother declined the bait. Diane had always required her children to think, to make important life decisions, for themselves. Nancy's independent nature was incompatible with anyone who tried to *tell* her anything, and Diane knew that her silence would force Nancy to think and decide for herself.

"I'm thinking aloud, Mom," Nancy said softly, a smile beginning to curl at the corners of her lips, "about having a baby."

"And?"

"I'm not sure if it's the right thing for John and me. We have a great life together, and it seems as though our friends who have children are run ragged, either because of sleep deprivation or over-scheduling. Things are uncomplicated for us, and

I've liked the freedom to do what we want without much planning. I like my job and want to keep flying. And I'd have to make compromises if we have a baby. God, I thought we'd made this decision already!" Nancy whispered with a breathy huff of self-exasperation.

"So, you want your life to stay the same," Diane paraphrased slowly, allowing Nancy to contemplate the possibility.

"No, Mom. I'm feeling restless. Like I'm actually ready for a change. But this is different from the restlessness I've felt when I've needed a new challenge in my career. And it's different than wanting to see or do something new. It's more like—like a scent is in the air. Like something good is going to happen if I act quickly." Nancy stopped, tears pricking at the corners of her eyes.

"And you've already returned your Publisher's Clearinghouse entry, no doubt," Diane teased, noting the threat of tears, "so it's not *that.*"

Nancy smiled broadly, gratefully. "Mom, there are so many reasons why it would be easier *not* to have a child. And I can't come up with a solid reason *for* having a child. But this seems to be the source of my restlessness. And I thought I'd figured out that question!"

"Seasons change, people change, Nancy. Maybe this isn't so very different than the restlessness you felt when you wanted to fly a different jet. Parenthood is definitely a career-decision, and not just an eighteen-year commitment. Your generation is much more in charge of your lives than ours was—or perhaps your father and I simply chose to believe that we were not masters of our own destiny."

Diane paused momentarily, then asked, "What do you *see* when you think about your life with a baby?"

Nancy cupped her chin between her palms, squinting at a patch of bedding beyond her mother's searching stare. "That's the problem, Mom. I can't *see* any part of it. I can see you and me, when I was younger. But I can't see me—or John—and a baby. I'm not like my friends who have kids," she explained. "They were always sure that they'd have children. And it isn't as though

I'm craving the chance to hold a baby. I've never really felt comfortable holding babies anyway. I'm not sure I have the 'maternal instinct' to be a good enough parent, and if I can't do the job well, I'd rather not do it at all—for my sake, yes, but more for the child's sake. Does this make any sense, Mom?"

"Nancy," her mother stated, grasping her daughter's hand firmly, "you have many gifts and talents. You are as loving a child—and an adult—as any of my children. I don't believe in the myth that the only women who make good mothers are the ones who've *always* wanted children. It fails to make room for the possibility that the child itself influences changes in the parents.

"And neither your father nor I were 'born' parents," Diane continued. "It was because we were responsible for each small, helpless, dependent baby that we became adequate parents, and because we were the beneficiaries of each child's guileless, unconditional love. Nancy, I may not have planned the details of my life as you and John have. I may have stumbled into my life because, for a variety of reasons, I felt that the conventional ways of the times were the *best* ways for me. But that doesn't mean that I was any differently equipped to be a parent than you are."

"But this isn't just a question of whether or not I'm up to the task."

"Of course it isn't," Diane agreed gleefully. "And the other parts of your struggle are much more important pieces of the equation. Actually, Nancy, I will happily be a sounding board, as your biased mother. But this struggle is for you and John. It would be unfair of me to do anything to take it from you two. Together, you'll make the right decision." Diane stretched forward to peck her daughter's pale cheek as she whispered fiercely, "You always have."

"I don't know, Mom."

"Then be still, off and on, as you struggle with this, and listen to your heart."

8:25 AM

"Diane, I'd like you to meet one of my partners, Ron Albers." John Williams facilitated the introduction as his pager beeped insistently.

"Pleased to meet you, Dr. Albers," Diane Cavanaugh greeted him warmly, offering both hands in welcome. "How lucky that John has arranged the red carpet treatment for me this morning!"

"Excuse me while I answer this page," John said apologetically, grabbing Nancy's hand for a quick squeeze and brushing a kiss across her forehead. "I'll leave you in Ron's hands—he'll have some questions for you, Diane."

Leaving the pre-op assessment room, John clicked on his cellular phone and punched in the familiar extension to Dave Johnson's office. The secretary answered, but the line snarled with static, despite the short distance between the Security Offices and the Women's Health surgical wing.

"I can't hear you," John called loudly, shaking his phone in a useless gesture. "What was that?" More static growled through the phone, followed by a high-pitched whistle that offended John's eardrum. Startled, he pushed the phone to arms-length in front of him. "I'll call back on another phone," he called into the receiver, not waiting a reply. *News,* he thought, *Dave has news.*

Returning to the nurse's station on the Women's Health wing, John rounded the desk briskly and stepped into the closet-size dictation room. Here, physicians dictated discharge summaries or consultation reports. By the end of the day, a crew of nimble-fingered transcriptionists would have stacks of neatly typed documents, ready to be inserted into patient charts. Noting the absence of competition for dictation, John tapped in Dave's extension, chuckling in awareness that the number—2677—spelled the word "COPS."

Dave answered immediately. "I have something I'd like you to look at, John. Need your opinion about it. When are you free today?"

"Not for a while. I'm in Women's Health checking on my mother-in-law. She's having some minor surgery today. Anyway, I need to get back down to General Surgery. Maybe at lunchtime?"

Dave's tone was grim. "I'm in meetings from 10:00 until 5:00, no breaks, and with JCAH and AHA site visits coming up, I can't rearrange any of them. You going to be around at 5:00?"

"Doubt it," John answered slowly. "I have plans this evening. Can you tell me about it over the phone?"

"No."

The pause following Dave's monosyllabic response was palpably electric, sending tingly shivers along John's spine. He mentally considered an alternative to the evening plans. *I can come back after dinner—I'll be out of here by 4:00, we'll open up Spazzi's at 4:30, and I can be back here by 6:00.* It would be less than what he and Nancy had planned as a gluttonous distraction for her mother. He tried not to hope that Diane needed general anesthesia, which would cancel dinner altogether. He would honor the agreement for dinner. "I'll meet you here at 6:00—will that work?"

"Six o'clock," Dave assented. "It'll take about twenty minutes to show you what I've got. Forty minutes, maximum."

"I understand that it's important," John acknowledged. "If you have a meeting cancellation, call me. Or page me. My cell phone is useless today—full of static and some sort of whistle."

Dave chuckled softly, in response. "Bet I can fix that! I may be the source of that interference, John. Can't tell you about it now, but I'll see what I can do on this end."

John felt the pucker of puzzlement cross his face as he hung up the phone. *What was THAT about?*

Shaking his head, releasing the tension, John briskly exited the dictation room and rounded the now-vacant nursing station. He reached into his jacket pocket and clicked on the cell phone. It was still full of static and the annoying whistle. Raising it to ten inches from his ear, the shrill whistle like a scalpel against his eardrum, John again shook his head with impatience.

He clicked off the phone and replaced it in the deep pocket of his lab coat. Unconsciously, he allowed his fingers to trace the contour of the buttons as he pondered the drug thief's proximity. He did not notice as Ron Albers and the pre-op nurse accompanied Diane into the Women's Health OR.

6:05 PM

John waved to Nancy and Diane as he pulled away from the restaurant. Thankfully, Diane had tolerated the biopsy well, with the help of light sedation and local anesthetics. Results of the biopsy would not be available for a week or so, and Diane was determined to move forward, rather than put life on hold. John wondered if his own mother had been like that, and decided that she must have been, perhaps for his sake. He had never seen her slow down until she was hospitalized.

He shook his head, willing himself to remain in the present. His mother's illness and Diane's situation were different stories, albeit within the same book of life: his. The thought chilled him, despite the warm evening air, and he warded away the demons by punching in Dave Johnson's number.

"Dave, I'm five minutes away—sorry to be late." John felt the psychological gears shift from social pleasures at the restaurant, to dark memories, and on to mental concentration regarding Dave's news about the diversion.

"No problem, I'll be here," he assured.

St. Catherine's was built in a Southern Gothic architectural style, featuring tons of white brick, three-story pillars and porticos at each of the entrances, acres of lush, green lawn, and manicured gardens, all wrapped in a tall, black, wrought-iron fence, the arched gates folded open in welcome. The hospital property sprawled across the equivalent of six blocks, much of it dedicated to parking, gardens, and office buildings, also of the Southern Gothic genre. None of the structures were taller than three stories, and none were larger than any of the Victorian mansions-turned-offices, which lined the nearby streets.

The hospital was initially dedicated to the health and medical care of Catherine Bassett Vonderheide, a beautiful woman from Savannah, Georgia, who had come north after her marriage to Cincinnati's billionaire entrepreneur, Edgar Preston Vonderheide, III.

Rather an orchid among even Cincinnati's finest roses, Catherine Vonderheide was chronically ill with a condition that defied diagnosis at the time. Her husband determined that he would build the finest hospital in the city, and then recruit medical specialists from the Mayo Clinic, Harvard Medical School, Johns Hopkins, and all the illustrious medical centers of the North American continent.

Architecturally, the structures favored the Bassett family home, and Catherine had a suite of rooms that represented *home* for the better part of her years in Cincinnati. In the end, St. Catherine's amounted to a shrine of devotion to Edgar Vonderheide's wife, and the center of medical excellence within the tri-state. Not even the Cleveland Clinic offered this combination of exemplary medical treatment within a five-star setting.

John palmed the steering wheel to the left, winding around to the east entrance. Across from the entrance was the physicians parking garage, designed to resemble a large carriage house. John slid the car into the nearest space, and dashed across the pavement, through the lobby, and into the main elevator, unconsciously counting the seconds required to reach the third floor Security Office.

Rounding the office entrance, John noted the war room effect that Dave had created. There were floor plans of both the main OR area, and that of Women's Health, taped to the wall. Multiple side-by-side dry-erase boards featured bold strokes of marker, listing the names of all employees who had worked in the main OR area last Friday. Color-coded elastic string stretched from a magnetic rectangle, each labeled with an employee name, to similarly color-coded push pins on the floor plan, thereby linking personnel to his or her assigned OR, or other areas nearby.

The colored strings delineated the jobs of each person: OR nurse, OR tech, Recovery Room nurse, Recovery Room aide, surgeon, anesthesiologist, nurse anesthetist, Housekeeping attendant, Maintenance staff, Pharmacy tech, etc. Some names had multiple strings routed from the dry-erase board to various places within the main OR area, which included a satellite pharmacy, patient prep rooms, twenty-two operating rooms, recovery rooms, a physician changing area, a nursing staff changing area, the scrub room, a centralized nursing station, and a family waiting room. Multiple strings indicated that the employee's job requirements took him or her to a variety of areas within the hospital.

John whistled in admiration of the detail. "You ever go home, Dave?"

Dave Johnson allowed himself a grin, "Only long enough to get my four or five hours of sleep. My wife would think I was fired if I spent more than a couple evenings a week at home."

John collapsed in the chair opposite Dave, rather tired than prepared for whatever news Dave offered. "What's happened?" he asked.

"A couple things. The latest is the report on what was in the syringes we found in the call room."

"And?"

"Limbotryl," Dave stated simply, leaning back in his chair, perhaps to better gauge John's response.

John stiffened, then leaned forward. "Limbotryl," he repeated, incredulous. "I'd never have guessed that."

"Why not?" Dave asked. He had his own ideas about why not, but favored John Williams' perspective as a professional who understands the narcotic.

John shrugged, gathering his thoughts, not as tired as he was a moment ago. "I guess because it's one of the big gun anesthesia drugs. It's great for long cases because it provides good relief without the side effects of nausea or hangover that you'd get if you used Sufentanil, or something else. But it isn't popular, in terms of drug diversion, for a couple reasons. It isn't like Fentanyl, which gives a quick rush without the somnolent effect that you'd find with some other narcotics. Addicts prefer a drug that's got a quicker onset," John added.

Dave nodded, looking at the report without comment. John

waited, contemplating what this could mean. Limbotryl added a perplexing piece to the puzzle. It seemed as if it belonged to another puzzle entirely.

"There's more," Dave added. "You noticed the static in the cell phones. It's probably feedback from some surveillance cameras I've set up in the OR workroom. If someone were diverting drugs, the easiest place to start would be the workroom, since it's unmonitored." Dave gestured toward the conference room down the hall, "Let me show you a video that was shot yesterday. It's set up in the conference room."

Ten minutes later, John was seated in the third floor conference room, stunned to be watching a video of one of his colleagues sifting through drug kits that were stashed in the Women's Health workroom until they were transferred to the Pharmacy Department for narcotics inventory.

"What do you suppose he's doing?" Dave asked.

John felt numb with shock at the sight, yet remained reluctant to condemn the admittedly suspicious rifling through drug kits as diversion.

"Is this video legal?" John asked grimly, hating himself for sounding like a lawyer who prefers to defend the guilty.

"It's public space. We have reason to suspect criminal activity. Risk Management approved the camera." Dave spoke softly, not the least defensive, cognizant that he was asking John to identify his partner and friend as a drug thief. "It's a clear image. We know who it is. We aren't sure about what he's doing. It doesn't look like he takes anything, based on my review of the tape, but his hands and pockets are outside the camera range. I need to know if he has another reason for searching those drug kits." Dave paused, looking briefly at the notes he had scrawled while watching the video originally. "Can you give me an opinion about what he might be doing?"

"No," John replied firmly.

"No opinion? Or, no comment?"

John felt the seafood minestrone turn bilious, lurching and burbling in his stomach. How could he answer the question? *What else could he be doing? Maybe he's looking for evidence of the drug thief, his own little investigation? Maybe he's looking for a good pen or his watch. I've taken off my watch a million times, and I've lost it in the OR, too. Since my back is to the wall clock, it's easier to track time if a watch is propped up on the drug tray, especially if I've got both hands occupied with lines and tubes.*

As the thoughts stirred, his stomach churned threateningly. John leaned forward in the upholstered conference chair, cradling his temples in twin pyramids formed by thumbs, middle, and index fingers. He noted the throbbing rhythm, normally imperceptible, now *staccato fortissimo*. An answer was expected, and Dave was being patient. Yet, the sock in the gut—represented by the possibility that a trusted colleague might have betrayed a nearly sacred trust—knocked the wind from him, and temporarily stole his voice.

Finally, John spoke. "Dave, we both see him rifling through the drug kits. We both know that someone has been diverting drugs. I can hardly believe what I'm seeing, and I'd like to tell you that maybe there's some reasonable excuse for what Ron is doing. There isn't. Or maybe there is. It's a long shot, but maybe he lost something during the surgery, maybe a good pen or a watch, or maybe he's playing detective. He's on our board, and he knows about the diversion. As to what he's doing, I don't know for sure," he looked up, meeting the intent gaze of Dave Johnson. "And neither will you unless you ask him."

"I *will* do that," Dave said quietly. "I just wanted to give you a chance to see what we have, and give you the opportunity to tell me that it might be something else."

Dave paused then, exhaling slowly, glancing at the freeze frame displayed on the television monitor. "I'm sorry it isn't someone else, John. It's hard to take. If you want, you can join us. Stu Adler will be there, of course, as will one of the Risk Management lawyers, when we talk with Dr. Albers tomorrow. It can't wait, you know."

John nodded, he did know. He wished he didn't.

7:00 PM

"Dave Johnson caught Ron Albers on film rifling through the drug kits," John announced without preamble.

"What! Today? While Mom was having surgery?" Nancy's eyes widened, and her lips parted in shock.

"Yesterday." It was an effort to speak, even in monosyllables.

"And?" Nancy asked from the center of the kitchen, hands braced on hips, her posture conveying disbelief.

John slumped in the nearest Windsor chair, not even taking off his jacket. He looked at Nancy, not really seeing her.

Impatient to know details, Nancy planted herself opposite him. A cautious intuition suggested that she tread carefully. Her heart thudded with trepidation at the possibility that one of their closest friends, their first choice for giving Nancy's mother anesthesia, was stealing drugs . . . was using drugs . . . was selling drugs? She took John's hand, stroking his fingers gently, feeling the bump of the wedding band she had given him several years ago, shortly after they'd vacationed with Ron and Sally Albers in St. Lucia.

The vacation had been sponsored by the Academy of Medicine, an all-inclusive week at the newly opened Wyndjammer Resort. The days had begun with sunrise walks along the beach, and often ended well past midnight, hours beyond the evening activity, whether crab races, casino, or karaoke. Typically, Ron and Sally closed the parties, the last to leave any gathering. *What did I miss? Was Ron ever away from the group long enough to do drugs?* Nancy wracked her memory, tripping through the years mentally as if flipping briskly through the pages of a photo album, searching for some clue, any shred of incriminating behavior that might have tipped them. There were none to be found.

"John," she said quietly, "in the video, did Ron actually *steal* any drugs?"

John shook his head, mute.

"You said he was caught going through the drug kits, right?"

He nodded, then met Nancy's gaze. "We have to talk with him in the morning."

"I'm surprised that Dave didn't do that already," Nancy mused.

John blinked, visibly startled. *Why didn't I think of that?* "I didn't ask him. I should have asked him. Dave always moves quickly on diversions. He risked a day, a diversion."

"Why would he do that?"

"Maybe because the film didn't actually show that Ron *stole* anything. Or, maybe because he had to talk to Risk Management. I doubt that it was only because he wanted me to tell him that Ron was doing something else."

"*Could* Ron have been doing anything else?"

"I wish I thought so."

"God, I can't believe this," Nancy whispered. "Do you think he'll be arrested after Dave talks with him?"

"Depends on what he says during the interview."

"But it's possible."

"Yes."

"Shit. It's just like last year . . . only worse. But really, John, it's not as if you've even given Ron the benefit of any doubt."

John looked at Nancy meaningfully, as if half begging to be convinced, and half cynically appraising her refusal to understand what he had shared.

Nancy raised her hand, briefly breaking eye contact, as if accused of extreme stupidity. "Hear me out, okay?" She lowered her hand, gathering her thoughts, organizing them as if preparing a persuasive speech. "What you know is that Ron Albers was searching through the drug kits. Others have done that before. You did it each time you lost a watch. Searching alone is not proof of theft."

She continued, raising a second finger as she enumerated each point. "Ron Albers has no history of drug use. Remember how Sally had to bug him to see someone about that neck pain that radiated down his back and leg? And Sally said he didn't even take any of the Percodan that was prescribed after he had the disc surgery. The guy doesn't take Tylenol for a headache, for godssake!"

She was lost in concentration, as if fighting for Albers' life. Her third finger lifted as John interrupted.

"Actually, your last argument is a perfect explanation for Ron to have *started* taking Fentanyl: quick pain-relief, short-acting to allow him to function nearly optimally at work, and easy access without having to see another physician."

"You docs are notorious for neglecting your own health: Physician Heal Thyself mentality," Nancy agreed. "But you don't know that's what happened, and it doesn't fit Ron's personality. Remember, he doesn't even take over-the-counter stuff. And most importantly, all of the drug kits you checked at the end of yesterday matched the drug record. There was no evidence of a diversion yesterday."

"Unless someone replaced the contents with saline—you suggested that, yourself," John argued.

"So check it out!" Nancy challenged. "This is our friend. So he went looking. That doesn't make him guilty of anything but being in the way of a hidden camera. And wouldn't Forrest Smith have fun with *this* in court! Ha!"

Smith had the dubious distinction of being one of Cincinnati's most visible First Amendment attorneys, one who would willingly tackle any civil rights abuse, even for the morally bereft Klan. Smith's tenacious pursuit of ideals penned by the authors of the American Constitution rendered him a colorful figure on the legal landscape. He was often misperceived as a sellout to ideals over principles. In truth, he was no sellout. But the hill on which he waged battle, without any regard for what might be politically correct or generally popular, was one on which few attorneys tread.

Nancy's arguments were not without merit, John conceded. "And I wish I *could* check it out," he complained. "But it's impossible to retrieve narcotics used in surgeries prior to today. As soon as Pharmacy examines the drug kit contents against the record, the remaining contents are disposed of. It's part of a strict narcotics procedure. Anyway, it's too expensive for the Lab to test every narcotic that comes back; that would be at least a few hundred tests."

Nancy sighed. "It's the fact that Ron was searching the drug kits that gets me, even if I don't think he's stealing or using drugs. He knew about the diversions, and he should've known better than to go through drug kits without someone else, just like the Pharmacy uses two techs to review narcotics that come back."

"You're right," John agreed. His eyes offered a challenge before he verbalized it. "I'm thinking about calling Ron tonight, asking him what he was doing."

Nancy did not breathe, surprised that John would consider this breach of Dave Johnson's trust. She contemplated John's motives to risk such a move. "So, if you call Ron, is it in the service of treating your partner as your brother?" This was part of the Hippocratic Oath, a promise each graduating medical student swore to uphold as the highest ethical code of honor within the profession.

"It's not just because he's a colleague. It's more because I feel I owe him the benefit of the doubt, both as my partner and as our friend, by offering him the chance to *explain* what he was doing. Better for Ron to hear about this from someone who knows him, rather than for him to be surprised as he's yanked from the changing room tomorrow—first thing, of course—and hauled into the Security Offices. I'd like to spare him that shock."

"Did Dave Johnson *tell you* not to speak with Ron?"

"No. He didn't have to. He's counting on what he considers to be my discretion, my good judgment, my wish to resolve the situation." John exhaled slowly, pausing in the midst of mentally rehashing the loyalty issues with which he struggled. "It would probably amount to interfering with a criminal investigation if I called Ron," he said flatly, tipping his head back, banging it lightly against the kitchen wall. "I think that's a crime."

"Maybe not, since it's not a *police* investigation," Nancy replied softly, still cautious. John was not an impulsive man, and his temptation to flee one trusted relationship to protect another signaled the importance of the matter. "So, this is about friendship, a relationship that supersedes any understanding you have with Dave Johnson."

"Something like that." John closed his eyes. "None of my options are good. If I let Dave keep the lead here, I may throw away a valuable friendship and partnership—possibly for no good reason, if Ron was looking for his Mont Blanc pen or something. If I call Ron and tell him that someone saw him rummaging through the drug kits on Monday, does that create a similar damage? You know, kill the messenger?"

John sat up straight, massaging his temples as Nancy gently flicked a stray curl from his forehead. He continued, "But that's not what bothers me the most: the part about Ron being pissed off because I'm asking him about it. What bothers me most is that maybe my judgment *is* off. Maybe Ron *did* steal narcotics."

"We can't expect to be 'right' about everyone, John. Quite frankly, I can't imagine Ron Albers stealing drugs for recreation. And if you want to be a friend to him, maybe it's enough to let the process continue, but stand by him, let him know—in front of Dave Johnson—that you don't believe he's stealing narcotics, that he can count on you to do whatever is necessary to protect his reputation. Maybe *that* type of friendship is enough. Maybe it's all that anyone should expect. A friend wouldn't expect you to violate a trust, even if the trust is implied rather than explicit."

Aware that this was easy for her to say, Nancy had only a glimmer of appreciation for the masters her husband attempted to serve: his concurrent obligations to his friend, the ethics of his Hippocratic Oath, the legal imperative to report colleagues suspected of substance abuse, the obligation—or was it more a professional courtesy? —to preserve the integrity of Dave Johnson's investigation. *Were there other competing masters,* Nancy wondered?

Sensing her husband's resistance, Nancy leaned against him, placing her cheek against his. "*We're* on the same team, you know. I'm not trying to tell you what to do, John. It's easy for me to say what is or isn't 'enough' to expect of a friend." She traced the outline of vertebrae that descended from the short waves at the nape of John's neck, gently scribbling a series of figure eights with her tapered nails.

John sighed. "I know, Captain."

"Will Ron be arrested tomorrow—I mean, if he admits that he stole narcotics?" Nancy queried, hoping to sustain their dialogue with a fact-based question.

"Probably," John replied with obvious pain.

"What about Sally? Who is going to tell her, if Ron is arrested."

"I don't know."

"John, think about it. Someone should be with Sally, if this happens tomorrow." Nancy turned his face toward her own, her demand voiced firmly. "*I* want to be with Sally if this happens."

John nodded in agreement. "I'll call you as soon as I can. Nothing may come of it. I hope that Ron has some damned good explanation." He vigorously rubbed his eyes, then reached over and looped a finger through a belt-loop of Nancy's jeans, reeling her into his lap and nuzzling her ivory neck. "Your mom okay tonight?"

Nancy nodded silently, sliding lithely, like a cat, from her husband's lap. She laced her fingers through John's, and gently led him from the kitchen, through the den, to the stairway. They ascended slowly, and Nancy prayed silently that they could both live with the path of least resistance.

No call was made. At least, not by John Williams.

9:05 PM

"It's me. Can you talk?"

"Just a sec." There was a muffled offer to finish helping with homework later, *after* completing this call. A click on the line signaled that another phone was picked up, the second click indicating that the first was hung up. "Okay. What's up?"

"There's going to be a meeting tomorrow. You're not going to like it, but we need to have a plan."

11:45 PM

John Williams stared at the bedroom ceiling. He couldn't sleep. His thoughts centered and swirled on what Dave Johnson had told him this evening. If what he'd said was true, then one of the most honest, trustworthy men he knew was responsible for this breach of trust. He didn't want to believe it. He didn't want to deal with it.

In the background of this drama hung a fact that he'd forgotten to share with Nancy: It was *Limbotryl* in the pair of syringes, the ones discovered beneath the phone in the call room a week ago. In a way, that was good news. It might mean that there wasn't an addict among the anesthesiologists. After all, what addict would want a drug like Limbotryl, one that knocked you dead for a while, when there were others that would allow a quick high without drastically impeding performance?

Did that mean that the syringes were accidentally taken from the OR? No, not if they were hidden beneath the phone. That was deliberate.

John tried to fall sleep by reading, then by taking a melatonin tablet, then by deep breathing, even counting sheep. The night was long. He did not rest at all.

Chapter Seven

THE ACCUSATION

Wednesday, April 10
6:50 AM

"Dr. Albers, as you know, there has been a problem with drug diversion. I'd like to talk with you about a surveillance film that was made on Monday." Dave Johnson opened the conference directly, his tone friendly, his demeanor open.

It was John Williams who appeared irritable, anxious, and guarded.

The assembled group also included Stu Adler, the President of the anesthesia practice, Barbara Westover and Richard Ostrader of the Cincinnati Police Pharmaceutical Diversion Unit, and Brinn Thomas, a hospital Risk Management attorney.

It's like a goddamn convention, John thought, unaware that Dave had called so many players to the table. *No, like an inquisition.* He fumed, more angry than frightened for Ron Albers. He preferred feeling angry to feeling scared, and he emotionally fanned the flames of his anger to preserve it.

If Ron Albers was afraid, he showed no evidence of it. He appeared genuinely puzzled. "What's this about? And why are Risk Management and the PDU here?"

"Dr. Albers, we have a video recording in which you are seen looking through the contents of drug kits that had been placed in the workroom after surgeries on Monday of this week." Dave retained a friendly tone, firmly stating the facts, subtly communicating that he and Ron were on the same team. "Can you tell us what you were doing?"

Ron's eyes narrowed and he nodded his head, but before he could utter a syllable, Brinn Thomas of Risk Management interrupted. "Dr. Albers, you are not required to answer any of these questions. You may do so, if you wish, or you may request counsel from your personal attorney. I represent the hospital, so I cannot advise you legally beyond what you have the right to do, or refuse to do."

Dave Johnson's expression never flickered, although the words *Doberman litigator* flickered through his consciousness. "That's right," Dave acknowledged in a measured tone, communicating both serious concern for Ron Albers, and friendly awareness that a little chat would clear up what must be a misunderstanding. Dave's gift for minimizing proved a valuable asset in his interviews, at least as a starting point.

Ron Albers looked at Stu Adler, then at John Williams, and finally back to Dave Johnson. "You think I was taking drugs?"

No one spoke.

"You *do* think I was taking drugs!" Ron was livid now, and a purple flush crept from the V-neck of his surgical scrubs to the peak of his forehead, where fair hair receded in wispy strands. "What *is* this, John? Stu?"

His words hung in the air, unanswered. Although Dave would never admit it at this point, before the meeting convened, he had asked Drs. Williams and Adler to remain silent during the interview. They were being permitted to attend a professional courtesy, but a clear boundary had been demarcated—this was *his* show.

Obviously out of the loop on this bit of information, Ron misunderstood his colleagues' taciturn silence as a confirmation of suspicion. "Well, fuck you very much, *pals*," he sneered at John and Stu. "I'll take the advice of Mr. Thomas and call my lawyer. This meeting is *over* until he advises me." Ron turned to face Dave Johnson, his eyes glaring blue lasers. "Am I working today, or am I being charged with a crime?"

Dave remained composed and amiable, retaining his reserved, natural demeanor. "You are not being charged with any crime, Dr. Albers. I am concerned whenever security films show *any* of the hospital staff looking through drug kits. You probably know, we even run film in the satellite pharmacies and in the Pharmacy Department's narcotics-disposal room. Just as in any circumstance when something appears out of the ordinary, we inquire about it. The fact that we do it with your colleagues present, as well as Risk Management, is to provide you with some measure of support. I realize this is a rude way to begin the day, and I regret that it's necessary. This interview is an opportunity to clear up any misunderstanding of what may have occurred."

"I've made my position clear," Ron stated again, his fury barely contained.

Stu Adler, ever the diplomat and statesman, spoke at last. "Ron, I understand that you would prefer to answer questions with legal consul present. Fine, fine," he said, waving his hand, as if acquiescing a moot point. "I'm sure we can straighten this out. But since you have endured a surprise attack—although none of us intended to attack you, just to resolve the questions that exist—and since emotions are running high this morning, I'd like you to take the day off. Talk with your lawyer. When you and your lawyer are ready, we'll have the interview. That right, Mr. Johnson?"

Stu, deferential and solicitous, glanced up to the head of the table where Dave Johnson rocked in the chair, his expression unconcerned, his fingertips gently tapping the wood-grain arms of the chair.

"Absolutely, Dr. Adler," Dave replied. "Here's my card," he spoke directly to Ron Albers. "Your attorney should call me as soon as you've talked. The sooner we resolve these questions, the better."

Dave's words and expression remained reserved, yet friendly, and belied the internal inferno that was building. This wasn't typical of his interviews, and to be within reach of some explanation, even a poor one, only to be served with delay tactics, stirred the acid in his stomach. Yet, Dave Johnson was a patient man. He would conduct his investigation in a pristine, legal manner, regardless of the time required. One can't rush art, and there was more than just a bit of artistry to investigative work. This one might be his personal Sistine Chapel.

Dave Johnson, the PDU investigators, and the Risk Management lawyer quickly dispersed, leaving John Williams, Ron Albers, and Stu Adler in the room. Ron continued to glare at his partners. "You could have had the decency to ask me about this before this morning," he accused. Not waiting a defense from either man, Ron continued, fueled by adrenalin. "It's a helluva way to treat a partner," he glanced meaningfully at John, implying that this was a violation not only of collegial partnership, but of friendship.

John could not dispute his partner, his friend. He agreed fully, and another wave of anguish surged from deep within his soul. It was wrong, he knew, to abandon a friend to investigative procedure. Maybe it was *more* wrong than to have disrupted, even contaminated, that procedure. He welcomed Ron's attack as confirmation of his initial instinct to call and warn him the night before. *Should have trusted my gut,* John reprimanded. Surely, his friend was innocent—*but then why didn't he just explain himself?*

"Ron, I'm sorry," John said quietly. "I wish it didn't happen." He refused to offer any defense of his actions. In a far corner of his mind, a small voice chanted repeatedly that he had done what was expected, necessary, and ethical. Its rhythm was like that of a distant drum, such that he knew it was there, although it competed with nearer voices and presences for his attention, such as the colleagues within arm's reach. Still, the faraway drum intoned rhythmically, persistently, patiently: a conscience at work.

John glanced over at Stu Adler, who suddenly appeared pale, his facial muscles slackened. Stu slumped in his chair, breathing deeply, then lunged for a plastic-lined trash can next to the wall and vomited into it, his shoulders shuddering with each heave, perspiration beading at his temples. John Williams and Ron Albers shifted into gear, all rancor set aside.

"You okay, Stu?" John asked, aware that his partner, obviously, was *not* okay.

Stu nodded, trembling slightly in the aftermath of his stomach's volcanic eruption. John grabbed Stu's wrist. His pulse was at full throttle, more than a hundred beats a minute.

What the hell is this, John wondered? He and Ron shared an uneasy glance, both men bewildered by their colleague's one-eighty turn of composure: calm and composed in the heat of the battle, violently ill when the attacking forces called retreat.

Ron helped John lower Stu Adler to a recumbent position. Ron then reached for a cushion from a leather sofa against the far wall, gently setting it beneath the older man's legs. Ron Albers was as surprised as John Williams at this turn of events, communicating his question via eye contact, not trusting his words.

"You coming down with the spring flu, Stu?" John asked casually. Several of the OR nurses had called in sick during the past two weeks, hit by a virulent flu that accompanied the fluctuating is-it-spring-or-winter weather.

Stu replied with a grimace, his feeble attempt at a smile. He shook his head. It was not the flu.

John tried again, "Anything else hurt?"

No, again.

Ron looked grimly toward John. "You'll have your hands full today, with *two* of us going home."

Stu uttered a grunt as he tried to rise, and then groaned in resistance to the idea of leaving. He fell back the couple of inches immediately.

"Maybe Stu needs to get checked out by one of the Medicine docs," Ron suggested to John. Their concern was growing, particularly in light of the rapid onset.

"No." It was a hoarse whisper. "You can't do this, Ron." Stu Adler looked directly at Ron Albers.

"Shut up, Stu," Ron said, attempting lighthearted humor that fell short of the mark. Then, he addressed John. "Let's get a gurney up here and take him down to Primary Care."

"I'll call," John offered, puzzled by the verbal exchange. He stretched from a squat to full-height, noting that Stu was again whispering that Ron "couldn't do this."

What can't Ron do, wondered John? *Get Stu checked out by one of the internists? Go home? Steal narcotics from the workroom? What was he talking about?* John snatched the receiver from the phone next to the couch, and arranged for his partner to be transported by gurney to the second floor outpatient offices. Hanging up, he turned back to Ron and Stu. "It's set. I'll call Jeannie, and she can meet you there."

Jeannie was Stu's wife, a registered nurse and the Executive Director of Compassionate Care, a local hospice organization. If anyone could get Stu to take time off and recuperate from whatever this was, Jeannie would be that person. She was forceful the way a tornado was windy, and John wondered whether Stu had honed his diplomacy skills out of necessity.

"No, I'll call her," Ron said firmly. "You're needed downstairs. Let me wrap this up. I'll go down to Primary Care with Stu until Jeannie gets here."

John paused, then nodded his agreement. "All right," he said, grasping for other words to convey support to his partner, the accused. "I don't think you were taking narcotics from the workroom, Ron. I don't like the way Dave Johnson set up this meeting, and I'll do whatever you want to help. I hope you believe that."

Ron Albers looked coolly toward his friend and partner. "We'll talk later," he said, noncommitally. "I'll call you at home tonight." Ron then broke eye contact, glancing at his watch as he re-counted Stu Adler's pulse beats.

John nodded, and then exited the room, stopping outside the door as the next question surfaced. What was he supposed to tell the rest of the group? It was one thing to explain Stu's "flu," but what was he to say about Ron's departure? As he contemplated the possibilities, Dave Johnson waved for him to wait from down the hall. Dave picked up the pace of his stride, as if worried that John might flee.

"Do you have a minute before you head back downstairs?"

"Not really, Dave," John replied, a chill in his voice.

"I'd appreciate a few minutes if you can get coverage sometime today."

"And I'd appreciate knowing when you decide to bring in the big guns, Dave. I understood that you, Stu, and I would talk with Ron today—oh yeah, and someone from Risk Management. You didn't mention calling in the PDU cops. I don't like surprises."

Dave held his position. "We can discuss this in my office—or back in the conference room, if you'd rather."

John glared at the Security Director. "One of my partners is on the floor of the conference room, pretty sick, and it's not the flu. Maybe the surprise offensive caught Stu off guard, too."

Dave blanched, appearing apologetic. "What's wrong with Dr. Adler? He was fine when the meeting ended."

"We don't know. He'll be checked out by one of the internists, but *he's* out for the day, too. There are at least a hundred OR cases on the schedule today, and as much as I'm concerned about who is diverting narcotics, I have a job to do." John walked away briskly, heading toward the quad of elevators. Dave Johnson remained at his side.

"You may not like the fact that I called in the PDU investigators—hell, you may not even like the fact that I asked Dr. Adler to join the meeting. But, this is *my* job, John. I know how to do my job, and it's not a team sport."

"You expected me to be a team player," John argued, his voice rising, gaining the attention of a Housekeeping attendant and a volunteer who was pushing the flower delivery cart. John lowered his voice, but his words bit deeply. "You expected me to let you handle talking with one of *my* partners, about a sensitive issue that *my* group has policies and procedures in place to deal with, but you never felt it was necessary to include me in the decision to call in outsiders? *Your job* may not be a team sport, Dave, but the understanding was that you and I were collaborating on this problem. I can play by almost any set of fair rules, but you'd better spell them out!"

Dave was not visibly moved by John's acrimony. "Let's take this to a quiet place, John."

"Later," John stated bluntly, raising his watch to see the time.

It was nearly 7:30 AM, and he *had* to get down to the ORs. He faced the Security Director squarely, crossing his arms in a divisive stance. "I'll let you know when things quiet down. Just stay away from Ron Albers until he talks to his lawyer. And stay away from Stu Adler, too. You've upset enough people this morning."

The ding announcing the elevator's arrival signaled the end of the confrontation. John Williams strode into the elevator and punched the button for the tunnel level, refusing to look at Dave Johnson. The closing elevator doors punctuated their dissension.

John would have to wait for the *other* news that Dave intended to convey.

8:00 AM

"When was the last time you ate something?" Drew asked.

"A couple days ago," Kathy whispered hoarsely.

"Well, no wonder you're so weak. You've got to eat something."

"Mommy! Daddy! You forgot to sign my reading folder!" called the little girl.

"I'll take care of it," Drew said tightly. "But you need to get out of bed and force yourself to eat something. At least try some soda crackers. You should be able to keep that down." Drew took the pencil and yellow folder from his daughter, quickly scrawling his name on the parent signature sheet. "Brush your teeth and run out to the bus stop. I don't have time to drive you today—I'm already late. Tell your brother, too."

"I will. Bye, Mommy. I hope you feel better." The little girl looked at her father, as if he might be able to promise that, today, her mommy would indeed be better. His face remained impassive, and the girl ducked out of the room, clearly disappointed, to complete the directive her father had issued.

"Kathy, you've got to pull out of this. I know it's tough, but I can't take care of the kids and keep up with my responsibilities at work." He stared at the hollow-eyed woman, this stranger, this shell of a creature that was once his vivacious wife. Her hair hung in limp tangles, lusterless, her face pale and dry as parchment, her lips chapped, even cracked at the corners. He watched her frown with effort to raise an ice-filled cloth to her lips, suck it momentarily, and then let it fall to the bed, still gently clasped in her hand. Then, she closed her eyes, turned her head to face him, and opened them to half-mast.

"I feel like I'm going to die," she said faintly.

"No, you're not going to die," Drew reassured firmly. "You need to take your medicine, and eat some breakfast."

His wife closed her eyes, as if shutting out everything and everyone but her misery. "We need you to be strong, Kathy. Just *try*," he implored. But she did not respond.

"Damn it," he muttered, striding angrily from the room and stomping down the stairs and into the kitchen. He dialed the office of Kathy's immunologist, and was greeted by a recorded message. The voice indicated that office hours did not begin for another hour, and to please dial the Academy of Medicine answering service so that the doctor could be paged, in the event of an emergency.

"Goddamn!" he cursed, clicking off the phone and slamming it onto the table. He stole a look at his watch, glanced toward the stairs as he considered his options, and then hastily picked up his briefcase, rushing out the kitchen door before he changed his mind.

7:30 PM

John Williams rolled his neck from side to side. He stretched his arms high overhead, nearly touching the acoustic ceiling tile, encouraging ligaments and fatigued scapular muscles to release their clench. An audible crack sounded his relief.

He was the second call doc, today, and he'd expended a full day's energy in the first hour and a half. Twelve hours later, he was beyond weary. His brusque statement to the OR staff that Ron and Stu were off sick had been greeted with surprise, and only his glowering, uncharacteristic ill temper stilled the questions.

He had a harder time explaining the absences to the other physician-partners, and settled on the same lie—for now—that both were sick and had gone home. Only Marty Devereaux, the group's Treasurer, and Dean Phillips, Board Secretary, knew the truth. They, too, believed the prudent course required telling a falsehood, and pleaded ignorance when questioned by surgeons and nurses alike. John, however, relied on the hectic OR schedule and a thundercloud expression to stave off questions and questioners.

Around 9:00 that morning, hoping for good news, Nancy had called him on his cell phone, enduring static that indicated Dave's security cameras were rolling. In further avoidance of colleagues, John had invited Nancy to join him for a private picnic lunch on the park-like grounds. During the brief lunch, John had shared the events of the early morning, incapable of enjoying the expansive view of blooming trees and tulips, or the lush, spring-green carpet of the hospital front lawn.

Nancy had listened sympathetically, saying much less than she wanted to. There was so much to ask, yet so little that her husband could answer. It was best to ask nothing—too much had already been asked of him today.

He did not verify the drug count, as he had previous evenings. Now, the Security cameras would capture any disturbance of drug kits. This saved John from spending another couple of hours in the satellite pharmacy and the Women's Health workroom.

The schedule for tomorrow was set, and he had intentionally scheduled Ron Albers and Stu Adler "OFF." It would be tight, and there was a good chance that he would need to go in for the morning. Typically, the second call doc joined the first call doc in having the post-call day off. However, when the OR schedule was filled and there were three docs on vacation, the second call doc often had to go in for several hours, gaining only an early out. Given that three docs were, indeed, on vacation—and two off sick—John planned to be in the next morning. He had to meet with Dave Johnson, anyway, and still had not responded to the Security Director's request to speak again, today.

Recalling their quiet lunch, John remembered to call Nancy and let her know that he was finished for the night. Nancy picked up the phone on the first ring.

"John, I'm on the other line with Jeannie Adler," she explained. "She wants to talk with you about Stu—and Ron, too, I guess."

"I'll call her back when I get home. I don't want to call on my cell phone."

"Drive safely, Doc," Nancy said quietly, clicking back to the other call.

John hung up without responding. He dialed Dave's extension, surprised when Dave actually picked up so late in the evening.

"No static," John noted. "Did you turn off the cameras, Dave?"

"For the night, except for upstairs," Dave replied evenly.

"I'm on my way home. Is there anything I need to know tonight?" John asked tensely. While he rarely held a grudge, the collateral damage of the morning's events loomed as a large, gaping wound.

"Ron Albers' attorney called this afternoon. We're meeting at his office tomorrow morning. Just wanted to let you know."

"All right," John acknowledged, his voice rising at the end, a question mark, waiting for more information.

"That's all for now, John. I'll talk with you tomorrow. How's Dr. Adler?"

"He's at home, now. I'll be talking with his wife in a while to see how he's doing."

If Dave expected John to elaborate, he did not convey that expectation. "My regards to Dr. Adler, when you talk with him," he stated simply. With a pause to indicate premeditation, he added, "I'm sorry for surprising you this morning, John. Dr. Adler, too." The words were sincere, although it was obvious that the Security Director did not regret his course of action. Instead, this was an example of Dave's preference to apologize after the fact, rather than to compromise his action plan.

Although fatigue-whipped and feeling less than gracious, John felt suddenly disarmed by the apology. It was the closest, he felt sure, that Dave Johnson would come to an admission that he may have been wrong. Was this what cops did to gain the confidence of criminals? John shook his head, burying the thought, puzzled by his wish to shift gears, searching for the anger that had burned so close to the surface all day long.

At a loss to respond, John tentatively replied, "Okay." But it wasn't okay. Okay was just a social amenity that would allow him to hang up the phone and go home. It was a social lie, and he would correct it later. He mumbled his good-bye and clicked off the cell phone.

Sluggishly, John pulled the scrub shirt over his head, allowing it to slide off his arms to the floor. *God, I'm tired,* he admitted. His usually quick, efficient motions were laborious. Placing his leaden arms over his head, tugging the rugby shirttail into place, he may as well have bench-pressed his body weight, or dressed while wearing thick ski gloves.

He reached within his memory for a Zig Ziegler snippet, something that would cue his body to re-energize. There were calls to be made, all of which would require energy, focus. Food would help.

John grabbed a mini-pack of M&Ms from a snack sack he kept in the locker. He counted the green and red candies, the ones reputed to increase libidinal energy, if no other. There were six, and only two brown ones. He permitted the indulgence in this popular college superstition: the more reds and greens, the sharper the senses grew, mental, sexual or otherwise. He might have prayed for a placebo effect.

Leaving the changing area, John noticed the clock. Eight o'clock. He steeled himself against further awareness of fatigue. If he acknowledged any fragment of it, his effort to tap into the power-of-positive-thinking would dissolve. He moved the conflicts of the day into a far corner of his conscious, and focused on the color red: power, energy. He mentally listed all the words he could think of that inspired energy, action, and purpose. His focus was complete, and he had no recollection of passing anyone in the hallways, or of any familiar landmarks along the drive home.

It was dark when he pulled into the driveway, but the screened porch at the far end of the house glowed with illumination cast from within the house, the low shrubs and brick patio softly, fuzzily resembling the luminous painting style of Thomas Kincaid. Nancy squatted before a large clay planter, a spade and a trowel in each of her gloved hands, surrounded by flats of impatiens, geraniums, alyssum, and vinca. She waved a greeting as John's car rounded the corner and paused while the garage door opened.

With quick thrusts, Nancy secured the garden tools in the vast pot, and peeled the slightly small gloves from her hands, shaking them until the finger sections were right side out. She then shuffle-jogged in her garden clogs to embrace her husband warmly.

"Working on the pots already?" he asked, his voice more chipper than when he and Nancy had spoken by phone.

She knew, then, that he was faking good cheer. Nancy wrinkled her nose playfully. "The aromatic elixir of my labor gives me away. I wanted to surprise you and have the pots done before I fly out for the weekend."

John slumped against the back of the car, dropping his arms dejectedly. He'd forgotten that Nancy was scheduled for a long trip, or actually a series of short trips that hopped from Cincinnati to Atlanta, and on to various cities along the eastern seaboard, keeping her from home for five consecutive nights. It was out of the ordinary for Nancy's flight schedule, a quarterly phenomenon that left both of them sleep-deprived and irritable.

"I forgot," John admitted.

"Thought so," Nancy answered, pleased to be reminded that she would be missed. "Mom's doing well today—she called this morning to say thanks for first class treatment yesterday. She slept well last night, and is feeling pretty good today." Nancy signaled John to follow her inside the house. "How about a gourmet dinner by Lean & Lively? I can zap some green beans, too."

He nodded. "I'll get a couple of beers from the basement fridge." He added, "Glad your mom's had a good day."

"I just wish she didn't have to wait so long for the results. That's the part that'll drive me nuts—*not* knowing."

John lumbered down the basement steps heavily, barely discerning Nancy's chatter. He tried to anticipate his conversation with Ron Albers. The possible words were not forthcoming. He could see only a color, crimson, and he could identify only a complex of crimson-tinged feelings—anger, shame, and guilt.

He crossed the basement to the sixties-era wet bar, the sole remnant of the former owner's bad taste. He pulled open the fridge door, revealing bottled beers and white wines. Barely reflecting on the choices, John pulled out two LaBatt's beers and kicked the door shut with his foot. He must have taken longer than he realized, for Nancy was shouting from the top of the stairs.

"Are you brewing it down there, Doc?"

"I'll be right up," he answered.

But Nancy was halfway down the steps and took the bottles from his hands. "Dinner's out and the green beans will be four minutes," she advised. "Looks like you've seen battle today."

"It's been a long one, and it isn't over," John sighed. "Ron said he'd call here tonight, and I want to check on Stu."

"Jeannie Adler called here around seven-thirty. Stu is resting, although he's pretty worked up about what Ron went through this morning," Nancy informed him briskly.

The microwave beeped, announcing that the green beans were ready. Nancy popped open the door, and in a series of quick motions she had scooped Chicken Carbonara and green beans onto two plates, and joined her husband at the table. As she shook open a cloth napkin and haphazardly dropped it in her lap, Nancy gave John a no-nonsense look.

"Let's take a break," she began. "Eat your dinner, drink your beer, talk to me about the school levy or anything else that barely concerns us—but not work. Just for the next fifteen or twenty minutes, deal?"

"You drive a hard bargain," John jested, the first waves of relaxation rolling across him as he drained half the beer.

For less than the recommended time, Nancy chatted while her husband simply ate. Nancy noticed that he seemed distracted, understandably so, but she overlooked his inattention, hoping that easy conversation would soothe him after the jarring work-day.

John pushed back his plate, signaling the end of this conversational diversion. "Time to make some calls," he stated simply.

Nancy picked up the dinner dishes silently, aware that she felt dismissed, yet equally cognizant that John intended no personal slight. She'd known him long enough to recognize that this seemingly terse and abrupt cut-off was a function of his stress. Once the challenging tasks were accomplished, John would resume his typically low-key, affectionate self. Patience, as a virtue, served Nancy well in these rare circumstances.

Hot water flooded into the sink, and Nancy sighed, basking her garden-weary hands in the wet warmth. As she bathed the dishes leisurely, the "mommy thoughts" returned. Perhaps, she reflected, her natural patience would allow her to be a mother. "Patience is an essential ingredient of parenthood," assured her sisters-in-law and several friends who had navigated the parental path.

The fantasy grew, and the plate became the child's face, the silverware became fingers and toes. It was almost unimaginable, the changes that would take place with a child in the house. What would she and John talk about? Would they lose perspective as they focused their energies on a child? Could someone who hadn't any natural maternal instinct be a good enough parent? Would it be enough to simply try her best?

Perhaps, Nancy reflected, she lived too much in her head on this issue. Possibly, it would be better to have *no* choice in the matter, to leave it to fate or what her grandmother had called God's will.

The approach of John's footsteps interrupted the reverie. Nancy was grateful for respite from reproductive ruminations. "Well?" she asked simply, showering the sink with the sprayer.

"Got Ron's answering machine, and decided to get another beer before I call Stu." John opened the refrigerator door and stared at the contents, willing the soft drink cans to transform into beers. He'd forgotten that all the beer was in the basement. "Want one?" he asked Nancy, closing the door to the fridge as he headed toward the basement door.

"No thanks, but I'd like to listen in on your end of the conversation with Stu. Can I eavesdrop?" she inquired with a smile.

John laughed and nodded as he descended to retrieve the beer.

Nancy's snoopy streak, which she reframed as curiosity or interest, amused her husband. Her request, tinged with a bit of self-conscious embarrassment, shook the gray-green mold from John's mood, and he treaded the steps more lightly, two at a time, on the way back up.

Nancy met him in the den with the portable phone in one hand, and a fresh iced mug—clouded from departing the freezer—in the other. Nancy then stretched out on the burgundy leather sofa, fluffing a chenille throw behind her head. She waited quietly, while John punched in Stu Adler's number and slowly reclined in an overstuffed corduroy club chair.

John cracked open the beer and slowly poured the amber ale into the frosty mug. On the seventh ring, Jeannie Adler picked up.

"How's Stu doing, Jeannie?" John greeted.

"He's better, John," she replied tentatively. "He's pretty upset about the way things were handled today."

"Me, too," John acknowledged. "Neither of us were prepared for PDU to be there, and for Ron to have been surprised—ambushed is what it felt like—was way out of line."

Jeannie remained silent, then offered confidently, "Ron wasn't surprised."

John's heart skipped a beat. "What do you mean? He sure acted surprised."

"Well, he wasn't," Jeannie answered tersely. "Do you and Stu ever *talk* before you go into these meetings?" she asked, clearly impatient. "Did you both walk into that meeting without any plan as to what would transact? You doctors—" she began, and seemed to think better of it. "Stu is just getting up. I'll put him on."

John sat forward, his face alert. In turn, Nancy sat up and leaned forward, curiosity piqued by her husband's red flag demeanor.

John heard Jeannie's exasperated sigh before Stu's tired greeting.

"How you feeling, Stu?"

"Oh, much better," Stu assured, attempting gusto. "A little tired. What a morning. I don't know what got into me, but I'm much better now." He paused briefly, but not long enough for John to gain the conversational lead. "Have you talked with Ron this evening?"

"No, his answering machine is on."

"Well, he probably needs the evening to himself. Rough day, what a morning," Stu repeated.

John argued with himself in the course of these seconds, weighing each argument in favor of—or against—asking Stu about Jeannie's puzzling statements. In a leap of faith, he decided to inquire. "Stu, Jeannie seems to think that Ron was aware of the meeting today, ahead of time, and that he wasn't surprised by Dave Johnson's attack."

Stu hesitated only a millisecond before replying, "Oh, Jeannie's intuition at work," he said reassuringly. "Didn't he seem surprised to you?"

"He certainly did," John agreed firmly. "But, what did Jeannie mean? About whether or not you and I had talked before the meeting?"

Stu answered smoothly, "I guess Jeannie thinks that you and I should have run that meeting, decided who would be there, that type of thing."

John could hear Jeannie's animated voice of protest, although he could not hear her words specifically. Stu had muffled the telephone receiver and was issuing some comment to his wife that John could not discern.

Stu returned to the phone. "Sorry, John. We doctors are about the worst managers, negotiators, and businessmen, as Jeannie is reminding me. But, I'm hopeful that this will all blow over quickly and we can move forward . . . ." his voice trailed off.

John frowned, raising his guard to red alert. "Stu," he said firmly, "This isn't going to blow over. I can understand that you're probably tired, and maybe we should have this conversation later. That's fine. But our group has a problem, since one of our docs has been implicated in a diversion."

"Of course, you're right," Stu replied agreeably. "I didn't mean to imply that there's no problem. Maybe we should talk about it tomorrow, John. Let's see what Ron and his lawyer have decided to do, and what Dave Johnson will do, okay?"

John felt uneasy. His sixth sense suggested that Stu was either too ill to deal with this tough issue, or worse—lying. He gambled on receiving a truthful reply to his next stern question: "Stu, what did you mean today when you kept telling Ron that he 'couldn't do this'? What couldn't he do?"

"Oh," Stu said, puzzled. "Did I say that? I don't remember saying that. When did I say that? Are you sure?"

John cut off his partner's protests. "You did, Stu. It was after the meeting, when Ron and I were trying to figure out what was the matter with you." John shook his head as Stu repeated the denials. "Never mind, Stu. We can talk about it later. I've scheduled you and Ron off for tomorrow. Don't push coming in—we've got enough coverage."

"I'll be in tomorrow, John," Stu said with certainty. "This little bug that I've caught is mostly over. No problem."

John paused, wondering if Jeannie Adler truly had reason to suspect that Ron was guilty of diverting drugs, or that someone had tipped him about the videotape. John felt compelled to make his own convictions clear, in hopes that they would dilute any of Jeannie's strong views. "Ron Albers doesn't use drugs, Stu. He doesn't steal drugs, either. I've known him as a friend for long enough to be sure of that."

"I'm sure you're right, John," Stu agreed readily. "Ron will probably be back with us tomorrow, and we'll be laughing about how ludicrous Dave Johnson's suspicions were."

John's eyes widened, and he held Nancy's gaze of intense interest. His partner, Stu, was completely out of touch. To imagine that anyone would be laughing about what had occurred earlier seemed a sacrilege of the worst kind. This conversation had to end, before John said something regrettable. "Well, just wanted to see how you felt this evening, Stu. Get some rest." Click. The connection was severed.

"Well," Nancy said firmly, "Based on what I heard you say to Stu, and the expression on your face, I can't wait to hear Stu's end of the conversation."

"He's either really sick, or out of touch about how serious this is," John replied, incredulous. "Stu actually said he thinks that Ron will be back tomorrow, and that we'll be laughing about how ridiculously funny this is—he didn't say funny, but that was the gist of what he was saying."

"What about your question, the one about what Jeannie said?"

John shrugged, "He blew it off to her intuition."

"No way!"

"I think Jeannie heard it. I couldn't make out what she said, but it sounded like she was ticked off by what Stu was saying." John took a long drag on his beer. Setting it carefully on the glass-topped curio table, he said seriously, "I think that Jeannie was telling the truth about Ron knowing something. She wouldn't waste her time saying something unnecessary—the woman can't even make social chitchat. She either thinks that Ron *is* diverting drugs and that someone tipped him, which means that she also thinks that Ron's an inveterate liar to have acted so genuinely surprised at the meeting."

"Or, what?" Nancy prompted.

"That's what I can't come up with," John said, both perplexed and frustrated. He gripped the beer mug and released it, then gripped it again and gulped a generous swig.

"What were you getting at, asking Stu about whatever he was saying earlier today?" Nancy asked.

"That's another weird thing," John answered. "When we were finished with the meeting and Stu got sick, Ron and I were checking his vitals. Then, Ron suggested that Stu get checked out by one of the Internal Medicine docs, and Stu said that Ron 'couldn't do this,' but I don't know what 'this' could mean. At first, I thought that Stu just didn't want to get checked out. Maybe he just wanted to go home and let the bug—or whatever he has—run its course. But Ron told Stu to shut up, kind of like he was joking, but it *sounded* as if he really meant it. Almost as if Ron didn't want Stu to say something in front of me."

Nancy crossed her legs, Indian style, and drew the soft, nubby chenille throw around her shoulders. The evening seemed chilly, now. "Do you think that Ron and Stu are collaborating to divert drugs?" she asked, aware that such high drama was generally reserved for prime time television, not John Williams' practice. Then, she corrected herself, "I mean, I can't really imagine *either* Ron or Stu stealing drugs. But maybe Stu at least called Ron to warn him about the meeting today. Maybe Ron didn't want that to slip out? After all," she reminded her husband, "You wanted to call Ron last night, yourself."

"You're right, I did want to call Ron," John admitted, struggling to name this warning signal that nibbled at his subconscious. "I don't think either of them is stealing drugs, but all of these weird comments make me question my own judgment. About them, I mean. Maybe Jeannie thinks that Ron *was* taking drugs from the kits. But why does she believe that Ron knew what was going to happen today?"

"The fact that Stu attributed Jeannie's comments to intuition, along with his complete refusal to acknowledge how serious this is, makes me wonder about *his* potential for taking drugs," Nancy commented.

"I don't think Stu is the type to take drugs," John disagreed. "But his comments were certainly off the mark."

"A mini stroke," Nancy suggested, mildly sarcastic. "Limited to the critical thinking areas of the brain."

"Hadn't thought about that," John mused, allowing a half-smile. "Makes me feel glad that I scheduled him off for tomorrow, even if it means that I have to go in for morning coverage."

Nancy gestured to the phone. "How about trying Ron once more?"

John nodded and shrugged simultaneously, signaling his ambivalence to make the call. Still, he would sleep better to have it done. It was ten o'clock, bedtime for he and Nancy, as she would be out the door by 5:30 AM, and John shortly thereafter.

He dialed Ron's number, heard the answering machine click on after four rings, and clicked off the phone without leaving another message. "Still not answering," he advised Nancy. "I'm not sure if I'd sleep better after talking to Ron or not, but I hate to leave this hanging."

Nancy nodded in agreement. "This is as much of a sleep deterrent as Mom's situation. It's going to be a long week. Or more," she added ruefully.

John rubbed his eyes, dead tired, yet almost certain that he would miss the delicious sleep that he needed to rejuvenate. He rose from the comfort of the overstuffed club chair, offering a hand to Nancy. Silently, they crossed the plank floor, flicked off the light, and proceeded to the stairs. Shifting scenarios darted through John's head, and something elusive nagged in the background. *I'm missing something important,* he reminded himself.

Nancy appeared to be equally lost in thought as they silently prepared for bed. When John exited the bathroom, Nancy was standing near one of the screened doors that led to a small terrace overlooking the greenbelt behind their property. The lace draperies danced in the cool breeze, fluttering up and out like a full-skirted ball gown without the benefit of a waltzing belle. He approached the doorway, and peeked through the screen to discern the object of his wife's attention.

Nancy pointed to the trio of deer, a doe and two fawns, which nibbled at the sweet hostas surrounding the stone and brick patio below. "Amazing that such beautiful creatures can be so destructive," she commented mildly. "I don't have the heart to chase them off. They seem almost fragile on those spindly legs."

John reached around his wife from behind, creating a jacket of warmth in the chilly breeze. He nibbled at Nancy's earlobe, mimicking the deer that appeared oblivious to the watchful presence of humans. Another night, he would have flipped on the exterior lights, or chased the deer from the house. He felt little esteem toward the garden-munching pests that overran the village.

Still, he sensed Nancy's hypnotic pleasure as she observed the mother and babies, and knew that he would not disturb the moment of enchantment to save the life of a hosta plant. Exhausted by the day of unresolved conflict and confrontation, John failed to understand this moment as a turning point in life.

Chapter Eight

TEAMMATES OR OPPONENTS?

Thursday, April 11
12:00 Noon

John Williams gently pressed the humps that formed the patient's lower vertebrae, locating L3-4 easily. He applied pressure around the site, stretching his left thumb away from his first three fingers. "You'll feel some cold," he advised, mopping the area with an umber-colored antiseptic, "And now a few pinches."

In less than three seconds, an eternity for the anxious patient, he had swabbed the area and injected Lidocaine to deaden the nerves. The patient was now ready for the syringe, its large-gauge needle hidden beneath a sterile cloth. The cloth was to protect the patient from awareness of what would be stuck into his back, and to protect the physician from squeamishly told tales of a cousin of a friend-of-a-friend of a neighbor, who had—allegedly—become paralyzed after receiving an epidural.

"My wife is the one in our family who has experience with this," the patient explained softly. "But I know a fella at work whose sister-in-law's neighbor wound up in a wheelchair after one of these epidurals."

Sighing softly, John launched into his well-researched explanation that, although he could not account for the specific sister-in-law's neighbor, a review of the anesthesia literature indicated that paralysis following an epidural was extremely rare—almost nonexistent. "This happened back in the 1940s, and they found out that a preservative in the medicine was the culprit. The medicine isn't formulated with preservatives these days, as a result. Hold still, now."

John reapplied pressure, stretching the skin taut, and smoothly inserted the needle into L3-4, alert for the sensation of "give" that signaled arrival at the epidural space.

In his intense effort to remain still, the patient held his breath.

"Go ahead and breathe," John instructed. "We're almost done."

He checked the needle's depth to ensure that he hadn't trespassed the boundary of the epidural space. Doing so would result in a spinal, rather than an epidural. Check. He pressed the syringe's plunger, and the contents of the barrel slowly compressed to make the journey into the epidural space, where it silenced the nerves that communicated *pain* to the brain. John deftly removed the syringe and slid a narrow catheter through the needle, inserting it into the epidural space so that the patient could receive a continuous infusion of medication. The patient, who was having knee surgery, would have pain control post-operatively, during which time his left leg would be encased in a device designed to exercise the knee's full range of motion. Without the epidural, such motion would be unendurably painful.

The patient breathed again, drawing several deep breaths, euphoric to have survived the procedure, which he had dreaded more than surgery itself. John smiled, recognizing this phase-two anxiety response. "I'm going to tape the catheter against your back, now," he advised. The man nodded in relief. "You'll start to feel a warm sensation in your legs—feel it yet?"

"I think so—yes, I feel it!" the man answered, as if surprised that John could predict the sensation that felt much like a warm bath, only on the inside.

John secured the catheter horizontally with three strips of white tape, and then placed two strips vertically on either side of the catheter, thus anchoring the horizontal strips. Finished.

"You're all set," John said as he packed up the remnants of the epidural kit. "I'll check on you in a few minutes, and then you'll see Dr. Franklin." He left the room as Mackenzie Franklin waved him into the hallway, and motioned "silence" with a finger to her lips. *What's up now?* Myriad catastrophes flashed through his mind in just half a second.

Mac's OR gown billowed as she sailed down the hallway to an uninhabited pre-op assessment room. Ducking inside, Mac whirled about to face John, and came to the point. "You've avoided all of us about what's happening with Stu and Ron," she said coolly. "I'd like to know if it has anything to do with the diversion."

Mac was easily half a foot shorter than John, yet her forceful manner made her seem taller. John fleetingly recalled the memory of Sister Mary Alfred, a parochial school nun and principal, whose four-foot ten-inch frame may as well have been ten-foot four, for the power she packed with the angel-maker paddle.

Refusing to tell Mac was not an option, and John would have revealed the events of yesterday sooner, had she asked. "Dave Johnson set up extra surveillance cameras. There's videotape of Ron going through the drug kits in the Women's Health workroom. Johnson called a meeting to ask Ron what he was doing, and Stu and I were there, along with Risk Management and a couple of the PDU cops. Ron didn't say anything, and was supposed to talk with his lawyer yesterday. I haven't heard anything, but the lawyer arranged a meeting with Dave Johnson for this morning."

"*Shit,*" Mac said reverently. She broke eye contact, unbelieving.

"That's how I feel," John acknowledged, sighing in relief to finally share the burdensome secret.

"Does anyone else know?"

"Sally does, and Nancy. Stu got sick right after the meeting, but he knows and so does his wife, Jeannie." John omitted the bizarre details of last night's conversation with Stu.

"It doesn't make sense that Ron would be taking narcotics."

"I agree. So why doesn't he just *say* what the hell he was doing with the drug kits?"

Mac studied the wall of the room pensively, without response.

John's pager shattered the thoughtful silence. He pushed the button that stilled the intrusive beeps, Dave Johnson's extension displayed. "Guess who?" John asked.

"Johnson," Mac guessed, with no trace of a question in the name she uttered. "You'd better fill people in so the gossip stops."

John nodded. "I've got to take this call first. Then I'll have a better idea of what to tell people. I also need to see who else needs lunch relief. I'll catch people after that."

Mac was already out the door, her gown streaming behind as she sailed purposefully down the hall. When she reached the room of the patient John had just seen, Mac turned at the door with the firm stare of a Sister Mary Alfred. "Call me later," she commanded.

John nodded, and with the agreement thus sealed, the formidable Dr. Franklin shoved open the door and greeted the patient.

John reached into the bottom of his lab coat for the cell phone. Four clicks and half a ring later, Dave Johnson was on the line, asking, "Are you on a cell phone?"

John acknowledged that he was, prickles of anticipation creeping across the nape of his neck.

"I'll be in my office. All day. When can you stop by?"

"Maybe in half an hour. I'm relieving people for lunch, and I'm early out after that. I'll see you then."

The men clicked off simultaneously.

12:25 PM

Dave Johnson studied his paper-laden desk, acknowledging that perhaps he had over-trained himself in the science of independent investigation. Had he risked allowing some other opinions, or at least some feedback, perhaps he would be dictating a report to close this diversion investigation.

He had erred substantially in his confidence that welding circumstantial evidence with expert questioning would lead to resolution. Still, he felt in his gut that his instincts were correct. He trusted his war room dry-erase boards, color-coded elastic bands, and computer printouts; but most importantly, he trusted his investigative instinct.

He had a collection of circumstantial evidence that linked Ron Albers to the diversion in the OR, and to the syringes found in the physician call room. He had captured Albers on videotape, searching through the drug kits in the Women's Health workroom. Each piece of information represented a portion of the paint-by-number picture that was lightly sketched at present. In time, the image would emerge in full-color and detail. The difference between this set of circumstantial evidence and that of previous diversions was *only* the professional position of the suspect: Ron Albers was a physician.

How could he ever hope to explain his change in course to John Williams? Last year, he had accumulated less evidence than this, and yet he had successfully elicited a confession from the CRNA who had pilfered narcotics from the OR. Actually, Dave realized, it was not at all the difference between a CRNA and an MD. The difference was that Ron Albers had stopped the interview cold. The nurse had felt compelled to complete the interview, and in the process, was snared.

He had less than half an hour to prepare his explanation, and Dave hoped that John Williams would not arrive for their meeting early.

12:35 PM

John Williams browsed the anesthesia lunch-relief schedule. Surprisingly, all of the names were highlighted, indicating that everyone had been relieved for lunch. He was free to leave.

He pulled off the lab coat as he made long strides towards the physician locker room. With his right hand, he snapped the pager button to the "off" position, and with the left, grabbed the paper hat from his head and stashed it in the nearby trashcan. He scanned the room, which was quiet at this hour. Most of the physicians were still in the OR area, and would not head back to the locker room until their cases were finished. At his locker, John concentrated on streamlining his actions, keeping at bay all curiosity related to the meeting between Dave Johnson and Ron Albers' lawyer. A few minutes later, he slid the clasp of his belt buckle into place, grabbed his jacket and laptop, and slammed the locker door tight. He threaded the combination lock through the latch, and shoved his palm against the bottom to secure it.

He glanced at his watch, noting that there was time enough to stop by the Pharmacy offices for copies of the drug records from yesterday. Then, he would see Dave Johnson.

At the Pharmacy Department, Doug Howard's secretary was on the phone, but handed him a pair of thick manila envelopes with a smile and a wave. The copies were enclosed, and John would key data into his home computer for hours this evening.

He dashed from the office, back through the maze of tunnels to the bank of elevators, where a single door was open in greeting. John tapped "3," counting the seconds that elapsed as he waited for the doors to close. The elevator ascended smoothly, not stopping at any intervening floor. He continued to count, which eased his impatience. At forty-seven seconds, he arrived at the third floor, and slid sideways through the still opening elevator doors, swinging his laptop sideways to accommodate the narrow space. He was halfway down the hall before the doors were completely open.

John entered the Security offices, nodding to Dave's administrative assistant, Katie, who was negotiating her boss's meeting schedule with another secretary. Glancing around the reception area as he waited, John again considered its war room décor. The clutter had grown since Tuesday. Bookcases and walls were lined with dry-erase boards. Piles of computer printouts, stacks of personnel files, and related investigative paraphernalia adorned every potential work surface. Save for Katie's desk.

"In here, John," called Dave.

John wondered how Dave knew that he had arrived. He hadn't even spoken a word of greeting to Katie. He entered the office, and took a seat across from Dave. While calm at outward appearance, John's inner core remained at red alert, fight or flight response awaiting the signal, whatever that might be.

1:00 PM

"Ron Albers stands by his story. He didn't take any narcotics. His lawyer and I have agreed that charges will not be pursued, and in exchange for my apology, in writing, they won't sue the hospital or me." Dave stated the case plainly, unemotionally.

For John, the news deflated his tautly held guard and countered his battle-readiness. "Why are you backing down now?" he asked, spreading his hands in a gesture of disbelief. "You were certain enough yesterday that Ron took narcotics, certain enough to call in Risk Management and the PDU cops. What's changed?"

Dave glanced down, refusing to feel the sting of the anticipated question. He looked back to John Williams, estimating the values of the man, the wisdom of candor with one who was a friend and colleague of the accused, one who was offended by the accusation itself. He calculated the risk, a mathematical equation that factored loyalty and moral courage more heavily than honesty or pride. It was the equivalent of moral calculus, its importance of exponential significance. A miscalculation would drive his investigation further into the ground. Negative numbers, negative resolution. He wavered only in the shadow of yesterday's miscalculation.

"I have prepared a letter of apology," Dave stated slowly, not answering the question. "Issuing it will solve a short term problem. It doesn't resolve the larger problem of the diversion, and I will keep an eye on the data that's being collected. You know I'm not a gambling man. I may have misjudged the process on this one, but my instincts are generally accurate."

John understood the message clearly. "So what happens next?" he asked.

"We return to standard operations," Dave stated firmly. "Dr. Albers returns to work. We continue to monitor staffing patterns,

narcotics usage, and areas where staff has access to narcotics."
Dave paused. "The hospital has authorized installation of surveillance cameras in the Recovery Room dispensary, as well as in each
of the ORs. And it looks like the hospital foundation will be tapped
for a computerized recordkeeping system." His mouth turned
up at the corners briefly, aware that for John Williams, this news
was the equivalent of learning that Santa was bringing *everything*
on the Christmas wish list. "You won't need your database much
longer," he added.

"Okay, you've surprised me," John admitted. "But what I'm
asking about has less to do with what *you* will do, or what *I* will do,
but whether you want to run this collaboratively or not."

Dave said nothing.

"There's been a breach of trust, Dave, and although you may
believe that you were just doing your job, your decisions have
had a serious impact on my group—on me, on Ron, on Stu. If
you want me to work with you, then I expect to make decisions
together. That includes decisions about who is included in the
loop."

Dave opened his mouth to speak, but John raised his hand
and broke eye contact, quickly interjecting, "Don't answer me
now. You need to think about this. If you want me to work with
you, you'll need to put all the cards on the table. If you want to fly
solo, I need to know. My group needs to know."

Dave nodded. "Agreed," he stated, reaching for his phone as
Katie buzzed and said that the Lab was calling. "The syringe contents," he added, motioning John to wait. A moment later, he
hung up, visibly disappointed. "They'll have a report tomorrow.
I'd called about the results, which should have been back yesterday."

John stood up quickly. "Then we'll touch base tomorrow."

"Absolutely," Dave assured.

They parted, each man contemplating the possibilities of their
partnership. Each was wary, for completely different reasons.
They remained united only in their unambivalent passion to resolve this question of narcotics diversion. For both, reputations

were on the line. Perhaps someone have to die before the men set aside protective concern for reputations and friendships, in search of painful answers.

2:00 PM

"I'm trying to catch people before they leave," John explained firmly, tersely. "There's been a lot of speculation about what's going on with Ron and Stu. I expect them back tomorrow. Stu has been off sick. He became ill after a meeting yesterday. At the meeting, Ron was questioned about being in the Women's Health workroom after hours. Security has been tightened because of suspected drug diversion. But the important thing is that Ron is not guilty of anything. He was ambushed, and the Director of Security has apologized, in writing. Until we knew what the Security Department intended, Ron was scheduled off. Questions?" John hoped that his tone would discourage questions.

Of course, it did not, for these physicians were more lion than lamb. Fortunately, most of the questions had been easy enough. Such as, what action the group would take against the Director of Security. The answer: none. Ron would have to take action, and could do so administratively, through the hospital's chain of command; or legally, through civil litigation. Dave Johnson had reason to inquire about Ron's presence; what had not been justified was bringing in outside law enforcement, and disregarding the Anesthesia Department policy related to such an investigation.

John felt relieved to have completed the individual contacts. Had he called a meeting, it would have been impossible to contain the fury this news generated. Thankfully, it would be Ron's call to press forward with a complaint against Dave Johnson.

Although far from satisfied with this outcome, John could not settle on exactly what bothered him so much—or *whose* actions: Ron's or Dave's? Perhaps the real source of tension was his own action; or more precisely, his inaction. As with a sin of omission, John's failure to intervene in the process the day before rendered him a culpable facilitator of—or an accomplice to—Dave Johnson's plan.

7:00 PM

John picked up the phone on the first ring. It was Ron Albers.

"I would have called you last night," Ron stated bluntly, unemotionally, "but my lawyer advised against it. He wanted to get through the meeting with Dave Johnson."

"I heard that Dave apologized," John said tentatively.

"Yeah," Ron acknowledged bitterly. "It'll keep the hospital and him out of court. But I'll be watching my back. My trust level is operating in negative numbers today. I can't believe that you and Stu allowed Johnson to run roughshod over the policies our group has in place."

"I wish I'd handled things differently," John stated firmly. "I don't think you were stealing drugs, but I'd like to know why you were going through the drug kits. That question hasn't been answered."

"I'm not sure you'd believe any answer I offered," Ron countered.

"Look, we've known each other long enough for you to realize that I'd believe whatever you tell me. What would you have told me if I'd called you the night before, to let you know what Dave Johnson intended for the next day?"

Ron hesitated. "I'd have told you the truth. And I would've been grateful for the courtesy. Especially since we probably would've agreed *not* to let Johnson run things until we'd exhausted the Anesthesia departmental process set up a few years ago, which I helped formulate as the policy committee chairman."

John contemplated this rebuke, and accepted its sting without flinching. "As I said, I wish I'd handled this differently. I owed you that. I'm sorry, Ron. I'd like to turn back the clock, and short of that, I'd like to know what to do to make it up to you and Sally."

"I'd like to accept your apology," Ron began, "but I don't feel very gracious right now. I believe it when you say that you'd like to turn the clock back and do things differently. I'd like to do that, too. Since we can't, and until I can sense some measure of trust between us, I'm not going to say 'That's okay, let's go on like it never happened.' I just can't do that now."

"That was exactly *my* dilemma when I watched the video, Ron."

"The difference is that you decided not to deal with me directly, to allow Johnson to proceed as if I were guilty."

John bowed his head penitently. Remorse weighed like a millstone around his neck. *God gives us intuition for a reason,* he thought to himself, *and I refused to use it this time. Damn.* Sighing heavily, he broke the silence. "Yeah. I blew it. I'd do it differently today, but that doesn't help you now."

"That's right," Ron acknowledged, his tone brittle.

A sudden flash of insight struck John dumb: by sustaining this tactic, Ron avoided the question of what he *had* been doing in the workroom, where the surveillance camera had recorded his rummaging. John struggled with how unapologetic it would be to push for an explanation, but felt compelled to ask.

"What *were* you doing in the workroom, Ron?"

John could tell that the question took Ron by surprise, and that any room for a conciliatory response was lost in the angry hostility that now rendered Ron speechless. John could almost feel the fury through the phone lines.

"You don't deserve an answer to that, and I don't answer to you!" CLICK.

Startled, John held the phone away from his ear, after Ron slammed the receiver into its base. Then, John tapped the off button on the cordless phone, considering the advantage offered by the old-fashioned telephones: the chance to hang up on someone with a bang. Ron had had the last word. It left John feeling hollow, as if he had failed a test this evening—for the second time. Most certainly, there would be no third chance.

As he contemplated the conversation, John decided that Ron, too, had failed a test for the second time. He had not answered the question; he had not explained his behavior. He had insisted, instead, on being treated as completely deserving of trust, despite graphic evidence to the contrary.

The thought crossed John's mind, *Who is being unreasonable here?* Yes, he had made a mistake by allowing Dave Johnson to handle the meeting with Ron. That should have been handled within the group, first, as set forth in the policy manual. Ron was not unreasonable to expect such procedures to be followed, especially since it was set up to permit the group to evaluate problem situations without the hospital's interference.

The oddity was Ron's tenacious refusal to explain his actions, to settle the questions. Ron could end this in a single explanatory sentence, John knew.

Why would he refuse?

Chapter Nine

RULES OF THE GAME

Friday, April 12
8:05 AM

Once again, the fifth-grade child helped the third-grader get ready for school, pack a lunch, and catch the bus. The front door slammed just seconds before Kathy heard the whine of the school bus brakes. The children had made the bus. Not that she could have done anything, had they missed it. She scarcely believed that she had survived another night, that life within this sea of pain was even possible.

Drew had called from the office late the night before, furious. "Look, tomorrow is the deadline, and I'll stay here all night, if necessary, to finish. If you aren't any better by the time I get home, I'm taking you to the ER. Your doctor seems to think that whatever medication you're taking is the strongest available. But if this is as good as it gets, you need a new doctor."

Kathy had not replied, but instead, had shut her eyes and turned her head from the phone, which her son held to her ear. She had said her piece two nights before: "If I'm not dying, then I'd rather *be dead*," she had whispered to Drew. There were no other words to speak. No strength to waste on words. Not even for her frightened children.

Marilyn had visited a few mornings back, and begged Kathy to reconsider the treatment. Speaking her mind had drained

Kathy of all reserves, minimal as they were. Yet, her will had prevailed, and she had accepted no treatment. Instead, they had collaborated on a video of her present state, and Kathy had stated those words of invocation, the ones she'd later repeated to Drew.

And then, darkness had descended.

Kathy had lost track of time. It was only the auditory cues, gleaned during more wakeful moments, which suggested to Kathy that one day had finished, and another was begun. The brother's shouts to his younger sister, the bang of the door, and the squeal of the hydraulics announcing the bus's arrival—which Kathy heard only minutes ago—were the first indications that a new day was here.

Drew, however, was not.

11:15 AM

Drew Martin kicked the orange bag that contained the newspaper across the threshold on his way into the house, kicking the door shut, in its turn. Exhausted from his all-nighter at the office, eyes burning with fatigue, he tossed the leather briefcase onto the sofa and walked heavily up the stairs, fearing what he would see.

The guest bedroom door was ajar, and his wife appeared to be asleep. Her chest barely moved, so shallow were her breaths. Her cheeks were pale and sunken, her parted lips cracked. Bruise-colored circles beneath her eyes emphasized her skeletal appearance.

"Kathy!" he said sharply. "Wake up! You're going to the ER."

No response.

"Damn it, open your eyes!"

Her eyelids fluttered briefly, and her chest rose sharply as she inhaled deeply. Then, she was still, save for the shallow breaths and the flicker of movement beneath her eyelids.

Drew lifted the bedside water pitcher, noting that scum had formed on the surface. *Shit!* When was the last time she'd had anything to drink? The cloth that had been filled with ice chips for her parched mouth lay on the floor. He picked up the crumpled cloth, now stiff and dry. He slammed the pitcher of scummy water and the cloth on the bedside table and shook Kathy's shoulders. "Wake up, I said!" He pulled her upright, and she gasped, eyes flying open in fear, pain, and shock. "You're going to the hospital, now."

Drew flung back the covers and placed one arm beneath her knees, the other around her back, lifting her with ease. *My God! She's skin and bones!* A chill of alarm ran down Drew's spine. *How did she get this bad? Why didn't I notice?*

It was the covers that had obscured her shrunken frame, he believed. She had isolated herself in the guest bedroom for the better part of two weeks; there was no way he could have known, especially with the work hours he had kept.

Mewls of discomfort, soft but persistent, were the only sounds that emanated from the emaciated form in his arms, and Drew softened his tone in a gesture of comfort, guilt-stricken and afraid. It was his wife's nearly autistic muteness that worried him most. Was she going to die? Had she been right, when she said she thought she was dying?

Drew gently lowered Kathy into the minivan, and raced back into the house for his cell phone and a blanket. He covered his wife before clicking the seatbelt into place. Then, he drove a circuitous route to the hospital, thus avoiding the potholes that dotted the major thoroughfares. Silently focused, he repeated the mantra, "I've got it under control. I've got it under control . . . ."

A well-ordered life had been the hallmark of their marriage, Drew believed, until recently. He had enjoyed the tidy division of labor, strategically devised and flawlessly executed until Kathy's illness wreaked havoc. *Damn this disease! Damn the doctors who can't even name whatever it is! Damn it, damn it, damn it!*

Drew fought the demons that suggested he did not deserve this curse. The arguments dueled in his head. On one hand, Kathy should buck up and fight this illness, whatever it was. If he accepted this admonishment, then Kathy was to blame for their crazy life. On the other hand, in his heart and head, Drew knew that Kathy was not to blame for her illness. Still, he hated to be the one who always picked up the pieces when she was so ill. But who else should? Who else would?

For the first time, as he clenched the steering wheel with white-knuckled fists, Drew acknowledged that he felt angry enough to smash the car into a tree. Yet, he would never permit himself the bestial luxury of violent temper.

He pulled out his cell phone and hit the autodial for Kathy's internist. They had spoken yesterday, and it had not been friendly. The internist had encouraged Drew to contact Kathy's immunologist, and the immunologist had assured that the medications he had prescribed were the best to be offered, and that he would re-evaluate Kathy at her next appointment. Now, Drew confirmed his action plan with the internist's receptionist: Kathy would be examined in the ER, and the goal was to have her admitted.

Then, he called the next-door neighbor, who agreed to have the children after school, and into the evening if necessary. Finally, Drew dialed his mother in Lexington, and arranged for her to come immediately. Nana would take care of the children this weekend, while he orchestrated Kathy's medical team. Next week, while Drew was at work or visiting Kathy at the hospital, Nana would get the children to school, oversee homework, drive to soccer and music lessons, and provide more than peanut butter and jelly or bologna sandwiches for dinner. It was all under control.

✦

By 1:00 PM, Kathy's internist had admitted her to St. Catherine's, her sixth hospitalization in twelve months. "She's dehydrated and anorexic, possibly because of an infection. We've run several tests and I should be able to tell you more in a day or two. Meanwhile, she's on intravenous fluids and we'll probably put in a feeding tube when she's a little stronger. You were right about bringing her in. But, why didn't you call sooner? Or, why didn't Kathy call?" the internist asked.

In measured tones, Drew reminded the internist that the immunologist had just seen Kathy a few weeks ago, and *that* doctor seemed to think he was offering everything possible. "Furthermore . . ." Drew recounted his long workdays, and pointed out that Kathy hadn't asked to see another doctor. The internist frowned, but did not comment further.

Drew slouched in an upholstered armchair, his eyes at half-mast as he studied the tubes and wires that delivered nourishment or monitored life within the silent, ghostly shadow of a woman, who lay still as a corpse beneath the bed linens. It was a terrible day. What must he do, what *could* he do, to retrieve their perfect life?

3:00 PM

The paging number was familiar enough. It was Dave Johnson. The aftertaste of battle lingered, and generated a sour flavor in John Williams' mouth. Sighing, eager to leave the hospital for the weekend, John methodically punched in the extension to the Security office.

Dave answered the phone, and proceeded to the point.

"The lab report finally came in on that syringe from last Friday's Code. It was Succinylcholine."

John did not breathe on his end of the phone. His adrenal glands fired up, erasing every vestige of fatigue from his body. *Somebody took the narcotic and replaced it with Succinylcholine.* It could be nothing else, and the acts of theft and deception nearly culminated in a patient's death.

Any residual rancor from the previous two-day battle evaporated. Rapid-fire thoughts of *who* and *how* and *why* intersected the realization that this situation was far more critical than he had thought. The *who* portion of the question had to be addressed, and as if reading John's thoughts, Dave asked to meet in the Security office, now, to review the schedule of people working in the area that day.

"I'll be right up," John agreed, grabbing the laptop computer from his locker to access his spreadsheet. Maybe Dave could see something that John did not.

Ten minutes later, John arrived at the Security Department reception area. Katie was not at her desk, and John peered through the doorway to the inner office.

"Is there somewhere I can set up my laptop?" he asked, skipping any social greeting. "There are a few things I've been tracking. I don't see any pattern, but maybe you will."

"Not much space in here," Dave acknowledged. "Try Katie's desk," he suggested, stretching a yellow elastic string to yet another spot on the foam core board, which depicted floor plans for the Surgery and Recovery areas. Although Dave did not often explain his methods or motives, he added, "I work best visually. The bigger the picture, the better. Looking at my computer screen doesn't always show me the big picture."

John nodded and retreated to the Katie's desk outside the door. He opened the computer and clicked the "on" switch. The machine purred in response. He gently nudged the sensitive mouse to "Staff" and double-clicked on the small bar below the keyboard. With another whir, the screen flashed to a black-on-white spreadsheet. This was organized to list personnel, the date and shift each person worked, the location to which he or she was assigned, patient assignments, and for the members of the Anesthesia Department, the type and dose of drugs administered.

Succinylcholine: how does a drug like Sux find its way to the Recovery room? John stared at the spreadsheet, willing it to answer. The names were there, but *who among them* would replace narcotic medication with a paralytic agent like Succinylcholine?

So intent was his effort to divine a method by which to narrow the field of suspects, John failed to notice the surge of energy that now replaced the fatigue of another tense day. His skin tingled, as if electrically charged. He believed with certainty that the information was *here.*

With a few taps of the keys, he commanded the computer to sort the OR staff by job description. Within a minute, the computer had generated a list of OR nurses, techs, nurse anesthetists, surgeons, anesthesiologists, pharmacy techs, and aides who transported patients on gurneys from the pre-operative area to the OR, then from the OR to Recovery.

Recovery! The thought triggered realization of his oversight: he hadn't captured the list of Recovery personnel, a major oversight, although they would have little access to Succinylcholine. That was strictly an anesthesia drug, one that paralyzed the patient for intubation, requiring the anesthesiologist or nurse anesthetist to ventilate, or breathe for, the patient.

Dave left the war room and frowned at the emerging screen of data John had pulled up on the laptop. "Any thoughts about how Succinylcholine could have gotten into that syringe?"

John's brow furrowed as he attempted to envision scenarios that would have allowed for this. He couldn't. "Sux is an OR drug. It has no place in the Recovery Area. It's a paralytic we use for intubation."

Both men silently contemplated the drug record. Dave pointed to a surgical notation indicating that a dose of Demerol had been given in the OR. "Any way that vial made its way to Recovery?"

"No way," John stated. "Those meds should stay in the OR drug kits. That way, Pharmacy can track the drugs by area. The pharmacy techs work in pairs, for quality assurance, and they check the drugs that come back from surgery in the kits against the drug record. Any narcotics remainders are disposed of by that team of pharmacy techs, and they'd have reported it if Succinylcholine came back from the Recovery Area, or anywhere other than the OR. If drugs could be transferred from the OR to Recovery, we might reduce the amount that's wasted, if it's unused, and it's been discussed with some of the expensive narcotics. But the risk for diversion or other problems is too great."

Dave nodded silently. "Just thought you might have some ideas. It's a baffling situation, and dangerous." Dave shifted his stance from studying the record to facing John Williams directly. "You asked me yesterday to consider how we can work on this together."

John glanced up, suddenly feeling guarded and somewhat remiss, insofar as he'd failed to obtain some commitment from Dave before they collaborated today. The news that Succinylcholine was found in the Demerol syringe had targeted John's defenses, essentially taking them out. Now, however, his defenses were remobilized.

Dave did not hesitate. "It's in the interest of patients, the hospital, and everyone concerned that we resolve this diversion. Especially with the stakes potentially being life or death. I'll collaborate with you, John, but with these limitations." Dave paused, lifting a finger. "First, I will share information with you that pertains to the investigation—all of it—if you agree to keep it confidential. That means that you don't share our discussions with anyone in your group."

Again, Dave paused, aware of the conflict this could create for John Williams, and searching the other man's face for resistance. He lifted another finger and continued, "Second, I will include you in the loop completely, unless I have reason to believe that you are personally involved in any aspect of this diversion—and I don't think you are," he amended quickly. "I will tell you directly if I think that you or anyone in your group is trying to conceal evidence or divert this investigation in any way. If that happens, I will suspend this gentleman's agreement."

John remained silent, absorbing these rules of fair play collaboration.

"Third," Dave continued, "I will include you in decisions as to who will be involved in any meetings or questionings. I will accept your input and consider it carefully. However, the ultimate decision about how to proceed with this investigation will remain mine. If we come to a juncture where you can't live with my decision, you can tell me and we'll have to work separately. But the main thing I'm suggesting is that you will have all the information I have. You will be in the loop, but investigative decisions will ultimately be mine. I'm the one who's accountable to the hospital Board. Can you live with that?"

John stared hard at the man who had been an ally, until recent events rendered him an adversary. Dave had presented his terms toughly, but fairly, and John perceived that Dave would collaborate with integrity. While he may not like some of Dave's decisions, it was worth the calculated risk to participate in the process.

"I can live with that," John agreed. "And I'll let you know if, at some point, I can't live with it. If someone in my group is involved with this, I want to deal with it now. But only within the bounds of our group's policy. The last time this hospital went through an accreditation site visit, we made sure that our group's policy of dealing with suspected drug diversion did not conflict with the hospital's. You agree to due process in that regard, and I will agree to your rules."

Dave nodded once and extended his hand. John took it, their agreement sealed. The rules of the game had been established.

Chapter Ten

EXAMINATION OF CONSCIENCE

Friday, April 12
3:20 PM

From behind the one-way glass, Captain Mike Daly watched his subject squirm and fidget, bubble and fester, the paint-stripper of an interrogation loosening his defenses. While he waited, Daly opted to pick up a PDU phone call, as the caller had asked for him by name.

"Daly here."

"Yes," the voice answered, "My father is a cancer patient, and I'm concerned that he's getting a medication that isn't legally prescribed. Can you help me with that?"

"I'll try," Daly answered, pinching the bridge of his nose as a headache formed in his sinuses. He hated these calls. Hospice organizations in the community were squeaky clean, and it bugged him when ambivalent family members had difficulty accepting that unfamiliar medications may be part of a patient's treatment plan. He knew a bit about cancer, having watched his mother die of it.

"I think that my mother, brother, and sister might be trying to euthanize my father with his medicine. As I mentioned, he has cancer. He probably shouldn't have lived this long, but he has good health insurance and excellent doctors."

The caller paused to breathe deeply. Then, with greater confidence, he continued. "There's some doctor who recommends giving my dad some pain medicine that could stop his breathing, as a side effect, I mean. My brother and sister are not concerned about that risk, and my father actually said that he wants to take the medicine. But I suspect that Dad is not mentally competent. After all, if he's agreeable to taking a medicine that could kill him, he certainly isn't making good decisions."

Daly interrupted, "You say that your father has cancer, right?"

"Yes."

"And that your father has survived longer than expected?"

"Yes, but that doesn't mean they should hurry the end along," the caller stated irritably.

"Of course not," Daly acknowledged. Wrong tact, he decided. Go for the feelings. "You are concerned that your brother and sister aren't looking out for your father's best interest?"

"My mother, too. She says that she's following my father's wishes."

"Let me backtrack with a question that probably doesn't matter a lot in the scheme of your concerns, but it's interesting to me that you asked for the Pharmaceuticals Diversion Unit. How did you happen to call us?"

"Well, I started out in pharmacy school, and actually completed half the program before I decided to switch to psychology. While I was there, you spoke to our ethics class. When I couldn't trace the medicines my dad was taking to our pharmacy, or to any of the physicians who are treating him, I thought it might be a diversion situation."

Daly remained silent, which seemed to make the caller nervous. He began to stammer. "I mean, I-I-I'm not *positive* that someone is diverting drugs to treat my father, but I was told it happens more often than anyone realizes, and since no one else seems to know where my dad gets these medicines . . . well, it seems like a possibility." After a pause, the man added, "So, you aren't going to do anything about it?" The voice was suddenly belligerent.

"I didn't say that," Daly responded, struggling to contain his impatience. "Have you talked with your father's doctors?"

"Yes, I've been on the phone all day, and reached all but one."

"And?"

"They agree that he should have whatever he needs to keep him comfortable, but they don't know anything about one particular medication."

"What's that?"

"Limbotryl. That's spelled l-i-m-b-o-t-r-y-l."

Daly stretched his girth to pull the latest edition of the *Physician's Drug Reference* from an overhead shelf. "Limbotryl," he repeated, flipping to the blue pages to check the narcotic analgesics category. "Don't see it. Hang on." He ran an index finger down another page, finding no such drug listed. "Are you sure about the name? There are a lot of drugs that cancer patients receive, and maybe it's under another category." Daly flipped to antineoplastics, cancer drugs. "Leucovorin, Leukine—no Limbotryl. Maybe you need to try the doctor you couldn't reach earlier."

The caller heaved a sigh of exasperation. "That doctor is with the home health care agency that's taking care of my father. He's not available during the day, and only returns phone calls. I left a message last night, but I don't want to wait if there's a risk that this drug could kill my father."

Good lord, Daly thought. *It's the cancer that's going to kill his father, not the drug!* To the caller, Daly said, "Right. So, how was the medicine packaged?"

"It's in a glass vial."

"And you found it where?"

"It was on my father's bedside table, with his other medicines. And there was a syringe, too. My mother said that she's supposed to fill the syringe and inject the Limbotryl into my dad's IV line whenever he asks for it. When I asked the oncologist why my father needed Limbotryl, he said he didn't know anything about it. Dr. Chaney told me to dump it into the toilet, and that he had already prescribed adequate pain medicine. He sounded angry, as if he thought one of us had gone behind his back to get extra treatment for our father. I don't know for certain, but I suspect that my mother did exactly that. And with my father already getting painkillers, it seems to me that my mom, my sister, and my brother are euthanizing my dad."

"I'm not a medical expert," Daly broke in, "but I've been through cancer with my mother. It was a tough time for the family, and I appreciate what you're going through."

"No, you don't!" snapped the caller. "You don't have any idea what it's like to be the only one who's concerned. I thought you'd be willing to help. My father has done a lot for this community, and he's earned the respect of most law professionals in this county!"

Daly set the *PDR* in his lap, his interest piqued. "I'm sorry if it sounds like I don't care. It's just that I'm not finding the information you need. You'll have to give me your name and number if you want me to dig a little deeper, and I'll need your father's name. I'm also going to give you the numbers for Pro-Seniors and the Council on Aging. They can advise you on the steps you can take if you're concerned that your father's interests or well-being aren't being considered by the rest of your family."

Daly flipped though the Hamilton County Social Services Directory to locate the numbers. The three-inch binder fell from his hands when the caller identified himself, and more importantly, his father.

"My name is Dan Warden. My father is Nathan Warden, *Judge* Nathan Warden."

✦

After hanging up the phone, Daly waved to Richard Ostrader, who had just returned to the office with Barbara Westover. Ostrader lifted a finger to Westover, a "just a sec" gesture, to which she rolled her eyes and slammed the office door. That, Daly knew, was for *his* benefit. It was her way of communicating that Daly, her former partner—in more ways than one—would never be her superior. Even if he was her boss.

"Hey, Richard," Daly called, straightening the cache of papers that had fallen from the social service directory. "Ever hear of a drug called Limbotryl?"

"Sure," Ostrader answered. "It's an anesthesia drug. Why?"

Daly disregarded the question. "Would a cancer patient need a drug like that?"

"You're asking *me*?"

"Just tell me what you know."

"If the cancer patient needs surgery, then the cancer patient probably needs anesthesia."

Daly was silent.

"Okay, I'll bite," Ostrader yielded. "Why does a cancer patient need Limbotryl?"

"Don't know, yet. Possibly for sedation. I know my mom was sedated, once the cancer got into her brain. She was a big woman, too much for my dad to handle when she got agitated and irritable. Her doctor had a visiting nurse give it to her."

Remembering was almost too much to bear. Daly looked at Ostrader pointedly. "See what you can find out, and keep it between us. I've got one of Snake's boys on the back burner. Catch me later, when you have something."

But Daly knew better than to follow up with Judge Nathan Warden, friend of law enforcement officers, bar none. He'd think of something to say to the son, something that would sedate the son, he decided with a chuckle.

3:45 PM

The thought had crossed into consciousness a year ago, when his father made a flight into health immediately preceding the trip to England for his older brother's graduation from Oxford. How could his father appear close to death for days on end, and then recover his sharp-tongued bossiness in time to order a travel agent to " . . . find three tickets to anywhere in Great Britain, just as long as I can get to my son's graduation. Make it happen." That was three days before the pre-graduation festivities commenced.

His dad was a wonder at getting other people to "make it happen," and that was his father's favorite directive, whether it be to his children, his wife, or any of the attorneys, clerks, bailiffs, or court stenographers who entered his court.

As a boy, Dan had avoided his father, fearing his anger and sarcastic reproof if he failed to "make it happen." He continued the avoidance even now, the geographic distance between Cincinnati and San Francisco forming a natural barrier.

When work brought him to Cincinnati several times a year, he would visit his mother while his father was in court, before the judge became sick. Since then, Dan visited only if his father was well enough to be serving from the bench, or too ill for company. On the latter such days, which his mother referred to as "difficult days," she would convey regrets on behalf of his father, adding, "But you may certainly come over and visit with me."

He'd always felt more comfortable in his mother's company. They'd shared a camaraderie that excluded his highly educated older brothers, who wielded executive power as naturally as Thor guided thunder. And their similar temperaments were thunderous as the god himself, a sex-linked trait that Dan failed to inherit from his father.

He'd *tried* to use the authoritative tone and the demanding, slightly sarcastic words that "made things happen," just as his father and siblings did. But the voice did not match the spirit from which it issued, and those to whom it was directed seemed to sneer—even laugh—at his attempted command. It was not an authentic voice, and Dan learned to trust the one that belonged to him.

While lacking volume and intensity, Dan Warden's manner of address was direct, quietly assertive, and friendly in tone. No one was more surprised than Dan to discover that his own voice had the effect of "making things happen," but with a bonus: people actually *liked* him, and were willing to go the extra mile because of his low-key good nature. Indeed, he was more a Dale Carnegie kind of guy than a Bobby Knight.

Sometimes, Dan wondered why he even *cared* if his father

was receiving illicit treatment. It was a path he hesitated to wander, contemplating his feelings for his father. In general, he respected his father, the kinship loyalty felt deeply, if bitterly. Dan was certain that he himself would be a different sort of father, more like his father-in-law, a reserved man who viewed quiet contemplation before speech as an indication of intellect and wisdom, rather than slow-wittedness.

In Dan's family, whoever made the fastest retort earned a guffaw of approval from their father. Strangely, it was Dan's sister, the youngest child and only daughter, who eventually became master of that game. Lisa, the name, speaks of softness, tenderness. But his sister was a skilled prosecutor who had earned the nickname "Barracuda-Black Widow-Doberman" from the victims of her skill. Dan could not imagine the trouble her future husband would endure, if she turned her skills on him.

Then, there was the memory of The Brain Game. Dan shuddered as he recalled—relived—the rules of play, in which siblings were pitted against one another, required to respond to rapid-fire trivia questions, points of philosophy, or issues of debate. Their father was the judge, and his approval was as prized as any Olympic Medal.

Dan had won not a single medal during his childhood, and had been labeled slow-witted by his father. He had been deemed a cautious thinker by his mother, who was of similar persuasion. While his mother did not contradict her husband or reprove him for his tactics, she did reframe his words in a more positive light. It was a bit of a joke within the family, that their father would invite his wife to rephrase his words more positively, whenever he made a particularly witty, sarcastic comment.

Dan sighed. Rehashing his family history would not help. It simply stoked the urge to flee the family that flung words like flaming spears.

Oddly enough, Dan acknowledged, he no longer harbored strong feelings about what was happening. The urgency and distress had faded, the zeal to protect his seemingly incapacitated father now waned. He felt disconnected from the flow of his parents' family life. Instead, the magnetic pull of his wife and her family drew him away from the Warden Family Rules of Engagement.

At least when he was feeling passionate that families could be different, he had *done* something, and it was positive. He and his wife created a family culture founded on respect, love, and support, not competition. *I made things happen,* Dan thought, smiling at the irony.

Still, he hadn't intended to identify himself, much less his father, to the police officer. Now that he had, surely there would be hell to pay.

That was the reason for the second trip to his parents' house: to let his mother know what he had done. And to voice his concern that the treatment might kill his father.

Dan struggled to rekindle the latter concern. When he failed to do so, he wondered if concern had been his real motivation to speak with the Cincinnati Police. He allowed the idea of vengeance to stand up and be counted within his conscience. Could he have been more intent on settling a score, or having the final word, via the interruption of his father's tightly controlled, well-planned, autocratically executed medical treatment?

He felt a mixture of guilt and glee, and more guilt because of the presence of glee. This wasn't the way he usually operated, and it felt as uncomfortable as the attempts he'd made to imitate his father, brothers', and sister's commanding speech.

Dan had failed to think through his strategy adequately, and this annoyed him immensely. He was generally a capable decision-maker, taking the necessary time to make informed, well-considered decisions. Especially those that affected other people. He consoled himself by rationalizing that the call to the Pharmaceuticals Diversion Unit was *part* of making his decision, a bit of research. Or was it?

No. Now, Dan admitted that his decision had been a knee-jerk response.

The night before, while visiting with his mother, Dan had been startled by the flurry of medical activity concentrated in his father's sickroom. As Dan observed the intravenous line that snaked from a vinyl bag to his father's withered, purple and blue forearm, his body responded with a flush of anxious heat.

Yet, it was when Dan overheard someone instructing his mother to administer additional injections whenever his father seemed wakeful—that's when Dan froze, cold with fear. Was it possible that his mother could and would follow such a directive? Would she give him a fatal dose, in the process? Shouldn't a medical professional be giving injections, if only to prevent an accidental overdose? Did his mother want his father to die? Wasn't she taking a huge risk, legally? Surely, this was not a legal process; even in California, it would not be legal.

Thus, it had been fear, numbing shock, and loyalty—more protective of his mother than his father—that spurred Dan to contact the police. He did not want to create trouble for his mother, but he did want to make sure that she neither harmed his father, accidentally of course, nor suffered any legal consequences for following such a medical directive: "Give him more of the medicine, if he begins to awaken tonight."

The mistake had been identifying himself, and more importantly, his father. Why had he done that? It was such a stupid mistake!

The police officer had answered his questions succinctly, lacking concern, in Dan's opinion. He'd expected outrage and action. The advice to contact his father's physicians had precipitated the notion that Captain Mike Daly viewed Dan as a meddling, disgruntled family member, not worth anyone's time.

It was the sense that he had been discounted, the feeling that he could not make things happen, that had triggered Dan Warden's defensive admission of their names. His father's name would certainly make things happen! Such had been his thought in the millisecond that preceded his quest for action. In effect, the mallet struck the stake squarely, the officer's shocked silence a testimony to the weight of Judge Warden's name.

What Dan hadn't counted on was the way his decision *would*

make things happen within the family. If he had granted this decision the same consideration accorded every other, Dan would not have given his name, and certainly not his father's. So, he had talked with his wife about what to do next, and called Mike Daly back, leaving a message: Dan conceded that he'd made a mistake about the treatment; that he'd spoken with his father's oncologist, and was now satisfied with the treatment process.

All that was left to do, for the time, was to inform his mother. If Dan could have avoided a confrontation with his mother, he would have chosen that path. The fact remained, confrontation was unavoidable.

He'd have to remind himself many times to stick to his purpose; to remember that he was not like his father and siblings; and that he would accept responsibility for his actions, the net effect of which might blacken his father's reputation for running his court with fairness, integrity, and intelligence. Dan had not considered this consequence, prior to the initial query, and that failure represented a serious oversight.

Sarcastic autocracy aside, his father was well regarded within the legal community. Just because that opinion did not extend unanimously to the Judge's family was no reason to publicly sully a reputation, and breach family loyalty in the process.

This was the Judge's most sacred rule of family life: although one might spar fiercely within the family circle, one never allowed an outsider to attack a family member without vigorous and immediate reprisals. It was a matter of family honor.

Daniel Warden had broken that rule.

5:30 PM

"Daniel, you had no right to do that!" his mother reprimanded, once again the strict German mother who had disciplined her children with the vigor of a field marshal. "This is not your business, and you are not in any position to make judgments. You don't see your father more than twice a year, and for you to sweep into town—right before your sister's wedding, no less—

and create havoc like this is unforgivable. I can't imagine what you were thinking."

Dan Warden's frown was as much a part of his facial features as his eyes. He'd frowned even as a child, a serious and shy child who preferred his own company and did not join in sibling play unless his father insisted. Perhaps the frown was his mask, designed to hide any feelings that might be labeled weak, or sissified.

His words were dispassionate. "Mother, you can't reasonably expect me to come here, see what's happening, and not have some reaction to it."

"I expect you to respect the decisions your father and I have made, Daniel. You may have any reaction you wish, and you may even share it with me. But you *never* should have called those people about your father's treatment. You may have cost him the opportunity to live as fully as he wants to, and I pray he doesn't find out that you are the one who's responsible."

Dan heaved an exasperated sigh. "Mother, this could kill Dad. And it's probably illegal. Don't you see that? Am I the only one in this house who thinks this is wrong?"

Mae Warden stood squarely in front of her second youngest child. "You are a smart man, Daniel," she began firmly, "but you have let down your father and me by speaking to the *police*, of all people, regarding something you know nothing about. It isn't your place to decide what treatment your father accepts, and it was disloyal of you to talk with strangers about this. And you were disloyal to me by telling them that you suspect I would do anything potentially harmful to your father."

Mae paused, momentarily. "Your father would be furious if he knew, and I will not let you speak with him until after your sister's wedding. He's been looking forward to finally being father of the bride. I won't allow you to ruin the day for him or Lisa. Do I make myself clear, Daniel?" she asked sharply.

Dan understood. She expected the, "Yes, Mother," response of a penitent child. Nothing else would be acceptable. His mother was not the sort who became weary of parental responsibilities.

Neither she nor her husband had been worn down by the passage of time, or by the succession of children. The standards of behavior that applied to the oldest child were applied equally to the younger four, and Dan anticipated a reminder of his "place."

"Mom, I'm not eight-years-old, or even eighteen-years-old. I can think for myself, and I know what's happening here."

"No, Daniel," his mother contradicted, "You have *no idea* what's happening here. If you did, you would comprehend how heartless an act you've just committed. Your father was so sick before these treatments he couldn't work from the bench. He became so depressed that I thought he might take his life. He was so miserable, he stopped eating, sleeping, even talking. Have you *ever* known your father to stop talking?

"You aren't here often enough to see what this illness is doing to him. You've never seen him come back from the edge of desperation, Daniel!" His mother's voice wavered, belying her emotional turmoil. "You should have spoken with me first, if for no other reason than the benefit of the doubt."

Dan looked away from his mother, dourly wondering if he had entered some time tunnel, now feeling every bit the chastised schoolboy. How did his mother do that? How could he, an adult, so competently navigate the psychological complexities of corporate mediation, taking down every potential adversary through gifted persuasion, and fall short of the mark with his own mother? Could she not understand what he saw from *his* perspective?

"Mom, you tell me what *you* would do, in the same circumstances. Would you ignore what plainly appears to be illegal, and take it for granted that Dad has made an informed decision about the treatment? He hasn't lifted his head off the pillow since I flew in, he's barely uttered a word to me, and I'm supposed to like—and support—this treatment because it will get him back onto the bench or let him play father of the bride? You did teach me to think, Mom, and I'm not convinced that these drugs will help Dad. *Illegal* drugs, I may add, which used to mean something to you when I was younger. Besides, it *is* my responsibility to advocate for him, as his son."

✦

As the words were uttered, Mae Warden stared at her child as if seeing him in an unnatural light, his flaws newly perceived, at once illuminated and magnified. He did not resemble the boy she'd considered like herself, in spirit and temperament. Indeed, he sounded like the other shouters in her family, although he hadn't raised his voice. It was merely the intensity and the conviction of his tone that sounded like shouting.

The effect of it was to render Mae quiet, a familiar family dance. The louder her husband roared, the quieter her voice would become. It was Nathan Warden's cue that his wife had heard enough. Their children had learned to respect the signal, as well.

Of all her children, she knew that only Dan feared his mother's mutism more than his father's blistering fury, for it severed him from her, such that she was present only physically, not relationally. Without the feeling of connection to his mother, the boy felt as if he belonged to no family at all.

Now, years later, in the growing silence following the stormy words, Mae understood that Dan had outgrown the habit of anxious withdrawal, his attempt to become invisible whenever his father launched his vituperative and his mother turned silent and cold as stone.

"Mom, how *does* Dad get this miracle drug that has allowed him to stay on the bench, go to Steven's graduation, and now to be the jolly host at Lisa's wedding?"

Mae remained still, certain that she could not trust this child, who was once so like her, with the answer to that question. She held her son's stare stubbornly, wordlessly.

"I'm glad if the medicine has given Dad more of a life," Dan stated softly. "Especially if it means that it's given *you* more of a life with him. But how is giving him this drug any different than using marijuana for pain relief? You remember how Dad went after that lawyer who tried to sell a jury on the idea that his client smoked pot only medicinally. And how about Dad's reaction to hearing that Walter Cronkite had helped his daughter get marijuana when she was sick? Doesn't it make sense, then, that I question Dad's willingness to go along with this?"

Mae Warden felt an unfamiliar wish to strike her son. Her way had not been to hit, but to retreat in cold silence, abandonment. Her husband had doled out the spankings. But suddenly, she felt a hot fury—so contrary to the cold indifference that typified her disapproval—a physical heat that she resisted with all her might. She trembled with the effort. The sole release, it seemed, was to lash out and smack her son, the one who used to be like her.

Why did he have to turn out like this? It seemed a betrayal, of sorts. Now, in a way, all of the children had become like Nate. She had no one to represent herself. It was as if she had contributed nothing to the gene pool. She may as well not have existed. And that's exactly the way she had felt for much of her married life, like a shadow in the wings of this vibrant man whose commanding presence and gift of oratory had attracted her, and then left her in the background when the courtship was completed.

Not that her husband was neglectful or unloving, just full of himself. Nathan Warden was a sun of a man, expansive, basking in his own light to the extent that he failed to see that of others. The rest of the family, the rest of the world, revolved around *him.*

For a time, when she was too young to understand about such people, Mae had thought that she was another sun, or perhaps his moon, bearing her own, steady rhythm of darkness and light, which complemented her husband's brightness. She was wiser now, and had adapted with the stoicism that was part of her nature, and that of her birth family.

Daniel had been a gift, when he revealed himself to be of like temperament. Mae had nurtured his gentle spirit, but only during private moments, so that Daniel would not bear the burden of sibling jealousy. In fact, the brothers and sister *did* notice the seeming favoritism toward Daniel, but mistakenly presumed its source to be Daniel's gender and birth order within the family, the youngest boy.

When did he become this stranger, she wondered?

Mae Warden turned from her son, both to protect herself from betraying strong emotion, and to protect her son from the possibility that she might actually hit him.

✦

Dan Warden recognized the wall that had emerged. He comprehended the degree of his mother's upset, and felt hugely responsible for failing her. Still, he knew he was right about this. Wasn't he?

Suddenly, he felt less certain. Old dances of childhood were difficult to unlearn. This incipient uncertainty typified the self-doubt that he'd often felt growing up, which he'd chalked up to a bad match of personalities. Whenever he was alone with his mother, whether as an adult or a child, his perceptions and feelings gained relevance, meaning. Yet, that reality became obscured, once his siblings or father entered the scene. Dan understood, as a teenager, that this situation prescribed attending college far from home. California was about as far as he could get without leaving the continental United States. And at Stanford, Dan had found a place for himself, and most importantly, people who were like him.

Now, he must return to California. Flee this place. Change the airline tickets. Skip Lisa's wedding. Simply go home.

And never come back.

He turned to leave, sealing off feelings of self-recrimination, refusing to acknowledge his mother, now shuddering as she attempted to recover her equilibrium. Then, behind her, framed in the arch of the hallway, Dan saw his father shuffle and puff as he attempted, in his weakened state, to storm the room, his IV bag held like a lantern, tubing looped from his forearm to the overhead bag. Dan froze, his mouth suddenly cotton-dry. It was the time-tunnel effect, just as when his mother had scolded him. Perhaps he had not outgrown the tongue-tied, timidity of his youth, in the presence of his father.

"Who, in God's name, do you think you are?!?" Judge War-den croaked hoarsely. "I'll make your cozy California life *hell*, if you've ruined the chance for people to get this treatment! You're no son of mine! Get out!"

"Nate! Get back in bed. I'll help." Mae turned to Dan, and might have turned him to a pillar of salt with her unforgiving glower. "Leave, Daniel. Now."

She then took the IV bag from her husband, placed her sturdy arm beneath his, and guided him slowly, gently through the liv-ing room to the library cum sickroom. Neither parent looked back.

Dan leaned against the front door, aware that he had been holding his breath. He breathed, once alone in the entryway, relieved to feel thirty-three-years-old again.

✦

The recollection of that confrontation, inevitable as it may have been, punctuated Daniel Warden's choice decisively. He would leave town; skip the wedding. It was easier to think clearly from within his hotel room, in the comforting presence of his wife and teammate.

Cecie had sighed in response to his suggestion that they leave, resigned that the Warden family would never be whole. Dan gave her credit for not saying, "I told you so." She didn't even com-plain about the childcare hassles she'd navigated in order for the two of them to make this trip for Lisa's wedding. Just one little sigh. Dan believed he was a very lucky man.

He looked at the telephone on the bedside table, consider-ing one last call to Lisa, who intended to wrap up work that day and drive directly to the rehearsal. She was such a gunner; so competitive, Dan thought, she couldn't even take off the day before her wedding.

The phone rang, startling him.

He answered tentatively, and then glanced at his wife, who ex-ited the bathroom with a bag of toiletries, mouthing, "Who is it?"

"What do you think you're doing?" the voice asked, furious.

Dan closed his eyes, then mouthed a response to his wife's query: "Lisa."

He wished he could think of a quick retort, smart and sarcastic. Instead, he said nothing.

"Dan! Are you there?"

"I'm here," he answered.

"Why didn't you come to me, if you thought someone was overmedicating Dad?"

"Because I thought you were supporting it."

"You assumed I was supporting it, and you took the quickest path to havoc. Just to clarify, you will not interfere with Dad's medical care. Dad wants this treatment, and it's not for you to play moral or legal legislator with his life. If you can't support it, stay out of it. He'll die having had the best chance to stay in the game; but it's not a game to him. He lives for his work . . . ."

Dan tuned out the rest of his sister's words. *How sad,* he thought, *to live only for his work.* Dan believed that he lived for his wife and children. How could it ever be enough to live only for work?

" . . . And taking this to the PDU, for godssake! I don't know how I'm going to fix this. But I'm begging you—and I don't beg anyone—stay out of this. Let Dad live on his own terms. Consider it a personal favor, or even a gift. But do what I ask. And I'll do what I can."

Dan said nothing, not even about his effort at damage control, backpedaling with the message he'd left on Mike Daly's machine. He contemplated the demand to bow out, attentive to the message beyond the words, for Lisa rarely asked, certainly never begged, but usually *told* people what to do. Was this his sister's version of desperation? Did it even matter, if it was? For some reason, it did matter, although he had not yet discerned why.

"I'm going back to California. I won't be at the wedding," he stated quietly.

Lisa sighed in exasperation. "You don't have to do *that*," she criticized. "This isn't about throwing you out of the family, Dan. Quit being so sensitive."

He smiled at the irony of her words. "Didn't you hear? I'm not a member of this family any more. The father's edict is final."

The silence on the other end confirmed that Lisa had not been informed of the order of banishment.

"Look, Dad's well enough to bawl me out, and he'll be in top form for your wedding. But he doesn't want to see me." Dan paused before articulating the real reason. "And I don't want to deal with him."

"Well, that's another issue. Can't argue with you there," Lisa said briskly. "Look, I'll do what I can here to keep this from erupting. Will you give me your word that you won't contact anyone— not PDU, not *any* legal authority, no one else—about Dad's treatment?"

"What makes you think I care about this erupting?" Dan asked, irritated that his sister presumed to have the upper hand, and that he was under her thumb. He knew with certainty that Lisa couldn't care less about the imposed banishment.

Again, silence prevailed at the other end of the line. Lisa Warden had not expected this response from her peaceable brother, the placatory sibling.

"What makes you think I'll just do whatever you ask—even if you beg?" Dan continued impatiently. "Did you ever once consider that I have a mind of my own? That I have my own opinion about this, and that I may not accept yours? Or Dad's?" Dan turned to see his wife waving her arms, a signal that meant, "Don't go there!" He looked away, already on the path. He would not accept his wife's warning, just as he would not accept his sister's justification for wrongful choices.

"Listen," Lisa said sharply. "You do what you will. I've *asked* you to consider this from a humanistic perspective. You don't have to agree with any of it. There are a lot of lives in the balance on this one, Dan. I hope you care if this blows up," she added quietly, "because Dad's quality of life depends on it. A lot of other lives depend on this treatment. Mothers and fathers who have young children enjoy family time because of it. Families are able to stay in their homes because it allows parents to function at work and meet the mortgage. You tell me, Dan. Is it worse to break the word of the law, if the goal is to protect the integrity of life? What about the spirit of the law?"

"You're preaching to the choir, Lisa."

"Not if this gets out of control."

Dan resisted his sister's arguments, mostly because they seemed oddly out-of-character, this empathic side of her personality.

Or, in the course of sustaining wounds throughout childhood—verbal "friendly fire"—had he failed to see the whole person of his sister, Lisa?

He admired her cunning, if it was that, hitting him where he lived by mentioning young families, the ones who stood to lose if he stirred this pot. What would he do if Cecie or Matthew or Allie—or even he, himself—were the potential beneficiary of an unorthodox and unsanctioned treatment? Would he permit Cecie to suffer? How could he allow his own children to suffer?

It was so much different, and difficult, to consider his tough father as a—sufferer? It was easy to back away when he thought about his own family, his wife and children. *How sad,* Dan pondered, *that I think of my father as separate from my family.*

He broke the silence, glancing back at Cecie, who looked too frightened to breathe for fear of what he'd say next. "I'm leaving, and I won't do any more damage. I don't necessarily agree with what you're doing. Or what Dad is doing. But, I live across the continent, and I visit when I'm doing business every other month. Your decisions don't affect me much."

Lisa interrupted, "But *your* decisions affect me, and a lot of others."

"I heard you the first time," Dan acknowledged. "I left a message with the PDU officer, explaining that I was mistaken, that I'm satisfied with the treatment Dad's receiving. I'm *not* satisfied, but it's a family matter. I'm no longer a family member, and I've said all I want to. The rest of the damage control is up to you." He lowered the phone receiver to the cradle, dropping it with a gentle thud.

On her end, Lisa Warden heard the click and sounded truly grateful when she said, "Thank you."

Chapter Eleven

THE DIAGNOSIS

Dave Johnson convened the video reviewers without ceremony. "This tape is from last week."

John Williams pressed his lips and jaw tightly, smothering a yawn. He had the logbook today, in addition to the group's vacation and work schedules. Any trades would be confirmed in the log. Anyone in the anesthesia group who showed up on video, but was not scheduled to work, would become a target of the investigation. The same was true for Hannah Gilbert's nurses.

"Stop a minute," Hannah murmured, flipping from the OR staffing sheets to Recovery, and then back. "It's okay. I have her down to float."

Dave frowned. "Let's track the float pool nurses. Not that this particular nurse deserves our suspicion. Just for the sake of information, since we have little else to focus our search."

"Her name is Casey Blanchard."

Dave tapped the fast forward button, and the tape zoomed ahead with a whir, punctuated occasionally by the blur of mouse-like creatures, which scurried in graceless motion to deposit or retrieve medication kits.

John jotted the name of the float nurse, not because he thought it relevant, but to ward off boredom. There was nothing unusual about last week's tapes. He wished that someone else would attend these screening sessions, believing that he had better things to do.

8:10 AM

Three days had passed since Kathy Martin's hospital admission. Her fever persisted, unresponsive to either antibiotics or Ibuprophen.

"Her immune system needs a boost," explained the internist. "I've called in a new immunologist for consultation. He will be in to see your wife later this morning."

Drew rolled his eyes. "What's another immunologist going to do for her?"

The internist remained patient. "I know you were told that everything that *could* be done was *being done.* Apparently, there's a pretty aggressive course of treatment that is usually reserved for patients who don't respond to standard therapies. It has risks. That's why it isn't prescribed as a frontline approach."

The prescription included intravenous antibiotics, a round of chemotherapy designed to keep Kathy's immune system from fighting healthy tissue, and high-power narcotics to tackle the pain.

Drew rubbed his eyes, blinking several times to hydrate them, and then nodded. "We have to try something."

10:35 AM

John Williams checked the break roster, noting that two more anesthetists were scheduled for relief. He poked his head into OR 8. "Larry, how 'bout a break?"

Larry Valentine nodded, and then delivered a succinct report on the patient's status.

While John monitored vital signs and adjusted the flow of anesthesia gases, the patient slumbered, oblivious to the nimble slice of the knife, the tugs of retractors, or the gasps of the suction tube. This was an easy surgical case; the patient was healthy, the surgeon was capable, and the procedure was simple. Consequently, there was an opportunity for John to flex his mental muscle about the decision to track float pool nurses, the path of a drug such as Succinylcholine, from the OR to Recovery, and at the front of his mind, Ron Albers.

The anesthesia assignment board indicated that Ron was covering this room, and John sighed with relief that their paths had not crossed yet. They would, soon, and John hadn't a clue about what he'd say, after the contentious phone call and precipitous hang up last week. No inspiration was forthcoming, and John shifted his thoughts to the other two issues, beginning with the tracking of float pool nurses.

It made sense to do so, in light of the frightening discovery that Succinylcholine caused a healthy young woman to code. Since "Sux" was not a drug used outside the OR, the most likely route to Recovery was via a floater.

Still, "Sux"—or any other OR drug—should never show up in Recovery. Why would anyone pocket a syringe of Succinylcholine? There was no use for the drug, outside of a medically induced respiratory paralysis, necessary for intubation. Or murder.

John smiled at his conspiracy theory. No, that wasn't what this was about.

But, what *was* it about?

10:55 AM

"Dr. Williams," Hannah Gilbert called from down the corridor. "Can you look at this record? It'll only take a minute."

John lengthened his stride, slightly irritated by the interruption. "Another problem with signatures?" he asked, taking the chart proffered by the Perioperative Nursing Supervisor.

Hannah nodded. "We need more than initials, and we need to distinguish between Dr. Adler and Dr. Albers. It's not just that the nurses don't know which doctor wrote the orders. JCAH requires a name," she smiled to take the sting out of her next words.

"A legible name. Not just a scrawl of initials that looks more like someone was trying to get the pen to work."

John sighed in acknowledgment. "I'll take care of it."

Even when the two physicians wrote their full names, rather than just initials, confusion was common: patients, nurses, and new physicians alike had difficulty distinguishing Albers and Adler. The names were just too much alike to the ear and the eye, especially when scribbled in patient charts.

He glanced down, perusing the record in front of him. He recognized the handwriting of Ron Albers, and noted that he'd used almost twice the amount of Fentanyl and Limbotryl that a short surgery required. Noting the patient's height and weight, John decided that, overall, it was in line with practice standards.

He'd become familiar with the judgmental review he gave his colleagues' anesthesia records. The laborious review, which he now did only a few times a week, represented the foundation of a database that showed him who used each narcotic. And most importantly, how much.

He handed the chart back to Hannah, who had noted John's intent expression. "What?" she asked.

John looked away. "Nothing," he replied brusquely. "Just checking how many places on the record we need to sign off. This one is Albers'. I'll talk to him, and I'll remind everyone else. Let me know if it continues to be a problem."

John turned back toward the ORs he was supervising, leaving Hannah Gilbert half-stunned by his abruptness. It was not his typical demeanor, and the nursing supervisor studied the record carefully, as if it held a clue to Dr. Williams' unusual behavior.

11:00 AM

John shrugged his shoulders, attempting to dispel the irritation that succeeded his encounter with Hannah Gilbert and the medical record. It reminded him that Ron Albers hadn't explained his cameo appearance on the videotape. The irritability persisted as he contemplated the chain of events of the previous two weeks. How odd, he considered, that the syringes were found in the call room on Tuesday; and the incriminating video of Ron was found the following Tuesday. What was happening on Mondays?

John tuned in more carefully to his surroundings, for today was Monday. If anything happened, he wanted to detect it today, not tomorrow. Immediate action promised results.

"John! We need you in here," called Mac.

Stirred from thought, John assisted with a difficult intubation, challenging because the patient was morbidly obese. His head could barely be extended to the degree that would allow the breathing tube to pass through the trachea.

Once the patient was intubated, a process that required two docs and three nurses, John traveled between three of his assigned ORs, checking patients' progress, and supervising anesthesia inductions. Around lunchtime, Mac relieved him.

"Anything new?" she asked quietly.

"Nothing I can talk about now. Maybe later this afternoon."

Mac arched her eyebrows, telegraphing intrigue. "Later, then."

John continued his review of last week's events, taking his lunch tray to the garden outside the cafeteria. The shaded park bench was less crowded than the veranda, and he chose solitude in which to analyze what had transpired. He recalled the exchange between Ron and Stu, when the latter was stretched out on the conference room floor. What was it that Stu didn't want Ron to do? Why did Stu act as if he didn't remember saying those words?

And later, why did Jeannie Adler say that Ron wasn't surprised by the early morning ambush that Dave Johnson had orchestrated? Jeannie's persistence, even from the background of the conversation between her husband and John, remained a puzzle.

In a moment of inspiration, it occurred to John that perhaps Ron wasn't surprised as much by the accusation as by the presence of police at the meeting. More importantly, John became aware that Jeannie's insistence that Ron *wasn't* surprised probably indicated that Stu had warned Ron in advance. And what did *that* mean?

1:15 PM

Diane Cavanaugh sat back in her chair, feeling as if she'd had the wind knocked out of her. "What does that mean?" she asked, when she'd recovered enough to speak.

Elise McKinley looked kindly, if somberly, at the woman in her office. A surgical oncologist who was perhaps a decade younger than the patient, Dr. McKinley had delivered this sort of news thousands of times. It wasn't actually *easier*, so many times later, but she had learned to do so with compassion, without becoming swallowed in the emotional maelstrom that often ensued.

It had been Dr. McKinley's experience that patients who reacted most strongly to the diagnosis fought the most fiercely, and often had the best outcome. The patients who reacted with numb shock tended to retreat into denial, delay treatment, and—depending on the type of cancer—often became mobilized to *do* something only "later," when there were few good options. Then, there were patients like Diane Cavanaugh, take-charge women who would happily do something, *anything*, but whose silent cancer eluded detection until the options were less likely to be curative.

This was the worst type of news Elise ever had to deliver. She especially hated to do so since Diane had ignored the recommendation to bring a family member or close friend to this appointment. They would proceed gently.

"What it means is that this is very serious. There are several stages of breast cancer, and each has its own set of treatment recommendations and outcome percentages."

Diane interrupted. "My husband died of cancer, as you may have heard from my son-in-law, John. I understand the seriousness and I vaguely recall some of the percentages. When I ask what this means, I want to know if there is any possibility that more surgery, radiation, or chemotherapy can cure it."

Elise nodded in gentle acknowledgment of the question regarding life or death. "Mrs. Cavanaugh, there is a range of strategies, from aggressive to palliative. As an example of aggressive treatment, we would operate to remove both breasts, and some surrounding lymph nodes. After that, we would start you on both radiation and chemotherapy. Or, we might begin with the radiation and chemo, and try to shrink or kill the tumor. Then, we'd do the surgery. Either way, it is a very difficult treatment course," she admitted. "We would monitor you very carefully, and there are things we can do to make you feel more comfortable during the chemo and radiation. You will need a lot of help, if you choose this type of treatment. It's the most aggressive of the options, but it also offers the best potential for getting rid of the cancer.

"Another option," Dr. McKinley continued, "would be to radiate the site after surgery, but not to do the chemo. It's not as aggressive a strategy, and it will still take you out of commission for several weeks. The outcomes are not as good as with the first approach, but some women prefer to take the radiation and keep their immune systems powered up with vitamins and other holistic remedies—and I use the term 'remedies' very loosely, Mrs. Cavanaugh. There is no scientific evidence that they work. I'm just becoming familiar with adjunct holistic medicine, and while some of the anecdotal information is impressive, I can't be sure that it's a good option for you."

"What do *you* recommend, Dr. McKinley?" Diane asked, her voice unwavering and determined.

"That depends on what you want to commit to. Can your family help you while you're having treatment?"

"Of course they *can*," Diane stated conditionally, "but I would rather handle this myself. When my husband was sick, he and I believed that it was better to keep our children *out* of the treatment process. I'd like to do the same now. My daughters could help with some of my errands, such as grocery shopping, but I would prefer to hire help, maybe a visiting nurse or an aide. I don't want to become a burden to my children. And I don't want to feel helpless or dependent."

Elise smiled. "I understand," she agreed. "Usually, families make decisions about the extent of treatment together. That's why I suggested bringing someone with you today. But, I understand your wish to make this decision yourself. Let's look at each part of the treatment, you can ask me any questions, and take a couple of days to think about it. If you would like, my nurse can give you a few names of home healthcare businesses, all of which offer many services." Elise paused to emphasize her next words. "In your situation, I believe that surgery is a critical first step. It should be scheduled right away. Once we've reviewed the other treatment options, you'll need to make a decision quickly."

Diane nodded, and then asked a question which Elise McKinley had not often heard during her medical career. Typically, she heard people say, "Do everything possible, Doctor." Today, she was asked, "What if I don't want to do any of it, especially the surgery?"

Dr. McKinley gauged the question's intent accurately, but elected to probe gently to confirm what she thought Diane Cavanaugh was asking. "It's really a critical first step in the process, Mrs. Cavanaugh. I would start there before using radiation or chemotherapy. You must have some concerns about surgery."

Diane nodded. "It isn't that I have any attachment to my breasts, per se, but I'm not interested in having surgery, and then radiation, chemo, or both, unless there is some measure of certainty that this cancer is survivable."

"I can give you the statistics, but I'll also tell you that the degree of success is just as much a function of attitude. When I was first practicing, I felt arrogantly comfortable giving my patients ratios and percentages. Then, when I had a little more experience, I realized that those statistics didn't take into account personality differences among my patients. I was totally unprepared to have a patient die when, statistically, she should have been cured. I was equally surprised to have a stubborn, determined patient survive against all odds. So, when I'm asked questions about survival rates, I usually mention this very important variable of personality, or attitude. It's not simple, this issue of prognosis, and statistics don't tell the whole story."

Diane nodded. "Well, I certainly fit into the stubborn and

determined category. And I'm an optimistic realist. How's that for a quick summary of my personality?" she declared with a laugh.

Elise smiled, a small chuckle burbling from her throat. "I'd say that's a winning combination of traits. That and a good sense of humor are wonderful tools to support recovery. So it surprises me that you would not want surgery."

"I didn't say that," Diane corrected, serious again. "I asked 'what if' I didn't want it. And my point in asking has everything to do with being in charge of my life. If I have the surgery and aggressive treatment, I wind up being out-of-commission for a while. I'll put up with it, if the prognosis is good. But, if the prognosis isn't good, I'm not willing to go through the trauma of surgery and treatment that may make me feel that I *am* dying." Diane leaned forward, folding her hands on the edge of Elise McKinley's desk. "If this cancer is not treatable for *most* of the people who get it, I don't want to waste my time with surgery and treatments. Do you understand what I'm saying?"

Elise nodded solemnly. She, too, leaned forward, placing her hands firmly on the desk blotter, then folding them to mirror Diane's. "I understand, Mrs. Cavanaugh," she answered quietly. "I cannot give you any promises, and we won't know exactly what the situation is until we get the lymphatic pathology report. It's more challenging to treat a diffuse cancer, compared with an encapsulated tumor. And, as long as the cancer hasn't spread to your lymph nodes, you can probably anticipate a normal life expectancy.

"However, if it *has* spread, the radiation and chemotherapy represent our best combat tools. That's as much as I can tell you."

"Well then," Diane stated briskly, "how quickly can I schedule the surgery?"

Chapter Twelve

TAKING CONTROL

Thursday, April 25
10:00 AM

The infection had been healed within days of the aggressive immuno-supportive treatment. Kathy had left the hospital with prescriptions and a follow-up appointment time. Although still weak, she could at least walk to and from the bathroom. The pain was less debilitating, yet powerful narcotic painkillers left her numb, swirling in a dense fog of semi-consciousness, a hallucination of dreams blended with reality. It was at this juncture, just days after leaving the hospital, that Marilyn and another member of the support group had visited.

Through the fog, Kathy heard them talk about the approaching summer vacation, asking about the children's camps. She blinked, and then widened her eyes, willing herself to listen, to comprehend their words. Perhaps they understood the strength of her effort, for they promptly focused the conversation.

"You know we can help you, Kathy."

As Marilyn mentioned the secret treatment again, Kathy barely recalled the resistance she'd felt previously. She closed her eyes, and then asked, thick-tongued, "Can't my doctor prescribe this treatment, without all the secrecy?"

Marilyn smiled regretfully and shook her head. "Your doctor won't," she said. "It's not available by prescription." She paused then, before adding, "I won't force the issue, Kathy. Sometimes, desperation is the only thing that lets a person commit to this treatment.

"You might want to pick up your pain journal again," Marilyn suggested. "Try writing about what you feel, the way we do in the support group. It sometimes helps to express the pain on paper." She said no more then, and left the room with the understanding that Kathy was not yet ready to commit.

Sunday, April 28
1:00 PM

Reluctantly, and without great expectations that the sacrifice would be worthwhile, Kathy Martin skipped two doses of narcotic pain-reliever. With less fog-headedness but more discomfort, she took a pencil in hand, attempting to master the pain by expressing it in writing.

"Sea of Desperation," by Kathy Martin

Pain, wave after wave,
Cyclical, unrelenting pain.
Pressure gathers momentum.
Throbbing rumbles of thunderous pain
Crest and then plummet,
Searing, jagged lightning strikes
Stab the body,
Then recede to suffocating pressure,
Until the next wave hits.

The rhythm is like that of the sea,
Undulating waves,
Crescendos that peak to
A surfer's delight,
A sufferer's nightmare.
Pain, as relentless as the pounding surf,

Relief just a matter of degree.
Ubiquitous pain,
Relentless and unforgiving.

Kathy put down the pencil, as Drew opened the door, announcing unexpected visitors.

"They've, brought us a week's worth of casseroles, blueberry muffins, and chocolate chip cookies," Drew said, amazed. "Thank you, ladies. This is a huge help to us, especially since my mother had to go back to Lexington. I can't tell you how grateful I am—we both are."

"It's no trouble at all," the oldest of the women murmured. "We simply wanted to see how Kathy was doing, and lend a bit of help."

"Well, I'll let you visit, and thank you, again" Drew said appreciatively. As he closed the door, he called, "Kiddos, we have homemade cookies!"

Kathy turned the pad over so that the women would not see what she had written. These gift bearers were from the support group, and she knew their mission.

In addition to the bountiful gifts of food, they offered encouragement to try the Magi's gift of healing. They coaxed her to take the elixir often, in hopes that her body's endorphins would be stimulated, that she would enter remission, and then be able to function as a person again.

Kathy closed her eyes, and the women ceased their whispers of persuasion. "I appreciate what you've offered to my family. But—"

The whispers became an annoying buzz, as the trio endeavored to convince Kathy. In the end, she pleaded fatigue, and asked for water and one of her pain pills. She opened her eyes, observing the shared glances of despair that they had not succeeded in their mission of comfort. Still, they refilled her cup from the pitcher of ice water, and retrieved a pain pill from the bottle, leaving with sorrowful expressions and the parting words that Kathy could always change her mind.

But they failed to understand her position, Kathy believed. She could not do what they asked. She had promised her husband that she would not take the treatment, for the family's sake.

Monday, April 29
7:00 PM

Kathy picked up the pen again, breathing deeply as she formed every curved letter, slowly, painstakingly, intent as a second grader learning cursive.

Lap, lap, lap;
Pain throbs against the shore of the body.
Crash, crash, crash;
Pain slams full force, hurricane strength,
Crushing both body and spirit.
Breathing suffers, rendered in
Desperate, shallow pants,
Automatic,
Free of conscious effort.

Ah, to be able to forget to breathe!
To finally still the pain,
And the body with it.
There's no choice.
Deliverance from pain is paramount.
Survival mandates a simple directive:
Escape the pain, hide, take the drugs;
No restrictions apply.

The days of calm seas have been
Few and far between.
Now, it is hurricane season.
Only death or remission
Will stem the tides.
Desperate. Can't eat, can't sleep.

How can the body be alive
Within this sea of pain?

When comfort descends,
Surely the body is dead,
For life is inextricably joined with pain.
Wave after wave,
Day after day,
As certain as the sun rises and sets.
Rhythmic.
Relentless.
How does one surrender?

Shall I give up? Or, give in?

She dropped the pencil, exhausted. Drew was working late, and his mother had returned to Lexington for a few days to take care of some business. There was no one else to help with the children, day-to-day. In that moment of quiet desperation, Kathy Martin ceded to the choir that chanted a prescription for restored health. She picked up the phone and dialed Marilyn. She'd take the drug, the Magi's treatment, for the sake of her family.

✦

Pain superseded any fear of what might be injected into her body. The Magi visited, tending to Kathy while Marilyn reassured the children, checked their homework and packed lunches for the next day. After the Magi left, Marilyn tucked in the little girl. The older boy insisted that eleven-year-olds didn't need tucking in. Both children appeared subdued, fearful and unhappy that their mother was so sick, unable to make them breakfast in the morning, or kiss them goodnight. Perhaps they felt a bit like orphans, with a bedridden mother, and a father who left for work before the children awakened and returned after they were asleep. In truth, it was worse than that. They believed their mother was going to die.

While Kathy and the children slept, Marilyn scribbled a note, indicating that she would return at 7:00 AM to help the children get ready for school. She also suggested that Drew ask his mother to return, unless there was someone else he'd rather ask.

Finding the note when he walked in at 11:00 PM, Drew felt too much sheer relief that someone had formulated a plan to resist any of the suggestions. He was grateful that this Marilyn, who he thought was a neighbor he hadn't met, had offered to help in the morning, and that she'd given him a straightforward task. Drew quickly called his mother, who assured that her business could wait, and that she would come first thing tomorrow.

Tuesday, April 30 – Friday, May 17

The next day brought shouts of glee from the children, who delighted in Marilyn's chocolate chip pancakes, as well as the news that Nana would be there after school. But it was Kathy who enjoyed the greater joy, following fourteen hours of deep, painless slumber.

The results of the Magi's visit were dramatic. The degree of relief surprised Kathy; she felt chipper and hungry. Still, she did not tell Drew or her mother-in-law the source of her healing, for she feared their disapproval. What would they think of her impulsive, desperate decision to accept this secret treatment?

Nana was a welcome help, and she greeted Marilyn and Mr. Stewart with a caddy of cleaning supplies when they arrived that afternoon for Kathy's next treatment. Nana presumed that they were both home health nurses, and she offered to write down any instructions they had for her. She thought it odd that there were none, but was reassured when, the next day, Kathy was able to join the family for meals and move about the house.

After the fourth visit, Kathy offered Nana grateful hugs, and then sent her mother-in-law back to Lexington. She proceeded to cook a five-course meal for the family, and after bedtime stories, back-scratches, and evening prayers with the children, Kathy lunged for her husband libidinously—surprising herself as much as him.

Life was better than ever. Drew did not ask how or why, but brought home flowers and limited his late nights to two per week. It was like a dream, a fantasy, and both the couple and their children clung to the magic of Kathy's flight into health, as if their lives depended on it. They did not question the source of such healing, for fear that the magic would end.

Monday, May 20
3:00 PM

Nancy Williams lowered the gear on the Boeing 727 jet, scanning both the instrument panel and the landing checklist. "Gear down," she acknowledged to the other pilot. The computer technology of this aircraft could land the plane flawlessly, and often did exactly that. However, among many other FAA requirements, pilots must execute a specific number of landings each month. Today, Nancy would land the big bird without computer-assistance, to meet the FAA standard.

She wasn't at all nervous, and preferred the challenge of landing without the computer, *real* piloting. It required concentration on variables such as airspeed, wind direction, altitude, attitude of the plane, and a measured titration of engine power, flaps, and aileron adjustment. So responsive was the aircraft to incremental shifts in any of these variables, that a firm but gentle touch was critical. Equally important was the pilot's kinesthetic awareness, which came less from physical sensation than instrument interpretation. It was a difficult concept to teach, but at some Zen point, based on instrument readings, the experienced pilot "felt" what small adjustments were needed to ensure a smooth landing.

With a gentle, synchronized bump, Nancy felt the rear wheels touch the ground and hold, the front wheel descending to a second gentle bump, which cued her to push the controls into reverse to slow the hundred-ton plane. Score one for a flawless landing.

"That'll do," said Captain Arthur Mason, seated to Nancy's right.

Nancy smiled, thinking of the farmer in the movie, "Babe." She and John had howled at the stoic Farmer Hogget's capacity for understatement.

"Thanks, Arthur," Nancy replied, offering a smile that had more to do with the Farmer Hogget recollection than Arthur's compliment.

Nancy felt a giddy rush of gratitude to be heading home. This trip had required four days away, four critical days this month. John would be home shortly, and they might even pull in at the same time. Nancy hoped that she had a window of opportunity yet today. It was hellish to be out-of-town during this fertile period, especially now that she felt an emotional commitment to having a child. Having made the decision, she expected to be pregnant immediately. Unfortunately, her work schedule had wreaked havoc with the orderly progression Nancy preferred in life.

Forward momentum, that's what today felt like. She would make her move the minute she crossed the threshold of their home, providing that John was there. *I'll call him from the car,* she decided.

Preoccupied with her vision of how the afternoon and evening would unfold, Nancy did not recall completing the docking and deplaning checks, her rote greeting of thanks to the passengers who passed by the cockpit door, or even the brisk walk from the flight crew room to her car. *She* was on autopilot, blissfully going through the motions as accurately as any computer-assisted landing, but in her own world of anticipatory procreation. Which, Nancy noted, felt entirely different—more compelling—than the urge to make love after a long period of abstinence.

Leaving the parking garage, she pressed the autodial for John's car phone. The clock read 4:10 PM, so he might be on his way home. A message indicated that the car and phone were turned off. Nancy punched in the speed dial for home, and the answering machine played. *Damn. One more option,* Nancy thought, *and then I'll page him.* She tapped seven numbers, John's cell phone at work, and heard the buzz of a busy signal.

Fighting the feeling that she was being thwarted, Nancy dialed John's pager and then hung up, deciding to try his car phone when she was closer to Cincinnati. She settled back, sliding in a CD that featured Bruce Hornsby and the Range, volume cranked so that she felt the bass in her spine. She would chill out a bit; take the edge off her disappointment at not reaching John, and contemplate tomorrow's day off.

Her mother had another round of radiation scheduled in the morning. Nancy would take her this time. Sandy had been in town to drive her mother for the previous rounds, but would be gone tomorrow for another series of business consultations.

Downshifting as she reached the I-471 interchange off of I-275, and then navigating the left lane exit, Nancy mulled over her mother's response to the treatments. After some weeks of recovery from surgery, Diane Cavanaugh had initially refused— no, she'd *stubbornly and insistently* refused—to allow either Nancy or Sandy to drive her to the radiation treatments. It was only when Sandy and Nancy had tearfully expressed feeling cut off from their mother that Diane had relented. Eventually, she accepted her daughters' arguments that they would be better company than Marilyn, an acquaintance from the cancer support group Diane and Jim had attended early in *his* illness.

This way would be much better, Nancy reiterated silently. A perceptible pebble of discomfort lodged within her belly, as she considered the prospect of accompanying her mother to the radiation session. *Will the radiation affect me? Is there any possibility that radiation would affect an embryo, if and when I get pregnant?* She knew that Sandy remained in the family waiting room while Diane received treatments last week. And she would do the same. *Still, could radiation leak in some bizarre way?*

Crossing the I-471 Bridge into Cincinnati, Nancy shook her head sharply to clear the neurotic rumble. She punched the CD selector, rowdy Beach Boys tunes to lift her mood and lighten her heart. Two tracks later, she spotted John's car merging into traffic from the MacMillan Road entrance ramp. Speeding up, she scooted over a lane and beeped the horn, reveling with laughter at the surprise on John's face when he looked over, half-irritated by the beep.

Nancy mouthed the words, "Beat you home!" and pulled ahead, just a bit over the speed limit. John declined the bait, but he did shift lanes, following several car lengths behind. *Never mind*, Nancy thought. She slowed to just over fifty-five near the Edwards Road exit, searching for the Cincinnati police officer who tracked speeders from the left berm. He was not there today.

Accelerating to sixty-three miles per hour, Nancy concentrated on arriving home before John. She would seize a few moments of privacy to freshen up, and to set the stage for their evening encounter. The rest of the day—and night—would be hers, his, theirs. She smiled broadly as she planned every minute.

6:00 PM

A picnic in bed was Nancy's idea of a festive reunion. She had tucked silverware into linen napkins, and set them on an antique silver tray, an anniversary gift from John two years ago. She added a pair of thin-stemmed crystal goblets, a corkscrew, and a bottle of ten-year-old Stag's Leap Cabernet Sauvignon. The Thai food, delivered by Take-out Taxi a few minutes earlier, was already upstairs on the warming tray.

"China, the Haviland china," Nancy murmured to herself. After all, Nancy reminded herself, this was a celebration. It wasn't everyday that a woman became pregnant, and she had calculated carefully. Today would be the day.

How did the old wives' tale go? If one wished to conceive a boy, it was advantageous to make love at the beginning of the fertile period; and to conceive a girl, it was more advantageous to make love toward the end of the fertile period. Was that right? If so, Nancy decided, then the baby would probably be a girl.

Not that it mattered to her, one way or the other; a good mother asked only for a healthy baby, without a gender preference. She pondered that perhaps the same held true for fathers, although they were generally known to want at least one son. Nancy wondered at the incongruence between what was expected of a mother and a father. It seemed that fathers were granted some slack, permitted to state any preference regarding an expected child's gender. Or was it only *good* fathers who were not as forthcoming about such preferences?

Whatever. Nancy gently lifted two Haviland Limoges plates from the tall china cupboard in the dining room. The pattern was a bit frilly for her tastes, but it was old and its history of serving many family meals appealed to John. The collection of plates, cups, saucers, and umpteen serving pieces had belonged to a family for three generations. Had they been capable of speech, these porcelain objects of art would have resonated with myriad voices, recounting many beloved familial tales. Nancy sighed, wondering if her husband was attempting to create, for himself, a sort of family history, with this representing the family china. Well, it would be part of *their* family history.

Nancy set the plates next to the linen-wrapped flatware. With a nod of approval, she grabbed a small vase of peonies from the kitchen windowsill, slid it onto a corner of the tray, and walked slowly, carefully, to the stairs.

John peeked out from the bedroom, smiling as he saw what Nancy had placed on the tray. "All we need are the silver candlesticks," he teased.

Nancy's eyes met his, wide and startled, chagrined to have forgotten something significant. "The candles! That would be perfect!"

John dropped his head and laughed aloud. "Would you like me to get the candles?"

Nancy evaluated their contribution to the overall ambience of the dinner, weighing whether or not it was worth the extra trip, by either of them, to eat by candlelight. Rounding the corner into their bedroom, Nancy wrinkled her nose and shook her head. "It' still daylight, anyway. Candles won't add much."

She set the tray on the trunk at the end of their bed, handing the wine and corkscrew to John as she fluffed their pillows and arranged food on the plates. "Anything new at work?" she asked.

John handed Nancy a goblet, nodding slightly. "Ron Albers has accepted a Pain Management position in Indianapolis. He's been a partner longer than I have, and he's leaving the group. I still can't believe it. He said that the money is great, and as director of the Pain Center, he'll have no call."

"Do you think he's leaving because of the . . . ." Nancy allowed the sentence to remain unfinished.

John frowned, picking up a plate of steaming beef, Asian noodles, and assorted vegetables in a spicy brown sauce. "I think that probably pushed him to some extent. But I can't say that he's leaving because of it. He's been pretty quiet at work. He does his job, but still doesn't talk to me. Stu told me that he thinks Ron will probably develop a rural network of pain services for people in the outlying counties. Stu even said that Jeannie would be all over *him* to get our group to do the same."

Nancy sipped her wine, allowing the food on her plate to cool. "I wouldn't think Jeannie's home healthcare business would see that as an advantage. She'd lose revenue if some physician were running the show. It's better for her, financially, if the patient's doc writes an order that one of her nurses can take care of."

John shrugged his shoulders. "There's a lot of money to be made in chronic pain, especially if you restrict the type of services offered. For example, if you offer steroid injections, you're going to make more money—and make more patients happy—than if you offer occupational therapy, physical therapy, and psychologists to teach people relaxation strategies. There's less overhead, and immediate relief."

"But not every patient needs a steroid injection for pain," Nancy interjected. "What about someone with a fatal disease? What about people like my dad, who couldn't get good pain control from traditional prescription meds?"

"There are epidurals, PCA pumps, and even nerve blocks that we could offer. But we decided that it makes more sense for us to concentrate on the people who are inpatients. We'd spread ourselves too thin if we started marketing anesthesia services to the general community."

"Hmmmm," Nancy mused, twirling Asian noodles around her fork, Italian-style. "Maybe Jeannie's interest concerns more than money."

"With Stu's income, she can afford to be philanthropic," John acknowledged. "But she can also make money offering services rurally. I don't know if it's true in the home health business, but the anesthesiologists at rural hospitals get seventy-five percent more than we do for the same unit of service."

"Managed care phenomena?" Nancy asked.

John nodded, "That's true for a lot of the specialists. You remember Alex Lynch? He moved his OB practice to some small town a few hours north of here because it was more lucrative." John Williams set down his plate, looking past the fuchsia peonies to Nancy. "But we have better things to talk about, right?"

Nancy grinned, slurping the last inch of a noodle, then patting her lips with the napkin seductively. Dropping the napkin onto the silver tray, she swung her legs off the side of the bed and swiftly lifted the tray to the floor. Climbing back onto the bed, she crawled over to her husband, ran her hands through his hair as she kissed his ear, and whispered, "Who wants to talk, at a time like this?"

Chapter Thirteen

TREATMENT

The process of receiving radiation was fairly straightforward, and her appointment had been uneventful, once Diane was in the room and positioned. The hard part had been seeing Nancy react, in mute horror, as the oncology nurse explained the treatment process.

And later, on the way home, Nancy's questions were blunted by what Diane suspected to be her daughter's aversion to knowing the details. Or, perhaps Nancy simply had hoped not to add to her mother's stress by appearing distressed, herself.

In truth, Nancy was her father's daughter. She may have inherited her daddy's iron stomach and fearless love of flight, but she also bore his expressive face.

To still Nancy's questions, and to avoid the clearly telegraphed distress signals, Diane closed her eyes for the duration of the ride home, physically and emotionally exhausted. Once there, Diane permitted Nancy to help her into bed, but nothing else. Diane *knew* that what Nancy needed was to be held and reassured that Diane was, and would be, fine; that the treatment wasn't nearly as horrible or as humiliating as it sounded. The staff was sensitive and professional. This was just one of those things one had to endure. Like having a pap test every year.

The heaviness of fatigue prevented Diane from expressing any such reassurance to her daughter, and she petitioned for forgiveness of this offense. So tired. Too tired. Dead tired. She would try another time. Nancy would have to understand, for now. Her mother was simply incapable of anything but escape into sleep.

Before slipping into the dreamless sleep of oblivion, Diane made a pact with herself to see this through on her own. She was tough enough to complete the treatments, but not if she had to contend with her daughters' distress. From here on, Diane would have Marilyn, or someone else she could hire, take her for the treatments. She would insulate herself from her daughters' fears, and she would insulate them from the details of the treatment process. Anything else was too much a burden.

4:30 PM

"I don't know how Mom can stand it!"

"You do what you have to," John said with a shrug.

"But can't you imagine how frightening it must be for her?"

"Nancy, your mom has cancer. The treatment is supposed to save her life; not offer her a convenience." He paused, and concluded, "There are worse things to go through."

"Like what?"

John Williams looked at his wife, aware of the danger zone in which they circled. "I don't know. Maybe I'm wrong. I'm going down to the workshop to strip that mirror."

He felt her eyes like lasers in his back. He felt bad about Diane, and didn't want her to suffer. But, he couldn't *do* anything about it. He was a do-er, and if he couldn't *do* anything helpful, he had nothing to offer.

Or, did he?

John lumbered down the stairs, winding around back to the furnace room that housed his circular saw, radial arm saw, and a pegboard full of tools, neatly arranged like steel soldiers. He considered the question of what he might offer, and what might be expected. It was easier to contemplate such a question in the stillness of his workshop. Here, he could ponder weighty issues of responsibility and relationship.

This situation was worse than when Iron Ace Jim was sick, for sure. Was it always worse when it was one's *mother* whose life was at stake? John shook his head, uncertain. He'd never known his father. He'd been three when his father died, too young to even remember the details of how and where; and he'd heard several versions of the story during his lifetime. Not that it mattered now, for he couldn't *do* anything about his father's death.

And later, when his mother was sick, he couldn't *do* anything, either.

The helplessness of the situation settled like a coal in his stomach. What did Nancy expect him to *do*? He wasn't a damned oncologist. He wasn't a psychologist. He sure as hell wasn't God.

John remembered God, in that moment. He wondered about God, and what He could *do*. Supposedly, God could do anything, everything. That's what the Sisters had taught him. God answered prayers. That's what the priests had taught him.

That's where they were wrong.

He had prayed, for they had told him that's all any of them could *do*.

And still, his mother had died.

And now, Nancy's mother might have to suffer to survive.

Prayers would not help, even if he believed it was something he could *do*.

Monday, June 10
7:00 AM

Weeks had passed. Shrouded beneath a plush, brocade comforter, her head supported by two king-size pillows, Kathy Martin barely noticed the emerging day, much less the season.

Beyond the sickroom window, a trio of young scarlet maples danced in the breeze, sunlight flickering through their leaves. Another mortal might have paused—despite misery—to behold this joyous view from the bed, enchanted by the graceful swaying branches, the flutter of sun-dappled leaves. Yet, the image was lost on the woman in bed, the one who knew nothing but pain—cyclical, unrelenting pain.

She had lived fully—magically—for weeks, following the Magi's treatments. However, as May turned to June, the enchantment had faded, ebbing as slowly as the tide goes out to sea. At first, it was the fatigue and stiffness, which Kathy refused to acknowledge. Then came the nipping pains. Eventually, the molten lava of throbbing pain soaked her body, leaving Kathy breathless, craving relief.

Which was where she was today. It was time to recommit, and the Magi would arrive shortly. Marilyn stood across the room, peering through the window, watching for the Magi's car. She turned to face the woman in bed.

"You need to take the treatments more often, Kathy," Marilyn reminded. "If you stay ahead of the pain, you won't get this bad, and it won't take multiple treatments to get you back on track."

"It's harder now that it's summer and the children are at home," Kathy explained.

Marilyn nodded. "I know. And it's trickier when your husband is around more."

"I don't like keeping it from him," Kathy snapped. "But it's either that, or . . . ."

They both knew: the video, which recorded her plea for mercy, for release. It represented the only other option, for Kathy could not—*would not*—live within the sea of pain.

Tuesday, June 11

Marilyn had returned this morning, after Drew had left for work. Kathy was still slumbering deeply, under the effect of yesterday's treatment. Marilyn had poured cereal and milk for the somber children, who were devastated to see their mother withering within the walls of the sickroom, again. Once the children were off to King's Island with a neighborhood family, Marilyn had consulted with the Magi. He recommended that Kathy rest for the day, but not to re-dose her until she could be evaluated, fully conscious.

When Kathy awakened, Marilyn was sitting in a rocking chair across the room. She said nothing. It was Kathy's turn to speak: to make up her mind and speak it.

At that point, alert and pain-free, Kathy decided what *she* would do. She would follow her heart, even if it pricked at her conscience. She could be a good mother, a loving wife, and feel like a human being with the Magi's gift. If Drew could not abide by her choice, she would protect him from knowledge of her decision.

That evening, before Drew returned from work, Kathy ate supper in bed and made a pact with Marilyn and the Magi. She would be responsible for diminishing her pain, and her husband would not be included within the circle of knowledge. "For the family's sake," as Drew would say.

Chapter Fourteen

CRITICAL ANGLE OF ATTACK

Wednesday, June 12
10:00 AM

The morning was as sultry as an August afternoon. Summer had arrived early this year, bringing dense, humid air, thunderstorms, and bursting blossoms that had not been expected for another month. Nancy Williams had barely finished planting annuals when she and Sandy had geared up for their mother's surgery and cancer treatment. Now, weeks later, her garden was a tangle of weeds, as oppressive to the flowers as the heat.

There had been precious little time to water and weed as she usually did. John had been caught up in tracking OR drugs, stripping the mirror, and flying. It was the first year they had not planted together.

Nancy pushed back a damp strand of dark hair, clamping a baseball cap over her head and pulling a ponytail through the back, above the adjustable plastic band. She settled on the foam cushion next to a basket of rubber handled garden tools, and pulled on a pair of dirty, blue gloves. She pulled the wild strawberry that had grown among the annuals, and then pitched it into a bucket, the rhythm lulling her into melancholy contemplation.

Sandy was with their mother this morning, and Nancy would visit tomorrow. It was frustrating, now that her mother no longer permitted Nancy or Sandy to come along to treatments. Only short social visits were allowed, no housework, and only a bit of help with errands or bills. She entrusted the housework to the capable women from Madeira Custom-Maid, and hired her nurse's aide for extra hours to run all but the most important errands, such as selecting birthday gifts for her grandchildren. That, Diane was willing to allow her daughters to do, but not much else.

The ensuing isolation, so unnatural and a bit frightening, reminded Nancy of the time when her father was sick and dying. Then, Diane had told her children that their father had requested the short visits, and only at the time of his choosing. It was his last vestige of control, their mother had explained, and she'd asked her children to respect and indulge their father's request. They had done so, the two sons with relief and the daughters with reluctance.

In retrospect, Nancy realized that it had been easier to respect her father's wish for privacy. They had been close, but not in the personal, emotional, female way of mothers and daughters, or sisters. Whereas Nancy had shared a professional love of aviation with her father, she had shared dreams and decisions, her deepest aspirations, and many a secret with her mother, over the years. In many respects, for the sisters, their mother was a best friend as well.

With Diane's self-imposed isolation, it was as if a door had been closed in their faces, as if their mother had abandoned her family in favor of illness.

10:45 AM

Ten minutes away, Diane Cavanaugh lay in bed, willing herself to remain still, as if asleep. Across the room, Sandy rocked in an upholstered swivel-rocking chair, reading from a collection of inspirational essays. *Perhaps Sandy will leave, if I pretend to sleep. I just want to be alone . . . no conversation, no questions, no one to see me.*

Diane attempted to consider her daughters' perspective, a mental exercise that creased her brow and defeated the effort to feign sleep. Thirty years earlier, there had been no such thought of excluding one's family from the circle of help. Providing or receiving such care wasn't necessarily greeted with joy, yet it was permitted and even expected. Nancy and Sandy never knew the details of the care required by grandmothers on both sides of the family, care that fell to Diane, because sons don't care for their own mothers in such an intimate fashion. And in the absence of daughters, as with Diane's in-laws, the care fell to daughters-in-law, and for a variety of reasons, primarily to Diane.

They just can't understand.

By virtue of being children, Diane's sons and daughters were protected from the exhausting rigors of caring for parents and in-laws. They remained innocent of the demanding, unwanted intimacy that comes with loss of faculties and functions. Jim Cavanaugh, who felt both guilty for his wife's burden, and helpless to assist her with this women's realm—he couldn't very well change his own mother's diapers—vowed that neither his children nor his wife would endure such responsibility again.

"That's what I saved for: the kind of help that will keep you my wife. Not my nurse," Jim had stated firmly.

Diane's lips parted in a half smile at the recollection. She'd understood Jim's edict as a measure of her husband's machismo, a facet of his personality that she'd known since the moment they'd met. He'd desperately wanted to be in control, to enjoy the dignity that comes from pretending that he needed no such help, if only by excluding loved ones from the intimacies of such care. In fact, it was only at the very end, while barely conscious, that Iron Ace Jim had allowed Diane to attend to his personal care, bathing him in bed, and combing his wild, silver mane. It was the only sort of nurturance her husband would tolerate, and Diane had embraced—needed—this opportunity to physically *care* for her husband.

Is that what Sandy and Nancy need? To physically care for me?

Even if the answer was *yes*, she must honor this pact with her husband—to keep their children innocent of parental care responsibilities. It was the right thing to do. Diane would not permit her daughters to flock about her, day and night.

Had the circumstances been reversed, she would have inserted herself in their lives, regardless of assurances that home health professionals would provide whatever was needed. Diane would have ignored such claims, decried them as false, or pleaded mother's privilege, had her daughters protested. *But that's different,* Diane argued silently, at once comprehending the hypocrisy. With that mental acknowledgement, Diane ceded to dreamless, restless, semi-slumber, the melodic hum of Sandy's voice forming gentle waves, distant background music.

11:50 AM

In the damp heat, Nancy contemplated the conflict. What reasons could explain her mother's refusal to see her, save for short visits, by invitation only? Why was her mother acting so standoffish?

Nancy switched from the dirty cotton gloves to yellow, rubber gardening gloves, reaching for spikes of thistle and dewed, fountain-like grass that had sprouted in great clumps throughout the beds that hugged the house. The nightly rains had left the soil wet enough that the weeds slid easily from the earth. It would take a while to clear them, but neither spade nor trowel would be needed. The repetitive task afforded her time to think.

This summer should have been different, Nancy reflected. She counted the weeks since their Conception Feast, as she referred to it—just over three, but no positive results yet. Still, there was hope, for there were no negative indicators, either. Nancy had hoped that she and John would be painting one of the bedrooms as a nursery, or shopping for a crib. Instead, John was determined to implement the computerized recordkeeping system, which would help track the drugs that continued to disappear intermittently. And she was scheming about creative ways to be involved in her mother's care.

She'd tried to talk with John about feeling left out by her mother, but he'd appeared puzzled by her wish to take on the responsibility.

If you don't understand it, I can't explain it to you!

Tossing a clump of crabgrass onto the walkway, Nancy wondered what her husband's response would be if it were *she* who had cancer. She shook the thought from her head.

Perspiration trickled from her forehead, down the side of her nose, like a tear. *It's too darned hot to be out here.*

Irritability began to form its own source of heat, and Nancy ripped off the gardening gloves, slapping them into the tool basket. Circling to the garage access, she shoved the basket into one of the cabinets, slamming the door once, and again when it bounced open. *Maybe I'm not as patient as I'd thought. Maybe it's just the heat and Mom's weird behavior.*

Before stepping into the kitchen, she kicked off the rubber garden clogs, and then headed to the refrigerator for a diet soda. Glancing at the answering machine, she noted the blinking red message light. Suddenly, picking up the messages seemed a worthy distraction, much better than sweeping up the piles of weeds which lined the walkway, especially in the high heat of the day.

It was Sandy. "Mom is really tired. She only wanted me to stay five minutes, but I read to her a bit before she fell asleep. It's one of those bad days. She asked me to let you know that she wants you to come some other time, not tomorrow. I know, I know, this is a bitch. We never see Mom these days. Let's meet for an iced coffee before we both go crazy. Call me." Beep.

Shit. Nancy slammed the can of soda onto the counter with enough force to create a bubbly brown splash. *This is selfish of Mom,* Nancy told herself. Yanking the phone from the cradle, Nancy hit the autodial to Sandy's cell phone. She skipped any greeting.

"I got your message," Nancy said tersely. "I'm getting pissed about the way Mom is acting."

"I'm not thrilled about it, either," Sandy replied, edgily. "I'm not sure there's anything we can do about it."

"We can talk to Mom about it, that's what we can do about it."

"Nancy, how are we going to talk to Mom when she won't let us visit? I agree that she's being unreasonable, but *she's* the one who's sick with cancer. She's the one who feels like hell from all the treatment. It's nearly over, well, halfway over. Hopefully, she'll feel more like her old self after this treatment series, or at least well enough for us to visit more often."

Nancy took the phone from her ear and stared at it with disbelief. How could her sister be so optimistic? Replacing the phone to her ear, Nancy felt impatience seethe through her entire body. She was tired of the heat, tired of her mother's obstinacy, tired of her sister's willingness to consider their mother's perspective like such a Pollyanna.

"Bullshit," Nancy stated bluntly. "She wouldn't let either of us get away with this. She'd remind us of how family sticks together, especially when the going gets tough."

"Nancy," Sandy sighed, "I'm tired. Just like you, I'm tired. If you have any inspired ideas on how to get through this, I'm listening. In the meanwhile, I'm going to count the days until Mom's last treatment. It helps *me*."

Nancy bowed her head, aware that Sandy was just as put out and frustrated, although her manner of coping with it was much different. *Patience,* Nancy thought. *Not my strong suit after all? Or just not today? Am I patient enough to be a mother, if I'm this aggravated with my own mother, who's sick with cancer?*

"Okay," Nancy said quietly. "Sorry to take it out on you."

"We're going to be a lot better off if we can help each other through this. If you need to get mad, do it. I'm not taking it personally. But Nancy," Sandy cautioned, "it's important that we respect Mom's wishes. If she needs the space, we need to let her have it. We have to figure out our own way to deal with it. She can't do more than what she's already doing."

"I know. At least I know that in my head, but it sure doesn't match what I'm feeling in my heart." Tears stung at her eyes.

"Same here," Sandy agreed. "Want to meet me for an iced coffee?"

"I do, but I can't," Nancy explained. "I haven't even showered yet, and I've been out gardening. How about lunch tomorrow, since I can't visit Mom?"

"I'll be out of town tomorrow, but I'll call you when I'm back."

"Okay. Thanks, Sandy."

Click.

Nancy gently placed the phone back in its cradle, walked up the rear stairs to the small room that had probably once been a Nanny Suite. It was now the guest bedroom, and Nancy considered asking her mother to come stay with them. No, she would never agree to that. Her mother was too independent to leave her own home.

Nancy crossed through the room, too hot with the sun beating through the large frame of windows that faced the rear of the house. The windows needed draperies, or perhaps balloon shades, Nancy decided. A baby could never nap in such a bright room. A ceiling fan would help move the air, too.

Distracted momentarily by the nesting urge, Nancy granted the self-nurturing baby fantasies. She'd leave the weeds where they were until later this evening, when it was cooler—eighty-three, instead of ninety-three degrees. Now, it was time to indulge in a long, tepid shower, and a nap.

4:15 PM

This was John Williams' least favorite part of flight instruction: practicing stall-recoveries. Bob Burke spoke softly, reassuringly, as John pulled back on the yoke, taking the plane to within a breath of its limits, daring it to stall. Bob had survived hundreds of student pilots, both military and civilian. Yet, that fact failed to comfort John, who felt perspiration dampen his shirt as if he'd just run a few miles.

Stall-recovery practice was a necessary component of pilot training, John knew. It was designed to educate the pilot both to recognize the indicators of an engine stall, and to regain control of the airplane at the stall point. Although John liked the idea of being well prepared, he hated performing maneuvers that tempted the laws of physics to put the plane into a death spin.

It was tantamount to asking to die: placing himself and the

plane in limbo, not completely in control, yet not quite out of control. He'd performed this maneuver several times, both in training for his private pilot license, and during the test with the FAA examiner. Today, Bob was simply reviewing the technique, a type of continuing education for recreational pilots such as John.

He felt slightly queasy, cotton-mouthed. His heart pounded both in his chest and ears. John gently pulled back the yoke of the plane, raising the nose gradually. He approached the ordeal slowly, cautiously.

Next to him, Bob sustained patient silence, for which John was grateful. A skilled, experienced aerobatics pilot, Bob thrived on g-forces and momentary weightlessness that challenged his kinesthetic awareness. But John failed to comprehend such an enthusiasm for risk, this intentional loss of control.

He imagined what Bob Burke might be thinking: that John was taking too damn long to get to the angle of attack, that critical junction at which the angle of the wing blocks the airflow that creates lift, causing the stall horn to shriek its high-pitched squeal, the yoke to shudder in protest, and the nose of the plane to shift rapidly from up to down, like a roller coaster on a straight, vertical descent—and how Burke loved it!

Christ, how does Nancy do this, John wondered? *In a jumbo jet, no less.* He continued to pull back slowly on the yoke, wishing he were maneuvering within the safety of a flight simulator. *That's how Nancy does this,* he reminded himself, momentarily forgetting that she had practiced stall-recoveries in small planes for years as a recreational pilot instructor.

Sweat tickled his left ear, but John ignored it, barely felt it, in fact, so intently did he watch his instrument panel for wing pitch, nose attitude, altitude, and airspeed. He was close. The stall horn would sound soon. The more slowly he pulled back, the more time he had to recover; the reverse was equally true, and John intended to give himself the widest window of recovery time possible.

"John, you've gotta' just *do it*," Bob stated firmly. "*Now.*"

John's heart rate accelerated at the command. He nodded

without looking at Bob, understanding that the instructor would not do it for the student, but that John needed to take the plunge, lose control—under controlled conditions—and regain it, sustaining faith in his ability to recover, as he'd done in the past. This was simply a review.

Gripping the yoke more tightly, John clenched his jaw and willed himself to pull back more drastically. Done! The stall horn squealed, the yoke shuddered in his white-knuckle grip, and the nose flipped from up to down, offering a view to the verdant earth from a nearly perpendicular perspective. *Shit! Shit! Shit!* John cried silently, the full-stall flipping his stomach, rushing blood to his head. With his fingers clenched around the quaking yoke— his death-grip maximizing control—he eased the yoke forward, attending to the instrument that verified the wing pitch, and sustained a vertical perspective to avoid a spin. To John, it seemed like a lifetime, but the moment flashed by, and the yoke settled from a shudder, to a quake, to a steady, familiar vibration. At the midpoint, the nose shifted back up, and the stall horn was silenced; disaster averted.

John exhaled residual fear, gratitude, relief, and a bit of carbon dioxide. It was over.

"Well done, well done," Bob commented, encouragingly. "Let's take it down. That's enough for a day."

John nodded, still too shaken for speech. Would he ever get over this?

Circling into the downwind approach pattern, John regained his composure, settling into the familiarity of landing the plane. He noted the beaker-like shape of the runway, an indication that he was at the correct altitude for final approach, then pushed the throttle forward to reduce engine power, and nudged the yoke forward to lower the nose of the plane gradually.

A moderate breeze stirred against the wings as the plane drifted downward. Green over green lights signaled that the plane was at the correct altitude to complete the landing on target. Landing short would put him in the middle of two four-lane thoroughfares; landing long would fail to provide adequate stopping distance, and he'd be in the trees at the far end of runway two-four.

After finessing the yoke to accommodate the crosscurrent wind, John glided the 'Four' onto the runway without a secondary bump. Then, he felt the warmth of exhilaration. Closure. Mission accomplished. God, it felt good to feel the ground below!

He taxied the plane to a row of small, single-engine aircraft near the airport buildings. There, he completed the shutdown procedure, and crawled out the right wing door. The fuzzy vibration of his pager startled John, as he leaped from the wing to the ground. He snapped the switch to see who was paging him. It was Nancy, at home. He would call her in a few minutes, after he had covered the plane, secured the parking harness, and closed out his flight plan, thus notifying air traffic control that he was safely landed.

Ten minutes later, he was cooling off in the air-conditioned building, the flight plan closed, a check written to Bob Burke for flight instruction, and his headset and clipboard stowed. As he zipped up the nylon flight bag, John observed Nancy coming up the walk, greeting Bob Burke with a quick hug. Bob then pointed to the building, indicating that John was still inside. They parted company, and John hoped that Bob had withheld any information about the flight.

"Hi!" Nancy called from the door. "What'd you guys do today?"

John shrugged to indicate that nothing special had occurred. "Most of the time was under the hood." He referred to the device that was worn over the head, obscuring all but the pilot's view of the instrument panel. It was designed to teach pilots how to fly with instruments only, ignoring signals from their bodies that hint to spatial orientation. The best pilots pursued this instruction and earned an Instrument Flight Rating from the FAA. Severe haze or unexpected cloud cover jeopardized the lives of pilots who had only a Visual Flight Rating. While he was not in hot pursuit of the IFR rating, John knew the value of such training. And it was not as grueling as stall-recovery practice.

"Well, how about dinner at Romano's?" Nancy asked, referring to their favorite Italian restaurant in Olde Montgomery.

"Sure," John agreed, pecking Nancy on the cheek. "I need to get a shower first, though."

"Oh, let's not go home," she complained. "You're fine."

"I stink, and I want a shower," John insisted. "We did some stall-recovery stuff after the hood training."

It was all the explanation Nancy needed.

Forty-five minutes later, they were nestled in a cozy booth at Romano's, sipping a 1990 Sterling Vineyards Cabernet Sauvignon, and sharing a large Caesar salad. The stall-recovery was still fresh in John's mind, and he wanted to ask Nancy about it. He would approach the topic slowly, as if it were no big deal, because he knew that Nancy found them an exciting challenge.

"How often do you have to review stall-recovery?" he began.

"Part of our regular simulator training includes engine loss strategies, which is different than stall-recovery," Nancy answered. "Why?"

John shrugged, crunching the crisp, bigger than bite-size romaine lettuce. He swallowed quickly. "Just wondered. Bob's been doing them with me almost monthly. It seems like a lot, considering that stalls aren't common."

Nancy nodded agreement. "That does seem pretty often. Did you ask him about it?"

"No," John replied casually. "I didn't think about it until today."

"Why today? Did things go okay?"

"Yeah. I mean, it was fine, but he seemed to want to take it faster than I wanted to, for some reason."

"Maybe he just wants to make sure you're more comfortable with stalls. You aren't exactly Mr. Adventurous, when it comes to this stuff."

"No joke," John agreed with a laugh.

"You know," Nancy said jauntily, "Stalls aren't such a big deal. Once you do enough of them, you get over the jitters. I guess it's an advantage to start flying when you're a kid. I can't remember feeling afraid of practicing stalls." She shrugged. "It's probably like the first time you stick one of those huge epidural needles into someone's spine. The idea of doing that nearly makes me sick, but you do it every day. It's the same sort of thing with stall-recoveries. Do enough of them and you get beyond the fear. You'll get over it."

John sipped his wine, not tasting it. He wasn't sure what he'd wanted from his pilot-wife, but simplistic reassurances didn't hit the mark. Never mind. They'd talk about something else. He hated to ask, but felt compelled, even at the risk of having to hear—and respond to—bad news. "So, what's new with your mom?"

Saturday, June 15
7:30 AM

Husband Kills Terminally Ill Wife

The front-page headline proclaimed this devastating news, launching a clamorous roar of opinion that raged throughout the Tri-state like the Yellowstone fires.

"Damned unnecessary!" sputtered Nate Warden.

Mae Warden looked across the room at her husband of so many years, wondering whether she would ever do something so desperate, for his sake.

Five miles northeast of the Warden's home, Kathy Martin and her husband shared Starbuck's coffee in the breakfast nook. Drew Martin had gone out for it, special.

Neither couple addressed the article. Privately, Drew swore a prayer of relief that Kathy was better. Kathy, on the other hand, wondered if Drew loved her enough to inflict such an act of criminal mercy, for her sake.

Across town, Stu and Jeannie Adler held hands, remembering the little girl in the pink tutu. It was easier than remembering her all grown up.

Stu's tears fell silently, while Jeannie's remained bottled. They understood the love that drove such desperation. What might they have done to find this man and his wife, before it was too late? They had found so many others in time, or at least had *bought* them time. Quality time.

In Carmel, Indiana, Ron Albers jogged past the park, which smelled of freshly mown grass. His nose wrinkled with each rhythmic breath, the fragrant grass clippings forming an allergic tickle, and he honked a great sneeze of relief. It was an hour earlier here. The newspaper, not yet delivered, would feature a page three article on the homicide. Still ignorant of that tragedy, Ron contemplated his new life.

It was satisfying to be here, settling into the Pain Clinic practice. Without overnight call, he'd been running more consistently. This move had been good for his health in more ways than one. It was easier to be a conduit from the relative safety of Indiana, and his circle of influence was growing. He'd met with the directors of several hospice-type agencies. They were of like minds, a sympathetic group of warriors battling the enemy called needless pain. This move was meant to be.

A hundred or so miles east, John and Nancy Williams argued vigorously about the subject of the article, Charles Hart. "Of course he did it because he loved her!" Nancy exclaimed. "How can you think that he just wanted her dead?"

"It's hard to watch someone die. Maybe he did it because he couldn't stand to watch her suffer."

"That's exactly why he did it."

"Then we agree," John stated, preferring to end this dangerous conversation.

"No, we don't. It goes to intent," Nancy insisted. "I believe his intention was to alleviate her suffering. He loved her too much to let her to suffer. You, on the other hand, believe he intended to alleviate his own suffering, and that his actions had nothing to do with love."

John shrugged. "I'll agree to disagree." He flipped open the Food section, and pretended to study the wine column.

Nancy shrugged, one of those "You're clueless" shrugs, irritated by her husband's narrow perspective.

Three miles north, just off Montgomery Road, Diane Cavanaugh set down the paper. It had been a bad week. She recalled weeks like this when Iron Ace Jim had been ill, times that he'd say, "I can't believe I woke up alive. How can I feel so bad and be alive?"

Of course, she'd had no answer then. Or now, when it pertained to her own health. Why weren't there better options for people who were dying?

Seventeen miles south, at the Hamilton County Justice Center, the subject of this consternation lay silently on a narrow, foam-padded bunk in the pod. There was neither a pillow nor a blanket. Charles Hart wore the blue-gray cotton shirt and slacks that marked him a prisoner. He'd expected to wear the stiff orange jumpsuits he'd seen on the inmates assigned to clear trash along the roadside. Perhaps the pylon orange outerwear was reserved for prisoner excursions, rendering the offender highly visible, both for his safety and that of others.

There'd been a lot of surprises in the past several hours, since he'd braved his first encounter with the coven of street druggies. The first surprise had been the ease with which he'd transacted a deal with the two men. They'd been easy enough to talk to, not strung out hippies or punks . . . .

"What you need, man?" asked the younger of the two men, the one wearing a red bandana around his head.

"Morphine. I want to buy some Morphine," replied the older gentleman from the car, rolling to a stop and lowering the window the rest of the way.

"Say what?"

"Smack, Du," interpreted the older fellow, who wore a faded camouflage jacket. *"The man lookin' for Smack."*

The younger, Red Bandana, stepped back and looked down the street. *"You da Five-O, man?"*

"The who?" asked the old man, confused. *"What do you mean?"*

The two on the street shared a glance, Red Bandana shifting his cool stare only to check out the other end of the neighborhood.

"Don't mind him, man," said Camouflage. "He don't mean nothin'."
Camouflage elbowed Red Bandana with a grin. "He cool, Du. Just a cool
ole man."

Red Bandana squinted at the old man, as if sizing him up for risk or
profitability. "How much you need, man?" Red asked.

"About this much," the old man answered, holding up an empty vial
of Morphine. He then opened his worn leather wallet, revealing two twenties, three tens, and two singles. "I've got this much. What can I buy for
this?" The man's voice trembled in anxious fear.

"We gotcha covered, man," said Red Bandana. "But Smack gonna
cost ya big."

It cost him dearly, every dollar in his wallet. Relief filled his heart as
he drove home. The hard part was over, even if the drug dealers had
probably bilked him. No matter, as long as he had what his wife needed,
he'd be their sucker. Now, all he had to do was give the Morphine to his
wife. Lord knew how badly she needed it. He would help her, finally.
That was the important thing.

Shifting on the unforgiving bunk in his pod, the man recalled
the second surprise last night, which had arrived in the form of a
uniformed police officer and one of the drug dealers. They had
rung the doorbell shortly after he'd given his wife the injection,
asking about his Morphine purchase and his wife's condition.
Hours had passed before he'd learned that the drug dealer at
the door was actually an undercover police officer. In the confusion of mistaken identities and sharp questions, his wife had died.
Just like that! He'd finally found a way to help her sleep peacefully, and she'd died. That was not a surprise; it was a shock.
There'd been an ambulance, a call to his son, and then a ride in
the squad car. As if his wife's death weren't surprise or shock
enough, he learned that he'd spend the night in a holding cell,
until he appeared before one of two judges for a bond hearing . . . .

Throughout the night, more than a dozen men joined Charles Hart
in the square, pale yellow, cinderblock room. Some were passed out, drunk;

most were simply subdued or sullen, a few of them already acquainted.
Next-door, catcalls and wails emanated from the women's holding cell; a
noisier, more emotional crowd represented Hart's neighbors.

The night had dragged on, seeming endless. He'd lost track of time
since his watch had been taken and stored with his wallet and other
valuables. It seemed a foggy, dreamlike horror. He wondered what the
children were doing? Who was telling the grandkids that Grammy had
died? Had his son found the folder, put together years ago, with all the
information about which funeral home to call, which priest to request for
the services, which cemetery to contact? He should be with his children,
and all of them should be comforting one another. How could this have
gone so wrong? She was supposed to sleep, not to die!

The next morning, he was taken before the judge. He was struck mute
with incomprehension; he was being charged with trafficking in narcotics,
and possibly murder. A lengthy discussion ensued between the prosecutor
and the judge, neither of whom seemed keen on setting a high bond, both
conveying thinly veiled sympathy for this naïve man, whose desperation to
help his wife landed him in jail.

At the end of the discussion, uncertain of what the judge had decided,
and not caring, Charles Hart passively submitted to the uniformed deputy's
lead. They crossed the hall, buzzed for admission to the immense intake
area, and proceeded to one of the metal computer desks. A stern African
American woman with silver, star-shaped studs on her curved, crimson
nails asked a series of questions, clicking the keyboard in rapid staccato as
Charles Hart responded blankly with name, address, phone number, place
of employment, next of kin, former arrests—of which there were none—
and medical problems. With stoic precision, the front line workers of the
Hamilton County Justice Center electronically fingerprinted Charles Hart,
gave him a cursory physical examination, issued him the dark drab pris-
oner uniform, and escorted him with several other men to a pod. Hart, in
his bewildered grief, failed to notice that he'd been "processed."

Alone on the bunk, he reflected that it no longer mattered
where he lived, what he wore, and whether or not he ate or
drank again. He'd rather just die and join his wife in heaven.
She was already there, to be sure. Strangely, he believed that

God would understand and forgive whatever crime he'd committed by giving his wife the Morphine. If only she hadn't suffered so much! He never would have done it, otherwise. He hoped their children and grandchildren understood that.

They were probably already in the visitor block of the Justice Center. Yet, he didn't want to see them, or more accurately, he didn't want to see their pain. The pain in their eyes would tell of the pain in their hearts. He'd had enough pain. If there had been enough medicine in the syringe, had he known *this* would happen, he'd have given himself the next injection.

Maybe he could just refuse his heart pills. He was already nine-tenths of the way to heartbreak. Maybe he'd just die of a broken heart. He prayed he would, soon.

Chapter Fifteen

ON BORROWED TIME

Monday, June 17
3:20 PM

Some rooms welcome their guests with warm colors, comfortable sofas, and authentic hospitality. Such rooms lack the homogeneous signature of a professional decorator, and often the furnishings are old, but not shabby. Lived in, without having outlived their usefulness. Such was the family room attached to Dr. Elise McKinley's office.

A towering fireplace, framed with antique blue and white Rookwood Pottery tiles, dominated the room. Oversized, tapestry-upholstered rocking chairs set on either side of the fireplace. Large floor-to-ceiling windows spread to the right and left of the hearth. Burgundy and navy Jacobean valences dressed the windows, pleated jabots descending symmetrically along each side.

Opposite the fireplace and rocking chairs, in the center of the room, a cafe au lait, club style sofa was draped with burgundy chenille throws. In front of the sofa, a broad walnut coffee table was set with a silver coffee service and porcelain cups. To either side, the widespread arms of two camel-colored corduroy chairs welcomed visitors.

Along the other three walls, paneled doors were flanked by rows of walnut-stained cabinets and bookcases. There, Elise McKinley displayed family photographs in assorted frames, including one of herself and her husband holding up a slick, silver-blue marlin. The shelves also showcased unique pieces of Wedgwood and Royal Copenhagen china, an antique ivory chess set, Italian mosaics on miniature easels, and oversized books featuring the many cities and countries to which the McKinleys had journeyed. Leafy plants—real ones, not silk—mingled with the treasures from around the world. No fewer than six tissue boxes were nestled throughout the room, easily accessible from any seat.

The floor was carpeted in a thick, Iranian Bahktari rug, which featured trees, birds, vines, and flowers, knotted in hues of cranberry, navy, hunter green, and camel, with hints of dusty Wedgwood blue, burgundy, and gold. For all the world, this room could be mistaken for the library of English gentry-folk. One could forget that this was part of a medical office.

There was not a hint of medical paraphernalia to indicate that a physician was part of the picture. All that was reserved for Dr. McKinley's working office, which was connected by a separate door on the right bookcase wall.

The rooms formed a square block, with egress from the working office to the hallway of examination rooms, and back to the reception desk. Patients entered the office from a small elevator vestibule. To the right of the reception desk was a doorway to the examination rooms. To the left was the main door to the comfort room, its grand fireplace opposite the entry, the sofaback to visitors. Once inside the comfort room, visitors would depart from the sliding door on the left bookcase wall, which connected to the small elevator vestibule. This allowed for private exits, especially following the delivery of bad news.

This room was for family meetings, and Elise McKinley drew on the room's ambiance to assist her in comforting people as she answered the tough questions that permitted patients and their families to make difficult, informed decisions. She'd wanted to be in this room when she first met with Diane Cavanaugh many weeks ago. But, Diane had come alone. It had seemed more fitting, in that situation, to meet in the working office, complete with medical diplomas and awards of recognition. Elise McKinley was wise enough to realize that the family room was not the best site for all of her patient consultations, bad news or not.

Today, however, the family room worked its comforting charm on the daughters of Diane Cavanaugh. They had requested a meeting about their mother, concerned that she saw them so infrequently, and only on her best days. Dr. McKinley had discussed the request with Diane, and encouraged the meeting. Diane would arrive shortly, and questions would be answered. While waiting in her working office, Elise took a moment to stretch her arms above her head, then to either side, lengthening the scapular ligaments that complained with tension.

"Mrs. Cavanaugh is here, Dr. McKinley," announced the intercom.

Elise bent slightly to tap the intercom. "I'll be right there," she responded, taking one last cleansing breath before crossing to the door that led to the family room. "Good morning, Diane," she greeted, before turning to the other two women. "You must be Diane's daughters. I'm Elise McKinley."

Nancy and Sandy stood to return the greeting. "Hello, Dr. McKinley," Sandy said warmly, offering her hand. "I'm Sandy Cavanaugh. This is my sister, Nancy Williams."

"Please, call me Elise. It's nice to meet you, Sandy and Nancy." Turning to Nancy, Elise commented, "I've worked with your husband, John. It's nice to meet the other half of the Williams team."

✦

It might have been a ladies' coffee, Diane thought, for all the introductions and the coffee and cookies that were spread on the walnut table.

"Please have some coffee—it's in the tall pot—or tea, if you'd like," Elise offered, "and I hope you'll save me from eating all of these cookies myself."

Diane observed a look that passed between Nancy and Sandy, not exactly puzzled, but *surprised* at the sociability of this consultation. They might have been silently acknowledging that meetings with doctors hadn't happened this way before, when their father was ill.

Sandy then accepted Elise's invitation, pouring coffee into English porcelain cups for her sister and herself, and tea for her mother. Diane accepted the teacup, intending to draw on its warmth for her fingers, declining to sip anything for the metallic taste in her mouth.

She smiled mildly, tired but clearly enjoying her daughters' reactions of understated surprise. Elise McKinley was not like most physicians, which was precisely why Diane had selected her.

It wasn't that Diane was looking for a Martha Stewart-type physician. Rather, she sought someone who forged connections with more than a professional interest; someone who attended holistically to mind, body, and spirit. Had her daughters asked, she would have told them that she was looking for the equivalent of a midwife. Someone who would not forget that she was a person, much more than a tumor. One who would insist on being called by her first name, " . . . and my first name *isn't* Doctor."

The women who had been attended by Elise McKinley were generous in their praise, but quiet in their voice, much like the women who were reluctant to name the favored babysitter, for fear of losing her to another family. Diane did not understand this type of selfishness, and would shout to the mountains about the wonder of Elise McKinley, if she ever regained the energy to do so.

✦

"You've collected treasures from around the world," Sandy commented, setting the coffee pot in place and handing a cup to Elise.

"Yes," Elise answered, smiling gratefully at both the proffered cup and the compliment. "My husband and I enjoy travel. He's English, and spent most of his boyhood in India. His father traveled extensively on business, and often took the family along. My husband has loved the nomadic life ever since."

"How do you manage to get away from your practice?"

"I block out two weeks twice a year," Elise answered. "Otherwise, he goes on his own, visits old friends, and brings me back a treasure or two." She smiled again, and sipped the one and only taste she would have during this consultation. "Now, I understand that Sandy and Nancy have questions. Diane, how would you like us to proceed?"

Diane waved a hand in delegation. "Why don't you answer the medical questions, Elise?"

Pausing first to be certain that this was what Diane wanted, Elise turned to Sandy and Nancy, gesturing with open palms for them to fire away.

Nancy started first. "How many more treatments will Mom need, either radiation or chemotherapy?"

Elise looked toward Diane, as if seeking permission to answer. Diane responded by averting her eyes. No answer was always some sort of answer, Elise knew. In this case, Diane had done far more than refuse to visit with her daughters. She had refused to share her own decisions. Elise began generically. "It depends upon the goal. If your mother's goal is to aggressively fight the cancer, which will weaken her further, then she has several more rounds of treatment, each spaced about a week apart. If the goal is to attack the cancer without diminishing your mother's energy, then we would proceed more slowly."

Sandy followed up. "If Mom has several more rounds, we're talking early fall before she's finished, is that correct?"

Elise nodded. "That's right."

"Mom," Nancy began, "If we can get you through the next several weeks, maybe you can look forward to having more energy by the holidays. But it would really help if you'd let us *do* something. At least stop in and see you every other day, or run some errands, do some laundry, anything at all. It feels awful not to be doing *something.*"

Diane sighed at Nancy's earnest plea.

Nancy plunged ahead, in the void of her mother's silence. "Mom, you know that Sandy and I are in town enough to at least help you with errands, groceries, driving you to appointments, that sort of thing. And it does *me* good to see you more often. Otherwise, I imagine the worst about what you might need, or who's driving you where. I'd really like to help out, but most importantly, just to visit with you—like always. It takes a whole lot more energy to worry than to help out a little. Does that make sense?"

Diane smiled briefly, and then nodded, her eyes stoic masks, darkly veiled, secretive.

Sandy placed a hand on Nancy's arm, her posture suddenly rigid, her eyes focused in a piercing stare, as if she were trying to read her mother's mind. Their mother closed her eyes abruptly, in response. All present knew that if the eyes were the mirrors of the soul, then closing them would keep silent—and secret—that which Diane refused to voice.

"Nancy, I think there are some other questions we need to be asking here, before we try to sell Mom on the idea of letting us help out more."

Nancy blinked twice, startled by the measure and tone of Sandy's voice.

Sandy turned to Elise McKinley. "What *is* the goal here, Dr. McKinley? What is my *mother's* goal?"

Elise sighed with a hint of relief. "Your mother has shared with me that her goal is to regain her energy, and to stop the treatments that make it difficult for her immune system to fight ordinary bugs, and which sap her energy in a way that she is no longer willing to bear." Elise paused before speaking to Diane, directly. "Would you say that I've represented your wishes correctly, Diane?"

Diane nodded a silent yes.

Elise continued. "It's important to recognize that the treatment takes with it not only the bad cells, but some of the good. The effect, of course, is that the body loses its resistance to infection; it tires easily, and rebels by not functioning as well as usual. For example, I hear frequent complaints about feeling tired but not being able to sleep. Or having bowel or bladder difficulties, swallowing difficulties, coordination problems, even confusion when having a conversation that requires rapid problem solving. These are typically resolved after the treatments are completed. They aren't permanent.

"But the side effects of the treatments are not the only reason your mother has chosen to stop them," Elise stated quietly. "During the treatment process, we monitor certain aspects of blood chemistry, and we perform periodic bone scans to evaluate the efficacy of treatment. We adjust the treatment accordingly. A week ago, your mother had a bone scan that indicates the cancer has spread."

"Which means what?" Sandy asked softly.

"It means that your mother had a very difficult decision to make. There are aggressive and experimental treatments available to treat the cancer. They are dangerous insofar as the treatment can actually make one sick enough to die. They are a good bet for people who are otherwise in excellent health, who have a cancer that's detected moderately early, and who have the determination to try everything. The difficult part of the decision," Elise said firmly, "is that the only other option is to keep your mother comfortable and as independent as possible. To focus on making the most of life, while nature takes its course."

Nancy's fingers gripped the delicate china coffee cup, blinking back tears, her face taut. She said nothing aloud, yet conveyed shock and fury by her tense expression.

A pair of tears rolled down Sandy's cheeks, her face otherwise calmly resigned. She spoke the dreaded words. "And Mom has decided to make the most of her time remaining."

Elise nodded confirmation. "Yes," she said, allowing them silence in which to digest the news.

Diane reclined with eyes closed, her left hand encircling the teacup, her right hand above the liquid, capturing whatever warmth she could. So distant she seemed from the others in the room, she might have already been dead, her body present, her spirit not.

Nancy broke the silence, her voice choked with outrage, the

pressure of anger constricting her vocal cords. "What were you going to do, Mom? Just let us figure it out at the funeral?"

It was a cruel question, designed to make her mother open her eyes, to *see* her daughters' pain, amidst that of the cancer.

Diane opened her eyes as slits, tilting her head slightly to make contact with Nancy. With obvious effort, which conveyed that, by comparison, death must be a blessed relief, Diane said, "I didn't mean to hurt you. Too tired."

With those gentle, whispered words, the first spoken with more strength than the last, Diane closed her eyes again.

✦

Nancy looked at Sandy, searching for an affirming collaborator, wanting to feel indignant at her mother's paltry explanation, but feeling ashamed instead. Her sister stared at the teapot trance-like, with wide, unseeing eyes. Tears dripped from her cheeks, her eyes forgetting to blink. Nancy felt sympathetic tears brook their banks, although she felt less grief than a bizarre mélange of shame, confusion, and self-pitying anger. Most surprising, she felt more sorry for herself, and for Sandy, than she did for their mother. How could that be?

Am I missing something, here, she wondered? *Why isn't Sandy ranting and raving? How can she just sit there, like she has no feelings? Weren't we just left out in the cold? Didn't Mom just lie by omission, and expect us to swallow it?*

Their mother had concealed important information, Nancy judged. That sort of thing was not done. It was a violation of one of their family commandments: Thou shalt not harbor secrets from thy mother and thy sister. Perhaps if she explained . . . .

"Mom," Nancy began steadily, "I know you're tired, and that's exactly why I'd like to help. We've always shared stuff, and I can't believe you'd keep something important—"

"Nancy," Sandy stated bluntly, her voice husky, "the point of this meeting was to find out about Mom's treatment. This is Mom's business, not a chance to indict Mom on charges of conspiracy to commit privacy."

"Sandy! Don't you realize that you and I were essentially dealt no-confidence votes, by being kept in the dark?"

"If this is what Mom gets for sharing, then maybe we deserve it."

"Don't you get it?"

Sandy stared at her sister pointedly. "Do you, Nancy? Did you hear what Elise said?"

Elise McKinley cleared her voice, assuming a matriarchal tone, choosing her words carefully and stating them with unwavering authority. "Diane, I see that you are exhausted. It's time for you to go home and rest. I'll call for a wheelchair, and one of my receptionists will help you into the elevator and to the car. I know that your aide is in the waiting room. But before you leave, I would like your permission to talk more with Nancy and Sandy."

Noting Diane's nod, Elise continued, "Your medications will need to be adjusted, Diane. I wasn't aware of how quickly your energy was being sapped. In this brief consultation, I've seen for myself why you may prefer to protect your daughters, and your-self, by hibernating. But there are a couple of changes we can make that will help with your energy. I'll call in the prescriptions, and I'll talk with you later today."

✦

Rising swiftly, Elise McKinley crossed to the doorway that led to her office. Tapping the intercom button, she quietly ordered the wheelchair and requested that Diane's aide, Amanda, come into the family room. "Also," she added, "Please write down the name and phone number of the patient support group that Marilyn helps run. Bring it along with the wheelchair."

Returning to the family room, Elise noticed that Nancy and Sandy now flanked their mother. Sandy was murmuring softly, gently stroking her mother's hand, having taken away the un-sipped cup of tea. Nancy was sitting at her mother's feet, leaning against the sofa, tears still threatening like storm clouds about to burst. The door behind them opened, and a receptionist backed in with a wheelchair, followed by Amanda, Diane's young aide.

Elise addressed Amanda first. "One of my staff will help you to the car. Diane should rest as much as she'd like today, but I'm stopping the medications that she has at home. I'll call in the new prescriptions, and if they can be delivered quickly, Diane can take them as directed on the label. She should not take any more of what's at home," Elise added for emphasis.

"I'll dispose of whatever's left," Amanda offered. "Is there anything else?"

"I'll call and see how Diane is, later," Elise stated firmly. "And I'll leave you with the name of a patient support group that has been particularly helpful to some of my patients. Will you please see that Diane calls them, when she's feeling up to going out?"

Amanda nodded and moved to the couch, helping the receptionist lift Diane from the sofa to the wheelchair. Her eyes at half-mast, hands slumped along the sides of the wheelchair, Diane looked the picture of a dying patient. In fact, she was a dying patient. But it was the medications that created the mask of death-like fatigue, and Elise knew that the medication switch would erase the frightening image they beheld now.

It was unfortunate, but some patients responded to very good medications this way. At least there were alternatives, Elise reminded herself. She called good-bye to Diane before resuming both her seat and her conversation with Sandy and Nancy.

"You must feel shocked by this information, as well as the way your mother looked today. You can see why she might find it easier to hide herself away. No explanations needed, no need to pretend, either for her benefit or yours. Now, a change in medications should help. But, I'll be more aware that your mother doesn't complain, and I'll ask her aide for some feedback, if your mother continues to limit your visits. Otherwise, I'll ask *you* about how she's doing. Are we agreed so far?" Elise queried.

Nancy and Sandy both nodded silently.

"All right. Now, there is also a patient support group that

meets once a week at various locations throughout the city. I've given this information to Amanda to give to your mother, but I'll give it to you, as well. There is a separate group designed to offer support and information to family and caregivers. I'm just guessing, but you may find it helpful to talk with other people who are going through this, if only to share information."

Elise McKinley leaned forward, looked each woman in the eye, and stated clearly, "I'm very sorry. I'd hoped that your mother would be one of the survivors. Your mother can be comfortable, alert, and fairly active during the next several months, and *several* can mean more than a year. But her cancer, now that it has spread, is not easily treatable, and she's tired of the treatments anyway. Please try to honor your mother's decision, whether you agree with it or not. If you would like to call me, I'll be happy to speak with you. Please share your concerns with me. And most importantly, do everything you can to take care of one another."

11:49 PM

Nancy curled up on her side of the tall rice-carved bed. John's even breathing suggested the bliss of sweet dreams. But she could not sleep. Her mother was dying. John did not know. She couldn't tell him yet. Tell him what? That her mother had decided not to fight? That life was not worth the fight? That her mother would not live to see them have a child?

At that thought, tears stung her eyes. Again. They'd threatened all day, but she had fought them and won. She was not ready to cry. Not yet. She couldn't explain why. It was as if she had to save the crying for the grief, for the actual loss of her mother.

But first, she had to stay angry, until she figured out what to do about the fact that her mother had lied by omission. Why? Did she feel that Nancy and Sandy could not be trusted to be strong enough to bear it, to bear up? How could her mother believe that only a stranger could be helpful? Especially since her mother had been so involved in caring for her father, when he was sick, and for her grandparents, too. What had Nancy and Sandy done, or failed to do, that they didn't measure up?

Questions without answers careened in Nancy's mind. They wound endlessly, and the perpetual motion made it impossible to sleep. Her head ached, and a dull, throbbing pressure in her lower back nagged for relief. With a small sigh of acquiescence, Nancy pushed back the covers and slid from bed to get a couple of pain-relievers.

As she opened the medicine cabinet, the air conditioner hummed to life, the gusty whoosh of chilly air startling her slightly. She shivered, gulping the pills in a single swallow, massaging her lower back. At once, sticky, warm fluid oozed between her legs. Nancy raced across the room to the bathroom and yanked down her panties. She stared with disbelief at the small pool of bright red blood that now dripped onto the variegated green marble, the complementary colors showing each at its most vivid potential.

Collapsing on the toilet, Nancy kicked off the bloodied panties in a burst of temper. Damn! Again! Or, not again. Anger, disappointment, and grief converged. The dam was about to burst. She'd been certain it would happen this time. So what if they had "tried" at the end of her fertile period? How many people became pregnant despite their best efforts to the contrary?

Another surge of blood pulsed into the toilet. Nancy flicked on the fan to mask her heavy sobs, hoping to insulate John from her painful grief, craving privacy and solitude in which to express this tumult of emotion. Nancy heaved a guttural groan of rage at her body's betrayal. Torrents of tears poured from her eyes, and her shoulders shuddered with despair. She bowed her head into her arms as she sat on the toilet, the potential for a new life draining from within her womb.

At that moment, she hated every pregnant woman on earth. She believed she was being punished for an unknown sin. Or perhaps this was the consequence she would endure for trying to control reproduction for too long. The toxic swirl of self-recriminating thoughts blended with the emotion of the day. She felt almost grateful that a child would not be conceived in its presence. At least she could wallow in her own misery, without the burden of having to console John, avoiding the obligation to respond generously to his efforts at comfort. It occurred to Nancy, briefly, that perhaps her mother had sought to avoid the same thing.

In the next room, John Williams stared at the ceiling. A pair of tears flowed from his eyes, tracing a path past his ears, to his neck, and onto his pillow. Instinctively, he knew what had happened. He understood the sense of loss, the grief. It had been nearly four months. It could take six to twelve. Or longer. He closed his eyes. The deep, rhythmic breaths eventually returned.

It was much later before Nancy slid beneath the covers, a cool washcloth over her forehead and eyes, a hot water bottle resting on her abdomen, and two Valerian herbal sleeping aids dissolving in her stomach.

Chapter Sixteen

SECRETS, RISKS, AND CHOICES

Sunday, July 30
7:00 PM

"My son thought the rest of the family was trying to kill me," Nate Warden stated deliberately. "Frankly, this treatment is the one and only thing that makes me feel alive." He paused, peering closely at the circle of seven, most of them old-timers within the group. He then gazed toward the newest member, a sixty-something-ish woman, who wore a wide-brimmed straw hat and a calf-length, cobalt blue beach shift. "My son actually contacted the police right before Lisa's wedding."

Diane Cavanaugh broke eye contact with the distinguished-looking man and adjusted her hat, wincing as the prickly straw rubbed against her nearly hairless scalp. She was an outsider, and felt uncomfortable in this circle of friends, a secret circle. They had been convened for her benefit, but she failed to feel grateful. Put-upon would have summed it up better. Marilyn had encouraged her to stay after a support group session to hear these unsolicited testimonials. The secret circle asked Diane only one favor: never divulge the confidences that were shared.

Diane had accepted the vow of silence, intrigued by Marilyn's hints of an underground treatment that would improve her quality of life, and possibly extend it, as well. Now, however, she felt irritated for allowing herself to be wooed by what were probably false hopes, furious with Marilyn for suggesting it, and disgusted by this man, a criminal court judge of all things, who admitted to breaking the law for the possibility of *really living* his life a bit longer. He had just finished explaining how he had set another target goal for himself, at least a year more, so that he could meet his next grandchild, due to be born around Christmas time. He admitted to being a controlling man by nature, accustomed to making things happen within the realm of the law. He acknowledged, as well, that it continued to be a source of moral dissonance for him to pursue treatment outside of those parameters.

At that point, Diane had sighed in frustration. His moral dilemmas had nothing to do with her. She had enough on her plate. It was tough enough to get through the day. She didn't want anything else. And she said so.

Looking to Marilyn with uncharacteristic surprise written on his face, Nate Warden folded his hands, as if in prayer. His motive, had he been asked about it, was threefold: to convey his humble respect for Diane as her own decision-maker, his reverence for the treatment that made his participation in life possible, and his apology for what appeared to be hypocrisy. Not that Nate Warden really believed he owed Diane, or anyone else in this world, an apology. Humility was just another concession or compromise to be made, a tithe of sorts, an expression of gratitude for what he considered to be his second life.

His expression faded from surprise to compassion. It softened his features, and hinted at Nate Warden's cherub-cheeked face in childhood.

Diane remained firm in her stance, glaring at the man of law and lawlessness. She did not want any part of this so-called treatment, and declared her intent firmly.

Nate Warden opened his folded hands and extended them, palms up. "I'm sorry," he said gently, softly. "I thought you knew." He paused, but none of the others filled the silence. He breathed deeply, and then stated, "This is an option of last resort."

Monday, August 5
6:06 AM

It wasn't often that Nancy and Sandy flew out-of-town on the same day, at the same time, much less on the same flight. Today was an exception, and they met at the Starbucks counter well ahead of departure. The scent of roasted coffee beans, chocolate, and cinnamon blended with the sizzle of sausage, bacon, eggs, and hash browns at the McDonald's across the way. The sisters shared a breakfast of giant blueberry muffins and café mocha, narrowly resisting the temptation of Cinnamon buns. The dull hum of early morning travelers, most in search of caffeine or newspapers, created a backdrop of white noise.

"Well, do you think Mom is any better on the new medicine?" Nancy asked.

"She's awake more," Sandy admitted, "And she seems to enjoy short visits. But no, she isn't *better*. I don't think it's reasonable to expect that Mom's going to really get *better*."

Nancy swirled the nutmeg-sprinkled cream in the oversize coffee cup, not meeting her sister's eyes.

"Maybe her medication needs to be adjusted, again," Sandy suggested. "It's only been a few weeks. Let's wait and see how she is when we're both back from these trips. Then we can think about calling Dr. McKinley. Elise, I mean."

Nancy nodded. "Did you notice that Mom's hair is starting to grow back?"

"Yeah. She told me it bugs her, especially when she wears that garden hat of hers."

"Well, she doesn't have to wear it for me," Nancy stated firmly.

"I suspect she does it for herself," Sandy countered. "She may feel more normal wearing it, especially when she's out."

"She doesn't *go* out, Sandy."

"Not much. But when we're there, it's as if she's 'out.' Maybe she thinks she's protecting us, hiding behind that hat as if we won't remember she has cancer."

"John is taking her dinner on Wednesday. He promised he

would, since Bob Burke can't fly that day. She'll be fine with what's in the fridge until then."

Sandy nodded, already aware of the plan. This reminder was Nancy's way of checking her list twice. It was especially challenging for Nancy when both she and Sandy were out-of-town, for Nancy believed that the family support was indispensable. Sandy, however, understood her mother's wish for privacy and space, and that with Amanda's capable assistance to Diane, the vacation from family would be emotionally restorative, too. *Or,* she wondered, *am I the only one who feels restored after such a break?*

The sisters chatted about nothing of consequence after that, ultimately partaking of their coffee and blueberry muffins in silence. Ten minutes later, they parted company, with Nancy checking in at the crew desk for the flight to Atlanta, and Sandy checking in with the other passengers.

7:22 AM

It was a sweltering dog day, the third in a row to qualify for Cincinnati's citywide heat emergency measures. The air was almost too wet to breathe, full of ozone and acrid, bitter pollutants. The fogged windows of the conference room dripped with condensation and unknown particulates.

Dave Johnson viewed the satellite pharmacy videotape with Hannah Gilbert and John Williams, the typical Monday morning routine. This would be the final tape review. They were all grateful. Mercifully, the hospital inaugurated the automated record-keeping system this morning. The previous three weeks of in-service training for physicians and anesthetists had highlighted bugs in the system. At this point, adjustments were in place, and everyone concerned prayed that the system would not need additional tweaking.

Yet, it wasn't this high-tech, computerized drug-tracking device that put an end to the weekly tape review meetings. Rather, it was the installation of a new lock on the satellite pharmacy door, and closing off the workroom with a similar lock. These locks were accessible only by swiping one's ID badge, and only certain badges were coded to allow access. A log sheet documented the reason for each entry, and required a signature. Dave planned to review the computerized log for the ID swipes, and the signature log sheets, as well. If anything appeared out of order, he and John would meet and review the videotape for that date. At three tapes a day, recording at extended play speed, Dave had collected a bookcase of tapes. None would be taped over until the end of the month, providing that there were no red flags in any of the tracking systems.

John felt irritated by Dave's paranoia. The obstructed access wasn't a huge issue, but it did slow down the process of getting what was needed. The badge scanner was sensitive, and denied entry unless the badge was swiped firmly in one direction, and neither too quickly, nor too slowly. It was, in a word, a pain.

Pain, and its control, was what John expected to manage. This was just the opposite.

The blue screen signaled the video's end, and Dave tapped off the television and VCR. "Nothing this week?" he asked.

"Nothing out of the ordinary," Hannah Gilbert answered. She shared a quick glance of mischievous pleasure with John Williams, like kids on the last day of school.

"We'll miss seeing you, Dave," she added with a wink.

He smiled at the joke. "Me, too. I know this has been a dull process, and one that hasn't helped us so far. I appreciate your time, both of you."

"No problem," John and Hannah answered simultaneously.

John added, "Let's hope our technological wizardry comes through for us, or that we enjoy the benefit of deterrence."

The group parted, and John prepared to leave for the day. He'd endured weekend call, gaining the benefit of a day off, the morning designated for a training flight with Bob Burke. Although Wednesday was their usual day, Bob was unavailable on Wednesday this week.

Already dressed in street clothes, John returned to his locker in the changing room to store his work cell phone. He sat on a bench and opened his electronic organizer, scanning his To Do list for today and the rest of the week. He jotted a couple other errands, quietly contemplating how to fit them into his schedule.

The door to the OR suites, located behind two other rows of lockers, opened with a squeak. "Just a minute," said Stu Adler into his cell phone. "Okay. Now when can you deliver it?" A pause, then, "Look, these people need it sooner than that. You know that, Ron."

John lifted his eyes from the electronic pad. Who was Stu talking to? Ron Albers?

With a whoosh and a squeak, the door to the OR suites was opened and closed again. Stu Adler was gone.

John shook his head, returning to his organizer. Anticipatory anxiety over more stall-recovery practice distracted him from the overheard conversation. He looked at the list on electronics gadget to justify canceling today's flight with Bob Burke. He found none.

Damn, he swore silently.

8:52 AM

John had come to dread Wednesdays. His flight instructor, Bob Burke, continued to torment him with practicing stalls, but with the added challenge of "the hood." This device, worn on the head, obstructed the pilot's view of everything but the instrument panel.

The hood trained the pilot to respond based on instrument readings, rather than visual or kinesthetic cues. Pilots needed this skill to navigate safely through clouds, fog, or rain. Inexperienced pilots tended to trust their kinesthetic awareness of the plane's attitude or pitch more than the instrument panel. Given the unfamiliar language of the instruments, the novice recreational pilot often resisted the instruments' cues. It was easier to trust the familiar gut-level intuition, for the gut communicated danger insistently, familiarly. Instrument training, beneath the hood, permitted the kinesthetic experience to merge with empirical data from the gauges and dials on the panel, rendering a pilot more capable of navigating in adverse weather or poor visibility conditions.

In preparation for the flight, with anticipatory queasiness, John lifted the flaps on the airplane wing, ensuring proper range of motion. Check. He then walked around to the other wing, assessing its flaps, as well. Check. Next, he ducked beneath the plane with a clear fuel-test cylinder, drew a sample of Avgas, and raised the cup to the light: clear, no debris. Check.

He argued mentally about the weekly stall practices as he set about the pre-flight safety checks. The training was for his personal safety, of course. Still, it was brutal enough to wear the hood and learn to accept the instruments as gospel truth. For Bob to add the task of stall-recovery practice was almost unbearable. Essentially, John decided, Burke had appointed himself pilot-therapist, electing to take his student pilot-client to the other side of fear through repeated immersion in this self-inflicted act of terror.

Continuing the pre-flight evaluation, John checked the prop for dings, and then removed the cap covering the pitot static tube. All clear. Check, check. He could refuse to practice stall-recoveries, he considered for the hundredth time. He could agree to the instrument training, only. This was really *his* decision. Did he want to train this rigorously for the benefit of being a capable, competent recreational pilot?

Finally, he approached the tail section of the aircraft, moving the ailerons to check for free movement. This instrument training was similar to the grueling oral Board examinations, which exacted its own blood-cost before conferring the highest anesthesia credential: Board-Certified. He had survived that ordeal, and had actually enjoyed the challenge of thinking on his feet. With instrument training, as with the tedious hours of study for the Boards, he'd do it. But he wouldn't like it. In his heart, he understood this as a test of Real Life—rather than aviation—this flying into limbo. Yet, he squelched the notion from conscious thought, unwilling to explore what that might mean.

9:15 AM

"Let's take it a little quicker this time," Bob coached, yanking his seat belt securely across his lap.

John nodded. His throat constricted, so much so that he did not trust himself to speak.

Looking squarely at the instrument panel, his vision beyond obstructed by the headgear designed to teach instrument-guided flight, John pulled back the yoke of the plane. Perspiration beaded his forehead and collected in his armpits, trickling down his back and behind his neck.

He sweated from fear more than heat. The ground temperature was already eighty-five, with a hundred percent humidity making it feel much hotter. Yet, at five thousand feet, the air temperature was a mild seventy degrees. A cool breeze circulated from the external air ducts.

Why am I doing this to myself? The question spun in his mind, relentless.

"Anytime, John."

He pulled back firmly, and was rewarded by both the stall horn's shriek and Bob's "Whoa there!" The small plane swiftly upended, and John struggled to hang on to the shuddering yoke and maintain the wing's vertical pitch. Teeth clenched, he fought the nausea that accompanied the roller coaster sensation. He discerned, rather than saw, the trees below. The hood blocked that view, but his instrument panel told the tale.

"Ease up, now!" Bob called. "More!" Burke put a hand on the yoke in front of him, just in case.

John eased up further, and the stall horn ceased. The plane quieted like a colicky child who has cried himself to sleep. He did not look at his instructor.

"A little *too* fast, that time," Bob stated sharply. "Let's go down."

The breeze now chilled John. He vowed never to fly post call again. Even though he'd slept decently last night, his reflexes were not as acute today. He'd taken the plane to the stall point much too fast, and the possibility of a death spin had been narrowly averted. He wondered if the close call was a function of his diminished reflexes, or if he was simply pushing back against Bob's pressure to proceed quickly. Either way, it was dangerous.

John yanked off the hood at two thousand feet, and landed the plane deftly, as if to compensate for the graceless stall. Neither man spoke. The silence allowed each a measure of time in which to manage the tough words that would come later.

10:00 AM
From the Journal of Diane Cavanaugh

I'm having second thoughts about taking the treatment. I feel well enough to pick up the pen, but I feel scattered, can barely focus. Not my eyes, my thoughts. I'm over the nausea, but feel so tired. If I could discipline myself to get up and change the CD—a Broadway tune, an overture, or something such as that. Energy begets energy.

Perhaps it would be a good thing, the treatment that is. The struggle concerns whether or not it's the right thing. Of course, it's not the right thing, legally. But, can I justify it on moral grounds because I don't want to be dependent?

This option would help me be independent. If the news is bad, at least I can be on top of things for a while. I say "if," as if I don't know.

Although I won't sleep, I'll rest. Too tired to write more. Writing in a journal has always helped me make sense of difficult decisions, situations, and problems. How will I do this, if I can't even gather the energy to put words on the page?

10:15 AM

"We can help your husband feel more comfortable, but I can't promise more than that. This medicine won't cure anything. But regarding your granddaughter, there may be a way to push her body into what looks like remission. Let me explain how we think this drug works . . . ."

The Housekeeping attendant, Edna, stared hard at the man before her. He was one of the doctors she had always trusted. Now, she knew that *he'd* been the one who'd left that syringe in the call room. It was . . . *unbelievable*. Yet true.

10:30 AM

"Maybe we should take a break for a while," Bob Burke said casually.

John paused, caught off guard by the suggestion. "Take a break," he repeated.

"Maybe pick up in a month or two. You've got your license. There's no reason to rush the IFR."

"I agree, but I can spare the time now."

"Maybe you should just take that time to fly VFR, build your hours, and we can schedule more IFR lessons next month. September is a beautiful time to fly. It's cooler, there's less of the heat radiation turbulence, and the trees, autumn colors and all, are quite a sight from the sky."

John paused. Did he want any more feedback? Should he push harder for the IFR time or an explanation?

"Bob, if you think I'm not up to IFR training . . ."

"No," Burke interrupted firmly. "It's not what I think that matters. It's what you think, John. All I'm suggesting is that you'll have an edge if you take the time to fly the plane and increase your comfort zone. The more you fly, the greater the comfort zone grows. Kind of like a well-tended garden. But, if you try to push things along in a garden, say with too much fertilizer, you'll kill off the crop. Don't kill the fun of flying by pushing so hard."

"It just seems as if working on the IFR is the next step."

"Not necessarily. You doctors are all alike. Must be that gunner mentality that gets you through medical school and internship."

"So, just fly under visual conditions?"

"Yes. Fly for the fun of it. Not for the next award."

John considered this, not certain that it was what he wanted to hear or do. How many times had he heard the advice to recreational pilots, "Go for the instrument rating. It'll make you a better pilot."

As if reading John's mind, Bob interjected, "Fly for the love of it, for the fun of it. It'll make you a better pilot. When you love doing something, heart and soul, you're more ready to take those learning curve risks, knowing that you'll come out okay on the other end."

11:00 AM

"Mother, just call Dad's secretary and arrange it," Lisa Warden commanded.

Mae Warden glanced into the room beyond, worried that her husband would overhear her end of the phone conversation and become angry, belligerent. Yet, she must watch him carefully, especially since he'd just received the intensive intravenous treatments last night. She would speak quietly, and continue to watch his breathing, now so shallow that she could barely discern the rising of his chest.

"Mother!"

"I'm right here, Lisa, and there's no reason to speak to me in that tone."

"Sorry. You know this is serious or I wouldn't bother to call. If you don't take care of this while Dad can't, it'll become complicated. Neither Dad nor I want to answer questions about recusal."

"I know that," Mae stated indignantly. "I don't want your father to hear this case any more than you do, Lisa. I'll make the call, but I can't file the paperwork for him."

"His secretary can expedite it."

"No one signs for your father."

"Trust me, Mother. He'll grant an exception. His secretary probably signs his name more often than Dad does."

"I'll take care of it," Mae stated quietly, firmly, ending the conversation. "I need to see to your father, now."

Lisa Warden set down the receiver. She understood her

mother's words, but more importantly, she understood their meaning. Mae Warden would not be pushed around. She would not be told what to do by anyone, especially if she believed it contrary to her conscience. Even at the risk of her husband's fury, she would not be bullied.

A chill of anticipatory defeat swept up Lisa Warden's spine. She shuddered and rubbed her arms briskly. A prescient glimpse of fate—her own and her father's—flashed swiftly through her mind: he would hear this case, and as Prosecutor, she would be the one to pick up the pieces.

Then, a sly smile crossed her lips. There was a way around her mother's risky self-righteousness. She would assign exactly the right Assistant Prosecutors to try the Hart case. Two could play at controlling the path of destiny, even if it tempted the flames of hell to singe her soul.

Chapter Seventeen

COMPASSION RECOVERED

Monday, August 19
9:00 AM

"All rise for the Honorable Judge Nathan Warden!"

Nate Warden breezed through the doorway from his chambers, slapping a file folder on the satin-polished walnut bench from which he presided. He glared at the lawyers, still furious that the rotating case assignment procedure landed *this* one in his court, bitterly aware of the irony that he should be the one to hear it.

He could have recused himself. Yet, how would he have explained his forfeiture of such an important trial, one that the media would cover with bloodhound pursuit and bulldog tenacity? To ask for recusal was to beg personal scrutiny. Once it was established that he had no personal relationship with the defendant, there would be questions about his motives. Judge Warden was known as a fearless arbiter of the law, so why would he beg off this trial? It was not worth the risk, he'd decided. He'd survived the "voir dire," the jury selection process. Somehow, he'd survive the trial. *Damn, damn, damn!*

"We have the case of State of Ohio vs. Charles Hart," the bailiff announced somberly.

Judge Warden blew a sigh of exasperation, a signal to all who knew his temper to behave well, according to the rules. He disciplined himself to use good manners, despite his irritability. "Good morning, Counsel. Proceed."

Scarcely registering the Prosecution's opening statement, Nate Warden studied the group assembled. To his left were the prosecutors, Mr. Ferrari and Mrs. Lemming. Both were dressed in dark suits, Ferrari's an off-the-rack wool pinstripe with a thin navy tie, Lemming's a sophisticated, charcoal silhouette, a pearly-pink silk scarf at the neck. The judge knew them as a competent pair. Ferrari and Lemming knew the ropes, and worked them as effectively as marionette masters. The dynamic duo was frequently assigned to high-profile cases.

Shifting his courtroom glower to the right, Judge Warden observed the defense attorneys, the unfamiliar Miss Anthony and her co-counsel, the flashy publicity-hound named Jerry Jacobs. The judge made an effort to keep his mouth rigid; it wanted to grimace in disgust at the man's penchant for converting court-room matters into public drama. Yet, it was the self-seeking qual-ity of Mr. Jacobs' case selection that offended the judge most of all. Jacobs didn't care about the family sitting next to him! He had taken the pro bono case because of the publicity it would generate for his prodigious ego.

A little voice, unbeckoned, whispered within the judge's mind, "It takes one to know one."

Judge Warden's mouth opened, as did his eyes, a flicker of surprise crossing his face. He resisted the voice and took in the new counsel, Miss Anthony. She wore a simple white blouse with her navy linen suit, a small gold cross on a thin chain draped in the V of her suit lapels. *Wholesome, idealistic, legal eagle for now,* the judge scowled in calculated thought. *But what will she be after a year of working for Jacobs?* He reminded himself that he must not hold the girl's affiliation with Jacobs against her. Still, she would have to prove herself in his courtroom. The girl leaned across Jacobs and smiled at the older man who sat next to her boss, nodding as if to reassure him that everything would be all right. *Pollyanna,* the judge mused. *You'll learn.*

His glance shifted beyond the older gentleman defendant,

to the men and women who shuffled and whispered before pass-ing a wad of tissues. The family appeared worried, possibly fear-ful. The women shared swollen, doughy features, and their red-rimmed eyes told the tale of tearful, sleepless nights. *Weakness,* Judge Warden diagnosed silently, grimly. The men wore stoic expressions, and it occurred to the judge that they could be his sons. They were the same age, but their suits were of a lesser cut and quality than what the Warden boys would wear.

Which confirms, he surmised, *that they have little means to defend their father, even if he deserves better.*

The small voice, like a guardian angel, whispered again. "Judge not, lest ye be judged."

Irritated, Nate Warden wondered at the origin of this con-trary voice. His conscience? It wasn't that he typically pre-judged the people who passed through his court. In fact, he prided him-self on his impartiality. Still, a ritzy, slick-dressing lawyer was as anathema to him as a poorly groomed one. Yet, he wondered, *Why this urgency to study the assembled courtroom players?*

The voice interrupted once more. "It could be you. Or Mae. Or Lisa."

NO! he declared silently. But the truth of this possibility was apparent. He'd read the pleadings, which were in the record, and the facts were plain. The man in front of him had purchased Morphine off the street, from an undercover narcotics officer, no less. He'd killed his wife by giving her an overdose of Mor-phine. He'd claimed that she was suffering, begging for more medication. No, he wasn't a doctor, and yes, he knew it was too soon to give her more. But she was suffering.

It wasn't so different than what the Magi offered, the judge mused. What would happen if *he* were in this court? Or Mae?

I shouldn't be asked to try such a case when I'm dying, myself!

But no one outside the family and his doctors knew that Judge Nathan Warden was dying. No one else suspected how this case might create conflict, or might be exposed to prejudice, as ev-eryone outside the family remained ignorant of the judge's con-dition. He received treatments on the weekends, most often, so that he could function in the courtroom throughout the week. It was difficult to keep up with case preparation, with weekends unavailable. Still, he managed. He maximized his weekday time through disciplined time management strategies, leaving precious little leisure for anything or anyone else. That included his family.

Would his sons take time from their hectic careers to sit in a courtroom if *he* were seated at the defense table?

No. He'd brought them up as warriors, honor and duty-bound to fight the battles of their professions: Business before pleasure. The one who works the longest day is the winner.

Is that what I wanted to teach them? It surprised the judge to own the thought, rather than assign it to the persistent voice that pestered him this morning. Yet, his question vanished—as if he had awakened from a now-forgotten dream—as Mrs. Lemming's strident tone jarred him from contemplation.

"This gentleman does not sell drugs," she stated caustically, "and we concede that point. But he *did* give drugs to another person, which represents a violation of trafficking laws. He gave these drugs to his wife. That constitutes drug trafficking. Magdalene Hart died. Her husband, the defendant, is directly responsible for causing her death. *That's manslaughter,*" she concluded, "and we will prove that beyond a shadow of a doubt."

Without missing a beat, Judge Warden called for the Defense to present their opening statement. Miss Anthony stood before the jury. Clasping a legal pad tightly between her hands, she began to introduce the Defense's case. It was a shrewd move, Judge Warden considered, that Jacobs opted out of the chance to perform, allowing his young, pure-of-heart associate to handle this part of the trial. It would offer triangulated symmetry, of sorts, with two women opponents arguing about the death of a third.

The youthful, passionate Miss Anthony now repeated Mr. Hart's words: "I didn't want her to hate me for refusing to give her relief when she was dying. And, if she died a little earlier, then she suffered a little less."

Judge Warden looked again, attempting to see the family

before him objectively. The man, the defendant, would have been called handsome, had he not worn the slack-faced expression of grief and despair. Wavy, silver hair crowned a creased, deeply tanned, leathery face that testified to outdoor work. Broad shoulders tapered to a trim waist, the inexpensive suit enhanced by the man's physical condition. Most distinctive were his hands: large and smooth, almost chiseled, with neatly trimmed nails, more like those of an artist than a laborer. The hands did not fit the defendant's weathered face or his bodybuilder physique. Had he earned the muscles by carrying his wife up and down the stairs of the cracker box Cape Cod cottage they called home?

Would I do that for Mae?

No. It was the voice, but it was also his heart. In such a situation, he would provide for all that Mae needed. But her care would never become his personal burden.

As the young woman spoke, Judge Warden became aware of the melodic notes of her voice, the alternating rhythm of her speech, the harmony of her every gesture. She conveyed passion about this situation, and framed the man's crime as loving, rather than criminal. She stated that, in this case, it was the word of the law that was criminal. Dropping her voice, which quivered with understated drama, she proclaimed, "This man was and is willing to sacrifice his life as a natural consequence of adequately medicating his wife. Yet, we will show that the defendant did not intend to harm his wife, but only to ease her horrendous pain. In the final analysis, her death was a terrible and tragic accident. The defendant acted out of a deeply felt duty, a moral obligation to *help* his wife. He was *not* attempting to take her life, and he is not a Dr. Kevorkian."

"*Objection*, Your Honor!" called Mrs. Lemming. "Killing is against the law. Defense counsel is presenting closing arguments, instead of—." She stopped abruptly, but retained eye contact with the ferociously correct Judge Warden.

He returned the stare, daring her to quote procedure to him, of all people. Yet, he also remained silent, aware that among the many reasons that he should not hear this case, personal bias was the greatest among them. He challenged himself to retain his rigid adherence to the rules. He cautioned himself against personal prejudice. *My situation has no bearing on this case. It must remain separate,* he counseled himself.

However, counseling professionals know that personal feelings can, and often do, affect the process. And in that moment, Judge Nathan Warden was not immune from this phenomenon of human nature.

"Let me see you at side bar," he ordered brusquely. With the attorneys gathered before the bench, Judge Warden lowered his voice to a menacing growl. "The Defense has every right to state their case. I'll grant some leeway." He leaned forward, pausing for commanding effect before addressing Mrs. Lemming directly. "Meanwhile, don't argue your case, Counsel."

Sophia Lemming lowered her glance, lips pressed tightly, jaw clenched, battle-ready rather than dutifully chastened.

Judge Warden stared daggers at the prosecutor, daring her to speak further.

Practiced in the arena of choosing her battles wisely, Mrs. Lemming returned to her seat without comment.

"Continue, Miss Anthony!" the judge ordered sharply.

Wide-eyed with surprise, the young woman rapidly, professionally, but unemotionally wrapped up the opening statement, disregarding the hand signals from her boss and co-counsel to slow down, sustain the emotion, and extend the drama. She swiftly sat down, blushing under the scornful glare of her boss, and the hot temper of the judge.

Shame on you!

Judge Warden ignored the voice. "Your first witness, Mrs. Lemming."

"The State calls Officer James Tieger."

"Do you solemnly swear that the testimony which you are about to give is the truth, the whole truth, and nothing but the truth, so help you God?" intoned the bailiff.

"I do."

"Officer Tieger," inquired Mrs. Lemming, "How are you employed?"

"I work in the 'Street Corner' Drug Unit of CPD. We work in conjunction with other drug interdiction agencies, like the DEA and RENU—that's the Regional Narcotics Unit—and we attempt to identify and arrest those involved in the sale, purchase, and use of illegal drugs."

"Were you working in that capacity on the night of June third?"

"Yes."

"On that date, and in your capacity as a police officer, did you have the occasion to come in contact with the defendant?"

"Yes, I did."

"Tell us about it."

"Well, I'd been working in an undercover capacity in Over the Rhine, near 13th Street, which is a high drug-volume area. Most of the dope boys in this area know me. And I know them. But I was worried when this older gentleman approached, the defendant," reported Officer Tieger, gesturing toward Charles Hart.

"Let the record reflect that the witness has identified the defendant, Charles Hart," interrupted Mrs. Lemming.

"It will so reflect," said the judge.

"Officer Tieger, you said that you were worried when the defendant approached. Please explain."

"I was worried more for him than for me, but he could've been a threat. I didn't know him, and he didn't fit into the scene. He picked a terrible place to shop for Morphine."

"And why is that, Officer Tieger?"

"It's deadly down there. He went to the heart of the traffic, when he could've gone somewhere else. But, not being streetwise, he went to where he'd probably heard most of the drug busts occur."

"Objection!" shouted Jacobs. "The witness is speculating as to what the defendant knows."

"Sustained," said the judge. "Stick to the facts and refrain from mind-reading."

"Specifically, what called your attention to the defendant?" Mrs. Lemming asked.

"He just seemed out-of-place," the officer stated firmly. "I knew he was in the wrong place when he asked if either of us—I was with one of the dealers we have under surveillance—if we had Morphine to sell. No one on the street calls this drug 'Morphine.' They would've said, 'Smack,' so I knew this wasn't the usual deal. He wasn't from the streets, and he wasn't one of ours."

"And what did you do then?"

"Well, I knew I had to follow through. Still, I wanted to signal the other guy that *I* didn't know this old man, if he wound up being a narc, which I knew he wasn't. The dealer I was with asked the defendant if he was the 'Five-0,' the police. When the defendant didn't understand the question, I said something like he wasn't trouble, just a cool old man."

"And?"

"Then, the other guy asked how much the defendant needed, and he held up an empty vial that was labeled 'Morphine.' The dealer I was with said it was okay, that we could help him. And the deal was transacted."

"For the record, again, would you please identify the person to whom the Morphine was sold?"

"It was the defendant."

Judge Warden interrupted. "Let the court record reflect that this witness has, once again, identified the defendant, Charles Hart. Proceed."

Sophia Lemming took a step closer to the witness stand. "Now, after this transaction occurred, why didn't you arrest the defendant?"

"I couldn't bust him on the spot because I'd blow my cover. So I got his license plate. After I'd finished my business in the neighborhood, I made a report. We ran the tag number through BMV to get a vehicle registration. We matched it with the driver's license database, where I was able to make a preliminary ID. The man had no record. With a name and address in hand, my boss asked me to accompany a uniformed officer to the man's house to talk to him."

"What was the purpose of that call?"

"Basically to ask a few questions. The man was obviously not an experienced narcotics abuser or trafficker. We just wanted to talk to him about the Morphine I'd sold him."

"Did you, at any time, enter the house of the defendant, Charles Hart?"

"No. He asked me to wait outside. He did let in the other officer, who was in uniform."

Mrs. Lemming glanced toward the judge's bench without making eye contact. "No further questions, Your Honor. Pass the witness."

Jerry Jacobs stood abruptly. "Officer Tieger, you are sworn to uphold the laws of this city, in fact the laws of this great country, are you not?"

"Correct."

"And it's against the law to sell Morphine on the street, is it not?"

"Correct."

"You sold Morphine to my client. In fact, you are no different than my client, right?"

"Objection!" shouted Sophia Lemming. "The Defense is using inflammatory questioning when he knows the nature of this law officer's undercover work."

Judge Warden paused before answering. He didn't like Jacob's tactics, but understood the strategy behind the question. "I'll allow it. Overruled."

Mrs. Lemming sat down as if pounded into place, stunned that Judge Warden, of all the judges on the bench, would permit Jacobs such latitude.

"Thank you, Your Honor," Jacobs schmoozed, smiling graciously.

The judge rewarded the man's smile with a frown of contempt, and Jacobs shifted his expression to earnest inquiry.

"Shall I repeat the question, Officer Tieger?"

"No. I remember it. The answer is that undercover officers are granted certain liberties in the interest of the State. Obviously, drug dealers aren't going to sell to a uniformed police officer. We use reverse buy snitches to move up the ladder and catch the drug addicts' supplier."

"And you recognized the defendant, Charles Hart, as being 'out-of-place,' as you put it in your earlier testimony?"

"That's right."

"Not an addict, not a dealer, not part of the drug scene?"

"Correct."

"And yet, you proceeded to go to his house with Officer Hastings, and then verbally harassed Mr. Hart until he let the uniformed officer into the home—"

"Objection!" Nicholas Ferrari snapped his pen on the table and jumped to his feet, locking eyes with the judge.

Judge Warden remained silent, his more treacherous strategy for conveying displeasure, and a signal for the lawyer to explain his objection. When Mr. Ferrari failed to do so, the judge shifted his frowning countenance toward the defense counsel.

"That's an issue for a motion to suppress. Move along, Mr. Jacob." As he'd done with Mrs. Lemming, Judge Warden leaned forward to drive home his point, certain that he had humiliated the defense counsel, who stared at his feet, comfortably supported by Italian leather shoes that cost the equivalent of four billable hours.

"Have I made myself clear, Mr. Jacobs?" the judge boomed.

"Yes, sir, Your Honor. I apologize for any slight against our *fine* police department," Jacobs said, mildly sarcastic.

"*Move on,*" commanded the judge.

Jacobs paused, as if gathering words cautiously, his hands folded against his lips, feigning prayerfulness. "Officer Tieger," he said at last, "did you not go to Mr. Hart's home with another officer on the night of June third?"

"Yes."

"And did you not identify Mr. Hart as the man who had purchased Morphine from you, earlier in the evening?"

"Yes, I told Officer Hastings—"

"And did Mr. Hart deny that?" Jacobs interrupted.

"No, he didn't say anything."

"And did you not demand to know who, in Mr. Hart's family, required a medication like Morphine?"

"I asked if there was anyone in his family who was sick. I didn't think the defendant used drugs, and he didn't know much about getting drugs, so he was probably pretty desperate to help someone he cared about."

"Well, I'm sure we're grateful for your intuitive analysis, Officer Tieger. But at some point, this man felt pressured to let one of you officers into his house."

"Objection, Your Honor," Ferrari stated firmly. "Again, that's an issue for motion to suppress, not this trial."

"Sustained," Judge Warden said wearily, losing the momentum that anger had fed. "Rephrase, Mr. Jacobs, and stick to the *facts*."

"Yes, Your Honor. I just believe it's critical to my client's case that—"

"Stick to the case, Counsel!"

"All right." Jerry Jacobs breathed deeply, staring at the intricate floral and trellis design of the courtroom's carpet, as if asked to do the impossible. "Officer Tieger, when you inquired about the health of his family, did not Mr. Hart say that his wife was sick, and that her medication was not working?"

"Yes."

"And did not Mr. Hart tell you that he had asked his wife's doctor to prescribe more medicine?"

"Yes."

"Officer Tieger, did you not insist on seeing Mr. Hart's wife?"

"I just *asked* if I could come inside and see his wife."

"You did *what?*" Jacobs assumed an outraged posture, as if Officer Tieger had committed an unpardonable act.

The officer remained silent, unflustered, well trained in the role of the witness during courtroom theatrics.

Judge Warden sighed loudly, but did not intervene. The prosecutors remained silent, and so would the judge. *God, I hate the way this lawyer conducts business. I hate what this defendant has to endure.* He bowed his head and circled his right hand, a warning to Jacobs to get his show on the road.

"Didn't Mr. Hart tell you that his wife was resting, since she had just received a dose of medication?"

"Yes. He said that we shouldn't disturb her, and that this was the first time in weeks that she'd slept."

"In fact, Officer Tieger, isn't it true that Mr. Hart said that he had to check on his wife?"

"Yes."

"And did he specify how often he was doing so, checking on his wife, that is?"

"He said he was supposed to check on her every half-hour or so, and it was time."

"At that moment, Officer Tieger, did you believe Mr. Hart was genuinely concerned for his wife's well-being, and that he felt obliged to care for her?"

"Yes."

"And does that not strike you as inconsistent with any intention to kill his wife?"

"Objection!"

"Withdrawn," Jacobs stated, having made his point, even if the jury would be instructed to disregard that question when considering his client's innocence or guilt. He continued, "So, Mr. Hart went inside to check on his wife and permitted Officer Hastings to come along, while you waited outside, is that correct?"

"Yes," Tieger answered.

"And shortly thereafter, didn't Officer Hastings tell you to call for an ambulance because the defendant's wife wasn't breathing?"

"Yes. I ran back to the car and radioed for an ambulance."

"Did Officer Hastings attempt CPR?"

"I was outside, so I couldn't see, but I believe he did because I could hear the defendant shouting, 'Keep trying! Keep trying!'"

"While you radioed for an ambulance?"

"It's procedure."

"And when the ambulance finally arrived, was Mr. Hart not

shocked about his wife? Did he not repeatedly state that his wife couldn't be dead, that the paramedics should keep trying to resuscitate her?"

"Yes," Tieger stated. "He was very upset."

"Thank you, Officer Tieger. No further questions at this time, Your Honor, but I may wish to call back this witness."

"You're excused for now, Officer Tieger. Call the next witness." Judge Warden glanced at his watch, grateful to be inching toward a recess. He'd grant one to the first lawyer who requested it, or at 11:15, whichever came first. Jacobs' theatrics and consummate arrogance were an exhausting performance to watch.

While the next witness was sworn in, Nate Warden studied the defendant and his family. The sons shuffled hands in pockets, searching for something, and the daughters wrestled with oversized handbags, one proffering a small pill case and more tissues to her father.

Miss Anthony was frowning, the judge noticed, and low muttering emanated from the defense table. Mr. Hart appeared ashen, his forehead and temples dotted with perspiration.

"Mr. Jacobs, Miss Anthony, let me see you at sidebar," the judge instructed.

Jacobs held up a finger, silently requesting a minute to size up the situation. Mr. Hart shook his head vigorously, as Miss Anthony pleaded with Jacobs, her request obviously seconded by Mr. Hart's daughters, who crouched nearby.

"Well?" Judge Warden inquired. If they wanted a damned recess, he'd grant it, all they had to do was ask!

Jacobs patted his client's back confidently, murmuring reassurances to the daughters who exchanged looks of disagreement. He then approached Judge Warden's bench.

"Is your client ill, Mr. Jacobs? Do you wish to take a recess?"

"No, Your Honor. We'll continue. Mr. Hart isn't sick."

"Very well, then. Proceed."

Mr. Ferrari questioned the other police officer, Hastings, obtaining corroborative testimony as to how the events of June third had unfolded. To the uninitiated, the laborious and slow process often induced somnolence, particularly for jurors. For Judge Warden, the languid pace was familiar, but he fought an unaccustomed stupor that threatened to blunt his edge. He disciplined himself fiercely. *Don't give in to it! Fight! Sustain the battle!*

"Officer Hastings, at what point in your conversation with Mr. Hart did he allow you to enter his home, to see his wife?"

"It was after we'd talked a while—maybe ten minutes or so—about my aunt who had died from cancer, and how tough it was for my mom, who was taking care of my aunt. We talked about how hard it is to watch family suffer, and how it isn't always cancer that causes pain. Then, he said he wanted to check on his wife. So, I just asked if he minded if I came along, just to see how his wife was getting on. He seemed to think about it, but he said okay."

"And did Officer Tieger accompany you, as well?"

"No, sir! The defendant said Officer Tieger should wait outside. I was the one wearing the uniform," Hastings explained.

Ferrari nodded in understanding. "And what did you see when you entered the defendant's home?"

"Mrs. Hart's bedroom was in back, near the kitchen. The room was dim, since the shades were pulled partway closed. It wasn't sunset yet, so I could see pretty well. I observed a woman in a crank-up hospital bed, with an IV in her arm and oxygen going. She didn't seem to be as restless as the defendant said she'd been."

"And what happened next?"

"I mentioned that she looked a lot more peaceful than some in my family had been, near the end. The defendant agreed with me, and said that this was the first real rest his wife'd had. He said that she used to moan and clench up in pain, day after day, until he'd given her the medicine that evening."

"Did the defendant specify which medicine that was?"

"Yes," affirmed Officer Hastings. "The defendant said that the doctor prescribed Morphine, and that what he bought was enough to let his wife rest, pain-free."

"Did the defendant say anything else?"

"Yes, sir. He said, 'I know it's wrong to try to get Morphine from drug dealers, but I couldn't let my wife keep hurting so bad, day after day, and the doctor won't give her anything else. I didn't have anywhere else to turn.' That's what the defendant told me."

The youthful officer, barely twenty-two, bowed his head. Judge Warden observed the witness closely. Tall and burly, clean-shaven, with a choirboy-pink complexion, the young man fidgeted with his hat, nervously. Warden discerned that the officer was new to the witness stand; eager to perform well, but agonizingly conflicted about this case. *Ah, it's good to have company* . . .

"What happened then?" Ferrari stated sharply.

"Well, the defendant said he was relieved that his wife wasn't suffering this evening, that maybe he'd get some rest, too. Then, he kind of looked worried—"

"But what did the defendant *do*?" Ferrari asked.

"Well, he checked the little oxygen tubes to make sure air was coming out, and then checked her pulse. I asked what was wrong, and he said he didn't know, but something was wrong. He sounded a little scared—"

"Officer Hastings, what did *you* do, at that point?" Ferrari interrupted.

"Well, the defendant said that Mrs. Hart wasn't breathing, and he couldn't feel her pulse. He asked me to check, to see if I could feel a pulse. I did that, and I didn't feel any. I used to be an EMT, and I checked her nail beds, which were blue, and even her lips were a little blue. It looked to me like she—"

"Did you call for medical assistance, Officer Hastings?"

Hastings frowned before answering the question, as if perturbed at the repeated interruptions. "Yes, actually I asked Officer Tieger to do that, since we can radio the request so quick."

"After you asked Officer Tieger to get an ambulance, what did you do?"

"I started CPR. I thought it was probably too late, but it's better to err on the side of caution. A person can have a very faint pulse and still be alive. It's procedure."

"In your estimate, Officer Hastings, did you do everything possible to save the defendant's wife?"

"Yes."

"Did the defendant object to you performing CPR?"

"Not at all. He said, 'Keep trying, keep trying.' And that's what I did, until the paramedics got there."

"Did the defendant say anything to you that would indicate awareness that the Morphine might have caused his wife's death, as in the case of an accidental overdose?"

At this question, Charles Hart moaned and slumped forward, just as Jacobs leaped to his feet shouting, "Objection!"

Two sheriff's deputies shot forward to help, gently lowering the defendant to the floor. The sons and daughters raced around the balustrade to tend to their father. All four lawyers blanched in surprise, speechless and frozen in place for several seconds. Even Judge Warden remained paralyzed momentarily, before the adrenalin kicked him into high gear.

The gallery crowd hummed with worry, the noise escalating to crescendo.

"Bailiff, call for medical assistance and clear the jury! Order in this court! All parties other than legal counsel and the defendant's family will clear this room. Now!"

In the swirl of voices, pleas, shouts, and movement, Nate Warden contemplated that perhaps this man, Charles Hart, did not, until a few moments ago, internalize the possibility that *he* had taken the life of his wife. Surely, Jacobs would have counseled his client about this! But, it seemed so fresh, so devastating, as if the defendant were hearing the possibility for the first time.

He's a man; he's not just a defendant, Your Honor.

Yes, Warden admitted, setting his jaw grimly.

From his bench, Judge Warden observed a trio of paramedics bursting through the courtroom door, clearing a perimeter in which to minister to the patient. At that moment, the judge understood that Charles Hart was not merely a defendant. He was a man. This was not a *case*, this was a life—a group of lives—held in the delicate balance of the scales of justice.

Only, in this instance, with respect to the life of Charles Hart, judgment would be rendered within a higher, more powerful court—one not of this world.

Chapter Eighteen

Confession

Sunday, September 15
7:00 PM

"If anyone had asked me a year ago, I would have told them that this treatment would give relief, but it wouldn't change your life." Nate Warden paused, frowned at the floor, then looked back at the group, noticing that the woman wearing the straw hat was back.

"It may not be everyone's experience, a changed life; but for me, changed it is."

Peggy and Marilyn, the group facilitators, exchanged looks before Peggy asked, "How is your life different today, Nate?"

"Well, let me tell you about something that happened recently. Of course, some of you know that I'm a criminal court judge. I'm known as a tough judge. You break the law, you'll pay for it. You come into my court unprepared, and you'll regret it. I tolerate no nonsense, and I operate with strict adherence to protocol. Just as a doctor has a bedside manner, a judge has a 'bench-side' manner. Mine is rigid, gruff." He smiled then. "I can be a pain in the hindquarters."

The group, enlarged to six compatriots, listened intently. Only Marilyn chuckled at Nate's self-deprecating attempt at humor. The rest barely cracked a smile at the man who was—and apparently not only with them—a curmudgeon.

"A while back, I had a family in my courtroom." He shrugged as he realized that, a month ago, he would have said he had a *case*, not a *family*, in his court. "Anyway, this older man was accused of killing his wife, who had a terrible, painful, wasting disease. His daughters and sons were with him, and this family looked as if they were dying, right in my courtroom. The man *did* die, on the way out of my courtroom. You've probably heard about it on the news, in the papers.

"At first, I thought it was a dirty trick for God to play on me, having this particular defendant's case assigned to my courtroom. But, I realize now that, if anything, God was hitting me over the head with my own hypocrisy. Here I sit, glad to take this treatment so that I can dispense justice from the bench, which is a good use of my talents. Yet, my court is one of black and white. Shades of gray are not permitted. I require the legal eagles to make their cases using that code, but I *live and work* because I don't hold myself to the same standard. Well, I could have recused myself. I could have transferred this case to someone else. But I didn't, mostly because I was afraid of having to explain my reasons.

"I've never done this before, but I believe I showed favoritism to the Defense that day. I saw that old man, who's actually younger than I am, and I thought to myself, 'That man has guts. He loved his wife enough to give her too much medicine to keep her from suffering.' I guess when you begin to operate outside the law, within those shades of gray, it affects your moral reasoning. It also pushed a button that doesn't much operate for me: compassion. And you know what else happened? It made me decide to call my son, the one who nearly destroyed this opportunity for *all of us.*

"I told him I was sorry for the name-calling, the threats, everything. I can't remember ever apologizing to one of my children. It was so important to me to always be right, the authority in the family. But I told my son that I was proud of him for speaking up on my behalf, out of concern for my welfare. I told him that, after our lifetime of battles, I probably didn't deserve for him to do something so loving; so forgiving. I didn't use those exact words, but I wish I had. They would have been more appreciative.

"So, if you're considering this treatment, realize that it might just change your life." Nate Warden smiled sadly, concluding, "And you might decide you don't mind shades of gray after all."

His words clinched the decision for Diane Cavanaugh. Redemption was available for all of them.

Chapter Nineteen

HOPES, WHITE LIES, AND MYSTERIES

Saturday, September 21
7:30 AM

Rasssppp! Kathy Martin yanked the surgical tape from her arm without flinching. Applying pressure at the site of the wound with her thumb, her index and middle fingers held like a scissor-clamp, she deftly plucked the intravenous catheter from the vein. There. It was out. She set the catheter in a plastic, kidney-shaped emesis basin, where the last of the fluid elixir dripped from the IV tubing below the shut-off valve. Next to the basin was a partially opened adhesive bandage, positioned for easy access. While sustaining pressure on the IV site with her thumb, Kathy snagged the bandage from its wrapper with her index and middle fingers, and nimbly centered the gauze part beneath her thumb. With two flicks of the fingers, the white adhesive backing floated to the floor, the bandage now securely pressed in place. Finished! *And all by myself!*

Smiling broadly, Kathy reclined across the bed and snuggled beneath the covers, daring the pain to return. It did not.

Focusing on the window, Kathy shifted her attention to the day itself. Shafts of sunbeams, which always reminded her of the path to heaven, reflected the bright autumn morning. Gold and scarlet maple leaves outside her window danced in dappled shadow across the bedroom wall. A mirror above the dresser caught and bent the light into tiny rainbows. Surely, those were signs that promised a better day.

She arched her spine until her body formed a crescent, her back cracking as it broke its long-held fetal curl. Her toes poked the sheet from its tucked in position beneath the mattress, and her arms arced over the top of the headboard. Relaxing from the stretch, she purred a blissful yawn, like a contented kitten, and shivered with delight at the serenity that came with the day.

Tossing back the covers, she fluidly sprang from the bed. With a quick snap of her right hand, the sheet and blanket that had covered her were now in place across the bed. Effortless. The healing Magi had come during the night, and Kathy had been made whole. She felt giddy with pleasure, almost high.

Energized, she planned her day. She'd start with a trek to the grocery and the local farm stand for fresh produce. Tonight, she'd offer a home-cooked supper for her husband and children. After the shopping, she'd attack the mountain of laundry that loomed from the basement. Glancing through the doorway to the hallway laundry chute, she noted the protruding pajamas, which hung like a limp flag. Yesterday, it might as well have been Mount Everest. Today, it appeared to be nothing more than an anthill—no more than four loads. She would have it finished by suppertime, before Drew returned from a weeklong seminar on the West coast.

It was better that Drew had been out-of-town until today, she reminded herself. He hated the risks associated with the Magi, and had even prohibited the treatment, although he enjoyed the sequelae of such visits. Had Drew been home, there would have been a fight. *Why does Drew resist,* Kathy pondered, *when he knows the power of the gift?*

But she knew the answer.

Three months earlier, Kathy had renewed her membership in life. She'd never felt better! She'd wasted so much time getting to this point, and for what? This treatment should be available to everyone who needed it, she'd decided. And until it was, she would serve within the underground forces that offered the healing elixir to dozens of people in the Cincinnati area—regardless of the risk—beginning with herself. Last night's treatment had restored her energy.

Sustaining regular treatments proved challenging, especially since they were done secretively. Drew's work schedule and out-of-town travel, as well as the needs of their two children, made it particularly tricky. King's Island season passes, including a transferable "Nanny Pass," had permitted treatments during the summer days, while Drew was at work. On those days, the sitter would feed the children dinner at the amusement park, tuck them into bed late, and provide Drew with the excuse that Kathy was sleeping in the guest bedroom because of severe cramps, allergies, or a migraine headache. For his part, Drew accepted these explanations seemingly without question. Perhaps the wonder of the many "good days" diminished his wish to delve further.

For that, Kathy was grateful. She quickly snapped up the sheet and blanket on Drew's side of the bed, twirling with pleasure as she allowed herself to *feel* every muscle, ligament, tendon, joint in her body. In another wave of giddy emotion, Kathy jumped into the center of the bed and laughed out loud. She felt alive!

4:15 PM

Nancy Williams tossed the standard flight crew luggage onto the bed and rapidly unzipped the main compartment, revealing a jumble of clothes from her four-day trip. Everything needed to be laundered, so she hadn't packed tidily.

Grabbing the clothes in a bundle, Nancy headed for the laundry chute. Pausing momentarily, she dropped the bundle, taking a long, silk nightgown from the pile and spreading it across the plank floor. She then scooped up the remaining clothes, and placed them on top of the gown. One edge at a time, Nancy gently folded the delicate mousseline around the other clothes, shrouding them completely, but leaving the lace bodice and lower edge of the gown trailing over the crook of her left arm and down towards the floor. Slowly, Nancy stood, and cradled the bundle, which resembled the form of an infant wrapped in an elegant christening blanket. She closed her eyes, taking in the sensation of weight, the draped fabric, luxuriating in a Madonna-like tranquility.

The calendar marked six months without contraception, and with every period, Nancy grieved with a waterfall of tears and wracking sobs. Finally, she felt ready to be a parent, and now all of her well-conceived plans were thwarted by Mother Nature's refusal to cooperate.

Keeping her grief private was a burden, but Nancy mistakenly believed that sharing it with her husband would depress him. She would try to protect him from that, at least.

In fact, John Williams would have been encouraged had Nancy shared her despair, for he had little idea how to reach out first. John did feel a sense of loss each month, although his was not a physical grief marked by tears. A casual inquiry of one of the fertility specialists—during a surgical procedure for which John had provided anesthesia—revealed that it might take a year or more to conceive. But that knowledge did not mitigate the pang of mourning. He felt a sense of urgency, as if Nancy might change her mind about having children if she didn't get pregnant quickly. It would have been a relief to know that, with each passing month, Nancy grieved as acutely as he did.

The rumble of the garage door opening startled Nancy from her maternal reverie. Bunching the ends of the nightgown into the center of the bundle, Nancy took several quick strides to the laundry chute and jammed the clothes into the narrow opening. The muted ring of the telephone called her back into the bedroom, and Nancy gave an exasperated sigh of impatience that the caller had interrupted her chance to greet John immediately.

"Nancy, it's Mom."

Impatience transformed into anxious fear. "Are you okay, Mom?"

"I'm fine, Nancy. I just wondered if you wanted to take a day trip to Shelbyville on Monday. It's a good time to do some early Christmas shopping."

Shelbyville was a couple of hours from Cincinnati, home of Wakefield-Scearce and a veritable treasure trove of antiques and unique collectibles. Nancy, her sister, and her mother typically made the trip to Shelbyville a few times a year, the autumn excursion occurring around Thanksgiving, two months away.

Did her mother want to move up the date because she was worse, Nancy wondered? Yet, if she felt worse, why would she suggest it at all? She shook her head fiercely to clear the thought.

"Hmmmm, that sounds tempting, Mom. I'm trying to remember what's going on next week. I'm upstairs, so I can't check the calendar, but I think that'll work. Yeah, why don't we go? Can Sandy go with us?"

"She's in New Orleans next week, and her travel schedule is really tight until early December. But, I have a list of things she's looking for," Diane added perkily.

Nancy could almost see the bounce in her mother's step, hearing it in her voice over the phone. *Amazing,* Nancy thought. Compared to how her mother had been dragging the past several weeks, this renewed energy inspired Nancy's hope for a reprieve from the damning diagnosis. Maybe it wasn't as bad as they had thought.

"And you're sure you feel up to a full day trip, Mom?"

"I wouldn't suggest it if I weren't," Diane said, her tone indicating that Nancy should know better.

"Then it's a date! I'll pick you up around eight o'clock."

"See you then, Honey. Love you, and love to John."

"Love you, too, Mom."

Nancy set down the phone gently, a small smile tugging at the corners of her mouth: perhaps God would spare her mother! *Please, God, spare my mother.* A fleeting thought interrupted: perhaps God would grant *this* request, rather than give Nancy and John a child. "Nonsense," she spoke sharply to herself.

Nancy re-zipped her luggage and rolled it into the large closet, where it would remain until she left on her next trip. Skipping down the stairs, she called out a greeting to her husband.

John was flipping through the mail, mostly solicitations and bills. He smiled, looking up to see Nancy still in uniform, her arms spread in greeting.

"Hi, Captain." He set down the thick stack of envelopes, and reached for a bear hug snuggle. It had been a four-day trip, although it seemed longer.

"I missed you, Doc," Nancy said softly, pulling back only far enough to look into his eyes without leaving the warmth of his clasp.

"Yeah? Well, I missed you, too." John pulled her close, seeking the soft curve of Nancy's lips, as familiar and welcome as a favorite pillow.

Temporarily sated, they released one another from the embrace. "What have I missed?" Nancy asked.

"Not much," John answered with a shrug. "Did you bid your schedule for next quarter?"

Nancy nodded, glancing at the calendar to note Monday's plans. There were none, except for the date with her mother, and Nancy would be back in time to prepare dinner—it would be her turn that evening.

"My mother called a few minutes ago, and she sounded great," Nancy reported. "She wants to make a day trip to Shelbyville on Monday."

John's eyebrows arched in surprise. "She must be feeling pretty well."

"That's what I think, too." Nancy bit her lip, hesitating to ask the next question for fear of a disappointing answer. Taking the risk, she asked, "John, do you think it's possible for Mom to be in remission?"

John sat heavily in one of the Windsor chairs at the kitchen table, and reached for Nancy's hand. Saying nothing, he pulled her to his lap, curving his arms around her arms and belly, wishing for inspiration so that he could reply helpfully, yet without creating false hopes.

He knew about the poison of false hopes. The way well-intentioned aunts and uncles, neighbors and priests, had offered words intended to comfort and protect him from full knowledge of his own mother's illness. As an adult, John knew that his protectors had meant no harm; the exact opposite, in fact. Yet, he marveled at how ill considered the remarks had been, from encouragement that enough prayers would help his mother recover, to assurances that God had a better plan for her.

Even as a twelve-year-old boy, John had thought the comments senseless. What better plan could there be for his mother, than to love and care for him, as only a mother can do? And since his mother ultimately *did* die, was he to believe that he had not prayed hard enough, frequently enough, with perfect-enough words of praise and invocation?

Since then, John had vowed never to demean anyone by offering false hopes. He now struggled with the conflict between keeping that promise, and soothing his wife and her wishful thinking. A deep, throbbing pain emerged in his gut. His demons were alive and well, blocking any creative inspiration. He felt Nancy wiggle in his lap, and was suddenly aware of how tightly, fiercely, he'd hugged her. As she lifted his face so that he met her gaze, he failed to marshal those demons that twitched in his countenance. Reflected in his wife's eyes were John's unsettled sorrow, anger, and anguish, discernable in the crease of his brow, the squint of his eyes, the clench of his jaw. How could he respond honestly?

Ever attuned to barometric changes, Nancy sensed the shift in her husband's emotion. She had first become aware of John's unmended grief as her father was dying, and came to understand her husband's increasing distance as self-protective. That's why he could not visit her father, especially at the end. He was still a newly orphaned young boy, when it came to the emotional aspects of losing one who is loved. Nancy's efforts to help him mend were met with stern resistance. The worst, for Nancy, had been when John coldly told her to quit trying to be his social worker. Later, he had apologized sincerely. He'd admitted regretting the words as soon as they flew out of his mouth. His urge to spew such venom was rooted in an instinct of emotional self-preservation. And, while admitting the dysfunctional response, John had likened his behavior to that of the jellyfish, which spews poison to paralyze potential predators. Nancy had touched a nerve that was too sensitive, and she then became a predator. His words had stopped her dead. Then, as well as now, Nancy wondered, *Is this an explanation or an apology?*

She sighed, dropping her hands from John's face. His answer, communicated silently, was clear. It wasn't simply the confirmation that, despite her mother's notable improvement, she would not survive this cancer. But also that she, Nancy, would be on her own emotionally. John could not help her with this one. Just as he could not help her manage or express her grief as her father was dying.

With a flash of insight, Nancy understood how easily John mobilized his energies when there was reason to hope. Yet, the minute they'd learned that Diane's illness was terminal, John had withdrawn, spending more time either at work or flying. Most recently, he'd taken sanctuary in his workroom, holing up while tending to the tedious task of stripping a painted mirror, its resplendent wooden frame constructed of pierced mahogany—a series of curls and whorls through which any background would be rendered elegant. John would remain invested only in that which held forth a promising future. She wondered, *Where does that leave us, if I were to get sick, like my mother?*

Nancy leaned on John's shoulders and pushed herself to a standing position, her arms and legs weighted with despair, the near-paralysis mitigated by encroaching, conflicted feelings: impatience with and compassion for her husband; irritation, pity, and anger that he couldn't just be supportive. Yet, there was also a maternal tenderness, an awareness of the little boy who felt abandoned by his mother and betrayed by God.

Resolutely, Nancy took a few steps back, as if to convince both herself and John that she was strong enough not to need him now. With her equilibrium reestablished, Nancy gave in to a quick peck on her husband's cheek. It was less than romantic, more an advance on the forgiveness she would need to extend to John for his diminished availability at this juncture. The kiss also served as a physical reminder that she did love John, despite his incapacity.

"I'm heading upstairs for a power nap," she said. Turning briskly on one foot, patting John's shoulder lightly, Nancy crossed through the family room and hurried to the top of the staircase, before the heaviness of her heart overtook her legs. Haphazardly shedding her clothes, she climbed into bed and burrowed beneath the comforter, creating a cocoon in which she cried herself to sleep. Alone.

Monday, September 23
8:00 AM

"Mom, you look great!" Nancy exclaimed, unable to conceal her astonishment.

"I must have looked pretty bad for you to sound so surprised," Diane Cavanaugh replied with a mischievous grin. "It feels like I'm back to my old self, in terms of my energy," she admitted. "I haven't felt this good in quite a while, and I intend to enjoy it."

Nancy followed her mother through the foyer of her condominium, the scent of lemon oil hinting of semi-annual stem-to-stern housecleaning. Nancy marveled that her mother, who had been in bed for the previous three weeks, had mustered the energy not only to take a shower and dress, but also to have her hair cut, nails manicured, and the house cleaned. She must have pulled out her craft supplies, as well, for a new, fragrant, eucalyptus wreath now hung above the fireplace mantle in the living room.

"What are you doing differently?" Nancy inquired.

"Oh, a little herbal this and a little herbal that," Diane answered lightly, if evasively. "But we need to head out quickly if we're planning to get home ahead of the rush hour. We can chat in the car." Diane grabbed a leather satchel from beside the sofa, and then pulled a heavy sweater-jacket from the front closet. "Let's go!"

Nancy nodded, eager for more details but willing to wait until they were on the road. *How wonderfully odd,* she thought. *Perhaps John is wrong about the possibility of Mom going into remission.*

Nancy recalled hearing about a book that documented miraculous, medically inexplicable cures of people diagnosed with terminal cancer. It wasn't the diagnosis that puzzled researchers, but the way in which the cancer mysteriously remitted with only dietary changes and herbal remedies. Despite a dire prognosis, the cancer had vanished without so much as leaving a fingerprint of its existence. *Perhaps Mom will be one of these people,* Nancy thought, her confidence in the idea growing with every moment that she and her mother were together.

While Nancy eased her car into the heavy interstate traffic, Diane dominated the conversation with chatter about Nancy's two brothers—one in Denver and the other in Washington, DC—their wives, and their toddler-age children. Nancy permitted her mother to rattle on, concentrating on the southbound I-71 vehicles that bottlenecked near the Redbank Road exit.

Her mother had maneuvered to avoid a direct response to Nancy's earlier question, and Diane's uncharacteristic avoidance bothered Nancy. Still, if her mother preferred to carry on as if she were perfectly healthy, without sharing any reminders of the disease that gnawed at her internal organs, then so be it. Perhaps, Nancy pondered, this was part of a New Age strategy in counteracting the disease process. Possibly, the act of surrounding oneself with positive people, while optimistically embracing life, afforded more complete healing. Maybe a holistic approach, tending mind, body, and spirit—in conjunction with courses of radiation and chemotherapy—offered this sort of renewal. *Maybe I should just be glad about it, and say nothing, just so I won't jinx it,* Nancy reflected.

Once the traffic flow returned to sixty miles an hour, Nancy tuned in to her surroundings, noting how the landscape was now adorned in its fall wardrobe. The leaves of the trees along the interstate corridor fluttered in hues of brilliant yellow, crimson, and harvest moon orange. Only generous autumn rains rendered such radiant color, exquisitely vivid against the backdrop of a rare cerulean blue sky. A light breeze stirred the colors, and Nancy found herself distracted both by her thoughts and the beauty of the turnpike tapestry. She felt compelled to interrupt her mother.

"Mom, have you ever seen such incredible fall colors? It must look like a Turkish rug from the sky, but I didn't notice it when I flew in on Saturday."

Diane looked startled, having been deep in a story about her Denver granddaughter's fourth birthday party, recounting the child's charming efforts to assist the magician. Recovering quickly, Diane scanned the jewel-toned horizon, nodding her agreement. "It reminds me of the fall your dad and I drove through Vermont and New Hampshire. Cincinnati doesn't see this sort of color tour very often."

When Nancy failed to comment, despite having interrupted the original thread of conversation, Diane asked, "Nancy, is everything all right?"

Nancy glanced over, disarmed by the question. A look of guilt crossed her face, as if caught by a mind-reader mother, while contemplating impure thoughts. "Oh, yeah," she assured her mother, attempting conviction.

"Oh, yeah—what?" Diane asked skeptically.

"I just noticed the scenery, that's all, Mom."

Diane smiled slightly, looking away. Nancy shared her father's open, expressive face, neither one able to disguise their feelings, nor play cards with a poker face. The thought that Nancy might be pregnant flickered in the back of Diane's mind. She frowned slightly, considering this possibility, but then shook her head in silent denial. No, Nancy would never be able to contain such news. It must be something else that distracted her.

With a twinge of guilt, Diane acknowledged that it might be her own subterfuge that worried Nancy. She wanted to keep her new treatments secret, especially if there was the potential for trouble. Above all, Diane wanted no one to feel responsible for her. She intended to remain in charge of her own life, with no burden placed on her children.

This intention was made with the strength of a vow. Diane did not want her children to have to care for her, as she had cared for their father. It wasn't as though she'd resented it. In fact, she'd been more than willing to do so, and preferred to keep Jim's care within her jurisdiction. The simple truth had been that Diane and Jim Cavanaugh were private people who took care of their own business. For Diane, it had been essential to remain in control of who saw Jim and when. With her as a gatekeeper, neither she nor Jim had felt compelled to put on any false smiles or pretenses. It had been far easier to wait until Jim was having a good day to suggest a visitor or two.

Well, that was part of the reason that Diane and Jim had kept his dying private. Another part had to do with preserving their children's memories of their father, Iron-Ace Cavanaugh, as a robust, fun-loving, adventure-seeking, Korean Conflict Ace pilot. To do otherwise would have shattered Jim's sense of himself. Now, Diane sought to protect herself in much the same way.

Of course, she had already permitted her aid, Amanda, and the people from Compassionate Care to attend her. It was worth the intrusion, Diane decided, for their intervention had resulted in the seemingly miraculous release from the discomfort, fatigue, and depression that had imprisoned her, confining her to bed.

Maybe I should talk openly with Nancy, Diane argued with herself. *No,* she countered silently. It would be better this way. As she had learned at the secret support group session, there were some who opposed such unorthodox treatments. There was too much at stake for those who stood to lose, should the nature of the treatment become known, herself included. Until recently, Dr. Elise McKinley had prescribed only narcotic painkillers and antidepressants, a numbing combination that had netted Diane a life-sentence in bed, with no chance of parole. Thank heavens for the change in prescription by Elise McKinley, and for Marilyn's team from Compassionate Care.

No, for now, Diane would keep her counsel. She would show Nancy the bottle of antidepressants that had done nothing to mobilize her physically or emotionally, but left her mouth desert dry and swollen. To these pills, she would attribute her renewed energy. Yes, it was a lie. *A white lie,* she told herself, *a protective device for both of us.* Diane reached over and patted her daughter's shoulder affectionately.

"I haven't shared my secret with you yet," she said, smiling brightly. "Elise McKinley gave me a prescription that's really perked me up. It's an antidepressant that seems to work on the body's response to pain or discomfort. Isn't it amazing what a difference such a thing can make?"

Nancy darted a quick look at her mother. "Antidepressant?" she squeaked.

"Yes," Diane stated firmly. "They're being used for people with different types of pain. It's quite common these days. Whenever I mention it to one of my friends, it seems that someone *they* know takes antidepressants as part of a pain relief regimen. I understand that it's very helpful for people with interstitial cystitis—you remember, Sandy dealt with that for a while?"

Indeed, Nancy remembered. But Sandy had never taken antidepressants, and her symptoms had abated over the course of three and a half years, disappearing as mysteriously as they'd arrived.

"Does it have side-effects?" Nancy inquired. "I knew a flight attendant who took antidepressants, and he sucked Life Savers and sipped Sprite like he was dying of thirst."

Diane waved her hand in a dismissive gesture. "Maybe a little dry mouth, but nothing serious. It's perfectly safe, Nancy. Now, let's quit talking about medicines and complaints or I'll feel like I've joined an old biddy complaint club. I wonder what Shirley has to show us in the silver vault today?"

Tuesday, October 1
3:00 PM

In the eight days since the trek to Wakefield-Scearce, Nancy had connected with only the answering machine at her mother's condo. Initially, she hadn't been worried. The image of her mother's apparent flight into health remained at the front of Nancy's mind. She hadn't even felt compelled to call from out-of-town, given her mother's wellness the week before.

Yet, now that she had been trying to touch base for three

days, this umpteen-millionth contact with the answering machine represented one too many. She hoped that her mother was just out Christmas shopping. Hanging up the phone impatiently, Nancy decided to drive over for a visit.

She grabbed a diet soda from the refrigerator and flung open the door adjoining the garage. With the punch of a button, the garage door hummed upward, a blinding glare of sunlight stabbing Nancy's eyes. It was almost hot, at nearly seventy-five degrees, unseasonably warm for this time of year.

Moments later, Nancy was en route, her thoughts focused on her mother. She failed to notice the autumn arc of brilliant yellow, orange, and crimson of the tree-lined roads.

Why doesn't Mom answer the phone? Nancy wondered. It wasn't like her mother to ignore messages for days on end. If Sandy had been in town, Nancy would have called to ask if her sister had spoken with their mother. This visit, though unannounced, was better. She would see for herself.

Nancy swung the car around the bend of Spooky Hollow Road, a bit too fast for the tires to withhold their squeals. Their complaint was lost on Nancy, so intent was she on getting to her mother's house. She headed north onto Montgomery Road, watchful of the speed trap at the car dealership, slowing as she neared the narrow lane opposite Bethesda North Hospital. Beyond the swath of evergreens that separated the busy street from the New England colonial townhouses, Nancy arrived at her mother's festively autumnal home. Miniature ceramic pumpkins, each electrified and featuring a different grimace, had been set in all of the front windows. A new grapevine wreath bursting with bittersweet was suspended below the fan window on the front door. It was a good sign, Nancy knew. It meant that her mother was feeling well enough to decorate for Halloween and the Thanksgiving season.

Nancy slid the car into a parking space, and briskly crossed to her mother's front door. The knocker was nearly obscured by bittersweet. Three stiff raps later, there was still no response. Shifting her weight from foot to foot, she impatiently punched the doorbell. *Come on, Mom,* she thought. Standing on tiptoe, she peered through the fanlight. A couple seconds later, an unfamiliar woman was tripping down the stairs that led to the bedrooms. Nancy's heart skipped a beat, but the woman was smiling as she approached the front door and opened it.

"Hello," the woman greeted warmly. "I'm Marilyn. I'm a friend of your mother. You must be Nancy." Without waiting for any comment, Marilyn continued. "Your mother has introduced me to all of her children through photographs, and that's the only reason I knew it was you. Come on in, now. It's a warm day for October, don't you think? Your mother is resting upstairs, and I just turned on her ceiling fan to cool the room a bit. You'll want to go upstairs, then. I'll just get my purse from the kitchen and be on my way." Turning briefly, Marilyn called up the stairway, "Diane, I'll see you tomorrow, but you call me if you need anything. Nancy's here now, she'll be right up."

Swinging an oversized tote onto her shoulder, Marilyn breezed through the door, gone before Nancy could respond with more than a polite murmur.

Shaking her head, Nancy headed up the stairs. "Hi, Mom," she called out. Rounding the corner at the top of the landing, Nancy beheld the sight of her mother, curled up in bed. Diane smiled wanly, lifting her hand in greeting. Her skin appeared pale and translucent, her veins like snaking rivers on a parchment road map. "Nancy," was all she said.

Nancy forced herself to continue forward, cheer plastered on her face despite the sick, heavy sensation in her stomach. "Mom, who was that whirling dervish, Marilyn?"

Diane nodded with a tired grin. "My friend. From the support group."

"You look tired," Nancy said with concern.

"I am a little tired," Diane admitted. "But I'm fine, otherwise. Maybe after a nap . . . ." The thought was left unfinished, and her eyes closed heavily.

Nancy bent to kiss her mother hello, then plopped into the overstuffed armchair that sat next to the bedside table. Warm sunlight from the west window bathed the chair, and its occupant, in a stream of dust motes and sunbeams.

Diane opened her eyes and smiled at her daughter. "You look like an angel, sitting there with the sun around you."

Nancy smiled weakly in return. It should have been a comfort, the warm sun and the cool breeze of the ceiling fan, the latter gently humming like summer cicadas. Yet, her stomach registered dread, making her slightly nauseous.

What was going on? Her mother had been so full of energy for the trip to Wakefield-Scearce. *Be calm,* Nancy told herself, feeling a surge of warmth accompany her pounding heart. *Think cool, blue thoughts. Feel the breeze of the fan,* she insisted. She would not let her mother down by expressing worry.

"Can the angel of domestic bliss get you anything, Mom?"

Diane shook her head. "Just a nap."

Nancy nodded. "I won't stay. I just stopped by to say hi. I called a couple times, and you must have been out shopping for those cute jack-o'-lanterns you've got on the window ledges. Wait 'til Sandy sees them!"

Nancy elected to make up excuses for her mother's failure to return the calls. It was an act of protectiveness, but Nancy hoped that her mother would offer an actual explanation, the truth. When she did not, Nancy felt a bizarre estrangement from her mother, as if there were scary secrets between them. In the half a minute since she had spoken, Diane's eyelids dropped again, and her breathing became soft, shallow. She was fully asleep.

Willing herself up and out of the chair, Nancy bent over the bed to kiss her mother before leaving. She would refill the water glass that set on the bedside table, and leave a note on the grocery pad in the kitchen. They would talk later.

Nancy picked up the glass and snatched a tissue to blot the ring of condensation that had formed on the table. Crossing to the bathroom, Nancy turned on the cold tap, rinsing the glass twice before filling it with very cold water. Glancing down to dispose of the damp tissue, Nancy noticed a capped syringe at the bottom of the otherwise empty wastebasket.

What's this? Nancy squatted on her haunches, and lifted the syringe from the wicker basket. She debated whether or not she should put it in her purse. She could ask her mother about it later. *Like I'm collecting evidence?* Nancy considered. Weighing the decision a moment longer, Nancy dropped the syringe back into the wastebasket, staring at it with uncertainty. What should she do?

Had Elise McKinley started a new medicine? If so, what was it? And why did it require an injection?

Nancy stood quickly, shaking her head vigorously to force the questions from her mind. Why did she feel so jarred, so anxious about this discovery? Perhaps it was simply because her mother hadn't been in touch about any changes in medicine. She would ask her mother directly, later.

Lifting the glass of water, Nancy returned to her mother's bedroom and placed the glass on an old issue of *Country Living* magazine. Marilyn might not worry about water rings on the walnut table, but Nancy did.

She stole another look at her mother's peaceful face. Finding reassurance in her mother's quiet, even breaths, Nancy left the room, closing the door with a soft click to ensure that the breeze wouldn't slam the door shut.

As she left her mother's house, she experienced the curious sensation that someone was watching her. She looked over her shoulder, scanned the parking lot, but saw no one, and there were no new arrivals parked. Shaking off the strange apprehension, Nancy jogged to her car, revved the engine, and scooted from the parking area to the main access road.

Had she looked in her rearview mirror, she might have seen Marilyn and Dr. Stuart Adler disembark from the hunter green minivan with the dark tinted windows.

5:00 PM

"Why would my mom be getting an injectable medication?" Nancy inquired, as she microwaved a pair of small Rubbermaid containers of grilled chicken and portabella mushrooms.

John shrugged his shoulders and wrinkled his brow to communicate—his mouth full of pretzels—that he wondered why Nancy was asking.

Nancy looked up from the steaming containers she'd pulled from the microwave, and smiled at her husband's effort to communicate wordlessly, politely. "Never mind," she said, dumping seasoned chicken and vegetables onto a pair of flour tortillas. "I'll wait."

John chomped the last of the oversized pretzel, and swigged a mouthful of cola to wash it down quickly. "If she couldn't take pain meds orally, she might get an injection. Why?"

Nancy frowned, not meeting her husband's eyes as she dashed a spoon of salsa, then cheddar cheese, and a sprinkle of black olives onto the fajitas. "I went over to Mom's today, and I found a used syringe in the bathroom wastebasket. Maybe it is for pain relief. Mom didn't look good today. She barely said hello."

John nodded stiffly. He knew what was coming: the beginning of the end, sometimes a very long end. He could feel his neck muscles tighten first, and then his back and arms. His fingers clenched in parallel response, gripping the handle of the frosted mug so tightly that they hurt.

He wasn't good at this. It was so much easier to help people when you could take personal interaction out of the picture. He'd never liked to dance for much the same reason. It was difficult to figure out how to respond to someone else's moves, although dancing with Nancy had been fairly easy, as she had a natural way of following *his* moves. But when it came to words, feelings, and especially painful emotions, John Williams tensed and withdrew. He did not want to go there. He didn't know *how* to go there. He said nothing.

Nancy handed John a plate, immediately comprehending his tense posture, and they took their seats at the kitchen table in silence.

While they ate, Nancy mulled over the significance of her discovery at her mother's home. John concentrated on each bite of food, fighting the urge to flee to the cloudless sky or to his workshop—anything but this draining emotional dance that seemed to require perfect words of support and encouragement to his wife, in the face of her mother's anticipated . . . . He refused to even conjure the "d" word, for the memories it evoked.

Wednesday, October 2
1:00 AM

The dream returned, with a twist. This time, John was in the plane with Bob Burke and a passenger: the nun from his recurrent dream.

"You must do whatever your instructor asks," said the nun firmly. "Your mother's life depends on it."

The script had varied, and John found himself arguing with the nun.

"Taking this to a full-stall won't help my mother," he stated abruptly. "You should be telling me to give her the medicine."

Bob seemed oblivious to the nun's presence, and to the conversation she was having with John.

"You must trust me about this," the nun insisted. "More importantly, you must trust God."

"What does the critical angle of attack have to do with my mother's life? My mother *died* years ago."

"You must face your fears. Force yourself beyond the comfort zone."

"How does that save my mother's life?" John asked, indignant.

The nun looked at him sadly, yet compassionately. "I can't tell you anything else. It's for you to discover, and it does no good to supply an answer when you don't even know the correct question." She paused, looking out the round window of the plane, toward the distant light. Then she turned back to face him. "Perhaps I can give you one more clue," she said.

The black robes swished from the rear seat, although the shift in weight did not affect the balance of the tiny aircraft. The nun wedged herself into the narrow space between John Williams and Bob Burke, who still seemed not to see her. Touching John's shoulder, she stated firmly, "Consider what every mother desires for her child, and whom your mother might have sent to love you. And take action."

She was gone, then. Bob Burke turned to face John and ordered firmly, "You just have to do it, John. Quit thinking about it and *do it*."

John pulled back on the yoke abruptly, too abruptly, again. The plane was momentarily suspended, upended in midair. "More throttle!" yelled Bob.

But John was paralyzed. He forgot what he was supposed to do. It felt like an eternity, yet it could not have been more than a second or two.

"Do it *now*, John!" Bob commanded, his hands already gripping the controls.

The left wing tipped down and the plane circled counterclockwise toward the earth. "Now, damn it! *Now!*"

The ground spiraled before them, and even Bob Burke could not regain control of the corkscrewing plane. The final image was of John's mother and Diane Cavanaugh waving from a large alfalfa pasture.

"Ahhhhhh!" he cried, as his legs shot out from the beneath the covers, his eyes popping wide open just before the moment of impact.

John's heart pounded in terror. His breath came in terse pants. Nancy stirred on the other side of the bed, pulling the covers closer.

It was so *real*, John thought. He sat up and glanced at the clock: it read 1:10 AM. Exhaling, he settled back against the pillow, his eyes refusing to close. He was too frightened to fall back to sleep. He was too afraid of the dark of his dreams.

Chapter Twenty

THE REVELATION

Thursday, October 3
6:45 PM

"I don't know, Sandy. Mom seems better, but it's as if she's hiding something. When I asked about her medications, she acted angry, as if I were some stranger nosing into her business."

Sandy Cavanaugh sat back in her chair, not touching her cafe mocha. "What does John think about the syringe?"

Nancy looked up with a wry smile. "John doesn't have an opinion that he'll express. You know, always good in a family crisis," she added, a sarcastic edge to her tone.

Sandy leaned forward, half conspiratorial and half authoritative, placing a manicured hand over the surprisingly untended hands of her younger sister. Smiling, she gently reminded, "John is still a little boy when it comes to this stuff. Be nice to him, the way you would if he were one of our nephews. There are other people who can help us with this."

Nancy withdrew one hand to stir the whipped cream into her cafe mocha, creating a whirl of white on sienna that reminded her of a hurricane on a satellite photograph. It was beginning to feel as if *she* were in the eye of a hurricane, with the news of her mother's terminal cancer representing the first front of gale force winds and torrential rains, and the present seeming more like the false calm before the back end of the storm unleashed its fury.

Fury, she thought, surprised to discover how well the word matched the emotions she struggled to contain. Fury at her husband, for his failure to remain emotionally connected when she needed him most; at herself for needing him, or anyone; at Sandy for her generosity of spirit toward John, when it was Nancy who needed—or at least wanted—the tender loving care.

Or, was Sandy right? Was it John who needed some mothering right now? *No, I need it.* Nancy indulged in self-pity at the loss of her mother's confidence. Why had her mother responded so angrily when Nancy inquired about the syringe? It felt as if her mother had cut her off. It was bad enough to know that cancer was going to steal her mother's life in the near future. She could not bear the thought of losing her mother's close company in the meantime. *And I'm supposed to mother John and understand how difficult this is for him. But who is going to mother me?*

Noting the tears pooling in the corners of Nancy's eyes, Sandy tightened her grip on Nancy's hand. "We can handle this, Nancy," she said firmly. "I know I've been out-of-town a lot the past several weeks. It won't get better until right before Christmas. But we need to talk to Mom. Drink up, and let's go."

Sandy squeezed Nancy's hand in a motherly manner, and then lifted her cup in toast of the plan. The sisters sipped in silence, and then left the cafe for the mild breezes of the Indian summer evening. They parted company at their cars, and with Sandy in the lead, proceeded north on Miami Avenue, and then northeast at Montgomery Road, toward their mother's home.

They arrived to a blaze of lights throughout the townhouse, and two unfamiliar vehicles parked in the closest visitor spots. Sandy was out of her car first, and nodded to Nancy, "Party going on here, or what?"

Nancy merely shrugged, and felt a surge of hope that her mother would be feeling well enough to entertain some friends.

Sandy pounded the doorknocker three times, and then turned the knob of the unlatched door, calling to her mother. "Hi! It's Sandy and Nancy!" Breezing through the entry hall, the sisters rushed to greet their mother, stopping short of the archway into the living room. While Sandy did not recognize the man and woman who sat opposite her mother, Nancy did.

Nancy was startled to see Stu Adler sitting in one of the wing chairs next to the fireplace. "Stu," she said with unmasked surprise. "I didn't expect to see you here." She quickly reached to hug her mother hello, adding a quick kiss to the greeting. "Sandy, this is Stu Adler, one of John's partners. Stu, my sister, Sandy. And you're Marilyn," Nancy said, recalling the vivacious woman who had been here when she last visited. "We didn't have much of a chance to meet when I was here the other day."

Marilyn smiled and nodded in agreement, more subdued than their first encounter. "Nice to see you again, Nancy. And it's nice to meet you, Sandy. I told your sister that it seems like I've come to know all of Diane's children through her collection of family photographs."

Sandy smiled amiably and extended her hand in greeting, first to Marilyn and then to Stu. "Pleased to meet both of you." Turning her attention to her mother, who was lounging on the sofa, an oversized pillow beneath her knees, Sandy offered a gentle but extended hug. "I've missed you, Mom. How're you doing?"

Diane smiled warmly. "I'm doing a lot better since Stu and Marilyn have been here. Don't you agree, Nancy?"

"I have to admit, Mom, you look like you're feeling better," Nancy agreed.

"Well, I am."

Sandy interrupted with a smile that allowed her to be nosy without being offensive. "So are you two responsible for Mom's flight into health?"

Stu nodded. "Nothing like good company to raise the spirits."

"So, what type of treatment is your anesthesia group providing?" Sandy asked. "Or, is this purely a social visit? I didn't realize you knew one another."

There was no immediate reply, and both Sandy and Nancy looked toward their mother expectantly.

Diane, in turn, looked toward Stu, then to Marilyn, as if searching for words. They met her gaze with unspoken permission to tell whatever she wished.

Glancing first at Nancy, but turning to answer Sandy, Diane said, "I'm taking a special treatment, and Stu and Marilyn provide it as volunteers. It's separate from Stu and John's anesthesia practice, and it's a wonderful option for people like me who want to *live* life, instead of being doped up. It's experimental or non-traditional, but Nancy, you've seen how wonderfully it works. Remember when we went to Shelbyville? You couldn't believe my renewed energy. And I felt even better when you said that."

Sandy interrupted, calmly. "What do you mean by *experimental*, Mom?"

"Well, this medication, Limbotryl, has been used safely for other purposes for years. But recently, it's been recognized as a great resource for people with cancer pain, and other debilitating conditions. It isn't something unknown or untested, Sandy. But it isn't *traditional* medicine, and it's outside of the mainstream for many reasons. Insurance formularies, FDA rules, all sorts of things. But it really helps me. You don't have to worry."

Stu rose from the chair, clearly ready to leave. "I'll let you ladies chat with your mother. If you'd like, I'll be happy to answer any questions you have later. For now, Marilyn and I have someone else to visit, to spread our cheer."

He smiled at his little joke, and Sandy smiled in return, from outward appearances a sincere smile. Nancy simply stared.

Marilyn patted Diane's shoulder as she crossed the room to leave. "I'll call you tomorrow, Diane. Enjoy this visit with your girls." To Nancy and Sandy, she reiterated her pleasure at meeting them, and then exited, nodding briefly at Stu as she pulled the door closed.

Stu took a few steps back into the room, appearing to search for the right words. "Nancy," he began simply, "John doesn't know about my volunteer work. Our work is outside of mainstream medicine, as your mother said. We may not have sanction to provide this treatment, but we believe it's the right thing to do. It's the best way I can help people who would otherwise have to choose between *this,* or the way you saw your mother suffering this past summer."

Stu paused briefly, including both of the sisters in an earnest look of appeal, his silence conveying passion for this mission. "It would be best to keep this private. We won't be able to continue our work, otherwise."

Nancy's bewildered expression conveyed her ambivalence at this entreaty. Sandy no longer smiled, but her expression remained stoic, inscrutable.

Stu then looked directly at Nancy, stating firmly, "It would be best to say nothing to John about this treatment. And I hope you will respect your mother's wishes, as well." He then left quietly, with a small wave to Diane.

Why, Nancy wondered, *did his words sound like a threat?*

8:10 PM

Nancy stared at the road, both hands gripping the steering wheel, as if she were fighting gusty crosswinds. The battle, however, was internal. With thoughtful intent, she played out a variety of scenarios, mindful as to how each might affect her mother. Perhaps she would tell John every detail, allowing the pieces to fall as they may. Or, she could say nothing, and do her own research on the treatment her mother wanted so badly. Yet, maybe she should just ask a few pointed questions, without any mention of Stu.

Stu. *That jerk! Who does he think he is?* Her heart quickened in anger at his words of warning, or threat.

She rounded the curves slowly all the way home, wanting to extend the journey so that all possibilities could be considered. As she neared the old bridge on Blome Road, a pair of deer darted from the woods and across the road. A third deer waited, its front leg cocked, poised to flee. Its eyes were reflected as an eerie green glow in the headlights' beam. Nancy had already slowed, in anticipation of the stop sign, and rolled to a gentle stop thirty feet from the cautious creature.

That's how I feel, she thought. *Caught in the headlights, and not sure whether to stay put, advance, or retreat.* She waited, the deer and the headlights in some sort of staring contest, the deer ultimately deciding to dash across the narrow road and into the dark cover of the thicket. Nancy wondered if the deer's courage was some sort of sign that would guide her choice of words when she returned home.

Allowing nearly half a minute to pass before advancing across the one-lane bridge, she released her foot from the brake. Gravity pulled the car onto the bridge and then to the other side. She accelerated only at the far end of the structure, proceeding uphill and around the corner, maintaining a residential pace of twenty-five miles per hour, alert for other deer in the woods that flanked the roadway. There was no traffic, and the four-way stop was a matter of form rather than function at this hour.

Slowing to pull into the long driveway, Nancy noticed that none of the house's exterior lights were illuminated. Although he was working a late call, John should be home by now, and surely he'd have turned on the lights. She frowned, slightly concerned.

Leaves scattered in the cool night breeze, parting the way for Nancy's car along the lane. Swinging the car in a tight arc, she tapped the garage door opener. John's car was indeed there, and Nancy slid beneath the still-opening garage door with scant clearance.

She would play this by the seat of her pants, with due caution, deciding what to tell John and how much to ask based on his response to preliminary questions about this medicine called Limbotryl. Much like the deer, she would not proceed unless there was some assurance of safety, especially for her mother.

After Stu had left, Diane had sternly advised Nancy and Sandy of her intent to continue the treatment. She'd reminded them that the medicine allowed her to be active, to function—for days at a time—as if she were normal. It was her decision alone, and even if the medication *had* risks, Diane would gladly assume them. "I have nothing to lose, and I have so much to gain while it's working at its peak," she'd stated firmly. "Leave the medical decisions to me, and don't do anything that will take this away."

Nancy slowly stretched a leg out of her car, turning back only to grab the wallet purse from the passenger seat. *God, I feel tired.* Touching her forehead, she ruled out the presence of a fever. Maybe she should just go to bed. It was only 8:30 PM, but it felt like midnight. This was no time to pursue a strategic conversation with John. She wasn't up to the challenge mentally or physically.

Relief penetrated her muscles as she decided to delay such a talk. She tapped the button to close the garage door, and pushed through the doorway leading into the back hall. Just beyond, she viewed the kitchen, now littered with newspapers, coloring books, pumpkins, and votive candles.

Looking up from a goopy pile of pumpkin pulp, John Williams smiled and waved a small carving tool in greeting.

"Hi, Captain. How's your mom?"

"Oh, she's looking better tonight," Nancy answered, surprised at how easily the fib slipped from her mouth, as if someone else were speaking. "Sandy must think I'm crazy to have been so worried. Nice art project you've got there, Doc. What's it going to be this year?"

John gently spun the pumpkin to reveal its fearsome jack-o'-lantern face, which resembled the Joker, an arch villain of the "Batman" television series. John collected children's coloring books for inspiration each Halloween. This year, it would be a Batman theme.

Nancy smiled indulgently, as if to a child, her mood shifting in response to the child's play in progress. "You should've been a plastic surgeon—not that I'd let you touch me with one of your little knives, if *that's* the outcome." She stretched her hands across the table, massaging John's head as she brought it closer for a hello kiss.

"I even have a Batman cape and face mask to wear while we pass out treats. You could be Batgirl," he added with a wicked grin.

"I could be Catwoman," Nancy warned, gently scratching John's neck with her longish but cracked, unpainted nails.

"Sure," John agreed cheerfully. "The silhouette is about the same."

"Aha! You selected your theme based on *my* costume."

"No, but I'll keep that in mind for next year."

Nancy chuckled, noting her husband's joyful immersion in this creative project. She knew that he would devote many more evenings to scooping and carving pumpkins, wrapping them gently in freezer paper and storing them in the basement refrigerator until the week of Halloween. While Nancy didn't mind dirt or soil on her hands, she hated the slime of pumpkin guts, and was happy that John enjoyed this return to childhood play. Actually, it was probably because he didn't get enough of such play that he committed himself to the pursuit of Halloween fantasy with such vigor and delight. *He* was the Martha Stewart of Halloween.

Nancy wished they lived in a neighborhood, rather than on this lovely but rural road, so they could enjoy more trick-or-treaters. Each year, John rented a fifteen-by-fifteen foot tent, which the rental company pitched near a small gravel turnabout at the foot of the driveway. Cars toting small children from this remote area of Indian Hill to the Clippinger-Madeira Hills neighborhood could pull up for treats amidst a thematically decorated tent. Nancy usually offered hot, spiced cider for the adults to enjoy, while the children ogled John's frightening decorative arts. His assortment of ghoulishly grotesque collectibles, fake eyeballs and the like, were especially popular with the third-grade male crowd.

This seemed an unlikely time to broach the question of Limbotryl.

Still, as she observed John ease the blade, creating precise incisions through the pumpkin shell, Nancy felt the re-emblazed anger at Stu burn within her stomach. She fanned the flame of—concern? No, it was *fear*, terror that her mother wasn't safe with this mysterious treatment. And that perhaps she had misjudged Stu as trustworthy. If that were the case, then what should she do? What *must* she do?

The bemused pleasure that had lifted her spirits as she walked through the door was now deflated, replaced by a heavy drape of gloom and fatigue. She longed for rest, for answers, for comfort. The urge to call her husband away from his child's play, to provide those answers and comfort so that she could rest, stirred her to cast caution to the devil and overrule her earlier decision *not* to discuss the medication.

"What can you tell me about Limbotryl?" she asked simply.

John looked up, surprised. "It's a narcotic that we use to put people to sleep. Why?"

Nancy collapsed in one of the Windsor chairs, shaking her head both to clear the cobwebs and to gather her thoughts. The commitment to this conversation had been made, and she now regretted it.

"Mom is taking Limbotryl. It's considered experimental or non-traditional for cancer patients, at least that's what she said. But it's allowed her to stay active, like going to Shelbyville. The other pain meds keep her in bed, or at least at home."

Still holding the small carving tool in his raised hand, John blinked and hunched his shoulders, the picture of being caught off guard. "I don't work much with chronic pain, such as cancer pain, so I'm not sure what they're using these days. I'm surprised that your mom likes it. It's a good anesthesia drug, since it has nearly zero incidence of nausea. But the bad part is that it hangs on a while, so people don't wake up as quickly as with Fentanyl or Diprivan. Really, I'm surprised that your mom feels that it helps her keep active, for just that reason."

"Mom says that she sleeps at first, but that she has a lot of energy when she wakes up. Kind of like a rest from all that her body is going through. Or an escape. I'm worried about how safe it is."

John sighed dejectedly as he picked up the collection of carving tools and dropped them into the sink. Flicking on the tap, he gently rubbed the sticky pulp from the small knives, shook off the excess water, and set them on the counter to dry.

Nancy felt the initial prick of irritation surge into anger toward John, who busied himself by cleaning his carving toys, instead of responding to her worry. In a sharp tone, she demanded, "Do you think it's a safe drug for Mom to be taking?"

John looked over his shoulder, ire in his eyes and tone. "We use it every day and it's safe enough for anesthesia, Nancy. I can't say how safe it is for your mom because I don't know the dosage or concentration she's getting. I don't know what other medications she's taking. And I've never even heard of it being used for cancer pain. I'll ask around, if you want, but I can't answer your questions or ease your mind because I don't have all the facts. Okay?"

Nancy's eyes narrowed, angry tears burning in the corners. Her throat tightened to contain a sob. "No, John, it's *not* okay. I don't *have* all the facts to give you. But you could at least make an effort to sound like you care."

"I *do* care," he insisted irritably. "What do you want me to say? Don't let your mother take that medicine because *I* don't know about its use in cancer patients? To be honest, if the medicine is being prescribed even experimentally, it must be fairly safe."

He abruptly broke eye contact, and angrily compressed the newspaper wrapping, filled with pumpkin pulp, jamming it into the trash compactor.

Fighting tears, struggling to remain composed, Nancy attempted to back away from her own hurt before responding. "What I want you to say is that you'll help me *get* the information. I want you to let me *talk* to you about my mom. I want you to hold me, even if you don't say anything at all."

Seeing her husband's uncertain expression, suddenly recognizing him as a very vulnerable, awkward adolescent boy, Nancy burst into tears. She gritted her teeth and clenched her jaw, to keep from screaming, "Grow up!"

Bowing her head in her arms, she shuddered with muffled sobs, furious with John for making her spell it out, furious with herself for wanting and needing his help. And, if she were completely honest, Nancy would have admitted to feeling furious with her mother for trying something unproven, and then asking for complicity in a treatment that might *hasten* her death. It didn't make much sense to worry about addiction potential in the face of death, but anything that would steal time from her mother's life was dangerous, in Nancy's view. *Why couldn't John understand?*

✦

Riled by the confrontation and uncertain about what he should do, John focused on the huddle of tears that sat at the kitchen table. He breathed deeply, arguing with himself about what to do next. He wanted to flee to the safety of his workshop, or the computer in his study, or even the hospital. He knew that Nancy wanted him to console her, but was she so angry that she'd push him away? Why could he not predict her response, after several years of marriage?

Reluctantly, he approached the shuddering figure of his wife, fighting the urge to run to the protective solitude of whichever cave he could get to first. While he wanted to soothe Nancy, he didn't want *to have to* soothe her. He placed his hands on her shoulders, massaging them gently, deciding that she was reacting badly. Intense emotion of any sort was unpleasant, and Nancy's tearful sobs weren't making it easy for him to help. Certainly, *he* hadn't reacted that way when *his* mother had died. And he'd been just a kid.

Was it possible that just going through the motions was enough to produce a heartfelt response, John wondered? Although, initially, he didn't really *feel* loving, by virtue of *acting* in a loving manner, he began to experience a powerful shift in his own emotional state. With every gentle squeeze and stroke, his hands and fingertips on her shoulders, the angry bitterness slid away. He marveled at the phenomenon, which he had never noticed before, and even tried to mentally justify his previous feelings to test the strength of this effect.

He'd lost the momentum, and was unable to conjure the outrage that he'd felt at Nancy's surprising outburst in the midst of his Halloween preparations. *Massage, massage, massage.* He focused on the word that described what he was doing. He began to relax, in turn, and was thus encouraged to sustain the motion.

The effect on Nancy was to ease the shudders, first to an occasional hiccup, then sighs, and eventually, to near somnolence. Without words, John let his hands communicate that it was time to head upstairs. Gentle pressure beneath Nancy's elbows encouraged her to stand. With a faint touch, he guided his wife through the kitchen and family room, to the stairway.

Seventeen slow, heavy steps later, they arrived at their bedroom. Nancy crawled into bed, too exhausted to complete bedtime preparations. By the time John had finished brushing and flossing his teeth, Nancy was asleep, curled into a small "s" on the near side of the bed. Upon rounding the far side of the poster bed, John gingerly lifted the covers and carefully climbed in, so as not to disturb his slumbering wife. The weight of exhaustion descended swiftly, as if he'd hit an air pocket and dropped five hundred feet within the space of a heartbeat.

It was rather an exceptional night, a milestone of sorts. John and Nancy Williams had fallen asleep in the same bed without a goodnight kiss, each curled near the edge of their respective sides. And while they would both sleep soundly, like children who've cried themselves to sleep, they would awaken unrefreshed, the by-product of unfinished business.

Friday, October 4
7:00 AM

Nancy Williams called out the items on the pre-flight checklist. Memory served her well, but policy and procedure mandated that pilots verbally reference the laminated and spiral-bound checklist. The pilot to her left, the Captain—not Arthur—voiced a brisk "check" to each citation.

Although nicknamed "Captain" by her husband, Nancy did not hold that rank as a commercial pilot. She was the First Officer co-pilot on the Boeing 727, traveling today to Atlanta, Orlando, back to Atlanta, and on to Philadelphia, where she would finish the day. With the distraction of work, the cape of leaden gloom lifted from her shoulders, and the torment of circling questions receded.

It was a relief to be away from home, a respite from worries about her mother. While focused on flight operations, Nancy felt less urgency to learn more about this drug, Limbotryl.

The name sounded ominous, like a threat. Limbotryl: it reminded Nancy of the sad little place the nuns referred to as Limbo, where unchristened baby souls resided outside of heaven's gates. Perhaps it sounded awful only to those raised within the Catholic faith of the 1960s—or earlier—to think that God might leave an innocent child outside of the Kingdom. As a schoolgirl, Nancy believed it to be a cruel act of banishment, something a loving God would never do. Was this medication just as capriciously cruel? What cost might be extracted of those who sought the miracle of Limbotryl's grace?

How easily she gravitated back to the worries, once the pre-flight checklist had been completed. Nancy sharply refocused on the next set of tasks. She steered her thoughts far from those that haunted her mind whenever she was home.

Her heart felt lighter with the benefit of challenging work. Geographic distance protected her from all reminders that another shoe was about to fall. And while her primary concern was her mother, she wondered if it mattered that, for the first time, she did not miss her husband at all.

Monday, October 7
6:30 PM

"Nancy, this is Mom's way of including us," Sandy Cavanaugh said abruptly. "If you don't want to come in, don't. But you're the one who's been so insistent on getting information about this treatment."

Nancy Williams sighed, exasperated. "Yes, but I want unbiased information. I'm not sure I can trust Stu and Jeannie Adler to give me the straight story."

"Fine. I'm going in." Sandy pushed the front door open and slid inside, shutting the door a bit harder than necessary.

"Is that you, Nancy?" queried Diane Cavanaugh.

"No, Mom, it's me," Sandy responded, bristling. She crossed through the entry foyer and proceeded to the living room.

"What's wrong?" Diane asked.

"Nancy isn't coming, Mom. She's having a hard time with this approach, and she's worried about how this treatment will affect you."

Diane frowned and snorted with disbelief. "Nancy knows how this treatment affects me! She's seen for herself how much more I can do when I've had it."

The door creaked open, and Nancy's footsteps tapped along the entryway tile. Another heavier pair followed, and the murmur of Stu Adler's voice resonated in baritone timbre.

Nancy entered the room first, the plush rose carpet silencing her footsteps, her face flushed, as if caught behaving naughtily. Distress and tension creased the corners of her mouth and wrinkled her forehead.

"Nancy," Diane greeted with worried hesitancy, "I'm glad you decided to come. Hello to you too, Stu."

"Hello, Diane," Stu greeted in return, taking a seat on the floral-upholstered Queen Anne chair, across from the sofa on which Diane reclined. "Nancy and I were just talking about how many things you're able to enjoy and accomplish these days."

"Yes," Diane agreed, "I *am* doing a lot more, Stu, and that's exactly what we need to discuss." Diane swung her legs around and planted them firmly on the carpet. "I want for all of us to talk about this treatment, and how it helps me to *live*." She looked from Stu to Sandy and Nancy, directing her comments forcefully. "Girls, I really feel *normal* with this treatment. And I want you to understand how important it is to me to do something normal in my life. Cancer is not normal. You know how it was for your dad, before he died. I wish *he'd* had this option. God knows he prayed for something like it, if not a cure. What can you possibly have against something that helps me this much?" she implored, sad eyes turned toward her youngest daughter.

Before Nancy could respond, a brisk, cheery voice fired a greeting from the front door. "Halloo!" With an accompanying door-slam, the staccato of thin-heeled pumps clicked along the floor, announcing another visitor.

"Here you are!" Vigorous as a stiff autumn wind, Jeannie Adler breezed into the room. She offered nods of greeting accompanied by naming each person in turn, granting brief eye contact to everyone in the room. She then turned to Diane, effectively dismissing the presence of all others. "Now, what's this about?" Jeannie demanded, the hint of a smile softening her brusque words.

"Nancy and Sandy would like to ask you some questions about this medicine I'm taking," replied Diane.

"Of course I can answer their questions," Jeannie stated firmly, with a dismissive wave of her hand. "But I thought there was really something wrong, Diane, when you called and said that both Stu and I needed to come. So, it's second thoughts in the family, or perhaps Doubting Thomases? Well, fire away!"

Sandy and Nancy exchanged glances, and then turned toward their mother to gauge *her* reaction to Jeannie. In turn, Diane's brow arched in surprise, then furrowed in mild irritation, but she said nothing. Stu bowed his head and sighed deeply, stroking the textured, silky fabric of his chair. Meanwhile, Jeannie looked expectantly toward Nancy and Sandy.

"How long can my mother take this medication and still benefit from it?" Nancy blurted.

Jeannie nodded. "You're asking about drug tolerance. It depends on the person, Nancy. It depends on how much medication the person needs, how often it's taken, and the duration of the course of treatment. Next question."

"Nancy was asking about *our mother*, specifically," Sandy interrupted.

Jeannie looked at Diane, as if evaluating how to answer this tougher question. "I don't know. Diane, it's like I told you at the beginning. We can do this repeatedly for months, even years, for some people. With those who have untreatable cancer, we can often go for a year. Some of our patients say that they believe this treatment has prolonged their lives, because they feel so *normal* for extended periods of time. It's as if the body fools itself into believing it's actually healthy."

Diane nodded in recollection.

Jeannie raised her eyebrows in question, a silent "Next?" directed toward Sandy and Nancy. Stu sighed heavily, again. Diane closed her eyes briefly, and sighed as well.

"What is the worst thing that can happen to my mother if she continues this medication?" Sandy inquired softly.

Jeannie nodded approvingly. "The worst thing is that it will no longer work. Your mother will become tolerant, and she will no longer enjoy protracted periods of normal activity. At that point, she'll have to resort to what we offer as standard medical treatment for untreatable cancer—yes, I'll tell you exactly what," Jeannie stated, raising her hand to still what she anticipated to be the next question. "It's Morphine. A great painkiller, but an s-o-b medicine that leaves people in a fog, imprisons them in their beds, constipates them to the point of bowel obstruction, and totally diminishes their ability to participate in life."

The last part of the sentence was more of a pleading croak, and tears pooled at the rims of Jeannie's eyes. "That's why I *do* this," she proclaimed, almost angrily. "I couldn't do it for my own parents, but I *can* do it for other people. Are you two so selfish that you won't allow your mother to enjoy a higher quality of life—"

"Jeannie!" The word was spoken in unison, a sharp reprimand by both Stu Adler and Diane Cavanaugh.

As if dashed with ice water, Jeannie shook her head. "I'm sorry," she said hoarsely, her voice a contrite whisper. "I should be used to this. I didn't mean to accuse you. I hope you'll forgive my bad behavior." With a lopsided smile, the uncharacteristic threat of tears returning, she placed her hand tenderly on her husband's shoulder. "Stu usually handles this part of what we do. He's much better at it. Please, just ask Stu. Whatever questions you have, he can answer."

✦

Stu Adler patted his wife's hand gently, lovingly, genuinely moved by her heartfelt penitence. This was not classic Jeannie Adler, bearing tears and apologies for her words and deeds. Stu knew that she must have been thinking of their daughter, Joy. It was about *her, Joy,* whom Jeannie felt most responsible, not her parents. He brought his wife's hand to his lips and kissed it, letting it go as she pulled away and left the room, the staccato of her footsteps followed by the muted thump and click of the front door.

A mournful silence descended. Even Stu Adler was at a loss for words, a swollen ache in his throat and heart.

Diane spoke first. "Stu, it'll be all right. Jeannie isn't herself today."

Stu nodded. "No, she's not. Thank you for understanding that, Diane. It's more than either of us should ask."

After a moment, collecting his thoughts, Stu leveled his gaze at Sandy and Nancy, the latter looking shell-shocked. "You and John didn't know us when our daughter, Joy, was alive," he said to Nancy. "Joy had Multiple Sclerosis and related health problems that progressed more rapidly than anyone expected. There wasn't Betaseron or Avonex back then." He paused, sighed again deeply, to still the thump of pain that made his heart feel as if it were bleeding to death. "But Joy didn't die of MS or its consequences. She committed suicide because she wanted a break from her body."

Nancy gasped in surprise, while Sandy lowered her eyes and shook her head sadly. "I'm so sorry," Sandy whispered.

Stu nodded appreciatively, pausing again to regain an emotional foothold, his eyes and nose prickling as he held back tears. Telling the story of Joy, and his failure, had not become easier, with time. He took a deep breath and cleared his throat before continuing.

"That's what we offer to people like your mother: a vacation from their bodies. "It's a risk, of course, because it's outside the realm of traditional medical practice, and I'm referring both to treatment and ethics. It's a greater risk because of the way we work. We require absolute confidentiality. I can't just write a prescription for your mother. The pharmacies don't dispense this drug. It's a surgical anesthetic. The idea is not just to treat pain, but to break the *cycle* of pain."

"And how do you do that?" Sandy asked softly.

Stu met her eyes. "By making them sleep. Deeply. For a long time, fourteen to twenty-four hours, depending on how severely debilitated they are."

"And how does this help?"

"We think that it stimulates endorphin production during REM sleep, unlike other surgical anesthetics, and that the endorphins trigger what appears to be temporary remission. We don't know for sure," Stu admitted. "But Jeannie and I decided that *knowing why* it worked was less important than *doing it,* if it could save a life."

"But Stu," Sandy continued, her modulated tone soothing against the grit of her words, "some lives cannot be saved."

Stu nodded his head with a small, sad smile. "That's true, Sandy. However, every life, if taken by God, rather than by one's own will, is a life—no, a soul—saved."

✦

"She's slept all day! Doesn't that worry you?" the mother asked, piqued.

"Not particularly," the father answered breezily. "What do you expect? We've been to the other side of the world and back. It's jet lag. If I had the option, I'd sleep until next year. She's just tired."

The woman abandoned the subject, for now. She would evaluate their daughter later.

When later arrived, the young woman awakened with cheerfulness and a steady gait.

"Look, Mom!" she called animatedly. "I don't even need my cane after all that beauty sleep!"

The mother smiled at her daughter, pleased to hear the joy in her voice and see the confidence in her steps. Perhaps the trip to Australia had worked some magic. Belated magic, she mused. The holistic healer they'd visited "down under" offered herbs and incantations, but the girl had not responded. In fact, she'd collapsed in bed, exhausted, her limbs alternately numb and burning with pain. Her blurred vision skewed images, as if she existed in a horror house, its trick mirrors creating nauseating vertigo.

This journey had been planned as a vacation extraordinaire, not a healing pilgrimage. Still, both parents had read separate articles about an Aboriginal shaman, proclaimed to be a miracle-worker. Perhaps, they'd agreed, the vacation could be extended to include a trek by Jeep to the outback home of this mysterious healer. To the despair of all three, the shaman's miracles eluded the young woman.

Until now, her mother thought, watching her adult child raid the refrigerator. Why now, the mother wondered?

Days later, the pattern of eighteen hours of sleep and only six waking hours began to concern the father. "She should be over the jet lag by now," he stated quietly.

His wife nodded agreement. "But she's better. Don't you agree?"

"Yes."

"Why should she be better? She isn't taking as much medication as before we left on vacation. Why now?"

The father had no answers, and neither parent would discuss it with their daughter, for superstitious reasons. If called to her attention, perhaps the daughter's condition would regress.

"Have you noticed," she asked her parents cheerily, "I'm not awake very much, but I'm in great shape, compared to before."

Her parents murmured agreement, exchanging glances uncertainly.

"What's the matter with you two?" the daughter asked, put off by her parents' reticence. "It's a lot better than feeling miserable sixteen hours a day, and sleeping for eight. So what if I've reversed the sleep-to-wake ratio?"

Nothing at all, her parents reassured.

At a quiet moment late that night, when neither parent could sleep, the mother articulated a question that circled within the father's mind, as well. "Do you think that she's right, that a reversed sleep-to-wake ratio might have caused this flight into health?"

"I've wondered about that, myself. I don't know. I can do a Medline search and see if there's anything in the literature about that."

"What if you could just anesthetize people who are ill, and let them sleep for most of the day? Would they heal?"

"Anesthesia doesn't give people that kind of sleep. It isn't REM or delta sleep. It's more like suspended animation."

"But, what if there were a drug out there, perhaps used for something else, but one that could take you through the sleep cycle. Maybe it's a matter of taking people through multiple sleep cycles." The mother paused, wracking her memory for the source of her next idea. *"I can't remember where I read this, but healing takes place during REM sleep. The body releases endorphins during REM sleep. Maybe there's a drug that could increase that part of the sleep cycle."*

She sat up abruptly, impassioned by a flood of possibilities that streamed through her mind. Each idea seemed a treasure in its own right, and as she sifted through the handfuls of jewels, she forced herself to pick up one gem at a time, calmly. Otherwise, they would evaporate from sight. *"If there is such a drug, maybe it could help with more than just MS. Perhaps it could treat chronic pain, cancer pain, and other diseases. It might not treat the disease itself, but it might offer a better quality of life, even if it was lived in six-hour increments. Right?"*

"I see where you're going," her husband assured, his wife's passion contagious. *"You said it before. The connection might be REM sleep."* He flung back the covers and motioned to his wife to follow him, the "A-Ha" of an idea germinating restlessly. He would check a reference book in the study, just to be certain.

"What is it?" the wife asked, breathless, her tone impelling the husband to spell it out. Quickly.

"We have a drug that produces REM sleep. When it was studied, EEGs showed that the drug created a brainwave pattern that's identical to REM sleep. It's the only drug we know of that does it."

"What is it, already?" the mother demanded.

The father whispered as he confirmed the reference. *"Limbotryl."*

7:30 PM

Stu left Diane's home forty-five minutes later, having shared his philosophy of—and justification for—the treatment. Sandy and Nancy had helped their mother into bed, and departed shortly thereafter, agreeing to meet at Ferrari's for a glass of wine and to discuss . . . *everything.*

Now, Nancy shook her head in disbelief, pondering the newly revealed facts that completed the drug diversion puzzle. *Stu is the one who's taking the narcotics. And Ron nearly took the fall!* The impact of this knowledge tumbled the wall of preconceptions about the men in her husband's practice, leaving Nancy dazed and incredulous within the rubble of this truth.

"I can't believe what we just heard," Nancy whispered.

"But did you understand what he was telling us?" asked Sandy gently. "This is his mission of mercy, and it's his way of making amends."

"Yes, but it isn't his mission that I have a problem with," Nancy replied, rubbing a knot of tension that throbbed in her neck.

"You know, Nancy, there are some things that we don't get to decide. We don't get to choose Mom's medical treatment. We only get to choose how we respond to Mom's decisions."

"But, Sandy, there is so much more to this than you realize. John's group has been investigating drug diversions for months, and one of his partners nearly took the fall for what Stu has been doing. I don't have all the details figured out yet, but do you realize that Mom could get in as much trouble as Stu or Jeannie? At this point, *that's* what bothers me most. Now that I understand about the treatment, I *like* the idea that Mom might live longer if she takes it. It makes sense to me that she could. But the risks . . . ."

Sandy Cavanaugh sipped her Chardonnay thoughtfully. She then set down the glass, rubbing lipstick from its rim. She permitted Nancy to think aloud. It was clear, in Sandy's opinion. The only person who could make this decision was her mother. The legal questions could be dealt with if and when they arose. Meanwhile, there was no reason to believe that any of the patients Stu and Jeannie Adler treated would risk their freedom to live more fully by informing legal authorities. The possibility that one of those patients might be a respected legal authority did not even cross Sandy's mind.

Indeed, she marveled at her sister's muddled thinking about this situation. Nancy was typically clear-headed, willing to search out the facts before drawing conclusions. Sandy wondered, *Is John's response to Mom's illness exacting a greater toll on Nancy than I've realized?* She debated exploring that path, saying nothing as Nancy continued to reason aloud.

"John would be appalled if he knew what Stu and Jeannie were doing," Nancy stated bluntly.

"What would he do if he knew?" Sandy tested.

"Since it's Mom who's involved, I don't know. I think he'd feel obligated to take a stand on it with Stu, but I don't know whether he'd do anything else. It's so strange, I feel like I don't even know John well enough to predict what he'd do."

Nancy averted her eyes from Sandy's keen gaze. She paused then, her expression pained, hesitant. "We're having some problems," Nancy admitted. "I feel like he's withdrawing, the way he did when Dad was sick. He seems to think that I expect too much of him. Quite frankly, I don't know if what I expect is too much or not. Is it wrong, or horribly *dependent,* to want your husband to offer a little moral support?"

Sandy tilted her head and raised her eyebrows, an expression of her own uncertainty regarding that question.

Nancy rolled her eyes and repeated Sandy's advice from days ago. "I know, I know. I should be nice to John, and understand that Mom's illness has brought all his demons to the surface. I should look to other people for support."

Sandy frowned. "I don't think I said *that.*"

"What?"

"The part about you looking to other people for support. I said that there were other people who could help us with information about Mom's treatment," Sandy clarified. "I'm probably the worst person to ask about whether or not it's in the spousal job description to offer moral support. It seems like the decent thing to do, but in this case, I think you have to do whatever's necessary to take care of yourself, Nancy. If you can't go to John without getting hurt and disappointed, quit asking him to do what he can't. And find someone who *can* offer you moral support. *I'll* try to offer you moral support."

Nancy blinked back tears. With a self-deprecating grin, she added, "*I'll* try not to be so needy. I don't know what's wrong with me, but it feels like everything is wrong. With Mom, with John, with work . . . ."

"What's with work?" Sandy inquired, her interest piqued by such a revelation.

"Oh, it isn't anything specific," Nancy stated slowly, as if just beginning to gather her thoughts about this aspect of life, too. "It's still fun, I like the people I'm working with, but it just seems like something is missing. I've never felt that way about my work."

Sandy shrugged. "Maybe it's just part of this whole phenomena of Mom being sick and John trying to distance himself from another grief."

"You know what gets me," Nancy said quietly, "and it's back to the subject of Mom's treatment. Stu and Jeannie Adler lost a *child*. They are doing this to give people an option their daughter didn't have, and they're risking a lot to do it."

Sandy nodded, unclear about what, exactly, Nancy meant, but certain that it was important.

"There is nothing that will bring back their daughter, and yet they risk so much for other people. I don't know that I could love *anyone* that much," Nancy finished.

"And no one is asking you to," Sandy assured.

Nancy nodded agreement. Yet, intuitively, she sensed that Sandy was wrong.

Chapter Twenty–One

TEMPTING FATE

Tuesday, October 8
11:45 AM

John Williams flipped through the stat sheets generated by the computerized record keeping system. The first page documented a patient code, the amounts of narcotics requested, utilized, and verified for disposal, and the anesthesia code. In the latter code, the initials MD preceded the code number for anesthesiologists, and RN preceded the code number for nurse anesthetists.

The information was succinct, lacking red flags that might herald drug diversion. John expected nothing else, otherwise Dave Johnson or Doug Howard would have convened a meeting before the report was distributed. The amount requested less the amount utilized equaled the amount returned for disposal, without exception.

So, what bothered him? Something seemed too—what? Tidy?

He scanned the Demerol again. Next, Fentanyl. And then, Limbotryl. Finally Sufentanil. The math was right, but there was a consistency that bothered him. The narcotic amount requested was the same as the narcotic amount utilized, but only for Limbotryl, and only for—John double-checked—the same MD code.

He peeled back the last page, which referenced the codes by

name. MD03 was Dr. Stuart Adler. Sighing as he folded back the pages, John immediately discounted the information as insignificant. Stu was a respected colleague, and just because he never skimped on the Limbotryl . . . well, that was no grounds for indictment.

Taking a fat, cushion-gripped pen from his lab coat pocket, John circled the number MD03. He placed dots next to all the other MD03 lines, and then worked the data from right to left: first identifying the physician, then the amounts of narcotic returned, utilized, and requested. In every instance, the arithmetic was accurate. Yet, for Stu's cases only, and for Limbotryl alone, there was no remnant to be returned to the Pharmacy for verified disposal—ever. *How could that be?* John almost always had unused Limbotryl at the end of a case.

Stu was outspoken and vigilant about his concern that patients receive adequate anesthesia, and he'd been incensed when the national news featured an anesthesiologist who was convicted of under-medicating patients to feed his Fentanyl addiction.

Addiction was not an issue, with regard to Limbotryl. Druggies liked rapid-onset narcotics, such as Fentanyl. Limbotryl was a good anesthesia drug, but it hung around in the body longer than substance-abusing health care professionals could afford; it would cost them performance. Stu wasn't diverting Limbotryl for any addiction.

Perhaps Stu erred on the side of caution; perhaps that's why his patients received all the Limbotryl requested.

Still, John wondered, why didn't the pattern hold for any of the other narcotics? And why did Stu request additional Limbotryl more than the other docs?

That's the problem, he thought, the idea cloudy in his head. There was something here, but he could not discern what it was, or what it could possibly mean.

2:00 PM

The nagging heaviness that besieged his gut begged for relief. Dr. Stuart Adler fumbled clumsily in both lab coat pockets, his fingers refusing to cooperate, despite their typical dexterity. The roll of antacids was gone. *Damn!* He cursed the timing. Today, of all days, was not the day he wanted to fight this blessed heartburn. He shouldn't have eaten the three-way chili for lunch. *Damn-it all!*

His irritation mounted, as well as the pain, like the flame rising from a blowtorch. With the flame in ascendance, the painful, burning pressure in his gut radiated through his chest, left shoulder, arm, and fingertips. He clutched his left arm with his right, gasping at the sudden burst of fire within, as if some remote device had touched off an explosion. *Lord, help me! Somebody help me!*

Surely he was screaming the words. He wondered, *Why is no one responding?*

Yet, he had not uttered a sound, save the brief gasp that accompanied the flaming, crushing pain. Two women passed, their backs to him, as he crumpled slowly to the ground, his mouth open in a silent grimace of agony.

He was having a heart attack, he was now certain. *Why didn't I figure it out sooner?* The air grew close, the hallway dimmed, and a cluster of white-clothed people rushed at him from all sides before darkness descended with an iron fist.

4:30 PM

"There's a complication, Diane, and I won't be able to give you a treatment today," Marilyn said reticently. "Stu had a heart attack. He's in the hospital, stable for now. Jeannie says the cardiologist will have more information in a couple days, but he's expected to make a full recovery.

"The problem is, our supply is low, so I can't give you another treatment for a while. I'm making arrangements for more, but it'll take weeks until we have as much as we need. Meanwhile, we'll just stretch out the interval between treatments." Marilyn's voice cracked, and she bowed her head. "I'm so sorry, Diane!" Her furrowed brow and glistening eyes spoke volumes of helpless, apologetic sadness.

Diane Cavanaugh heard the tightness in Marilyn's voice as fear, and perhaps anxiety, that the brave man she admired and worked for might die. Compelled to comfort the distressed woman, Diane shook her head, chin tilted up to convey determination to make the best of the situation. "I'll be fine, Marilyn," she assured.

Marilyn sighed. "It seems the clients are the ones offering reassurance, today. I appreciate that, Diane. But you need to know where we stand, in terms of your treatments. What I can offer may not keep you as active as before, but it should offer some reserves. I have prescriptions for a narcotic pain reliever, and you should take it as soon as you feel the pain coming on. Don't wait until it hits full force or you won't get good enough relief. Do you have any questions?"

No. Diane shook her head slightly, a sympathetic smile raising the corners of her lips.

Marilyn nodded, attempting a smile as well. She was grateful to Ron for sharing his supply. He was the only one Marilyn could think of to call. Jeannie was tied up with Stu's health crisis; she could not be expected to do anything else. For now, Ron was checking with others who might be able to sell enough to sustain the Adlers' patients. However, the network was small. Marilyn prayed that the overseas connection Ron mentioned would respond quickly.

6:30 PM

"Why can't they get more of the medication?" Nancy asked, plopping next to her mother on the sofa.

Diane winced, feeling the impact as if *she* were the sofa. She knew it was time to take a pain pill. This was what it felt like at the start of the pain cycle, the prodromal effects. "I don't know. Maybe it's because . . . . I just don't know, Nancy," Diane finished lamely.

She felt exhausted. The pressure grew to nips of pain. "I need to take a pain pill. Would you mind getting me a glass of water and some crackers? It's easier on my stomach if I have something in it, before I take a pill."

"Sure," Nancy agreed, jumping up enthusiastically, pleased that her mother was asking for help. "Maybe John can do something about it. I wonder if the hospital is short?"

"Well, don't say anything about this to him," Diane called toward the kitchen, a stern warning in her tone. "We agreed not to mention this, Nancy. Remember?"

"I know, I know." Nancy opened and closed a pair of cupboard doors, quickly retrieving the salted soda crackers and the water glass on the counter. "You've done so well with the medicine, Mom. I just thought—well, never mind."

7:30 PM

Sandy had just arrived, and Nancy reiterated her suggestion.

"No. I won't let you do that," declared Diane.

"She's right," agreed Sandy. "If we say anything, if we even hint about it, your husband becomes an accomplice."

"But he could help. He'd want to help," Nancy pleaded.

"He'd want to help, and he'd be afraid to help," Sandy argued. "It's a terrible bind to put him in, and I can't believe you'd do that to him."

"Look at Mom, and tell me that we *shouldn't* do something. And Mom, if it were me, you'd pull every string and bend every rule, taking a chance that maybe, sometimes, it's okay to do the wrong thing for the right reason."

"But it's *not* you, Nancy," Diane stated firmly. "It's me, and the relationship is different."

"You are family, Mom."

"By marriage, not blood," Diane reminded.

"Mom is right, Nancy. If John were asked to do this for you, it would still be a tough decision, but he'd have such a personal stake in preserving your quality of life—"

"You're forgetting that John and I are related by marriage, not blood, too. I disagree with you, Sandy. He would do this. I'd bet on it. It would be his chance to do for our mother what he couldn't do for his mother."

Sandy shook her head impatiently. "You don't appreciate what you're asking, Nancy. And I can't believe you see yourself as *less* related to John because it's by marriage rather than blood."

"I didn't say that!" Nancy corrected tersely.

"You implied it."

"Stop it! Both of you." Diane had heard enough. How long had it been since she'd had to issue that command to stop the squabbling? Fifteen years? Twenty years? The words belonged to another time, eons ago. She was a younger woman then, and she'd been healthy, up to the challenge of battling children. Not now, not now. It would be easier to simply fall asleep and never wake up. Yet, she couldn't sleep for the pain. Even with the narcotics, which she'd taken an hour ago, she didn't rest well. Still, narcotic pain relievers were better than nothing.

"I'm sorry, Mom," Sandy said softly. "We'll let you sleep. Can I get you anything?" ·

Diane shook her head, her eyes already closed, her fingers curled around the edge of the blanket, hugging it to her chest, praying that the drug would numb the pain and lead her into a deep, peaceful slumber.

Nancy looked first at her mother, and then at her sister. Both wore tight expressions that creased their foreheads and locked their jaws. They might have been twins, as alike in their stubborn demeanor as in their single-minded pursuit of the circle of silence. It had been promised, a condition of ongoing treatment.

Nancy had promised, too. Yet, with Stu and Jeannie tied up with their own life-or-death drama, didn't that change the picture? Wasn't it reasonable to explore other options? Isn't that what Stu and Jeannie had done for their daughter? Wouldn't any daughter do the same for her mother?

·

Wednesday, October 9
6:30 PM

Nancy flipped the pages of the travel magazine, willing her mother to wake up and need something. She was on vacation the rest of this week and next, yet the glossy photographs of purple and white Alpine mountains, azure Caribbean seas, and sassy red hibiscus gardens failed to touch her spirit of adventure. She slapped the slick periodical onto the bedside table, sighing with restless boredom. She needed to *do* something.

If only John were already part of this secret! If only there were no secrets. Secrets were dangerous, she believed. Perhaps that was the best reason to divulge them. Take away the power of the secret by revealing it; get off the perilous, slippery slope on which one treads, precariously and vigilantly.

Secrets also created estrangement, and the last thing Nancy wanted was to intensify the distance she already felt from John. She must convince her mother to include John in the circle, or they must abandon the circle. Those were the only choices, and the latter was not an option—her mother must have these treatments. It might permit her to live long enough for the next miracle drug, the cure. Her mother must live.

7:20 PM

Diane Cavanaugh stirred slightly beneath the blankets, a soft moan drifting from her lips. The barest movement sent shrieks of lightning pain through her limbs and spine.

Nancy was there, hovering. *Why won't she just go home?* Nancy was saying something, but her words were thick, and they echoed hollowly, as if replayed on a tape at slow speed. Diane closed her eyes, uncomprehending. *Nancy should articulate more clearly,* Diane scolded silently. But she wondered if it was Nancy or the medication that created this warped, underwater conversation.

Of course, it was not a conversation at all, for Nancy did all the talking. Diane blinked and nodded, as if in response, but truly, she could not make out the words. It was as if she floated beneath the ocean, the depths of water obscuring the particular words, so that all she heard were sounds.

Time elapsed without meaning. Had Nancy been talking for a minute or an hour? Diane did not know. She could not make her way to the surface. She forced herself to blink and nod, if only to assure Nancy that she was all right.

"All right, Mom." Nancy smoothed her mother's sheet and blankets, gently tucking them around her shoulders and arms, an embrace of swaddling warmth. "I'll get more towels from the dryer, and I'll tell Sandy what you've decided."

For Diane, only the last phrase rang clear, a momentary surfacing from the ocean depths. *What?* Diane wondered, *What have I decided?*

✦

Whether attributable to angels or serendipity, events conspired to delay bringing John Williams into the circle of silence. Sandy had been called in to pick up negotiations in San Francisco, after a colleague was hospitalized with severe food poisoning. In the meantime, Marilyn had negotiated for a special visit from the other Magi. Two days later, Diane was strong enough to get out of bed. By the weekend, when Sandy returned from California, Diane was moving about the townhouse, not quite energetic, but pain-free, and euphoric with the results.

Saturday, October 12
12:50 AM

Sandy Cavanaugh kicked three newspapers and a basket of mail to the side of the front door of her historic condominium, creating a path in which to maneuver her wheeled luggage. Once through the tall entryway, she tapped the heavy, paneled door with her heel, closing it a bit too loudly for this time of night. The walls shuddered at the resounding thud. Sandy winced, both in fear that the plaster walls would send forth showers of chips and powder, and in apology to anyone who may have been disturbed.

What a trip! She'd managed to settle the negotiations during the past few days in triathlon fashion, both in terms of time required and ground covered; her workdays had lasted seventeen and a half hours. It was good to be home.

Her colleague, Ed, remained hospitalized with something other than food poisoning, but she was off the hook—for now. The vice president had warned that she may need to pick up several of Ed's consultations, and hinted that he might have an illness serious enough to keep him out of commission for months. Sandy's initial reaction was concern for Ed and his family of eight, three of whom attended pricey universities. He was too good a negotiator to lose for several months, and Sandy offered a silent prayer that his health would be restored.

Her secondary reaction to the boss's news was a silent groan of agony, as Sandy realized that covering Ed's consults would nearly double her travel between now and Christmas. If she'd had the energy, she would have cursed.

Instead, she stood the luggage upright in the entryway, and entered the small study to the right. The old wooden floorboards creaked beneath her feet. Sandy imagined them as old women, rheumatic and plaintive in greeting her return. Atop the walnut desk, the answering machine light blinked to indicate several messages.

Ah! I didn't even call in for messages! I hope Mom's all right.

With the tap of a button, the machine spouted an offer to clean her chimney, a reminder to vote for Issue 3, whatever that was, and updates on her mother from Nancy.

The latter messages, while generally positive, disturbed Sandy. "Hi, Sandy. It's me. If you're picking up messages, call me. Mom has decided to talk with John. Marilyn arranged a treatment for Mom—called in a bunch of favors, I guess. Anyway, let's touch base before we take Mom's groceries over on Saturday. Okay? Bye."

Beep.

"It's me, again. Sorry. It's Thursday, and Mom is feeling better. Don't call her until you talk to me, please! I hope you get this message before you're home. Bye."

Beep.

"Sandy, it's Nancy. It's Friday evening, and I guess you aren't home yet. At any rate, remember to call me before you talk to Mom. If you get in late tonight, leave a message on our machine. We can pick you up to get Mom's groceries around nine o'clock, if that's okay with you. Call me first!"

Beep.

It was neither okay with Sandy, nor comprehensible, in light of what her mother had said about this issue on Tuesday. How could her mother have changed her mind? *Why* should her mother have changed her mind? She lifted the phone, hit autodial, and tapped her nails against the receiver, as if to speed the connection. What should she say? She glanced at the phone, noting that it was nearly 1:00 AM in Cincinnati; she was still on California time. She clicked off the phone just before it rang.

Forget calling tonight, she thought decisively. It was already Saturday. In several hours, she would visit her mother, and find out for herself.

9:30 AM

As planned, Nancy and John picked up Sandy at nine o'clock, and they proceeded to the local farmer's market. The list of produce and grocery items had been divided among the three of them, and they separated to shop more efficiently. As Sandy rounded the first aisle, Nancy was waiting, her cart empty.

"Did you get my messages?" Nancy asked urgently.

"Yes. I didn't pick up any while I was gone. Sorry about that."

"No problem. I'm just glad we're *doing* something."

"Hmmmmm," Sandy murmured, concentrating on the selection of Jonathan and McIntosh apples stacked in gleaming military precision. She would not permit Nancy to bait her into a discussion until after Sandy had spoken with their mother.

Nancy set down the potatoes cradled in her arms, staring with disbelief at her sister. "Aren't you thrilled that Mom was able to get a treatment, and that she's willing to explore other sources for the medication?" Nancy set the potatoes in her cart, crossed her arms, and tilted her head, waiting for Sandy's response.

Sandy continued to study the apples, as if one might be more perfect than another. She noted Nancy's insistent posture, with a sidelong glance, but refused to meet her sister's stare. "I'm looking forward to seeing Mom. I'm glad she's feeling better today. Is John getting the chicken soup and beef bouillon?"

Nancy frowned. "Did I say or do something to offend you, Sandy?"

Sandy looked up, meeting Nancy's challenge directly, eye-to-eye. "No. I'm sorry if I seem distracted. I'm tired. And I'm really surprised about Mom's change of heart. I just need to see her, and find out for myself what she's thinking. And I could use about twenty-four hours of sleep."

Nancy smiled then. "I'll bet you could've slept all day. Maybe John and I should've just done the shopping and let you sleep."

"Well, this won't take long," Sandy demurred, "and I want to see Mom anyway."

"I'll hustle John with his list, and meet you at the checkout lane," Nancy offered.

Sandy watched as Nancy turned with a grin and jogged over to the soup and cracker aisle. She marveled at her sister's display of assurance. Did Nancy really believe that Sandy would agree to include John in the circle of care? Had Nancy forgotten her vow of secrecy?

Meanwhile, Nancy collected chicken broth and soda crackers, confident that the morning would unfold according to her plan, and grateful that her sister had no subversive notion to undermine this strategic opportunity. Everything was under control.

10:45 AM

They had just dropped off a sack of fresh produce from the farmer's market, and Diane returned the kindness by offering either mulled cider or coffee to her two daughters and son-in-law.

"Coffee!" All three chimed in unison, breaking into laughter at their unanimous caffeine craving.

Moving slowly, deliberately, but independently, Diane gathered three mugs and filled each with freshly brewed coffee. In her own mug, she poured half a cup of hot cider. Coffee left a bitter residue in her mouth these days, and she'd given up the habit in favor of mulled cider or very weak blackberry tea. She arranged all four mugs on a tray. Then, she added spoons, napkins, and a plate of sugar cookies decorated with candy corn. She was stalling, and knew it. Still, she puttered with a small carton of milk from the fridge, slowly pouring a quarter of it into a creamer.

She'd been surprised, at first, when Nancy had outlined her plan. Where did Nancy ever get the idea that Diane wanted John to get the medication? *Was I so out of it that I told her so?* Perhaps. The medication she'd taken—not the treatment, but the narcotics that left her dull, foggy, leaden—might have caused her to forget such a conversation. Nancy had been adamant: Diane had agreed to bring in John, and it was the only way for Diane to get the treatments often enough.

It would have been so much better if the out-of-towner, who provided the last round of treatment, could continue to help. Diane smiled as she recalled Marilyn's pale-faced shock when Nancy had greeted the man by name. The secret enterprise, complete with inauthentic names to protect the guilty saviors, had been compromised. Yet, Marilyn had discerned immediately that neither Diane nor Nancy, who had greeted the man with a vivacious hug, would jeopardize the miracle this man extended at such grave, personal risk.

Diane wondered how she could ask John to do the same. Yet, if she didn't, short of uprooting from this community, and relocating in the middle of the next state, what sort of life was left?

Diane shook her head, still uncertain. *No more stalling,* she insisted silently. She took the tray firmly in two hands, steeled for whatever came next.

11:00 AM

"Ah, here she is with the coffee," called Nancy cheerfully. "Mom, I can't believe how much better you seem today."

"Thanks, I do feel better."

Nancy continued. "John, remember how I was telling you about how weak Mom was on Tuesday? How she just moaned and couldn't get comfortable in bed, even with the Morphine? Well, look at her today!"

John lifted his mug of coffee, looking slightly embarrassed to be put on the spot. "Here's to you, Diane, and to more good days like this."

Sandy was quiet, but smiled as she lifted her mug.

"John," Nancy continued, "Mom has the opportunity to continue with a treatment that offers her a better quality of life than what she gets with Morphine or other big gun narcotics."

A slight chill of panic swept through Diane, as she watched her younger daughter sustain the lead in this drama. That's what it felt like, too: A drama, a performance, an improvisation. Diane knew that at least one person had not been cued: John. And what about Sandy? Had Nancy assigned Sandy's lines, too? Would Sandy be willing to speak them? *Am I willing to speak the ones Nancy has scripted for me?*

No, Diane decided, as she intentionally tipped her mug, spilling the amber liquid onto the cream tablecloth. "Oh, we'll need to clean that up right away," she said firmly.

Sandy dashed to the kitchen for paper towels, and helped her mother sop up the cider.

"Nancy, will you help me get this cloth into the wash tub to soak?" Diane asked.

"Sure, but just let me finish. This treatment is cutting edge—"

"John," Diane interrupted, "Jim and I were always private

people when it came to our health. Although I am happy to have the opportunity to still be active, there's no reason you need to know all the gory details of my treatments. Actually, there's nothing gory about the treatment, itself," Diane added, feeling as if she were chattering nonsensically. "It's nothing more than an injection every so often." Turning to Nancy, Diane gazed with steely intent at her daughter, as if to say, *Let me handle this.*

Nancy returned her mother's stare. This wasn't the script they'd agreed to.

While Sandy silently cheered her mother, Nancy blushed crimson in a medley of confusion, embarrassment, and anger that her mother would suddenly shift gears without speaking to her first.

John looked from Nancy to Diane, and then to Sandy, his bewilderment apparent. None of the women would meet his gaze. He had no idea what was going on, neither the plot nor the lines.

Diane rescued him gracefully. "Let's not talk about sickness and treatments while I'm obviously feeling so well. It's such a nice morning, so let's just visit a bit over some more coffee. John, would you mind tossing this cloth into the laundry closet for me?"

"Be glad to," John affirmed with relief.

"I'll get more coffee." Diane rose to get the carafe from the kitchen, leaving her daughters in a tense silence.

"Sandy," Nancy hissed. "Did you talk to Mom first?"

Sandy looked coolly into her sister's accusatory eyes. "No, I did not. But I think Mom is right, and if she wants to keep this her own private business, I'm going to respect that."

Diane and John returned to the dining room, and silence descended until Diane finished pouring coffee. Had the drama concluded, Diane wondered, or was this merely Act I?

Chapter Twenty–Two

BLOOD IS THICKER

Thursday, October 17
4:00 PM

"Mom, you need to reconsider. Why do you insist on accepting two good days, one mediocre day, and four days of misery? Especially when there's an alternative!" Nancy spoke sharply, frustrated. "Please, let me talk to John."

"No. Sandy agrees," Diane whispered hoarsely.

"Sandy isn't being realistic, Mom. I can't understand why you two can't get it through your heads that suffering like this is unnecessary! There is no reason in the world not to at least give John the benefit of the doubt. Is it possible that you don't think John is compassionate enough to help? Is that what this is about? You don't believe he cares enough to bend the rules?"

Diane heard the fear in her daughter's voice, and remembered the two-year-old child who'd raced to her parents' bedroom and clambered onto their bed, terrified of the "noisy crackers," her word for thunder or firecrackers, which boomed from the heavens. The same emotional tone, fear before tears, loomed now.

"Nancy, I trust John," Diane assured. "But this is about more than bending rules. You know that." The effort to speak exhausted Diane, and she fought to stay on top of the water, not to sink below, into the depths of Morphine seas.

"Mom," Nancy stated thickly, blinking her eyes rapidly, "If you really trust John, then you'll let me ask. Just ask him. Please, let me."

What are my options, Lord? Diane forced herself to stretch out her hand, to reach Nancy physically, for her child needed reassurance. But what could she say? Hadn't she explained her position? Or, was she wrong? Was this a sign that should be heeded? Diane recalled the story of a man who arrived at Heaven's Gate, furious that his faith in God hadn't saved him from a treacherous flood. God responded, "When you were up on that roof, who do you think sent the boat and the helicopter?" *Am I declining the lifeboat or the rescue helicopter, if I don't ask John for help?*

It was nearly impossible to think. Pain gnawed at her bones, and the Morphine swallowed her whole. Perhaps Nancy was right, and this was the only option. *I can't think straight. It's easier to say yes than to try to think, or to fight. If I don't give up, perhaps it's time to give in . . . .*

"All right."

Nancy leaned forward, as if she hadn't heard right. "What, Mom?"

"I said it's all right. Ask John. Tired now. Tired." Diane's hand drooped in Nancy's palm. Ceding to the effects of the narcotic cocktail, Diane closed her eyes, falling slowly, languorously, into the depths of the sea. It was a relief to surrender. *Please, God, send me an angel. Grant me relief, or release . . . Amen.*

Sunday, October 20
2:30 PM

Although Diane had voiced second thoughts about her decision, once she'd received another treatment on Saturday, her tone had been ambivalent. Attuned to the ambivalence, Nancy had insisted on bringing John into their circle, reminding her mother about what she stood to lose without the miracle drug. In turn, Diane had gently reminded Nancy that to involve John was to put him in a difficult position, and that she did not want John to feel as if he had to *choose.*

Earlier in the day, after driving her mother to Mass, Sandy had insisted that Nancy come over to discuss this plan. Sandy could scarcely believe what had been negotiated between her mother and sister just days ago. She'd agreed with Diane, and encouraged Nancy to allow the treatments to proceed without John's awareness, allowing him to see Diane only when she was ostensibly healthy—the good days. Nancy had argued that it wasn't realistic, and that John was old enough to face real life. She'd confronted Sandy, as she had confronted her mother, regarding the issue of trust. In the end, worn by Nancy's persistence and determination, Diane and Sandy had shared a tentative glance and a sigh of resignation.

"What do you want, Mom?" Sandy now inquired gently.

Pausing only momentarily, Diane restated her doubts about the plan, but agreed to it. "Perhaps we should just ask. It's a lot to ask. But perhaps Nancy is right . . . ."

Nancy believed that it would be best if John could see Diane in high gear, both to overcome John's natural skepticism, and to convince him that the end justified the means. As Nancy set forth her plan in detail, her mother and sister irritably questioned every aspect, their doubts shouting from behind their actual words.

Nancy answered every question and doubt with confidence, determined to implement The Plan. Ultimately, a dinner date at Diane's home was set for the following Sunday, the week of Halloween.

Sunday, October 27
7:00 PM

Dinner at Diane Cavanaugh's was typically casual-elegant fare, never fussy, and always delicious. Tonight was no exception. She had prepared a hearty sausage-zucchini soup, homemade corn muffins, fresh Caesar salad with anchovy dressing, made from scratch, and a chocolate-almond torte for dessert. Far from appearing exhausted by the effort, Diane exuded joyful energy. To her family, she appeared well, possibly healed. Surely, such glowing health denied the existence of untreatable cancer.

They were finishing dessert when Nancy slid her glass dessert plate toward the center of the dining room table, pronouncing, "Mom, that was delicious."

"It certainly was, Diane," John echoed, with an appreciative smile to Diane.

"John," Nancy began, "Mom has the chance to receive a set of treatments that will allow her to continue to do everything she has been. I wanted you to see for yourself how beneficial they've been."

Diane gave an embarrassed cough, but smiled at John and Nancy. She then glanced at Sandy, who was tracing a design in the melted chocolate left on her dessert plate, her face going taut beneath her mother's gaze. In that moment, Diane knew she had made a terrible mistake, allowing Nancy to use this as some sort of show-and-tell format to convince John that he should support the treatment. And Sandy knew it, too, Diane discerned. That's why Sandy could not bear to look up from her plate. How could she stop this, now?

✦

Nancy continued her well-rehearsed presentation, her eyes focused on John. "With this treatment, Mom gets great pain-relief, without the side-effects of most narcotics. Stu Adler is even helping us. At least he *was*, before his heart attack."

John turned to face Nancy, who was seated at his right. "What's Stu doing?" he asked, incredulous.

"He provides the medication for the treatment," Nancy explained.

"Through the home healthcare business that he and Jeannie run?"

"Yes," Nancy replied, licking her lips, nervously aware of her husband's puzzled attention. She didn't dare look at either Sandy or her mother, or she would not be able to continue. Sensing her mother and sister's disapproval, Nancy steeled her nerves with a deep breath. They would see how right she was about this, she knew, once John had a chance to digest the information. While Stu recovered from his heart attack, John would administer the injections, and Diane would be able to enjoy all of her traditional holiday plans.

"Anyway," Nancy went on, "I was thinking that you could do this until Stu is back on his feet. You could give Mom the injections. It wouldn't take long, and it would allow Mom to enjoy Thanksgiving."

"Can't one of Jeannie's nurses give you the injection, Diane?" John asked innocently.

Nancy watched as her mother stared hard at John, as if keenly evaluating her son-in-law. Diane answered his question simply. "No, John. This is a very private, secret part of Stu and Jeannie's business. And I am asking you to keep this confidential."

"I'm confused," John acknowledged. "Why all the secrecy?"

Nancy intercepted her mother's look, which silently offered to explain the situation, if Nancy preferred.

But Nancy did *not* prefer that. She knew how to approach her husband, and she did not want her mother to paint a picture of criminal treachery. The good here definitely outweighed the bad, and it was crucial to emphasize the positive attributes of this treatment.

Nancy elected to start with the outcome, then allude to the process. "John, there is a way for people who have terrible illnesses or chronic conditions to have a better life, if they take this treatment. It offers a type of remission, and there are a lot of people in this town who are living more fully—able to work, to play golf and tennis, to take care of their families, and to seem *normal*—because they take this medicine. You would want me to take it, if I needed it, wouldn't you?" Nancy did not pause, aware of John's discomfort, sensing his fear of a trap regardless of his response.

"Of course you would," Nancy answered for him. "It's really a wonderful thing, but it isn't approved for this type of use, yet. You can see for yourself how much of a difference it makes for Mom. It's probably only a matter of time before this becomes the gold standard of treatment for a variety of illnesses, but we can't wait for the FDA and the managed care folks to pull it together. Mom needs it now, and it would help if you could give it to her."

John broke eye contact with his wife and turned to his mother-in-law, surprised at Sandy's silence throughout this exchange, and understanding it as a no-confidence vote for either he or Nancy. He could not tell whom. "Diane," he said uncertainly, "I don't know what this medicine is, but I'm guessing that it's Limbotryl. Nancy asked me about it, and I've never heard of it being used for treating cancer pain or any other condition. Is that the medication we're talking about?"

"Yes," Diane answered.

"I can't prescribe it for you, Diane," John stated. "It isn't a drug that's used, to my knowledge, outside of the operating room. How does Stu manage that?"

Diane took a deep breath, and raised her hand to Nancy, who was poised to answer first. "John, it's Stu's private supply. I don't know where he gets it, and I really don't care. But I feel terrible that I've allowed you to be dragged into this discussion. Nancy, you made some compelling arguments to get me to agree to this, but I believe it was a bad decision. Now, you are in a horrible position, John, and it's completely unnecessary. I'm sorry, John, for involving you. I wish we'd simply enjoyed our dinner and conversation." Diane stood and began to clear the dessert plates from the table.

"Mom!" Nancy exploded. "You haven't even given John a chance."

"He shouldn't *have* to be given a chance, Nancy," her mother rebuked. "It means now that he also has to *take* a chance. If you don't understand the kind of dilemma this must be for John, then I can't explain it to you."

"Diane, I may not be able to help with *this* treatment," John stated, "but I could certainly recommend some options that we've heard about from the chronic pain people. It's a branch of anesthesiology, and it includes other professionals. Like psychologists, occupational therapists, massage therapists—"

Diane interrupted briskly, but with a smile that conveyed appreciation of John's effort. "I don't need a psychologist or a massage. I have a bad disease, and I've made my decision about how I'll live the rest of my life."

Her next remarks were addressed to Nancy. "I will never forgive myself for allowing this conversation. It was a bad idea, and I feel responsible for jeopardizing the future of these treatments by bringing John into it. I wish I'd respected my intuition, Nancy. I wish I hadn't allowed you to convince me of what I knew was wrong."

"But, Mom," Nancy pleaded, "John still has to hear all the benefits. When he does, he won't feel any differently than I do about this being the right thing to do."

John stared at his wife, incredulous. "Do you really believe that, Nancy?"

"Of course I do," she said confidently. "You just need time to get the facts about what the treatment is, and how dramatically it improves not just Mom's life, but the lives of people who have Multiple Sclerosis, Rheumatoid Arthritis, Chronic Fatigue Syndrome, and God only knows what else, but *lots* of diseases. John, don't you see how it's just a matter of time before it becomes standard treatment? Doesn't the fact that it *works* make a difference? And it isn't *you* who is on the line. It's Stu. He's the one providing the medicine, not you. You'd just be administering it. If we hadn't told you the *name* of the medicine, would that make a difference? If you thought it was Demerol, would it be a no-brainer?"

John's mouth was compressed in a tight line, and his cheek muscles twitched as he clenched his jaw. He looked from Nancy to Sandy, who had quietly observed the unfolding discussion. "Where do you stand on this, Sandy?"

Sandy met his eyes with clear determination, obviously having settled her conscience long before. "John, I believe that my mother is capable of making her own decisions about treatment. I support whatever she decides, and *I* can damn well give her the medication, myself. That's where I stand on this. And I agree with Mom that it was wrong to involve you. I am *very* sorry about that."

"Sandy!" Nancy exclaimed in irritation. "How can you *say* that? You and Mom make it seem like I railroaded you into this terrible idea, and that you feel that some terrible injustice has been done to John as a result. John is a big boy, and he has enough life experience to understand that sometimes decisions are complicated. What you do for family sometimes takes decisions out of the realm of yes and no, right and wrong. When it comes to someone you love, you move out of the simple truth about black and white, and into those shades of gray. John knows that. You just don't give him enough credit. He hasn't *said* that he won't help. But for godssake don't push him away without letting him say where *he* stands on this issue."

"Maybe I should answer that, Nancy," John said softly, an edge of warning in his tone. "I stand to lose a *lot* if I'm involved in this. If I don't report Stu Adler, I'm essentially an accessory to whatever crime he's committing by giving this treatment to patients." He read the shift in Nancy's expression: she was appalled by her husband's words. He guessed that she would have phrased it as betrayal, and one did not betray family, especially since they were the only family John had. Yet the doubt on his wife's face posed the silent question: "Or, would he?"

John continued. "I understand your loyalty to your mom, Nancy—"

"Obviously, you *don't*," Nancy declared angrily. "And it appears that Sandy doesn't, either. But what's important to me, right now, is what you intend to do about this. Do you feel compelled to report Stu? Do you realize that it will end my mother's treatment? And the treatment of many other people who have benefited from Stu and Jeannie's courage to *risk* it all, for people they don't even know? Did you know that their daughter, Joy, committed suicide because she didn't have this option, and that they do this *for free,* in her memory, so that others can be spared such desperation?"

"Can I say something?" John asked impatiently, furious that

his wife had orchestrated this entire evening with its hidden agenda, embittered that she didn't have enough confidence in him to discuss it privately. Or, had that been what she was trying to do the night he was carving the pumpkins? "All I want to say, is that I will do anything I can, *within the law,* to help your mother."

To Diane, he said, "I will look into research protocols for you. If NIH is researching this drug for use outside the OR, I'll see what I can do to get you into the study, even if we have to stretch the truth a little. But, I *cannot* give you this 'treatment,' Diane. I just *can't.* I'm sincerely sorry. If that makes me the bad guy here, then that's the way it is. But this is *not* disloyalty to you, Diane. And it's not disloyalty to you, either, Nancy."

John turned to his wife, intending to take her hand as a gesture of comfort, despite the fact that he was pissed as hell about her tactics. He *did* understand the desperation she felt about protecting her mother's well being. If he'd been able to, he would've done so for his own mother. But a twelve-year-old boy doesn't have the same moral and ethical obligations as a physician.

He reached to take Nancy's hand, and was stung with surprise when she slapped it away.

"Don't tell *me* that this isn't disloyalty," Nancy snapped. "I don't know you anymore. You don't want anything to do with family loyalty unless it's in good times. You are a fair-weather friend to this family, John Williams. You do what you have to. But I pray to God that you don't feel some urge of conscience to trade your family for the seven pieces of silver that your Code of Ethics amounts to."

"Well, I don't think I have to *choose*, Nancy," John said, his voice terse, anger at the boiling point. "I won't be reporting Stu, at least not for now. But I resent the way you set me up tonight, and I'm not going to discuss this with you here. We can talk about it at home."

Nancy Williams stood, staring at her husband intently, then marched to the front door of her mother's condo. John Williams went to follow, but diverted to the kitchen, where Sandy and

Diane were washing the dishes. He hadn't even noticed them leave the dining room table.

"I'm sorry," he said softly. "It was really a wonderful dinner, Diane. And, I'm really sorry."

"Thank you, John," Diane said, smiling sadly as she rinsed the last of the dishes. "*I* am more sorry than I'll ever be able to tell you."

John nodded, unsure of what else to say. He waved farewells to both Diane and Sandy, who appeared to be crying as she loaded the dishwasher.

He ducked back into the hallway, and walked to the front door, where Nancy waited with her arms crossed defiantly. "Let's finish this at home," John stated firmly, opening the front door and pausing on the walkway for Nancy to join him.

"You're the only one leaving, John," Nancy stated with calm fury. "I'll be home to pack a bag tomorrow. We have nothing else to discuss."

Bam! The door slammed with a shudder in his face, packing a forceful blast of air that punched him like a fist.

✦

"So. You refuse to do it." It was a statement, not a question. The mother stood in front of the teak swirl that served as her desk, arms crossed in a position of defiance.

"I can't get it without stealing!" the father shouted. It was odd hearing his voice elevated. Such was not their custom; it was not his custom, especially.

"Order it from the manufacturer. Create a phantom study—or maybe it won't be a phantom study. We'll run it from the business. This is for our daughter, for godssake!"

Monday, October 28
1:00 AM

John Williams snapped the tab on the pop can, unaware that he had been sitting in the dark kitchen for nearly five hours, the meal at Diane's like a last supper. Dread, loss, failure, and defeat lurched in the pit of his stomach.

Had he screwed up his entire life by voicing his opposition to the plan? Actually, he told himself, he hadn't directly opposed the plan, but wanted Nancy and Diane to consider other avenues. There were so many serious consequences of their plan, negative consequences.

John reflected that Diane had been right, when she'd told Nancy that it was a mistake to ask her husband's opinion. Diane had the benefit of her nearly religious conviction that this was the right thing to do, so there was no shade of gray for her. This was the best plan for her. She would not spend the rest of her life in a narcotic-induced haze when she could enjoy short "vacations" from her body, followed by a pause in illness that felt like remission because of the normalcy of activity, appetite, and sleep.

Diane's words formed the only rebuke John had ever witnessed his mother-in-law deliver. They stung, especially since one layer beneath the rebuke of Nancy's plan was the wordless accusation that John had let her down; and that she'd expected it. Or was he misreading his mother-in-law? Did Diane truly believe that it was wrong to bring him into the secret circle? If that were the case, he hadn't let down anyone. Although Nancy would argue the point.

The scene had been ugly. Nancy had told John—furiously, through the door—to leave her mother's condo. Then, she'd punctuated the order with the declaration that she'd be back, but only to pack a bag.

Obviously, John decided, Nancy could endure her mother's rebuke. Blood *is* thicker than water, he reminded himself. What Nancy could not endure was his refusal to consider that, sometimes, it's acceptable to do the wrong thing for the right reason.

He pondered that moral question, taking a long swig of cola, and belching with a blend of satisfaction and self-disgust at his choice to release it, unrestrained. He asked himself what conditions might encourage him to break the law, legal, moral, or otherwise.

In the end, there were no clear answers. He wondered what he'd do if it were *his* mother. *Don't go there,* a voice in his head commanded. Perhaps, he considered, Nancy was working under the faulty assumption that because *she* had struggled with the moral and ethical dilemma, and because of *her* conclusion that she could support the course of treatment, her physician-husband would accept and support it, as well. *But, how could she think that?* He could not fathom Nancy's reasoning.

He also could not fathom her behavior, from orchestrating this dinner meeting to refusing to return home. *She'll come back,* he reassured himself. *Nancy will come home.* The thought of asking Nancy to come home did not cross his mind. From the beginning of his relationship with her—and all preceding girlfriends— John declined to be the pursuer, but chose to be the pursued. He would not inflict himself on anyone; he would wait for an invitation. If Nancy needed space for a while, fine. He would not interfere.

Swigging the last ounce of pop, John headed upstairs. Unconsciously, he counted the steps to the second floor, and from the landing to the bathroom. There, he brushed the sickeningly sweet cola from his teeth and breath, and then climbed into bed, descending into sleep quickly.

His dreams that night tortured him with boredom. He was about twelve, sitting—waiting, waiting, *waiting*—in a meadow resplendent with tall, golden stalks of wheat-like grass that swayed in the breeze. Boredom shifted to pain, the waiting like a punishment, an undeserved timeout, until he was rescued by the vision of a nun from his boyhood days at Madonna of the Hills School.

"Where are you supposed to be, young man?" the nun asked sharply, assuming that he should not be sitting in the field, bored and thinking of nothing.

When John failed to find his voice, the nun bent down to look him in the eye. Her veil flowed gracefully from a heavily starched wimple, and fluttered in the breeze. She smiled then, suddenly more like an angel or a bride than a nun, and said, "Maybe this is where you'll need to *be* for a while."

Then, the nun's face became his mother's face, but only for a second. When he awakened, it was with the sense that there was something important he must do. Yet, he could not recall *what it was* that seemed so urgent. The images and the urgency haunted him off and on throughout the day.

10:00 AM

Nancy returned home, well after John had left for work. Steeling herself against sentimentality, she gathered clothes from the highboy and stacked them in a large leather suitcase. She marched purposefully to the closet, where she gathered four pair of shoes, one of each color: navy, brown, black, and red. As an afterthought, she grabbed her cross trainers, as well. She carried the unwieldy stack of ready-to-topple shoes back to her bed and dumped them onto the comforter, stuffing socks into each pair before loading them into a smaller leather suitcase.

She then returned to the bathroom. Opening the lowest drawer of the former sideboard, she tugged several gallon-size freezer bags from a box, and proceeded to unload the mirrored medicine cabinet. She then tossed the collection of cosmetics, toiletries, and sundry incidentals into the sturdy, seal-able bags.

Satisfied that she had what she needed, Nancy exited the bathroom and crossed to the cedar chest, selecting several versatile sweaters that could be mixed and matched with jeans or leggings, which she had already packed.

Forcing her mind to remain focused on the task, Nancy refused to look at the room with anything but a practical eye: packing essentials only. She did not look at the photographs above the fireplace mantle, or the wedding album on the window seat, or the antique prisms suspended before a small, circular window in the bathroom. Anything remotely associated with John or their marriage must be viewed with a wall of dispassion, nothing more than an object in the room. She would not be distracted by feelings today.

Walking back into the closet, Nancy lifted her uniforms from the rack and carried them to the bed. *The* bed, Nancy thought, not *my* bed; not *our* bed.

She unzipped a leather and tweed suit bag, and deftly swung the hangered uniforms into one side, gently tucking the rest into place before re-zipping the bag. She unsnapped a shoe compartment, and crossed back to the closet to get her work shoes, comfortably ugly oxfords that completed the pilot uniform.

With another snap and a zip, the job was done, and Nancy began the first of several trips to haul the luggage downstairs and into her small Honda. It would all fit, of course, and Nancy marveled at how little she truly wanted or needed at this point. She wanted no reminders of John, whom she deemed incapable of loving beyond the "good times" of the marriage vow.

Refusing to look further, Nancy slammed the trunk shut. She did not remember that the indoor plants needed water, or that her favorite outfit was still in the laundry bin. If she remembered that, she would remember other things, and then she would not follow through with what she felt she *must do.*

Thursday, October 31
7:00 PM

John Williams whistled the Charlie Brown theme song as he lifted the heavy, putrid, trash compactor bag from the steel housing. He'd been home for an hour, and the scent of rotting pumpkin guts had assailed his nostrils the second he'd crossed the threshold. Without the malodorous physical reminder of last week's final frenzy of pumpkin carving, this might have been the Halloween that didn't happen.

When pulling into the lane earlier, he hadn't registered the fact that the local party supply crew had pitched the tent at the end of the driveway, as scheduled. It was only the olfactory assault that had reminded him that the Williams' roadside tent of horrors remained dark, abandoned.

John had scrambled to slice open twenty bags of Snickers, Three Musketeers, and Milky Way candy bars, dumping the booty into a trio of black, plastic caldrons. He'd then trucked the candy caldrons, loaded inside Nancy's garden cart, to the end of the lane. Finally, he had unloaded the dozen carved and wrapped pumpkins from the basement refrigerator, and made a second trip with the garden cart to the tent. There, each pumpkin had been unwrapped and illuminated with a votive candle. The candlelight and the soft glow of a camping lantern were all that announced and illuminated candy offerings for Trick-or-Treaters.

It was a half-hearted Halloween attempt, much less than his usual extravaganza of the grotesque, but John comforted himself with the two-pronged philosophy of "Better Late than Never" and "Something is better than nothing." He nibbled a Snickers candy bar, searching for comfort via a chocolate-induced endorphin surge. Television ads for "It's the Great Pumpkin, Charlie Brown!" precipitated more whistling. John recalled Nancy's hip-wiggling dance, triggered whenever she heard the tune.

Nancy. He put up a wall against the thought. It was enough to tend to the business of rotten pumpkin innards, hauling out the trash—moving the scent of decay from the kitchen to the garage—and creating a bit of Halloween for the kids who'd come to expect fearsome entertainment at the Williams' tent.

An hour later, with trick-or-treat officially over and the chores completed, John collapsed on the leather sofa, exhausted by work, depressed by solitude, abandonment. He watched as Charlie Brown explained, optimistically as ever, how the Great Pumpkin would rise over the pumpkin patch . . . .

How can anyone be so optimistic?

He reached to the counter and tapped the answering machine's "play" button, a necessary distraction in the face of the unanswerable question about optimism, only to be greeted by optimism personified.

"Hi, Cousin John! It's Mary Claire. Remember me? The one who always got us into trouble? Well, I'm comin' in from St. Louie for 'A Christmas Carol,' and I'll come haunt you like the ghost of Christmas past if you don't come to a performance. Nancy, too. I'm about dyin' for Skyline chili and Graeter's ice cream. Can you believe I haven't tasted the stuff in nearly seven years? God, we're gettin' old. It's been too long, Cousin John. Call me back soon at . . . ."

John smiled as he recalled his fireball cousin, the one with the golden curls and peach complexion, who looked like an angel, and acted like an imp. Mischievous humor marked her a hellion, but her guile and cherubic features left her unscathed by the nuns, and admired by peers who'd watched her stir up trouble, and survive without a blush. Now an actress who performed in regional theatre throughout the Midwest, Mary Claire had given her strict and stoic parents—John's maternal aunt and uncle—plenty of reason to pray for her soul.

" . . . Now, don't forget to look at your calendar!" Mary Claire called cheerfully from the machine.

Beep. "Hello, John. This is Stu Adler . . . ."

John's heart skipped a beat as the second message began.

"I'm out of the hospital. Got out today. There's no permanent damage to the heart muscle. They'll watch me like a hawk, and I'm not supposed to drive, but the medication I'm on seems to agree with me. And it's important to talk privately, soon. Anyway, I'd like to come over tomorrow, say late morning. There's something we should talk about—work related—so if you're free, I'd appreciate the chance to interrupt your post-second call day off. You don't have to call me back unless you're busy tomorrow. I'll just plan on seeing you, otherwise." Beep.

Stu Adler. Bile crept up John's esophagus, burning like a torch. What did *he* want, of all people? *He's done enough damage to my family!* John breathed deeply, exhaling the fiery rage that the last message rekindled.

If the man hadn't just had a heart attack, John would phone the bastard right now, give him an earful about ethical practice, and inform Jeannie—who'd probably answer the phone, control freak that she was—of Stu's intent to drive against doctor's orders. And that's just where he'd *start* with that woman . . . .

John glanced at the television, where hearts of passion filled the screen, and Sally swooned at the prospect of spending an evening in the pumpkin patch with Linus. Angrily, he pointed the remote control at the set and snapped the off button. Love wasn't like that, he knew. Love wasn't even based on faith. He'd learned early in life that it wasn't a good idea to count on anybody, much less someone you couldn't see, or something as ethereal as the Great Pumpkin.

It was best to count on only himself.

Chapter Twenty–Three

SAINT OR SATAN?

Friday, November 1
5:00 AM

John Williams rolled up in bed and massaged his temples in an effort to still the jackhammer pounding of his conscience. Kicking off the covers, he slid out of bed, and muttered a wish that he were simply nursing a hangover. Anticipating confrontation was much worse. Yet, he felt compelled to do it. A part of him was eager for it, especially when the guilty party had asked for it.

He trudged eighteen steps to the bathroom, where the cool marble chilled his feet. He flipped on the ventilation switch and crossed to the shower, setting the lever to hot and letting the water run until it steamed. He pulled the string of his pajama slacks, allowing them to fall to his ankles in a heap. He then stepped out of the puddle of clothing and into the steam, numb to the jets of water that sought to sting him awake.

Reaching for his razor, John rehearsed what he would say later today at the confrontation. He tried several approaches, none of which felt right. He wished that someone else would write his lines, or prepare his script.

Curiously, he realized, he'd never considered *not* confronting the person who had crossed the line. In his mind, that was not an option.

He'd contemplated sharing his hunch with Dave Johnson. Not too long ago, he would have taken the clear course: tell all and let the Drug Diversion cops intervene. Yet, now, the people involved included both family and a respected colleague and friend. Worse yet, two of them were in fragile health.

John did not want the responsibility for ruining not only a career, but also what would amount to several persons' lives. Still, there was the moral and ethical imperative to report what he suspected. *Act decisively,* he coached silently, guiding the razor gently across his jaw. *The law is clear. There is no alternative.* The razor glided smoothly over his chin, and then a bubble of blood reflected in the mirror. *Damn it!* There had been no resistance to hint at a nick, but the blood was proof enough.

He rinsed the blood from his chin, and with quick, brisk strokes, pulled the razor over his right cheek and jaw. Deliberate care hadn't prevented a nick; he'd simply get the job done, imperfect a shave as it was.

As for the confrontation a few hours hence, he would tread lightly. Stu had been discharged from the hospital only yesterday, and John had no interest in precipitating anyone's heart failure.

Why the hell does he want to see me? Why did he ask for this meeting?

9:30 AM

In the far corner of the garage, John daubed the intricately carved mantle with a turpentine-soaked sponge brush. Lifting the brush momentarily, he watched the paint bubble, recoil, and peel itself from the antique walnut. The chemical reaction was mesmerizing.

A moment later, he refocused his attention to clearing the peeled paint with a soft cloth. Each swipe of the festering paint yielded great satisfaction. Like wiping the slate clean, revealing what was hidden beneath the surface.

That's what he hoped would happen this morning.

The gentle hum of an approaching car signaled that perhaps

it would happen soon. The car engine idled briefly, and then cut off all together. The slam of a door and purposeful footsteps concluded this prelude that announced Stu Adler's presence.

"Morning, John," he greeted with reserved cheer.

John set down the cloth and nodded to his partner in return. "Stu. Glad to hear you're out of the hospital."

"Yes. Thanks."

"You must be feeling okay, to drive I mean."

"Yes, well, what the cardiologist doesn't know won't hurt him." Stu paused, studying John's refinishing project intently. "Nice mantle you've got there. Did it come from the Wooden Nickel?"

"Actually, we found it at a place in Chicago called Salvage One. Lots of pre-demolition treasures there." John wiped his hands on a moist diaper wipe, twisted the cap onto the turpentine can, and re-wiped his hands.

"If you're at a good stopping point," Stu said casually, "I thought we might take a drive. There's someone I'd like you to meet."

"I can stop now," John agreed hesitantly. "What do you have in mind?"

"An acquaintance of mine said she wanted to talk with you." The query as to whether or not John would come remained unspoken.

John considered this, aware that to refuse would require him to directly confront this partner and friend, who had just suffered a mild heart attack; had just been released from the hospital; had been restricted from driving, and yet believed that this meeting was important enough to disregard not only the cardiologist's orders, but those of his fierce wife.

John remained silent, still contemplating a course of action as he tidied the workspace in the garage. Stu appeared content to study the carved griffins that bracketed each end of the old mantle, relaxed in the manner of a man who is unafraid to acknowledge breaking a rule in favor of a principle. It bothered John, this apparent presumption by Stu that the morality of his mission superseded the law. Indeed, this perceived arrogance served to stir the still hot embers of John's anger, and he launched the offensive, heedless of Stu's heart trouble.

"I'm not interested in meeting any of your outpatients, Stu, if that's what you have in mind."

Stu looked up, apparently surprised to hear the acrimony in his partner's voice. "You presume to judge me without the benefit of hearing my case? You were certainly hard on Dave Johnson when he did that to Ron." Stu sustained eye contact in challenge.

"The difference is," John responded quickly, "I'm not an investigator charged with keeping the hospital's patients safe, and your motive is to influence me so that I don't inform Dave Johnson of my suspicions."

Stu nodded in agreement, "I see your point, and you're right about my motives. If you can look Nancy's mother in the eye and tell her that you don't want her to have the best cancer pain relief with the fewest number of side-effects . . . ."

John felt as if he'd been socked in the stomach. Stu knew that John and Nancy had argued about this very issue: her mother's treatment and comfort. And Nancy had taken a private matter to one of John's colleagues. His shock was mixed with a sense of betrayal that Nancy would not only lie by omission, preceding the dinner at Diane's house, but that she would then take it back to the perpetrator of this moral dilemma was beyond comprehension.

Stu read John's mind with uncanny accuracy. "Don't blame Nancy for doing what any child would for her mother. She tries to serve two masters, her love for her mother and her love for you. The conflict requires her to choose between helping her mother to live, and her wish to protect you from having to compromise your ideals." Stu clearly wanted to say more, but instead remained silent.

John's adrenaline surged, blood throbbing hotly in his chest, temples, and fingertips. "I'd never let Nancy's mother suffer," he snapped. "And you're resorting to cheap shots to suggest that I would."

Stu shook his head impatiently. "John, you'd never let her

suffer, but would you be willing to risk your livelihood so that she can be pain-free without side effects that limit her freedom?"

"What are you saying, Stu? That Limbotryl is the only way to control pain without side effects? That's garbage and you know it. And if it's true, then any physician could, and should, prescribe it for every cancer patient who needs it."

"And what if it's not on the formulary for non-surgical use, John? What if we know, anecdotally, that this is the best medicine we can offer. But the insurance companies say they won't pay for it? Morphine is a cheaper drug, and corporate giants don't care that it leaves you living in a fog, not to mention all its other side effects. Your mother-in-law might be able to come up with the cash to pay for more expensive pain relief. But there are lots of people who can't. And even those who *can* afford it don't get good pain-relief without side effects. Those are the people I help."

Stu appeared to realize that he was losing this battle, and that John would need to be approached more gently. He spoke softly, apologetically, and pleadingly. "I regret mentioning Diane as a starting point in all this. Please, John. Let me take you to meet a young acquaintance of mine, probably your age. Her situation is nothing like Diane's, and yet it's similar in many ways."

John scrutinized his partner in the full light that beamed through the open garage door, shrouding Stuart Adler in an ethereal halo-like light, an incongruous image. Emboldened by Stu's apologetic plea, John stated, "I don't want to be sold your brand of medical ethics, Stu. And before I meet anyone you've treated with stolen narcotics, I want you to justify how helping one person live comfortably outweighs the risks of killing someone else."

A puzzled look crossed Stu's face. "What are you talking about?"

"I'm talking about pulling up narcotic and trying to cover the diversion by adding what you thought was saline, but was actually Succinylcholine." John was pumped, and he quit caring about caution. "A thirty-two-year-old woman nearly died because someone pushed Sux, instead of saline, into a Demerol vial. If she hadn't survived the code, you'd be a murderer, Stu."

"I don't know anything about that," Stu said angrily. "You don't know how I work, and I certainly don't push saline or Sux or anything else into a Demerol vial. I don't give these people Demerol. God gave me a brain and a will to use it, and your cocky arrogance to accuse me of murder—"

"So, how *do* you work, Stu?" John butted in tersely. "How do you manage to cover the fact that you've diverted so much narcotic?"

"You don't deserve an explanation," Stu replied. "But I'll tell you how I work, if only in the hope that you won't try to keep me from helping Diane because you view *me* as some bumbling moron who can't tell the difference between Succinylcholine and saline! I don't bother to refill the vials. I just record that I used the entire contents for the patient's surgery. The syringe stays in my pocket. The empty vial matches what's on the drug record. Simple as that, John. No need for any other subterfuge."

"That's why you use more Limbotryl than anyone else in the group," John whispered.

"How do you know that?"

"I started tracking things when we found the syringes in the call room. Now, the Datex system can track who's using what in the OR."

Stu nodded without comment.

"So, what about those syringes in the call room?" John asked edgily. "Were those yours, after all?"

"Yes," Stu admitted. "I'd forgotten the syringes in my lab coat pocket. I'd gone home for the day, but went back for one of Jeannie's patients. Anyway, I went back to my locker for the syringes, but didn't have a pocket large enough to put them in—one of those warm spring days when I'd forgotten to bring a jacket. I held the syringes behind my hand as I left the locker room, which was deserted at that time of the evening. Went into the office to grab a bag to carry them in, and then I heard someone putting a key into the lock, so I ducked into the call room. Whoever it was must have changed their mind about coming in, because they just pulled the key out of the lock and left."

"Then why did you put the syringes under the phone?"

"I wanted to go to the conference room, you know where Shelly tries to recycle those paper bags stacked next to the microwave?" Stu waited for John's nod of understanding.

"Well, I didn't know if whoever had tried to come in would come back, so I just set the syringes under the phone, in case they went into the call room. I decided to grab the paper bag and some journals to give my presence after-hours a measure of reason. But, in comes the evening Housekeeping attendant, and she goes into the call room to clean. Edna had been there earlier in the day, and I couldn't figure out why someone was coming to clean at that late hour. So, I waited quietly for more than an hour, and that Housekeeping attendant never came out of the call room. After a while, I heard light snoring, and I knew that it'd be awhile before I could get in, so I just left. I still can't believe someone from Housekeeping would risk having the on call doc walk in and see her *sleeping* in the physician call room," Stu recollected in surprised admiration.

John gave a sardonic laugh, half amused at the meandering story. " Maybe they scoped out the surgical schedule for the night and knew the coast would be clear for both the nurse and doc from Anesthesia."

Stu grinned faintly, "Maybe. If it had been Lockhart instead of me, he'd have busted in the room and hauled them up to the Housekeeping supervisor." Stu shook his head, saying, "Wish I'd had the inspiration earlier. Any other questions, John?"

John pressed further, given Stu's capacity to tolerate interrogation.

"How do you explain that young woman who coded after routine surgery, where the syringe had Sux instead of Demerol?"

"I can't explain it with any certainty," Stu said. "Unless there's someone in the OR or Recovery Room who has a use for Demerol, and is either desperate or careless."

John considered this, his pulse returning to normal with Stu's explanation for the call room mystery. He believed Stu about the Sux, and despite his intent to resist pat explanations, John accepted Stu's story.

As well, an uncharacteristic curiosity about this person his age, a beneficiary of Adler's diversions, captured John's imagination. Seeking out the black or white of the issue was suddenly impossible amidst this swirl of plausible explanations, within both the gray area of compassionate medical practice, and the gamut of emotions that arose now that his family was involved.

John tried and failed to recreate the anger he'd wanted to unleash at the man whose actions had fractured his marriage, and tested his professional courage. He would sort that out later. For now, John would agree to meet Stu's patient-client.

"About this person you've helped," he began.

Stu held up his hand to stop the question. "See for yourself. She's waiting for us."

10:30 AM

Kathy Martin greeted the two men at her front door with an infectious grin. She was grateful for the opportunity to show a skeptic how far she had come, with regular treatments. It was the least she could do to return the Magi's kindness.

"Come in, gentlemen," she welcomed them. "I've set out some refreshments in the family room. Follow me."

John Williams glanced at Stu Adler, not understanding what this seemingly healthy, energetic woman had to do with treating cancer pain. Stu read the puzzled expression on his partner's face, and raised his index finger, gesturing that answers would be provided within the next minute or so.

"Have a seat on the sofa, if you will," Kathy suggested, sitting on a recliner-chair off to the side, opposite an entertainment center. "Those chocolate chip cookies aren't just for decoration," Kathy added. "Please help yourselves while I pour you either lemonade or coffee—cream and sugar?"

"Black," Stu and John responded simultaneously.

"You gentlemen are certainly easy to please," Kathy responded cheerfully. "Now, where shall we begin, Mr. Stewart?" She addressed her question to Stu Adler.

Stu looked toward John and quickly explained, "We offer everyone the option of choosing a pseudonym. I call myself Mr. Stewart. Kathy knows that's not my real name."

"I actually refer to Mr. Stewart as the Magi," Kathy said, at once serious.

"I'm sure I haven't earned that title," Stu corrected gently. "But what I'd like you to do, Kathy, is tell my friend here a little about what your life is like without regular treatments."

"I'll do better than that," Kathy offered. "I have a video that was made at one of the lowest points in my life. A friend of mine recorded it for me, as a document of sorts, and anytime I consider discontinuing the treatments, or rescheduling for another time, I can review it. It reminds me that I have to make time for the treatments, because otherwise I risk returning to this state." She leaned forward to emphasize her next words, intending them specifically for John. "I'd rather die and be done with it than ever have to be this sick again."

"May I ask about the nature of your illness?" John queried, his words hesitant.

"You'll see," Kathy answered. "You may not recognize what it is specifically, and that's really the least important thing. What's important is the level of disability I suffer without intermittent 'vacations' from my body."

Kathy plucked the remote control from the shelf of the entertainment center, and clicked on the TV and videotape player. She perched on the arm of the recliner, manipulating buttons until the tape showed a date from earlier in the year.

The next frames showed a woman that John would not have recognized as the one who sat before him today. The woman in the video was obviously malnourished, her eyes and cheeks sunken, her arms and lower legs skeletal. Her hair had fallen out in patches, and her lips were cracked and bleeding.

A moment later an anonymous voice explained the scene. "This is Kathy Martin, age thirty-six. Kathy has suffered with chronic pain and fatigue for the past several years. She has been evaluated at St. Catherine's Hospital in Cincinnati, Ohio, as well as at the Mayo Clinic and Johns Hopkins Medical Center. Kathy has received a variety of standard treatments aimed at controlling her pain and symptoms, including steroid injections, narcotic pain relievers, biofeedback therapy, massage therapy, hydrotherapy, occupational and physical therapy, and psychotherapy.

"At this time," the narrator continued, "Kathy cannot get any relief from the oral narcotic pain relievers, and she can no longer even swallow oral medications. She has become anorexic over the past four weeks, partly because she is too nauseated to eat, and refuses a feeding tube. Kathy has choked on even soft foods, due to her weakened state, and is able to sip only small amounts of clear fluids, such as water or diluted electrolyte fluids, such as Pedialyte. Kathy wears postpartum sanitary diapers, as she is unable to tolerate most incontinence garments. She has not been able to ambulate even with assistance for the past week and a half."

The screen darkened momentarily, as if the camera had been turned off and switched back on. The screen showed a close-up of the woman's shrunken face, and the narrator inquired, "Kathy, what is it that you want?"

The woman's reply, although only a hoarse whisper, was audible.

"I want to die."

Kathy Martin snapped the stop button to freeze the frame. She stared hard at the image, as if recommitting it to memory, and then turned to look at John Williams and Stuart Adler. "That is what I am without help," she stated quietly, emphatically. "That is what I will not allow myself to be ever again. I will make myself die first."

"What type of home health or hospice services did you try?" John asked, unconvinced that she could not benefit from the advanced treatment options provided to people with chronic medical conditions.

"Ha!" Kathy snorted. "Home health offered to take my pulse, change my pads, and run an IV, that's what they offered. I don't qualify for any of the hospice services. You see, I'm not actually dying, although to look at this video one would think otherwise."

"Have you ever taken Morphine injections for pain?" John persisted, wondering about drug dependency as an issue for this woman.

"Yes, and I was sick as a dog," Kathy replied earnestly. "I couldn't move, not even to turn my head in bed, without vomiting. I tried all sorts of injected narcotics, all legally prescribed and administered. None of them did anything but knock me out. But, my insurance company paid for them, because I was being offered standard, FDA-approved medical treatment. When I first received Limbotryl, I approached the insurance company about paying for it. They said that it was not FDA-approved for that use, that it was a drug used for surgical anesthesia, not chronic pain management. Believe me, when I felt better, I tried everything to get treatment provided through proper channels."

"So, how was the Limbotryl different for you?" John asked, "I mean, that should have knocked you out, too."

Kathy's expression became animated as she spelled it out for the skeptic before her. "Of course it did, at first. I was out for hours, completely pain-free. My body was allowed to get into REM sleep, and there's some evidence that it's during this sleep phase that the body releases endorphins and takes care of restorative functions. I call it a 'vacation' from my body. And when I wake up, following a treatment, I feel better, lighter. My muscles are less leaden; my joints bend without complaint. I'm still fatigued, but better.

"When I was as sick as you saw me there," she pointed to the freeze-frame on the TV screen, "I needed several rounds of this process before I was able to get out of bed and move around. But, after being sick for so long, I got a burst of energy that just wouldn't quit. My husband couldn't believe the difference."

She became somber immediately. "My husband does not agree with this type of treatment. He believes that taking it is a form of drug abuse, that I'm risking prosecution. It's tough for him. He likes me to be well. He likes to run our family life within the rules of the kingdom, and yet he can't have it both ways."

"So, what are you doing?" John asked.

"I'm taking the treatments without his knowledge." She stared hard at John, then cocked her head as she stated, "I won't say he doesn't *know*. He's a smart man, so surely he suspects. But he doesn't know from me, and there's no treatment when he's home, so as far as he's concerned, I'm following the rules."

There was a lengthy silence, and the haunted face on the TV screen, tight with pain, lent an eerie, foreboding aura to the otherwise comfortably cheery family room.

John Williams looked at the floor as he gathered his thoughts, and without looking up asked, "Why did you make this video? Just as a reminder to yourself?"

Kathy waited until he glanced up, until he committed with his eyes to hearing her out. "I made that tape for Dr. Jack Kevorkian. To request his services."

John was not prepared for this revelation. His stomach churned threateningly, and he ran his hand across his forehead and down his face, attempting to erase the vision.

Stu patted John's arm, "Think I know how you feel, John. I felt something like that when I heard about it. Kathy, tell my friend why you didn't go through with that plan."

Kathy took a deep breath. "I met with Dr. Kevorkian. He is a very compassionate man, and he knows how to deal with people who feel desperate. The media may paint him as a vulture, but he's a kind, gentle man with people like me. He agreed to help me, if his review of my medical information confirmed that this was the best I could hope for.

"But I have this friend, Marilyn," Kathy continued with a smile. "Marilyn told me that I didn't need to quit this life. She promised that I could have as much treatment as I needed, but that I would have to sustain the treatments regularly for the rest of my life. She encouraged me to consider taking the treatments while my husband, Drew, was either at work or out-of-town. Marilyn and my Magi here saved my life," she whispered, tears glistening along the rims of her hazel eyes. She made no effort to wipe them away or apologize for their appearance.

"Is there someone you love who could benefit from this treatment?" Kathy asked gently.

John shook his head, "No, uh . . . I don't know."

Stu rose from the sofa and crossed to the recliner, offering a brief hug to Kathy. "Thank you for meeting with us today," he said warmly. "The world is a better place because you're here. I'm glad you chose to stay with us."

"My family is, too. Me too, of course!" she added with a laugh.

John had risen, understanding that the meeting was over. He walked over to Kathy Martin and extended his hand. "Thank you," he said. "I hope you stay well."

"With the gift of this Magi, I expect to stay well for a long time." She smiled graciously, holding John's hand in both of hers as she said, "If I can help, please call me. I consider it part of my mission in life to help others in similar situations. It's my way of paying back the gift of having my life handed back to me . . . *whole.*" She squeezed his hand gently.

John nodded in reply, not quite trusting his voice at that moment. He was not typically emotional, but there was nothing typical about this encounter. He'd now met someone who'd faced Dr. Death himself, and sent him away. Kevorkian was always the enemy, in John Williams' book. To offer people another option so that they could choose life . . . well, that was what John thought the medical profession and hospice organizations provided. Shame that he didn't know better burned in his heart.

The drive back to John's home was silent. Stuart Adler allowed the younger man a quiet space in which to assimilate all that he'd heard, all that had been shared, and the many shades of gray that exist between black and white.

This was no debate that could be won on oratory, alone. It would require compassion, moral courage, and most importantly, humanity of the soul.

Chapter Twenty–Four

EVICTION

Sunday, November 3
Dear John,

I am so sorry for agreeing to the "surprise attack" on you last week at dinner. It was unforgivable, and I cannot imagine why I didn't see how wrong it would be from the start. You've been asked to bear an unthinkable burden: to choose between doing as Nancy asks, and doing what you pledged in the Hippocratic oath.

You must do whatever your conscience tells you to do, John, even if it means that this treatment ends. Sometimes, we can take the backdoor for expediency. But when that door closes, it's time to open a window. Perhaps it's time for this treatment to be studied rigorously, scientifically. Certainly, it's time to stop sneaking around, all secrecy and subterfuge. I've told Stu Adler that I won't take any more treatments.

In addition to my request for your forgiveness, I do have another request, John. If you could find it in your heart to meet with Nancy, I'd be so grateful. She has her father's stubborn Irish heart, and she refuses to contact you despite my pleas. She is furious with me for stopping the treatments, although she knows that I've always made my own decisions in this area.

You and Nancy have created a wonderful life together, and I don't want to be the cause of this estrangement. If I can help to mend this hurt between you, I will feel relief from this guilt that's more painful than anything—because it's deeper than a physical pain. It's pain in my soul, my spirit. I don't write this to have you share in my pain or my guilt, John. It's mine, alone.

You are in my thoughts and prayers.

Love,
Diane

Tuesday, November 5
Dear Diane,

Thanks for your note. I've left several messages for Nancy, but she won't take my calls, and so far she hasn't returned them. Please don't feel responsible for our problems.

I know that we can always count on your love. If you wouldn't mind passing on the enclosed letter to Nancy, I'd be grateful.

Fondly,
John

Tuesday, November 5
Dear Nancy,

We need to talk. I am sorry for what your mom is going through, and for what you are going through. I'd like to work this out, but I can't do it alone. Please call me at home or at work as soon as possible.

Love,
John

The Williams' Answering Machine:

"Hi, John. This is Sandy calling. It's November 7th, around 8:10 PM. Mom asked me to call and let you know that Nancy is flying through the 10th. I'll give her the letter when she gets back in town. Hope you're fine—call me when you can. Bye."

Sandy Cavanaugh's Answering Machine:

"Hi, Sandy. It's John calling back. It's 7:00 on Friday. Just returning your call. Thanks for the message. Hope your mom is doing well. Bye."

The Williams' Answering Machine:

"John, hello. Diane Cavanaugh calling. Nancy is back in town. She's staying here. Thought you might be able to stop by. Take care, John."

Diane Cavanaugh's Answering Machine:

"Hi, it's John. Nancy or Diane, if you're there and can pick up . . . . I guess you're not home. Well, call me back when you can. It's 6:15 on November 13th. Bye."

The Williams' Answering Machine

"Are you ignoring me, Cousin John? It's Mary Claire calling . . . *again.* I'm rehearsing for 'A Christmas Carol,' and won't leave this town until we get together. I've got a couple tickets for a Thursday night performance for you and Nancy. *Call me,* or I'll just show up on your front door! It's Thursday, November 14th, and I've been here for *days.* You doctors must work all day and night. My boyfriend and I will stop by later this weekend, even if we have to drag you out of the operating room at St. Kate's. I'm haunting you, Cousin."

Friday, November 15
8:10 AM
From the Journal of Diane Cavanaugh

There comes a point at which I have to choose what is right, or at least define what is right. It's so much harder today. There's less guidance and the boundaries are more tenuous, less defined, shades of gray, rather than a distinct barrier between right and wrong. It was easier when I was growing up, when we could count on that solid black line, whether it was drawn by the priests or our parents or the community at large.

And these days, people rely more on their capacity to control a situation than their capacity for faith. It's as if God has nothing to do with it, when really, God has everything to do with life. However, in our diverse world, in order to get along, what is substituted for an authentic understanding of "Truth" is a suspension of any rules, or guiding principles. After all, we do not wish to be offensive by declaring that something is indisputably "wrong." That would be narrow-minded of us. Judgmental. Intolerant.

And what must God be thinking from on high?

Surely He must note our lack of moral courage.

And what part have I played in my child's control strategies for living? Have I taught her, unwittingly, that it pays to plan for every moment in life? That a well-controlled life is the only one worth living?

What about the value of flexibility? Not moral flexibility, but the capacity to roll with the punches. And to have faith, rather than a set of control strategies, that we will meet whatever challenge comes our way.

Did I forget to teach each of my children about commitment? Persistence? No, I taught those lessons, and I thought my kiddos had learned them. But when the going gets tough, today's children seem to feel it's permissible to run away. What would their lives have been like, had I done that when they were little, when Jim and I seemed to be on a collision course for disaster? They act as if they don't remember it. Perhaps they don't. Perhaps they ought to be reminded.

I don't know. When do we parents stop raising our children?

I thought I was finished. If so, with at least one child, I've failed. Does that mean I have a responsibility to finish the job? Or do I just ask forgiveness?

Surely I failed to teach that marriage is less about living happily ever after with one's soul mate, than navigation and negotiation of the uncharted territory that represents what's left in the marriage ten years later. What I wanted to teach them was that, whether it's ten years or two, whenever the honeymoon is over, you pray that loving one another will be enough. And I wanted my children to know the delight, after fifteen or twenty or twenty-five years, when your children are more independent, that you might rediscover why you got together in the first place. To quit too soon is never to know that joy of rediscovered love, romance. Not that it happens that way for everyone, but I feel blessed that it did for Jim and me.

The pen feels heavy today. My heart feels heavy, too. But otherwise, I am well.

I am well because I chose to allow someone to do something wrong—illegal and immoral—so that I could control the quality of my life. Even though I've stopped those treatments, the benefits are sustained—for the moment. Do I deserve the highest possible quality of life? Of course. So do we all. But at the price of one's soul? At the price of someone else's soul? As we conspire in silence about this wrong, we exact a toll on both our souls. I wonder what penance there is for such a sin?

And what do I do next?

Of course, I know. I said it at the beginning. I decide what is right. Not as in "right for me," but as in "authentic

*truth." I probably won't like it. The truth may set me free,
but it may also hurt like hell.*

I will not sell my soul in the process.

*If I have failed to teach my children all of the lessons
I'd hoped, I'll do my best to succeed in teaching them to
have faith, to trust God enough to turn my life over to Him.
I'll not ask anyone to damage his or her divine soul, that I
might escape the painful truth. It has nothing to do with
deserving better. It's a matter of being able to face God
whole, or as whole as I can be, given the damage of a
human lifetime on the soul. It's a matter of being true to
myself.*

*Whatever harm this inflicts on my child, who so clearly
wants me to do things her way, I am sorry. But it's my life,
my decision, and my soul.*

11:00 AM

Diane Cavanaugh blended the granular bulb food and the
richly amended soil with a trowel. Then, taking an empty four-
inch plastic pot, she scooped the nutritive soil from the miniature wheelbarrow, and tossed it across the freshly planted bulb
garden. The parallel furrows that formed a Celtic cross, and the
dual rings surrounding it, were now obscured. Purple, yellow,
and white crocus bulbs, as well as the miniature daffodil bulbs,
hid well beneath the surface, tips up, awaiting the winter hiber-
nation and the springtime thaw. They would be patient. Diane
was not.

A thunderstorm menaced across the valley, some miles west
of the airport that was just beyond the ridge. The day was unseasonably warm, as much of this autumn had been. "My timing is
good," Diane stated firmly. "I may not feel well enough to do this
even next week, Jim. And the rain that's coming will soak the soil
and release the bulb food. Today was the perfect day for this
project."

It was a comfort to come here, to talk with Jim, and to listen for any whispers of divine inspiration that proved he was listening, on the other side of The Gates. She always felt better for the quiet, contemplative conversation with Jim. He'd always been strong, in a quiet way. Even now, she borrowed his strength by remembering it deeply, as she tended his grave.

"So, you see where we are," she announced, having finished telling him . . . everything.

Silence. Thunder rumbled, and then silence returned. Even the birds remained mute under threat of the storm.

"I'm sure there's more, things I can't possibly know, but won't you help me, Jim? Help me to know what to do."

She felt no response now, no presence, unlike earlier this morning, when she'd begun to tell the whole story. Where was he? Had she lost him at some point along the way, as she was telling the story?

Diane sighed, tossing the trowel and spade into a woven basket, and then lifting the wheelbarrow to empty the remaining soil and bulb food onto her husband's grave. *Surrender,* she heard in the stillness of her heart. She paused, hoping for more, something specific. Silence. Only silence prevailed, amidst intermittent grumbles from the sky.

Sighing again, Diane took a garden rake from the floor of the car, and proceeded to level the dirt, retracing the Celtic cross design and the rings surrounding it. *There. They'll be lovely next March.*

"Jim!" She now felt his presence. "I thought you'd left me."

I'll never leave you.

"You know, I may not see these blossom in the spring."

Surrender the details.

"I remember you always used to say, 'Don't sweat the details.' Is that what you'd say now?"

Yes!

"I wish you were here, Jim. I wish you could just talk with our daughter."

I've already said I would, don't you remember?

Diane sighed. "Well, it's always good to talk things over with you, Jim. I hope you'll like what I've done here, when it blossoms next spring."

I can already see it. It's beautiful, Diane. You'll see.

"Nancy gets back from her trip on Sunday. I think it's time for me to have a talk with her."

Sunday, November 17
7:30 PM

"Nancy, you can't expect me to be complacent about this. You have to deal with John directly, whether you're ready to or not. You can't just stay here and pretend you aren't married. Your father would never have allowed it, and I can't allow it, either."

Nancy Williams rolled her eyes, her back to her mother so that Diane could not see the reflected frustration. "Mom, this is between John and me, and I'll deal with it when I'm ready. Right now, just let me take care of you. I'll call John when I get back from my next trip."

Diane Cavanaugh forced herself to sit in bed, although the effort made her nauseous with vertigo. Taking a deep breath, she swallowed the bile in her stomach and tried to talk sense to Nancy. "You are *not* on this earth to take care of me, Nancy. I have an aide, a housekeeper, and a nurse who check on me, take care of me, etc. I don't need you to be my nursemaid. If you want to do something useful, go talk to John."

"My marriage is *my* business. I know you feel responsible, for some strange reason, for our separation. But it isn't your fault or your responsibility. It just happens."

"I'm not trying to pry," Diane said tremulously, tears shining in her eyes. "I just don't want you to ignore John when he's making the effort to reach out to you. Isn't that what you want him to do?"

"What I wanted him to do was to support the treatment you were getting. He decided not to do that. As far as I'm concerned, that tells me that John places his professional interests above family interests. If that's the case, his priorities aren't in the right place."

"But he's trying to put family first, *now*, Nancy," her mother argued. "Won't you at least call him?"

"No, I won't."

"Punishing John because *I've* decided not to accept additional treatment does no good. You are bitter, and that bitterness grows like a cancer."

"I am not bitter. I may be disappointed, possibly even more than a little angry about the way things have turned out, but I'm not bitter. And I'm not trying to *punish* John," Nancy retorted.

"Then, what *are* you trying to do?" Diane asked.

"I'm just trying to survive. I do what I have to do each day. I go through the motions. It helps me feel better to at least have some purpose and routine to my life."

"This is the first *real* test of your marriage. Your father and I had *real* tests of our marriage, and we struggled to make things work. Perhaps you think it wasn't as dramatic as what you and John are dealing with, but they were important issues to us. I hope that we taught you well enough about the importance of commitment, whether it's easy or difficult."

"Look, Mom, John hasn't even come to visit in the three weeks since we had dinner here. If he really wanted to work this out, he'd be staking out your house. What about *his* level of commitment?"

"He has called. He has written. You have done neither." Diane closed her eyes and pulled the covers up to her chin. "I'm tired. Let's not talk about this any longer."

"It'll be all right, Mom," Nancy said gently, setting a fresh glass of water on the bedside table, and taking a seat on the chair nearby. "I'm tired, too. I'll turn in soon."

"Nancy, one last thing," Diane said softly, her eyes open and direct. "I think it would be best if you didn't stay here. I have the help I need, and I feel that I'm somehow *keeping* you here. I'd like you to pack up within the next three days. If you and John can't share that big house, then you can make some other arrangements. But I can't feel like I'm contributing to this situation by having you stay with me. I'm truly sorry, dear. I *do* love you."

Eyes wide in surprise, the fatigue of the three-day trip forgotten, Nancy leaned forward in the chair as if she hadn't heard correctly.

"I do love you," Diane repeated, "but you'll need to leave. Do you understand?"

"No, Mom, I don't understand," Nancy answered, stunned.

With effort, Diane opened her eyes and attempted to explain, again. "If you stay here, you have an excuse to avoid the problems that you and John are having. Then, I become part of the problem, or *more* of the problem. If you can't stay here, then I'm no longer part of the problem. I won't agree to be part of the problem. That's as well as I can say it, Nancy."

Diane closed her eyes again, thoroughly exhausted.

Numb with disbelief, Nancy struggled to recall any turmoil in her parents' marriage. Had it truly existed? Even if it had, what about all the lessons her parents had taught about taking care of family first, such as their grandparents? What about blood being thicker than water, and always being there in tough times? Did her mother mean that Nancy's first family was her husband, and *then* the family in which she'd grown up? If so, then Nancy would receive precious little support, watching her mother die. John had already made that clear.

Her mother's deep, regular breaths indicated that she was asleep. Nancy left the room, hearing the click of a key in the front door lock that signaled Sandy had arrived. Sandy would be horrified, Nancy thought, recalling her mother's words of eviction.

"Nancy?" Sandy called softly.

"Right here," Nancy replied in a stage whisper. "Mom's asleep." Nancy shook off the shock, rubbing her arms as she descended the stairs slowly, her distress evident.

"What's happened?" Sandy asked, worried.

"Mom's okay. It's not that," Nancy answered, addressing what she believed to be Sandy's first concern. "You'll never believe what Mom just told me."

"What's that?"

"She wants me to leave. She says that I should pack my things and leave within the next three days. Can you believe it?"

"Did she explain *why* she's asking you to leave?"

"She thinks that I'm staying here to avoid dealing with John. Doesn't she realize how much I can help—*have helped*—by being here? What about those "Family First" lectures she and Dad gave us? Like how it was more important to plan our summer vacation around the family reunion, and taking care of Grams and Gramps?"

Sandy remained quiet.

Nancy crossed the tile hallway to the living room, and plopped onto the sofa. "The thing is," Nancy continued, "I don't *feel* as if John is family. Not the way you and I are family, or the way Mom is family."

"Nancy, have you even *responded* to John's letter or calls?"

Giving her sister an irritated glance and curling her arms around her knees, Nancy felt that Sandy, too, was behaving less like family. What was wrong with her mother and sister, all of a sudden?

"John blew it, Sandy. He had a chance to do something important for us, and he refused. For all I know, he's reported Stu and Jeannie Adler, and made lots of other lives miserable—not just mine. That's not my definition of family loyalty. If John had been willing to think outside the narrow little box in which he lives his life, Mom would still be taking the treatments, and she'd be doing what she wants for Thanksgiving. She'd be getting ready for the holidays instead of staying in bed all day," Nancy complained.

"If wishes were horses, then beggars could ride, Nancy," Sandy said, returning the volley of irritation. "When we were growing up, Mom and Dad took care of each other and of us. They settled their disagreements, and there were plenty, but they didn't run away from home. I know this is probably the last thing you need to hear tonight, but your idea of this mythical, happily-ever-after family life isn't part of the real world, Nancy. You have a husband who wants to make things better, who has taken the lead by calling, even *writing you a letter,* for godssake. He may be flawed, but so are we all! What I'd give to have a guy so flawed!"

"Is that what this is about?" Nancy asked belligerently. "You want what I have, and it's not as bad as I make it out?"

"No, Nancy," Sandy said coldly. "What this is about is exactly what Mom said. You're avoiding John and you're using Mom as some shield to protect you from dealing with your problems. You won't even *look* at your piece in the problems. How do you think *you'd* feel if John had orchestrated an evening to ambush you with some serious moral dilemma? And yet, *he's* still trying to get in touch with you!"

"So, I'm the bad guy. It's all *my* fault."

"I didn't say that. I said you have a piece in it. So do I, because I didn't kick and scream and do whatever was necessary to keep that stupid dinner from happening! At least I shouldn't have been there to be a part of something I *knew* was wrong. And I will be sorry the rest of my life, especially if you and John throw away what was a good marriage. So he has problems with death and dying. So he doesn't know how to do the supportive nurturance thing. It's tough for *lots* of people, Nancy. And it's a better problem than someone who has problems with fidelity, or honesty, or responsibility."

"I don't know what to say," Nancy said, angrily. "I didn't expect my own *family* to be so unsupportive, no so unappreciative."

"Nancy, when you married John, you *added* him to your family. He is family. The sooner you get that through your head, the sooner you can get on with the real-life, grown-up job of working things out. Not running away. Not hiding behind your mother's skirts."

"Sandy! I can't believe we're having this conversation. You're my sister, for godssake! And I would have said that you and Mom and I have a deeper family tie than I have with John."

"Then you and John really do have problems." Sandy stood to leave, handing an envelope to Nancy with John's return address label in the upper left corner. "He's started writing and calling me, as if I have some influence over you. I'm sorry, Nancy. I still believe that Mom is the one to make decisions about her treatment. It isn't right to hold John responsible for the fact that she's changed her mind. Frankly, I think she's a ballsy gal, and that she's taking a higher road than you are."

Sandy paused briefly, swinging her purse over one shoulder with a flourish of impatience. "I'm leaving for some out-of-town consults, but Mom *does* have people lined up to help her, Nancy."

Without another word, Sandy crossed to the hallway, and quietly left the townhouse.

Nancy Williams felt very alone and abandoned. She curled onto her side, punching the sofa in fury. A tightly clenched moan escaped her lips, as a storm of tears poured forth from the depths of her soul. The letter from John fluttered to the carpet, the fourth that she had refused to open.

Monday, November 25
11:30 AM

John Williams poked the macaroni on his plate, not taking a bite. It was the week of Thanksgiving, yet he felt no holiday cheer.

Nancy had been gone for weeks, and he'd been surprisingly— no, shockingly—persistent in the quest to pursue, retrieve, and resolve his marriage. He had written nearly a dozen letters to Nancy, sending them in care of Diane or Sandy, and later to Nancy's furnished apartment. He'd even driven there a couple of times, but Nancy's red Prelude hadn't been parked in the lot.

Sandy had called him about Diane's request that Nancy leave, and tried to explain it without making Diane appear heartless. John had appreciated the vote of confidence from his in-laws, but remained demoralized by his wife's refusal of any contact.

He hadn't reported Stu and Jeannie Adler, although he felt certain that the Adlers continued the subterfuge, the treatments, for their *other* patients. That certainty spawned guilty remorse that his mother-in-law now declined Limbotryl's rejuvenation. Such a vital woman should revel in the fullness of life. How unjust, that the best of palliative medicine served to imprison Diane in a dopey haze, when something better existed. John admired Diane's classy spunk, refusing the treatment Adler offered. Yet, it was more than just spunk; it was courage. She refused to make John choose between protecting the secret treatment, or exposing both his mother-in-law and a colleague to the law of the land.

Of course, he'd have to choose; but his choice would not alter Diane's intention to stop the illicit treatment. John wished he had the guts to take a stand, one way or another: either report Stu and Jeannie's drug thefts and illegal distribution, or join their restorative enterprise.

It was easier to let it alone, to think about it later, especially since Diane had refused further treatment from the Adlers. Inaction, indecision, represented a choice, John knew. The question that nagged at him was this: *Am I a moral coward?*

For a while, he struggled with the possible outcomes of reporting versus not reporting the Adlers, each with its own price to pay. Either way, he felt as if he were in no-man's land, and tried to name it. Was it Limbo? No, that was an arcane reference to what was once believed to be the permanent residence of unbaptized innocents. *This* no man's land imitated Purgatory, a waiting place for souls not yet ready for the Kingdom of Heaven, but where redemption remained possible. Yes, he decided, it was in this sort of place that his spirit resided.

To focus his energies after work, John began writing a research protocol that would allow patients with cancer pain to receive treatment that put them into extended R.E.M. sleep, to evaluate whether the restorative and healing attributes of that sleep stage would diminish pain and allow more normal activity. He'd contacted the director of oncology at the University's Barrett Cancer Treatment Center, and they'd completed a literature review. Interest piqued, the director offered to negotiate a collaborative study with both the UC Anesthesia Department and the Neurology Department's Sleep Clinic. Funding would come from an NIH grant, applied for by the Barrett Center, the Anesthesia Department, and the Neurology Department, jointly. The project looked favorable, and John had begged off of several evening visits to Diane in order to meet with the UC colleagues after work.

It was easier to become immersed in the project, than to see Diane's health wane. He hated himself for this weakness, but justified it with reminders that he was doing something for a greater good. And Sandy had passed on messages that she and her mother were grateful for his proactive interest in the treatment, which John accepted as absolution for his absence.

"Are you going to poke that macaroni to death or eat it?" Mackenzie Franklin set her tray next to John's, immediately digging into her own creamy, golden mound of pasta.

"Hi, Mac," John greeted. "It's better warm."

"It *was* warm when you sat down," Mac reminded him. "You're missing the best part of comfort food, if you let it cool off." She watched as John returned to poking the pasta, a look of sympathy crossing her face. "Why don't you come to our house for dinner tonight? We're having the kids' favorite—rotisserie chicken, potatoes and gravy, and string beans. Oh, and caramel apple pie for dessert. Let me tempt you, John."

"I don't know, Mac. I have a lot of reading to do for this study we're trying to set up. I was planning to get a lot more done tonight."

"You can still read," Mac assured him. "Just eat dinner with us. You'll be out of our house by 7:00, maybe 7:30, with plenty of time to do some reading. Just say yes." She patted him briskly on the shoulder. "I'll bug you until you say yes."

"Okay, yes." John looked up with a grin that would have been called shy, but it was just slow because those smile muscles were seldom exercised these days. He'd developed a vertical furrow between his dark eyebrows, and gray crescent shadows beneath his eyes.

"Deal," announced Mac. "The great thing about having a nanny is that she can put simple stuff on the table, so all we have to do is open a bottle of wine—or you can have a beer, if that's your pleasure. Just try to *eat* the food, or you'll set us back with our table manners. We have to give the kids a good example, you know?"

John glanced at Mac sharply, her words evoking an unintended flicker of pain. The fact was John *wanted* to know. He'd had high hopes—once Nancy had decided she *did* want a child—that he would have firsthand knowledge of the requirement to set a good example, and everything else concerning children and parents.

But that wasn't to be, and there was no sense stewing about it.

For now, he'd look forward to having no decisions to make about dinner, and he'd enjoy the laughter of Mac's infectiously joyful children.

7:15 PM

Nancy Williams dug the toes of one foot against the heel of the other, wedging it tightly to avoid untying the laces. She kicked off the shoe that reluctantly loosened its grip, noting the scuffs of abuse. She repeated the action, challenged by slippery stockings that failed to grip the heel of the other oxford. Irritation energized her momentarily, as she struggled for release from the bondage of dress code footwear.

"Ah!" With a whoosh, the foot was free. Before the next flight, she'd have to get a shoeshine. Company policy required almost military attention to all uniform garments, including shoes. Yet, tonight, she failed to muster the energy to care.

Although it was not late at all, exhaustion that bordered on childlike, pre-meltdown fatigue prompted tears of frustration to prick at the corners of her eyes. Hunger registered as a dull ache, although she'd eaten only an hour ago: a hot, soft pretzel with gooey, golden, processed cheese.

Nancy scanned the still unfamiliar room that now represented home. A nubby, multi-colored, silky-tweed sofa rested against the creamy white wall, a woodland scene framed in brass overhead. Twin side chairs, striped in navy and hunter green fabric, flanked a small fireplace. Opposite the entryway was a sliding glass door, which became a mirror of the room at nightfall. Darkness outside conspired with the lamp-lit interior to obscure a small, sheltered balcony beyond the glass panes. To the left was a galley kitchen, wallpapered in a faux brick pattern. A tiny, wrought iron, glass-top table and two chairs rested in an alcove, where a small overhead window afforded scant light on even the brightest days. To the right, a narrow hallway led to the bathroom and bedroom.

The bedroom. Nancy avoided looking toward that door. She'd slept in the bedroom only once, her first night in the apartment. It was no more foreign than a hotel bed, and she'd expected to adapt readily to the new surroundings, given her out-of-town experience as a pilot. Such was not the case with this bed. She refused to contemplate why this mattress, if *it* was to bear the blame, was so different from others that afforded rest.

Since that first night, she'd slept on the sofa. It's broad arms and loose pillows beckoned, plush and comforting as a mother's lap, a mother's bosom.

Nancy missed her mother, wanted her mother; craved her mother's lap, like an overtired child. But her mother had been strangely withdrawn, reserved. It was more than simply illness that kept her mother so distant, Nancy believed. She reminded herself that, as a grown woman, she was no longer a child who needed the physical comfort of her mother. Still, these childlike longings for nurturance irked her, and refused to be sated by massage, food, conversation, sleep, or exercise.

She sighed heavily, stifling a yawn, and yielded to the sofa's embrace. She then pulled a blanket from across the arm of the sofa, arranging one of the loose pillows beneath her head, and cradling another between her knees so they would not wear the red badge of pressure marks in the morning. Other days and other flights had been more hectic than today's, but sleepiness blanketed her like a down comforter: not too heavy, and just cozy enough for her to slip into the depths of dreamless, delicious sleep.

She did not awaken until 8:00 the next morning.

Chapter Twenty–Five

THANKSGIVING

Wednesday, November 27
8:15 AM

"Nancy, it's Mom," called the voice from the message machine. "Your brothers' families will be in late this evening, and I hoped you'd be able to come over first thing tomorrow morning. We can help the children frost sugar cookies—I made a bunch with Gram's old turkey cookie cutter—and we'll watch the parade, of course. I've invited John, too. He hasn't seen the boys or his nieces and nephews in quite a while, and without people of his own . . . well, he's coming, at any rate, but only for dinner." Beep.

The machine paused to announce the date and time of the call, then proceeded to the next message.

"Nancy, just to finish my message, you don't have to bring anything. I know you're flying today, but try to come as early as you can tomorrow. The kids are looking forward to seeing you, and your brothers, too. Sandy is bringing a friend, and they're coming early. He's a widower, and has a boy in fifth grade and a girl in third. It'll be great to have all the little ones here. See you tomorrow, Nancy. Bye." Beep.

Nancy pressed the erase button, stunned to think that her mother had invited John for Thanksgiving dinner. *How cozy,* Nancy thought cynically, *Sandy can embark on a new romance and I can pretend to be happily married, all over a Norman Rockwell Thanksgiving dinner. No way, and no thanks.*

Fortunately, her mother expected Nancy to fly today, and would not expect to hear back. The thought of a quiet day in this anonymous apartment, void of any personal artifacts, gave rise to nauseating claustrophobia. Suddenly, Nancy noticed all the flaws of this mediocre interim housing. The carpet was colorless, the slats of the vertical draperies were bent, the lime-encrusted faucet dripped, and the walls were either bland, or they were horribly covered: imposter brickwork papered the wallboard kitchen, and apartment issue, dull-white paint coated both the living room and that *unmentionable* room in which she'd never sleep, again.

The phone rang in Nancy's hand, and she nearly dropped it. She waited for the message to record, in order to screen the call. "Hi, Nancy. It's Sandy. I'm calling about Thanksgiving. Mom invited John, and I hope you'll still come. I'm not going to tell you that you *should*, but—well, you know Mom. Anyway, I'm contributing my own little drama. I'm bringing a guy I met at a conference. Can't wait for you to meet him. He's got two kids, and arrrrrgh! I can't believe I'm doing this! We just met a few weeks ago, and he and his two kids are coming to Mom's Thanksgiving dinner! I must be nuts. Call me as soon as you can so—" The answering machine cut off with a rude beep.

Holy shit! Nancy smiled at her sister's uncharacteristic, flustered hyperbole. Sandy hadn't invited a man to Thanksgiving dinner in years, not since college. Nancy considered the distraction that would offer, shifting the focus that would otherwise be on she and John.

John. She felt giddy, light-headed, slightly nauseated as she imagined him celebrating Thanksgiving with the rest of her family. It reminded her of the early years, when just seeing him made her heart race, and the accidental touch of his fingertips set her limbs on fire.

What have I done? Nancy pondered the question from the safety of the sofa, her surrogate comforter, gazing beyond the sliding glass doors in search of an answer. The barren slate sky and naked, leafless trees mirrored her emptiness. *What's John doing today? Right this second?* Nancy fluffed the blanket before burrowing beneath it. *Does he miss me?* She shivered, willing away the thought, firmly reminding herself that she did not miss him. Or, did she?

She waited for the phone to ring, for Sandy to complete her message. Yet, the phone remained silent. It was tempting to call back immediately. A few weeks ago she would have, and they'd have giggled and carried on like twelve-year-olds.

Today, however, she was supposed to be flying, according to her mother, who was misinformed. Compared to sitting in this unimaginatively furnished apartment, another day of hectic, pre-holiday flights appealed to Nancy's spirit of avoidance. There was no way she could go to Thanksgiving dinner if John would be there.

The thought returned, unbidden and judgmental: *What have I done?*

Nancy directed her thoughts to the suffering her mother stood to endure, given John's refusal to help. She recalled that disastrous pre-Halloween dinner when her plan, so lovingly conceived, had exploded; shattering her marriage and fracturing the filial bond she shared with her mother and sister.

It's not my fault.

Really. It wasn't. John had made his choice, and she was simply accepting his decision not to be a fully vested member of the family. What reasonable person would ask her to overlook John's refusal to step up to the plate, when her mother's health depended on it?

It's more complicated than that.

Nancy frowned in annoyance as the thought manifested, almost audibly. What was this, some sort of Jiminy Cricket-like conscience? If so, it was wrong.

Nancy flung the covers across the arm of the sofa and launched herself from its depths. Decisive action would silence this troublesome, challenging voice. Snapping up the phone from the coffee table, she punched in the number for flight staffing. "Hi, it's

Nancy Williams, 727 FO. I'd like to request a trip-trade or open flying for today and tomorrow."

"We have two open trips," responded the Crew Desk clerk, "but they're long ones. Won't get you back until Sunday."

Nancy didn't hesitate. "I'm free," she assured. "Just give me the route options, if there's a choice, and sign me on."

Satisfied that she was acting decisively, rightly, Nancy negotiated the arrangements, thankful that she'd avoid the family holiday, as well as the close encounter with John.

November 28, Thanksgiving Day
5:00 PM

"I want the drumstick!"

"No, you always get it. It's my turn!"

"Look, guys, there are two of them. You can each have one."

"No, I have six of them! I decided to make three small turkeys so that all the kids could have a drumstick, if they want one."

"Mom, you think of everything!"

"I've had a little experience in the drumstick negotiations of children."

"I get to break the wishbone!"

"There's enough for *all* of us to do it. Grandma said so."

"We never did this, did we?"

"Every year!"

"I get to do the wishbone with Jenny!"

"No, *I* get to!"

"Enough already, you two! It's time to pray."

"Can't I start? I'm starving?"

"How can you be starving after all those cookies?"

"Go ahead, Elizabeth. Let them start. We can pray once everyone gets through the line. God will understand if we're not quite in sync. How about if you take these rolls out to the buffet?"

John Williams handed a dinner plate to the other odd man out, Tom Anderson. The two shared an immediate affinity, sensing common ground insofar as neither was a Cavanaugh. Tom was the assistant superintendent at of one of Cincinnati's premier, suburban school districts, a former social studies teacher and soccer coach who'd taken the girls' high school team to the nationals. The men connected around their common grade school, Madonna of the Hills Elementary School. Tom had graduated from the school three years ahead of John, and had attended public school after that.

"I had Sister Joan Cecelia in eighth grade," Tom recalled wryly. "She was the nun who like to tell gory stories about the most horrifically martyred saints. My parents decided she was reason enough to enroll me in public school."

John laughed appreciatively. "My aunt and uncle thought Sister Joan Cecelia was the teacher every boy needed, and they made sure that my cousins and I were assigned to her class."

"Are your cousins older?"

"Yeah, except for one cousin, Mary Claire. You might have known my cousin Paul. He would have been there at the same time you were."

"Sounds familiar, but I can't place him. I *do* remember Mary Claire. She was in all the Christmas plays as the angel. The nuns loved those long, gold curls and blue eyes."

"Believe me, she wasn't an angel, but she was my favorite cousin."

"What's she doing now?"

John sighed, and a look of panic crossed Tom's face, as if fearing that he'd stumbled on bad news or touched a raw nerve.

"It's okay," John assured. "I just remembered that she's in town for 'A Christmas Carol,' and I owe her a call. She didn't die or anything." He cringed at his choice of words, glancing toward the kitchen to see if Diane had heard. She hadn't. He reminded himself that he hadn't wanted to come for Thanksgiving dinner, but he'd hoped Nancy would be here. He had risked looking Diane in the eye, knowing that she was dying, and that she'd sacrificed a worthwhile treatment to preserve his integrity. It was a worthy risk, given the opportunity to see Nancy and talk. He tried to squelch the disappointment that she was not here.

Despite Nancy's absence and his own reluctance, John admitted that, in all, being here wasn't difficult. No one discussed Diane's illness, the kids ran around as if nothing was wrong, and Diane appeared little different than four weeks ago at the pre-Halloween dinner fiasco.

Most importantly, no one even mentioned Nancy's absence.

John continued his explanation, hoping to put Tom at ease. "Mary Claire is an actress in St. Louis. Not my aunt's idea of a Good-Catholic-Girl career. She's done some experimental theatre in St. Louis, and a variety of local and regional plays. She's been pretty successful here in the Midwest. Of course, she's honed her dramatic streak since birth. It was always a riot watching her work on her parents, when we were kids."

"Ah. It sounded like she wasn't around any more."

"Well, she isn't, really. She's been in Chicago and St. Louis. My aunt and uncle—the ones who raised me—died about fourteen years ago, and we weren't really close. There wasn't a family reunion tradition or anything. I sort of adopted the Cavanaughs as my family, and I hate to admit it, but I've lost touch with my cousins."

John twisted the stem of his wine goblet, eyes averted, looking up in time to see Tom staring back intently, concerned. John coughed a laugh of embarrassment. "Bet you never thought you'd get to know me *this* well!"

"In my book, that's a compliment," Tom chuckled.

John shook his head. "Too much information."

"I don't know," Tom said, tilting his head in mock skepticism. "I figured I'd be in the hot seat today, new boyfriend with kids and all. Trust me, it's better to be on the listening end."

John grinned appreciatively. "I've been part of this tribe for a while. I'd eat and run, and never come back, if I were the new guy being grilled and filleted."

After sharing a laugh, the men silently studied the emerging picture of this lively family as they gathered around the dining room table, plates brimming with sliced turkey, sage stuffing, mashed potatoes, green beans, and carrot pudding. Tom's children giggled at the naughtiness of John's much younger nieces and nephews, mimicking their caveman-like waving of drumsticks.

John wondered if Tom was recalling other such celebrations, ones with his wife, before she died. As the recollection of Thanksgivings past swirled in his memory, and how different this one felt for Nancy's absence from it, John wondered if perhaps today's feast offered Tom Anderson and his children a steppingstone toward happier family holidays—not as they used to be, but still happy. Beyond that, John wondered if Tom felt any sense of disloyalty about taking that first step. His own loyalty issues popped into the foreground, and John quickly interrupted the disturbing reverie with a question.

"So, Tom, you think the Bengals have a shot at Super Bowl XXX?"

8:15 PM

The evening was a success, Sandy believed. Tom's children and her nieces and nephews had played like longtime friends, despite the age difference. Every hilarious family anecdote was recounted: the time James, then a teenager, crawled through his sisters' bedroom window at three-thirty in the morning, only to be greeted by Sandy—as if he were a burglar—with a baseball bat! And the time their parents had rented a Piper Cherokee to fly the children to Oshkosh, Wisconsin, for the annual Experimental Aircraft Show. The morning had been exceptionally hot and humid, and turbulence brutally rocked the small aircraft. All four children had thrown up, and their parents spent the day cleaning up—instead of enjoying the air show. Then, there was the incredible day that Elizabeth and Annie delivered the first grandchildren on the same day at hospitals hundreds of miles apart. The cousins were affectionately referred to as "the twins." "And remember the time . . . ." Stories and laughter abounded.

Sandy watched Tom out of the corner of her eye. He and John discussed something intently, but she couldn't discern the topic over the competing noise. She smiled and nodded at her brother, pretending to comprehend what he was saying, miles away as she took in the big picture of this three-ring circus. Just the thing for Tom and his children: a crowd of roisterous Irish raconteurs, noisy and high-spirited children, and a feast of comfort food.

If only I could come up with a prescription for Nancy and John, she thought with regret. It wasn't as if she were responsible for her sister's happiness, yet she felt an obligation to do something. What that might be, Sandy hadn't a clue.

The glow of springtime love distracted her, as she caught Tom's eye momentarily. He winked, and she returned the signal, flushing slightly, caught in the act of watching him. Maybe it would be her turn, finally, for a lasting relationship. Strangely, this one had blossomed easily. *Too easily,* she thought.

Three weeks did not render a relationship serious, certainly. Yet, this one had the trajectory of "serious." Already, Sandy could mentally finish Tom's sentences. He could anticipate hers, as well. They enjoyed the same foods; the same movies, too: anything with Tom Hanks or Meg Ryan, and nothing with Arnold Schwartzeneger except "True Lies;" and they even shared a sentimental fondness for boastfully cheerful Christmas letters.

Tom came to her with a family package: three for one, two dependents included. Given the natures of his children, Sandy was not deterred.

Yet, she was not convinced, either, that this was the path she'd take. Her mother's words echoed the wisdom of patience, when Sandy had expressed reticence about inviting Tom and his children to a holiday dinner. "If you're brave enough to walk down the road a bit, both of you will know if it's meant to be. What's the worst that can happen?"

The worst, to Sandy, was the intensity of being the first post-loss love. The phenomenon was especially grueling with divorced men she'd dated, leading Sandy to institute a personal rule *never* to date anyone with less than two years of what she termed "post-loss independence." Tom had barely made the cut, his wife having died not quite two years ago. She'd battled breast cancer for five years, diagnosed during her last pregnancy. It seemed that Tom had completed the course in post-loss independence early, perhaps because of the duration of his wife's suffering.

Maybe, Sandy considered, the greatest risk of walking this road with Tom was that he'd quit the relationship, rather than gamble on losing anyone else to the disease that stole his wife's life—and theirs together—the same disease that Sandy's mother battled. The genetically linked risk was obvious.

They hadn't broached that hot topic in this early phase. It was enough to navigate the dating game with children.

Tired children, it seemed. Her brothers and sisters-in-law gathered their broods, promising a quick dip at the hotel pool in exchange for cooperation. Sandy joined the cacophony of "I love you," "Sleep tight," and "See you in the morning." Bear hugs and quick kisses punctuated the family salutations, until even Sandy was exhausted.

She glanced back at Tom, grateful that he'd waited to make an exit, rather than rush out with the herd. He balanced a stack of coffee cups and saucers in each hand, nodding for Sandy to check out his children, who were in various stages of somnolence. Sara was curled up on the sofa, mouth parted in deep slumber. Ted blinked his eyes repeatedly, as if willing himself to stay awake for the end of some television show.

It was time, Sandy knew, for another transition: from the party, to bedtime at home. Twinges of pain dwelt within any transition, she decided, whether it was accepting the loss of the festivities for essential rest, or the loss of a familiar life for essential growth. Staying on the path, walking through the fire of accommodation and change—that's what defined life, did it not? And what kind of life would it be, she wondered, to ignore the potential richness for fear of loss?

Friday, November 29
1:06 AM

Nancy Williams dreamed that night, one of the few dreams she ever remembered. She and her father shared a quiet Thanksgiving dinner, off-duty but aboard a transatlantic commercial flight. They were the only passengers.

Somehow, the food was exactly what Nancy's mother prepared each year, not airline fare. There was the obligatory turkey, and her father had a huge drumstick, as usual. As well, they savored mashed potatoes and gravy, sage stuffing, green beans, sweet potatoes with nearly burnt marshmallow topping, carrot pudding with cinnamon-sugar sprinkled on top, and caramel apple pie with hand-cranked vanilla ice cream for dessert.

For some reason, Nancy did not feel satisfied, despite having eaten more than her share of the feast. She remained hungry, even starving. When she mentioned it to her father, he looked puzzled.

"Maybe you need something else," he offered.

"Like what?" Nancy asked.

"Don't know," he answered. "Maybe you aren't looking for food to fill you up; maybe you need something else."

Nancy laughed at her father's absurd comment. "Like what, Dad?"

"Like forgiveness."

"What do you mean? I haven't done anything!"

"We've all done things, Nancy."

"What have I done that requires forgiveness?" It was only a hint of a question, more a statement of challenge.

"You didn't fly the plane."

"When?"

"Right now."

"Dad, we're off duty. I'm not supposed to fly the plane." Was her father demented?

"You're always supposed to fly the plane. You promised."

"That's physically impossible. You know that can't be done, Dad! What are you trying to tell me?"

"When you promise to fly the plane, you agree to do it in sunshine or rain, breezes or gusting winds, day or night, smooth skies or turbulence. For the whole flight, you'll fly the plane, and you'll set it down as gently as you can at the end of it all."

"And just how long is that?"

"A lifetime."

Chapter Twenty–Six

Photos, Memories, Wishes, and Dreams

Saturday, November 30
1:10 AM

The dream returned, and once again, it was memorable.

"You haven't finished your turkey. Hurry up! It's time to break the wishbone."

"Dad, I don't make wishes anymore. I'm all grown up."

"Oh," Jim Cavanaugh answered, disappointed. "That's too bad." He paused, then added, "I've never stopped making wishes. Seems like a death sentence, telling someone they can't wish anymore. Especially if it's because somebody else thinks they're too old!"

He sounded angry, and Nancy patted her father's hand in comfort. "I don't think you're too old, Dad. I didn't mean it that way, really. It just seems like such a little kid thing to do, and I'm not a kid anymore, you know?"

Her father shook his head, uncomforted.

"I remember," she recalled sentimentally, "when I was about ten, and I wanted to break the wishbone with Sandy, but James and Steven got to it first. You scolded them for taking it, when it had been promised to Sandy and me. Then, you asked me what I would have wished for. Do you remember that, Dad?"

He nodded, smiling. "I remember. You said you weren't supposed to tell, but that since the boys already broke the wishbone, there was no sense keeping your wish secret."

Nancy smiled. "And then, I said I'd have wished for a pair of lace-up roller skates."

"And I made your brothers spend their allowance to buy you a pair, since they stole your wishbone. You never know what sort of luck might come with the bigger piece of a wishbone. And sometimes, you don't need the wishbone at all."

8:45 AM

"Look what I brought!" shouted Lindy from across the flight crew lounge.

Nancy looked up. "What?"

"A wishbone! I know it's queer, but I love to break these things. I've actually gotten what I wished for, breaking these stupid bones."

"Well, don't spoil your record now," Nancy teased.

"No way! I always win. Come on, break it with me."

"God, I just had a dream about wishbones last night," Nancy chuckled. "My dad wanted to break the wishbone with me, and he thought I was making fun of him for being such a kid."

"Who wants to grow up, when you can make your wishes come true?"

"I'm with you on that," Nancy agreed.

"Okay, wait until I think of something good."

They paused, knuckle to knuckle, thumbs to wishbone, contemplating the riches of wishes from which to choose. Strangely, the words, "Fly the plane," flew into Nancy's head. Lips parted, she thought about the hundreds of wishes she might make: that John would change his mind and help her mother, that her mother wouldn't die, that Limbotryl would become a miracle drug for everyone who needed it . . . .

"I've got one! Ready?"

Nancy frowned in concentration, squinting her eyes tight. "Not yet. Just let me think."

"Fly the plane."

"What did you say?" Nancy asked, her eyes flying open, incredulous.

"Nothing! Hurry up! We've got to fly this plane in a few minutes, and I want to wash my hands after we break this thing."

"Right. Okay." Nancy closed her eyes again, but it was impossible to focus on a single wish. She opted to heed the words: "Fly the plane." Quite simply, she wished to fly this plane, to land everyone safely. "I've got it now."

"Go!"

Thumbs pressed from each side, fingers cocked beneath the slender arc of the wishbone, a pair of wishes stated silently, and CRACK! The bone snapped in two.

"Oh," Lindy sighed in disappointment.

Nancy stared in wonder. The larger half of the wishbone was clenched in her fist.

Thursday, December 5
1:00 PM

"When you were about six, we moved to Rockford, Illinois. Your dad had a wonderful opportunity to manage the local airport, and he began to develop a regional air show while he was there. That's a picture of your dad with Governor Ogilvie and the mayor of Rockford. It was taken at the inaugural air show. There's another one of Dad with all the political dignitaries at a ribbon cutting ceremony for the new building." Diane Cavanaugh paused to sip crushed ice in fruit juice.

Nancy looked up, then flexed her fingers, cramped from writing. She set aside the oversize faux leather memory book, filled with photos and handwritten tales of the Cavanaugh Clan.

This was how they spent the days before Christmas: Diane recalled the details of years past, while Nancy and Sandy alternately transcribed those memories for posterity.

Diane's collection of photographs documented every major event. During the autumn months, Diane had scavenged through the old family slides, and selected hundreds to convert to prints. Autumn had been a good time for her to tackle the project, early autumn at least. Diane had lovingly mounted nearly half of the photos onto heavy, cream pages, with room for narrative to the side and below. This family folklore would be her legacy, shared with her grandchildren, and even great-grandchildren, someday. She would not meet those descendents, however, and persevered with each detail, that they might know her and other ancestors of this generation. It was, Diane knew, a faulty attempt at immortality. She wondered how many generations—or how few—might pass along the family memory books, before this labor of love were put out with the garbage.

Diane had kept a diary since high school, and stacks of spirals from those early years, along with some floral print journals that she'd later received as gifts, collected dust on the upper shelf of her bedroom closet. Reading them had rarely crossed Diane's mind, until she committed to the wish: to leave behind the Cavanaugh family story. She spent hours, days, perusing the faded, crackling pages, noting the shift in handwriting as the girl who wrote with full, rounded letters grew into the woman who penned in elegant, long-lettered lines.

The journals filled in many forgotten details, and the handwritten pages revealed more than the thousand words that a picture might tell. They reminded Diane, painfully at times, how many things she'd wanted to do, and hadn't. Hurts were resurrected. In contrast, joy was the overwhelming theme of the photos. Who wants to capture anything but Kodak moments? But her journals went deeper than any photograph. It bore testimony to both the sun and the shadow of life, the rich blend of bright and dark, the tapestry of all hues within the spectrum of a complete life. That would include the good times and the bad, and the dull grays of unmemorable days in between.

The goal, for Diane, had been to record the history, and then dispose of the journals too personal to share. They were for her alone, and the act of putting words on the page had served to clear her mind, settle questions of the heart, vent anger, and purge what might have become hate. Her journals were not simply a chronicle of daily events, or even a genealogical document. Otherwise, Diane might have passed them on to her children.

Because these thoughts and words were so personal, Diane felt compelled to edit responsibly, selectively, what would be conveyed via the photo-narrative memory book. The fact that this was revisionist family history did not concern her, at first.

Throughout the pre-Christmas season, Diane had felt too fatigued to write the narrative, too drugged to do more than scrawl. Thus, she'd asked Nancy and Sandy to assist in getting the words onto the pages.

Today, it was all Diane could do to remember and speak for brief periods. This had been a long session. Diane's throat was parched to soreness, and Nancy's fingers were cramped, nearly numb. It was too much for either woman to continue.

"We'll pick this up later, Mom," Nancy suggested, standing and arching her back in a cat-like stretch. "Hmmm," she muttered, glancing with curiosity at the next page of photos, which documented the family birthdays during that year in Illinois, 1969 to 1970.

Typically, there was a photo of the birthday boy or girl, wearing a plastic, jeweled crown, flanked by parents, Diane always holding the homemade cake with candles lighted. It had been a tradition to mark each birthday this way. Yet, as Nancy studied each of her siblings' birthday photos for that year, she noticed her father's conspicuous absence. He was not featured in *any* of the photos, and the Cavanaugh birthdays stretched throughout the year. Nancy's was in March, Sandy's in June, James' in August, and Steven's in October.

Nancy flipped to the page where the 1969 family Christmas photo should have been mounted. Instead of the obligatory picture of the family, pajama-clad in front of the Christmas tree, the spot featured a collage of snapshots: the children opening gifts and sitting before the tree, favorite gifts held high. Her father was in none of those pictures, either. Oddly enough, the photos featured the Pleasant Ridge house, not the new home in Rockford.

These photos, sandwiched between pages of pictures with completed narrative, offered no clue as to why Jim "Iron-Ace"

Cavanaugh was not included in the holiday images. *How strange,* Nancy mused, wondering if her father's job had kept him from celebrating with his family. *Where was Dad, in 1969? And why weren't we in Rockford?*

Given how vividly Nancy recalled his attendance at birthdays and holidays, it was almost unimaginable that her father had not been there during that year. She would ask Sandy, who would have been eight-years-old that Christmas of 1969. Perhaps Sandy remembered about that holiday without their dad.

Or later, she'd ask her mother. Perhaps they'd collaborate on that section next. Nancy would find out then. Or, did her mother intend to omit narrative on those pages? Perhaps it would be best to talk with Sandy first, to glean what she could from her sister's memory.

Meanwhile, she'd rest, along with her mother. She could nap for hours on these quiet days off; days spent tending the family memory book at her mother's bedside. Nancy wondered if Sandy felt as lazy, on days that she wrote narrative for their mother.

Maybe it's just the blues, Nancy considered, pulling a thick afghan over her shoulders and scrunching the sofa pillow beneath her neck. *It's just the stress of Mom being sick,* she decided. Certainly, this was not an indication of depression, was it?

2:45 PM

"When do you suppose you'll stop having this dream?" her father asked patiently.

Nancy grinned, "Do you s'pose it'll stop if I just 'Fly the plane,' Dad?"

Her father returned the grin. "Yep."

"I don't even know what that means. I *am* flying the plane."

"No, you're just a passenger. You're going along for the ride, but you aren't taking any responsibility for flying the plane."

"Let's be frank, Dad," Nancy insisted. "This little metaphor you're playing with has nothing to do with my job, and every-thing to do with my marriage."

"Right!" Jim Cavanaugh glowed with enthusiasm as his daughter finally linked the dots, viewing the picture for what it was.

"And you think that by living in a separate apartment, by refusing to take John's calls and letters, I'm refusing to fly the plane of marriage. And that I've reneged on my promise to fly through smooth skies or turbulence, rain or hail, or dark of night, right?"

"Right. But you're mixing your metaphors. If I were a postal worker, I might have told you—"

"I know, I know, I know, Dad."

"No, you don't, obviously."

"Dad, if you know this much, you also know that John is the one who started this, so it's really up to him to fly this plane—it's his responsibility. He refused to help Mom, and she's going to suffer because of it."

"We all have to suffer, Nancy. It's life. But it's also a matter of degree. Your mother can handle whatever comes her way. The question is, can you?"

"This isn't about me."

"No, not entirely. Although your actions speak as if you believe otherwise."

"What's that supposed to mean?" Nancy snapped, irritably.

"Your mother's treatment is about your mother. Your mother's decision not to involve John is about your mother. It's not about you. But, throwing up a wall that stalls or crashes your marriage *is* about you. And others." He stopped, suddenly stubborn.

"What others?" Nancy asked sharply.

Her father looked through her, more than at her. He might have been straining to see events in the future, and his face brightened at the prospect.

"What others?" she repeated.

"You know, we're the only two people on this aircraft."

"So?"

"Do you think that pilot and co-pilot have committed to flying this plane, whether they have to deal with bad weather, a hijacker, or a mechanical failure?"

"Of course!"

"Even though it's just the two of us on board? And I'm dead, so nothing's going to happen to me."

"It doesn't matter how many or how few passengers are on board, Dad. They'd do it to save themselves. Even if neither of us were aboard, they'd fly this plane and land it safely, however long the journey."

"Funny you should mention that," her father mused. "What if the pilots think their destination is Copenhagen, but they have to put down in London for an equipment failure?"

"Well, they'll do what they can to land in London safely, fix the plane, and finish the trip."

"And that's what you need to do, too. Now, your mother has her own plane to fly. Let's say she's faced with a different sort of equipment failure, one that isn't repairable. What then?"

Nancy leaned back in her seat, looking away from her father. She knew what he was after, but couldn't say the words.

He said them for her. "Then, her destination may not be Copenhagen after all. And her journey may be shorter."

4:30 PM

Nancy awakened sluggishly. She'd slept for nearly two hours. Her mother should have had medicine an hour ago. With a surge of adrenaline that attended this realization, Nancy tossed back the afghan and leapt off the sofa, amazed that she could feel both the tidal wave of energy, and the magnetic pull of deep, luxurious slumber.

When Nancy reached her mother's bedroom, Diane was sitting upright in bed, making small notes on the pages capturing the Cavanaughs in 1969. Diane glanced up, almost perky, compared to her exhaustion earlier in the day.

"I thought I might try to fill in a little of this myself," she explained somewhat sheepishly, as Nancy walked through the door. "It's not that I don't want your help, but I like to do it, when I feel up to it."

"No problem," Nancy said breezily, wondering if her mother had other reasons. "Just let me know if you want me to take over."

Diane nodded, frowning slightly.

Nancy cocked her head, looking across her mother's lap to the page on which she painstakingly printed tidy block letters, as if each word were gold; significant, precious, worthy of thoughtful consideration before being "spent" on the page.

"You're going to get a hand cramp if you don't ease up on that pen," Nancy said with a chuckle.

"Yes, well, it's a bad habit," her mother admitted, setting down the pen and massaging her fingers and palm. "I tend to hold the pen too tightly when I'm thinking. It's easier when I write free-prose in my journal. It's not like I have to worry about a picture-perfect sentence for that.

"*This*, however," she said distinctly, gesturing to the album, "is a document for our family. I feel as if I have to get it *perfect*. Or at least just right." She tapped the pages lightly, then picked up the pen again. Pausing, Diane frowned at the book, appearing to conclude some difficult decision as she handed the pen to Nancy.

"Don't write anything, yet. Let me tell you about these pictures. Then, you can tell me what should be written in a permanent document of our family life."

Nancy raised her eyebrows, intrigued. Sitting softly on the bed, she waited for her mother to begin.

"I created this memory book almost as an expression of gratitude for being given such a good life. I wanted to be sure to represent as many of our blessings and good times as possible. For my grandchildren, I wanted a photo history, so that the little ones will know a bit of your father and me. So, this started out as a happily-ever-after family history."

Diane paused again, choosing her words carefully, as if a witness at an important trial. She continued: "But then, I decided . . . in fact, it just came to me while I was resting, and it seemed like such a good idea, that it inspired me to start right away." Diane's voice became pressured, fueled by the passion of her inspiration. "What I decided is that it's important to acknowledge that we've weathered some difficult times, too. The fact that we've survived them, *intact*, is just as much a blessing to be remembered. It's too easy to forget what you've learned, or how you've grown, if all you do is remember the moments that look like something out of a television show. I was thinking, all of a sudden, that this narrative was starting to resemble something from 'Father Knows Best.'"

Diane regarded the Christmas, 1969, photo collage, asking "Do you notice anything different about this set of pages? Other than the fact that you and I have filled in pages for the years before 1969, and many of the years since?"

Nancy nodded, steeling herself for the unexpected.

"What's different, then?" Diane prompted.

Nancy hesitated, then asked, "Is it the fact that we don't have our usual birthday picture with you and Dad?"

"Yes. And how about Christmas?"

"Dad isn't in any of the pictures," Nancy stated softly, the hint of a question in the lilt of her voice.

"That's right," Diane whispered. "I was determined to show the Cavanaugh family celebrating in full gear. I wasn't going to let his absence ruin the magical family history as it was being made in 1969, or even now, twenty-seven years later."

Diane glanced out the bedroom window at the approaching dusk of a short winter day. "That's a type of sickness, Nancy. It denies reality, it denies strength, tenacity, perseverance, negotiation, compromise, and most of all it denies a commitment that became enduring love. I've decided it's more important to have the record include *that* as part of our family legacy. If I don't include it, our family history is incomplete, and you'll never know to be grateful for the life that we wound up living. Also, you'll never know that sometimes you have to fight for what you want, as if your life depended on it. And that there's often a reward for doing so."

Nancy shifted on the bed uncomfortably, sensing that she was about to be enlightened in a way that would challenge her to reconcile with John. But what did John have to do with any of this? She elected to remain quiet, raising her guard to protect the will to make her own decisions. She was old enough, capable enough, to have the lives of two hundred passengers entrusted to her flight skills. Surely, she was also old enough and capable enough to navigate the turbulence within her marriage.

Diane shifted her gaze from the window to her younger daughter, and laughed appreciatively. "You've had that expression since you were a stubborn toddler, and there's a photo of your dad with the same expression when he was a boy. I know when you go stubborn on me, Nancy. Just hear me out, and then make your own choice, as you always have.

"That fall, your father accepted a position in Rockford, Illinois, without consulting me. He signed a contract to have a realtor sell our house in Pleasant Ridge, and came home with a bottle of champagne and the announcement that he'd taken a fabulous offer to manage an airport in Illinois, and that we'd be moving there within a month. He showed me the salary agreement that he'd been offered. It was twice what he'd been earning, and it included life insurance, a retirement plan, and wonderful health insurance that even included dental care. Not everyone had such generous benefits back then, Nancy, and your father believed that he'd just secured the family's fortune by negotiating this incredible package."

Diane looked away. "All I had to do was jump for joy at our great luck. But all I wanted to do was jump out of a window. I was not the jubilant, supportive wife that some of the other photos suggest. I was bitter, angry, and vengeful. My vengeance played out in subtle ways. I never managed to keep the house quite tidy enough for the realtor. I couldn't find a single house in Rockford that met my requirements. So, your father chose a house on his own, signed the loan documents, and moved us to Rockford before the Pleasant Ridge house sold the next spring. I couldn't believe he'd do this. But for some reason, instead of telling him off, I lost my voice. Maybe, at that point, I was trying to be a good wife. But, honestly, I think I was partly in shock and partly too angry to talk to your father.

"He tried everything to make me love the new house and our community. He bought family memberships to the swim and golf club, hired a decorator who wallpapered and furnished the house in high style. Yet, I was determined not to like that place. It was as if the more your father cajoled, the more I dug in my heels. I'd had no voice in the decision. He hadn't even asked my opinion about moving four young children away from the only place they'd known, from their grandparents, their friends, their home.

"So, I cut him out of our celebrations, just as he'd cut me out of this important life decision. I dragged my feet so that you children could spend one last Christmas in the Pleasant Ridge house. Your dad stayed in Rockford."

Nancy seized this moment to respond. "Mom, that's no different than what John and I are going through now. How can you tell me that I should respond to John's decision to cut us off from the treatment that could give you more good days, and possibly more time, when you made the same choice back in 1969?"

"The difference is that you don't have to repeat mistakes I made. Your father and I made another mistake by failing to acknowledge that tough year with you children. Maybe if we'd been more open about our problems, as well as our effort to resolve them, you'd realize that there are many options. Not just one. You don't have to leave physically, as you've done, or emotionally, as I did."

"Well," Nancy said firmly, "I won't discuss my marriage, and I'll handle it my way. Just as you handled yours."

Diane raised her eyebrows, smiling at the rebuke, not the least bit injured, as if Nancy were a hissing kitten, struggling to assert itself. "I wonder how things would have turned out for us, for you, Nancy, if I'd stayed on that path. I wonder if a thirty-year-old mother of four, with only a couple years of college and no skills, would've been able to offer you and your brothers and sister the stability and standard of living that allowed you to make your own path. What if I'd just quit the marriage?"

"That's different, Mom," Nancy retorted with exasperation.

"We don't have children." As she said the words, she felt a warm flush creep from her neck to her face, classic evidence of a lie. *But I haven't lied! We don't have children,* Nancy insisted silently.

"As if children are the only reason worth working out problems," Diane responded distantly, looking as if she were viewing her life as it might have been, in the tradition of George Bailey or Ebenezer Scrooge.

"My point, Nancy, is that part of our family history is this terrible year in which your father and I nearly lost everything we'd worked for, and the fact that we survived it and went on to become stronger. *That's* the real legacy. I want my children and grandchildren to know the kind of stock they're from. Cavanaughs don't run away, they face their problems. Perhaps not right away, but eventually. We're strong enough to do it, and we're better for it."

"And would you be giving me that advice if John were beating me?"

"Let's not confuse the issue, Nancy. We aren't talking about abuse. We're talking about your husband, who has never mistreated you or anyone in our family. We're talking about a conspiracy to bribe him to forget the Hippocratic oath, and to sell his soul to the devil, in exchange for a few good days for me. John isn't the bad guy here, and though you may disagree, your view of the situation is skewed.

"You are so much your father's daughter. I hate to see this part of *me* in you. I wonder what would happen if you were as determined to make things right as your father was, once he understood the impact of his independent decisions?"

The question hung in the air, unanswered. It was essentially unfair, Nancy believed, as the circumstances were so different. To Nancy, the difference was more a matter of life and death: her mother's. And whereas her father's actions excluded her mother, John's actions excluded only himself. Furthermore, they felt like a betrayal of the family's interest. How could her mother even think that the situations were parallel?

Friday, December 6
1:25 AM

The nights became a source of both irritation and comfort. The dream repeated, and then progressed. As usual, Nancy and her father were seated in a jumbo jet above the Atlantic Ocean, the sole passengers, ferried by anonymous pilots.

"You have to be very careful about this decision."

"You mean my promise to fly the plane?"

"Yes. Especially because of the special cargo that's on board."

"Us?"

"Not just us."

"There's more than just one life in the balance?"

"By George, I think she's got it!"

Tuesday, December 10
9:30 AM

"July first, give or take a couple weeks either side," the doctor announced joyfully.

"*That's* the special cargo," Nancy whispered.

"What's that? Special cargo? It certainly is!"

Nancy smiled wanly, bemused at the irony of this timing, which could not be worse. Or could it? She'd be on vacation for the remainder of the first trimester, through the Christmas holidays, and that would allow her to spend more time with her mother.

She could almost hear, even feel, the blast of her father's reproachful protests: "I thought you *got it*, Nancy! What's it gonna' take?"

But all she could contemplate was, what now?

Wednesday, December 11
1:00 AM

"I was hoping you'd be here tonight."

"No you weren't," her father challenged.

"If you know so much, why didn't you tell me about this directly?"

"There are some things—lots of things, actually—that you have to figure out yourself, Nancy! And I thought you'd done that. Well, you've made progress, but there's more. I can't do it for you. I can only point you in the right direction."

"And offer a few well-directed clues?" she added mischievously.

"Well, it's working, isn't it?"

"The timing isn't great."

"Timing is everything!" her father shouted, gleefully.

"If so, then *this* isn't perfect timing."

"There you go again, thinking you can control every little detail of life!"

"Dad, you're the one who taught us, 'Fail to plan and you'll plan to fail.' Remember?"

"I wasn't right about everything," Jim Cavanaugh grumbled. "So learn from my mistakes."

"What mistakes?" Nancy jested, certain that her father would be hard-pressed to come up with any, save for what her mother had shared the week before.

"Ask your mother. But you should have a little faith, and quit trying to make everything perfect." He remained stone-faced, implacable.

"Nothing's perfect," Nancy mused softly, "And more importantly, no *one* is perfect."

"Quit trying to make me feel better. Don't say things that make me think you understand."

"If you know so much," Nancy challenged mildly, "How come you don't know when I'm being *perfectly* serious?"

Chapter Twenty–Seven

UNINTENDED CONSEQUENCES

Thursday, December 12
9:30 AM

Julia Hannigan swept past the reception desk briskly, barely limping, and nodded to the secretary who was fielding calls. She smiled broadly, if unintentionally. The giddy rush that accompanied a flight into wellness, preceding the return of casual indifference to her health, was rooted in the power of last weekend's endorphin surge. The past few days, she'd had energy enough to run a marathon. She felt grateful enough to shout prayers of praise.

The secretary waved a greeting, eye-to-eye, connecting one call and immediately clicking to receive the next.

What a difference, Julia mused, *to have people look me in the eye, rather than avoid me.*

It was true, given human nature, that most people found it easier to perform a dance of avoidance, than to attempt contact that might be awkward, unwelcome—or even embarrassing. Usually, Julia participated in a similarly avoidant dance. This served to protect others from the self-imposed responsibility to conjure a supportive response to bad news. In kind, this mechanism protected Julia from the equally self-imposed tendency to soothe the flustered sympathetic.

Today, however, Julia's smile was the unconscious manifestation of self-actualized pleasure, a natural consequence of rejoining the world, *whole,* re-establishing full membership in the lives of her family and colleagues. She crossed the lobby on steady legs, her arms capably cradling a thick sheaf of invoices and intra-office mail. She then wound through the maze of eighteen cubicles to her desk at the Fields & Strauss Electronics Company, and plopped down the stack of invoices that needed immediate attention.

As a customer relations "special problems" agent, Julia was responsible for contacting clients whose order was incomplete, late, or for any reason undeliverable. It required a finesse that came naturally to her.

She rolled back her chair and flipped through the intra-office memos, deciding to check on any essential meetings and issues before beginning her telephone calls. The last piece of correspondence announced a mandatory, company-wide drug screening for the next day.

Muffling a gasp, feeling as if the wind had been knocked out of her, Julia collapsed on the chair and grabbed her planner, slapping it open to the monthly calendar. She counted back to her last round of chemotherapy—that's what *she* called it. Only three days. Would that be time enough for it to clear from her system?

O God, O God, O God, she prayed silently. *Not when everything is finally getting back to normal.*

She would call the nurse. The nurse could get the doctor to request that she be excused, on the grounds that the drug he prescribed *would* be detected. No, he wouldn't be able to do that, she realized. But he *could* provide a letter explaining *why* they would find that drug in the screen.

O God, O God, O God. Please, don't let this be a problem, not now.

She would have to call, soon. Privacy was an issue, given the arrangement of the cubicles. She couldn't call from here. She'd have to wait until lunch and call from a phone booth. There was one next to the Shell gas station. *Okay. Breathe. I can handle this,* she coached herself, willing it to be true.

Julia pulled the invoices from beneath the stack of memos, and then set them down. She needed a manual task, one that didn't require much brainpower, but a project that would isolate her in the cubicle, away from people who might take note of, or contribute to, her jangled nerves. Scooting closer to her desk, Julia logged onto the computer, and brought up the quality control checklist she was revising for her boss. It wouldn't take long, but it would distract her until she could leave for the earliest possible lunch break.

The next hour and a half crawled along, seemingly at the pace of evolution. She finished the form revisions, filed dozens of invoices marked "complete," read her mail, cleaned out her desk, and made two trips to the coffee dispenser. It was still a bit early, but she'd deal with queries if they came up.

She slid her chair beneath the desk, pulled her satchel over one shoulder, and then briskly navigated through the maze of walkways to the reception area. Again, the secretary was taking calls, and paid no attention as Julia pulled on her coat and signed out for lunch.

Ten minutes later, Julia stood outside of the Shell station, her right index finger pressing on one ear to block the competing noise of traffic, her left hand holding the phone receiver tightly to her head. A chilly, late-autumn wind sent knives of shivers up her spine, and down her limbs.

"This is Julia Hannigan. I need to speak with the nurse. It's important." There was no mistaking the urgency in her voice.

"This is Jeannie. What can I do for you, Julia?" asked the dynamo on the other end of the phone.

"I just found out that my company is doing a random drug screening tomorrow. I'm worried that they'll fire me, if I still have some of the medicine in my bloodstream."

"We've run into this before," the nurse stated calmly. "I'll check your chart, and we'll be able to gauge whether or not it's going to show up. It's been a few days since you last had the medication, Julia. You probably won't have even trace amounts. Hang on."

Julia felt irritation creeping in, taking the place of fear. Just when things were going so well, there has to be a random drug screen. *Please, God. Please, God. Please, God. Let it be okay. Let it be okay. Let it be okay.*

Julia always prayed in sets of three. Her mother had taught that doing so invoked the immediate attention of the Blessed Trinity. Julia was committed to using every measure available, superstitious or not, to summon the power of her spiritual protectors.

She'd become more religious since her illness. Actually, Julia had always felt a spiritual connection, but hadn't practiced formal religion since leaving her devout parents' home—until she'd become so debilitated that all she could do was pray. Later, at the worst times, she became too distracted by pain to pray. At that point, Julia learned to judge her relative wellness based on her capacity for prayer, and she fulfilled the promise of more intent prayer with each step toward health.

"Julia." The nurse returned to the line. "I have your chart here. Your last dose was Sunday, four days ago, which means that you should have no trouble. The longest this medication would be detectable in urine is two to three days. If it were a blood screen, instead of urine, it could be detected. But the reason you're doing well is because you're on a three-times-a-week schedule. Do you want to skip your next dose? That's set up for tomorrow evening, anyway, so it won't affect the drug screen."

Thank You, Thank You, Thank You, God. Julia closed her eyes and breathed as if she hadn't done so in minutes. "I don't want to miss the next dose," she replied gratefully. "Thanks for looking this up. Things at work are great, and I can't afford to lose my insurance."

The nurse responded brusquely, as if she hadn't the time for appreciative chitchat. "You just do your work, and we'll do ours. See you tomorrow evening." Click.

Julia stared at the phone receiver, startled by the nurse's abrupt tone. This woman had always been businesslike, and had told Julia and her husband that this facet of the business was a personal mission. It was a way to honor the memory of her daughter, who'd committed suicide after years of suffering with a chronic illness. Had the daughter received the medication that Julia took, the nurse's daughter might still be alive.

Neither Julia nor her husband, Len, would ever forget the words or tone of that initial consultation. "Don't even think of this as charity. This is free to you because it's free to me. And if my daughter had gotten some of it, she might have been able to tolerate living. She might even have lived well. Just don't ever discuss this with anyone else. It's a matter of your life, and my peace. Am I clear?"

Julia and Len had been nearly mute with shock and fear, but had nodded assent and lived up to the agreement. They understood the power of the medicine only after the initial treatment, and having seen its impact, were willing to agree to almost any contract. The surprising conversation took place *after* that miraculous first dose, for the nurse knew that she could not rely on patients to keep the confidence unless they'd experienced such dramatic relief.

That was why she worked this special intervention backward, with the medication following a word-of-mouth referral, and the formal consultation afterward. The risk of losing the elixir of life itself made it easy for patients to agree to terms, such as not even disclosing to one's personal physician that this medication was being prescribed. In most instances, even the most cautious and skeptical of patients or family members became willing participants in the deception, for to see the outcome was to believe in the beneficence of the treatment. They assured themselves that the family physician did not need to know, since another doctor administered the drug, anyway.

As the sun broke through pale gray cloud puffs, the wind ceased its tormenting chill. *It's a sign!* Julia Hannigan cracked a smile, feeling as relieved and successful as the kid who gets away with a forged note to play hooky. It would all work out, no one would be the wiser, and she'd be all the better for it.

Yet, what she didn't realize was that someone else was about to wreak havoc with her happily-ever-after ideas.

Friday, December 13
2:20 PM

The youthful blond brushed back the hair, which swept across her face: thick, long bangs that blended into a modified bob. She glanced furtively over her shoulder, and then lifted her wrist to check the time. Perspiration formed dewy beads across her lips, which were dry by comparison. She licked her lips anxiously, then opened the Workroom door with a flourish of purpose, as if she had business there.

As expected, the room was empty. She crossed to the far corner noiselessly, and proceeded to rifle through the contents of a drug bin. Here were the remnant medications, used during morning surgeries. She smiled, noting the familiar, distinct markings of Dr. Franklin's vials. Plenty of Fentanyl left. She could feel the pounding of her heart escalate to a gallop, apprehension mounting with the risk of discovery.

Her desperate *craving* for the drug's soaring relief fueled the anxiety that seemed to whistle in her ears, pound in her heart, and tremble in her fingers. The desperation was borne of drug tolerance; she needed more and more of the narcotic to achieve—and sustain—the high. She felt physically discombobulated during the anxious process of getting the drug, and she also became careless.

Time was not on her side, she knew, and her fingers worked clumsily as a result of her fear. She was not a cool-headed thief. Frowning, she rapidly pushed other drug vials aside, searching for more Fentanyl. She had a three-day weekend, and much would be needed. Her breathing was rapid, almost panting, and she felt another round of moisture break the skin beneath her arms. She might have just climbed several flights of stairs. But such virtuous activity was not the source of her sweat and rapid respiration.

No more? There were typically forty or more remnant vials by this time of the day. Nevertheless, she had six. That would have to do. Almost out of time. God only knew how badly she needed a hit. She would come back, she decided. Change of shift offered another opportunity, or even after that, before the Pharmacy picked up the bins. There would be more Fentanyl used today, and she'd augment her stash later.

Shaking her head nervously, she grabbed a syringe from her lab coat pocket, and uncapped it with unsteady hands. *I need this now!*

As agitation blended with anxious fear, her hands became tremulous beasts, which refused to cooperate with the essential task: *get the drug, get the drug, get the drug.* Pressing her wrists against the counter to steady her hands, she filled the syringe with the contents of those six remnant vials, and then plunged the needle into her arm, not bothering to swab the area with disinfectant. She exhaled deeply, the anticipation of relief mingled with a sense of accomplishment, success bearing a cool breeze that chilled her damp skin. She steadied her hands against the countertop before capping the glinting silver needle that delivered peace.

Still, the job was not done. If she simply tossed the now empty remnant vials into the bin, Pharmacy techs would note a discrepancy and the theft would be discovered. It was unlikely that anyone would attribute the discrepancy to her. In fact, the anesthetist or anesthesiologist who had administered the drug during surgery would be held accountable.

Yet, it was essential *not* to call attention to her theft, or measures would be instituted to curtail her supply. That would be devastating. Surely, she would die if that happened.

To cover the theft, she would replace the liquid pleasure with something else. Typically, she used saline. It was easily available, and it was not tracked, as it had no medicinal value. In her early thefts, she would empty and refill one vial at a time, cautious to mark the fill spot with her fingernail, injecting the fluid until it reached exactly that spot. This time, however, she felt hurried, tense, on edge, and jittery. In her haste, she'd emptied all the vials at once. In a moment, she'd cover her tracks.

For now, she would revel in the quest fulfilled, the effect

achieved. Confidence and optimism born of the narcotic high rushed through her body. Perhaps there *was* plenty of time to complete the process.

Yet, she remained a bit tremulous as she grabbed the vial thought to contain saline. She inserted a fresh syringe, and drew up the fluid until the barrel was full. The final step was to insert the needle into each of the six remnant vials, careful to leave exactly the amount documented in the drug record.

But she'd been sloppy early in this process. And the false confidence that attends a drug induced high dissuaded this nurse from making a cautious second check of the vial's contents, a rare and serious nursing error.

It would be weeks before her error was caught, and she would inadvertently repeat it later in the day. Her weekend stash was not what she'd thought: what she took for Fentanyl and Demerol was actually saline. And what she thought to be saline was, in fact, a paralytic called succinylcholine, used for surgical intubation. Although the consequence to the young nurse would be the absence of a soothing or invigorating weekend high, there would be an unintended ripple effect—potentially lethal—that would impact the gift of the Magi.

6:55 PM

A leisurely pasta supper with his wife separated the two calls this evening. The first, made on the way home from work, had been the home of Ann-Marie Travis. The family lived on an isolated patch of densely wooded land, the sole farmhouse amidst a sprawl of 1960s ranch style homes. The Magi did not feel comfortable there, and seldom stayed more than fifteen minutes. Ann-Marie was a pleasant enough woman, but she spoke only reticently. Her husband was even more reserved, brooding, bordering on mistrustful. The Magi did not know if Mr. Travis was suspicious of doctors in specific, or strangers in general. Nevertheless, if Ann-Marie wanted this treatment, the Magi would provide it. Young mothers like Mrs. Travis needed it.

Yet, despite the treatments, her health was failing, the effects of Lou Gehrig's disease making it nearly impossible for Ann-Marie to take nourishment. Dietary supplements hadn't curbed the anorexia that whittled her five-and-a-half foot frame from one hundred sixty to one hundred five pounds.

The Magi sighed, recognizing that there wouldn't be many more treatments. Ann-Marie knew it, too. She gained less and less from each treatment, perhaps even nothing at all. Still, she continued to ask for it. Perhaps the small gains were worthwhile, whatever they might be, but the Magi never asked Ann-Marie to defend her request.

As for her husband, the Magi noted that, with his wife and family, Mr. Travis was a soft-spoken man of few words. He worked as a mechanic at his father's garage, and asked no questions about the nature of Ann-Marie's treatment. If he noticed that the elixir brought less and less respite, he did not comment. And surely, he noticed, for he was a bright enough man. More likely, and quite simply, he wouldn't waste anyone's time, or his own breath, by stating the obvious.

During the treatments, Mr. Travis would allow the Magi to set up the intravenous line and inject the first round of medication. However, Mr. Travis would pick up from there. He did not care to have Marilyn or Kathy—or any stranger—in his house overnight, and Ann-Marie voiced no preference to the contrary. He typically arranged for their three children to spend the night with his sister's family. That way, Mr. Travis could provide the injections every four hours throughout the night, the children would be looked after, and no outsiders intruded upon his home.

This was always the way the Magi had worked with the Travis family, and the only way they would work with him. The Magi left several syringes of the elixir, specifying dosages and his intent to return the next day to evaluate what else Ann-Marie might need.

In contrast, the Magi's second visit and final treatment of the day progressed more typically at the Hannigan home. Although the children squealed and raced rambunctiously through the house, chasing a cat dressed in doll clothes, neither Julia nor Len minded the noise. Julia had prepared for bed, and called a final goodnight to the children, who shouted the same salutation, in return. She smiled at Len, Stu, and Marilyn, the latter of whom prepared IV tubing for Julia's overnight treatment.

"Ready for La-La Land," she quipped.

"Night, Sweetie," Len said tenderly. He kissed Julia on the forehead, and then stroked her free hand. "Remember me in all those good dreams you'll be having."

Julia chuckled, guiding Len's hand to her lips for a quick kiss in return, while clenching the opposite fist to pump up the veins in her left forearm. The Magi was gloved and ready to swab the area with disinfectant before inserting the IV needle and catheter, from which the elixir would flow into Julia's bloodstream.

Since Julia was trying to maintain a full-time work schedule, Friday night treatments worked best. She would sleep for nearly fourteen hours, then take mini-doses at 8:00 PM on Saturday and Sunday. The mini-doses were nearly as effective as a two-day full treatment. The gains were realized without the consequence of losing an entire weekend. The greatest benefit: she lost no work time during the week.

While this system presented a lot of responsibility for Len, especially throughout the weekends, they had decided the blessings were worth the sacrifice. Usually, Julia could take the treatments for a few weekends, and then take a break for four to six weeks. Once the MS symptoms worsened, she'd call for another round of sessions, and the Magi would visit.

As he adjusted the flow of the IV, the Magi contemplated how uniquely patients responded to treatments. The patients' medical conditions differed, they took various other medications, and they came to him with a multitude of emotional, mental, and spiritual presentations. That complex of dynamics contributed to the challenge of managing this type of care. And that challenge, along with the outcome, was what sustained the Magi. There were no cookbook recipes to follow with this elixir. Just well judged trial and error.

Now, it was time to inject the elixir. The catheter in the IV butterfly would remain in Julia's arm throughout the weekend. That way, Marilyn could provide the appropriate dosage of medication, even once Julia awakened and no longer needed the IV fluids. She could irrigate the site, something that Len could have done, too. However, Len was happy to have Mr. Stewart and Marilyn take care of the technical aspects of care.

The Magi pushed the syringes to the side of the carton, looking for the telltale markings of Dr. Mackenzie Franklin. It was a bonus to get her syringes, as he would know what was inside the barrel without labeling the ones he'd substituted in the drug kits. *Strange,* he thought, frowning a bit as he picked up one, and then another, of the syringes. *That shouldn't be,* he told himself. The barrel of two syringes featured a pair of red X-es, which was Dr. Franklin's standard marking for Succinylcholine.

Medications were often similar in appearance. What looked like harmless saline could also be a brain-numbing narcotic, or even a toxic paralytic. That's why Dr. Franklin marked her syringes so precisely.

It probably saved Julia Hannigan's life.

This realization caused the Magi's heart to thump wildly in his chest. His throat constricted in fear at the egregious mistake. How *could* he? He did not know. But now, he needed to locate a syringe with Limbotryl for Julia. She and Len sensed his flustered impatience, and exchanged nervous glances.

"What's wrong?" Julia asked firmly.

The Magi paused, uncertain what to answer. He held up the syringes. "These aren't the medication I need. I don't know how they were mixed in with the others. Give me a moment to locate Limbotryl."

He resumed his search through the dozen syringes, finding only one labeled in Dr. Franklin's style. It was the only one he could trust. Or, could he? If the *marked* syringes held Succinylcholine, it was possible that some *unmarked* syringes contained the same thing. He would not risk that.

No, he would not risk *any* of the syringes. It was too dangerous. His was a mission of life, and he would not play Russian roulette with his patients. At once, he wondered about the syringes he had left with Mr. Travis. *Dear God, please let those syringes hold Limbotryl!*

Decisively, he packed the carton of syringes into a leather case. "We can't proceed tonight, Julia," he stated abruptly. "If I can't be certain that I'm giving you the proper medication, I won't give you any."

Marilyn paled at his words, uncertain what had gone wrong.

Len and Julia shared another look. "What's wrong with the medication you brought?" Len asked softly.

The Magi sighed, debating what to tell them. He opted for the truth, for he was in a hurry and could not think of anything else that would calm the couple. He felt compelled to drive back to the Travis home to check the other syringes—quickly. He looked at his watch, bemoaning the lost time at supper with Jeannie. However, four hours had not quite passed. Surely, he'd be in time. He'd call from the road to warn Mr. Travis against giving his wife *any* of the medication.

"There are two syringes marked to contain something other than Limbotryl. It's a medication that would stop your breathing, Julia. I don't know how it got into this supply, and I need to get rid of all of this, because I can't guarantee it's what you need. I'm sorry."

He closed the leather bag quickly, and directed Marilyn to disconnect the IV tubing from Julia's arm. "Keep the butterfly in place," he ordered. "If I can get some Limbotryl later tonight, I'll be back. Otherwise, just irrigate it and cover it until tomorrow. I need to check on one of my other patients, now. Really," he emphasized, "I'm terribly sorry. I can't imagine how this happened."

In a flurry, he swung on a jacket, grabbed the medical bag, and hustled through the door, which he slammed with a shudder that shook the house.

Len and Julia Hannigan murmured polite reassurances to Marilyn, who was speechless with surprise. The couple inquired what would happen if the Magi couldn't get the medication Julia so desperately needed to function, to survive.

Marilyn said nothing, uncharacteristically, shaking her head in bewilderment. She would call Jeannie as soon as she attended to this IV. Surely, everything would be all right. It was a wish, a plea, a prayer.

8:15 PM

"What's the matter with you?" Jeannie asked irritably. "What's happened?"

Stuart Adler choked on his words, his throat constricted with fear, nearly swollen tight; tears crept down his cheeks as he held the wallet of photographs in one hand, while clutching a cell phone in the other. *How did this happen?*

"She *died*," he gasped, hiccupping a sob that generated a fresh flood of tears.

"Who died?"

"Ann-Marie," he whispered.

"She's *dead?*" Jeannie's voice was incredulous. "Did you even get to give her the treatment?"

Self-recriminating grief took hold of his core, and he struggled to silence another series of sobs. He remained silent until the shuddering ceased, then tried again. "That's what *caused* it, I think," he squeaked. "Not the Limbotryl." He paused, forcing himself to breathe deeply so that he could convey the horrible details. "I don't understand it, but somehow, Succinylcholine wound up in my carton of medications."

"No!" Jeannie barked. "Stuart, this can't be! How did *that* get into the carton?"

"I don't know. I didn't even notice the markings until I was getting ready for Julia's treatment."

"You didn't give her anything." It was a statement, one that dared him to answer affirmatively and expect to survive her wrath.

"No!" He was angry, now. Did she think so little of him that she'd suspect such incompetence, once he'd discovered the problem?

"You should have called Ann-Marie's husband and told him not to give *her* anything," Jeannie accused.

"I tried," he said between clenched teeth, "and the line was busy. I got over there as fast as I could. What else would you have me do?"

She ducked the question. "What did her husband say when you got there?"

"Her husband didn't react at all," Stu answered, reactivating his own surprise at such a stoic response, especially by a spouse. "He just said something like, 'Now she's in peace.' He didn't cry, he didn't ask what happened. He just called his sister, told her that Ann-Marie died, and asked if the children could still spend the night with their cousins."

"Unbelievable! What about arrangements for the body?"

"I took care of it. She'd talked with the people at Burns and Beckman a while ago. They're handling arrangements."

"What did you put on the death certificate?"

Stu stared at the photo of his expressionless daughter, wiping a tear that had dripped onto the plastic cover. He was guilty, guilty, guilty. He felt sick enough to vomit. He had killed his daughter by *not* offering her the elixir. Now, he had inadvertently contributed to the death of someone else because he *did*. And his wife was asking about arrangements for the body, and what he had written on the death certificate.

If I had a gun in this car, I'd use it, he decided silently.

"I said," Jeannie repeated, "what did you put on the death certificate?"

He sighed. "Heart failure."

Heart failure, he mused. *Where is that chest pain, now that I want it? Heart failure would be a blessing, a lot less messy than a gunshot.*

At the other end of the phone, the woman's eyes glittered with tears. She rarely allowed herself tears. But she heard the desperation in the quietly uttered words, and feared the incipient loss of him, too, if she didn't act quickly. She would have to go and take care of this. Stuart couldn't handle death, at least not unnecessary death. She would need to isolate him, protect him, until they figured out what had happened.

It was a *terrible* accident. It should *never* have occurred. *Why did it occur?* Jeannie wondered. If he'd accidentally pulled up the wrong drug . . . well, she didn't want to pursue that possibility.

They would deal with this, reminding the family of what good had been offered, if only for a short time. No, not they; *she* would remind the family. She'd send her husband home, before his emotions got him into trouble. Their work *must* remain protected, confidential, even in the shadow of this horrific, accidental death.

Meanwhile, she'd pitch the stash of vials and syringes he'd be bringing home. Whatever was in them was a toxin, not an elixir.

She'd follow the partner's advice—sound advice that her husband had refused to consider, until now? Perhaps this was the moment he'd reconsider. There was a way to order the elixir from overseas via the Internet. The partner would take care of it; he was computer savvy. They would *know* what was in each vial, and it would bring healing. Not death.

Perhaps the trafficking of such substances *was* illegal. They would cross that bridge . . . .

For now, Jeannie was determined to have the *exact* medication intended for their patients. And she hoped that this weekend would give her enough time: to deal with the unanticipated death; to console the grieving family—for surely, in his strange way, Ann-Marie's husband grieved; and especially, time to tend to her husband's emotional recovery.

She was a tough woman. It was hell to lose a daughter, their only child, but she'd survived that trauma. She'd remind herself that this was not coward's work. Indeed, to sustain the mission of healing, she'd wage fierce and relentless battle against her husband's demons. For, despite her sharp, unsympathetic words, she loved this gentle man. Most importantly, she could not risk losing him, too.

Chapter Twenty–Eight

REMORSE

Saturday, December 14
9:30 AM

"Stuart, we need to take some initiative. I've talked to Ron, and we can purchase some of his supply. It won't be much, and we won't have enough for everyone. But we can develop our own little triage system to determine who *needs* it the most, and who'll *benefit* the most. The others may lose a bit of ground, but it can't be helped until we initiate our own supply request."

Jeannie Adler sat at her desk, a ten-foot asymmetrical swirl of teak, hand-rubbed to a satin patina. A pair of faux leather letterboxes and thick patient files obscured half of the surface. Across the table, Jeannie's husband slumped in a black leather chair, silently studying the grain of the desk. He seemed not to have heard his wife's pitch.

Sighing, Jeannie backed her leather chair from the desk. She rounded the corner and crouched next to her husband, gently turning his face toward her own. "Stuart," she whispered. "It's not your fault. We've always checked those syringes carefully, and the ones you left her husband were correctly labeled. I can't explain why she died, Stu, but we have to move on. Please, listen to me."

Blank eyes turned mournful, her words having the opposite effect of the comfort intended. Stu looked down, severing the brief contact that Jeannie had made.

"Ann-Marie was a tough patient," Jeannie went on, deciding that a circuitous path might better reach him. "You told me, two visits ago, that even Ann-Marie seemed to know the treatments weren't giving her the boost she needed. Didn't we agree that she was near the end?"

It was a rhetorical question, and Jeannie expected no response. She would simply retell the story, as they both knew it. If necessary, she would also retell the story he hated to hear: the one about Joy. That real life nightmare, revisited by Jeannie's occasional telling of the story, always spurred Stu to action. He needed to be mobilized, quickly.

"Ann-Marie knew, and that's why she talked with the people at the funeral home. She wanted to take care of it—like housekeeping—so that her husband wouldn't have to worry about it. She wouldn't have taken that step if she didn't have some idea.

"It's so hard at the end," Jeannie said, as if thinking aloud. "I try not to feel it, and it's always easier if I'm very busy. It's almost effortless if we have a new patient, because then I can simply focus on their progress." The words reminded her that a low supply of the elixir would diminish the chance for redemption, especially if they couldn't treat new patients.

"Stuart, I'm going to pick up the supply from Ron later today. I have six nurses making weekend calls, all Medicare home health. Kathy and Marilyn will have to cancel the group for prospective patients. No sense meeting if we can't offer them something." Jeannie squeezed her husband's hand, and then gently stroked the raised veins, blue-gray ridges amidst a liver-spotted plain of tawny peach. She wondered when they'd become old enough to earn liver spots, and studied the pattern of light and dark as she prepared for the final effort.

"We've done a good job, Stuart. This is what we do to honor Joy. She'd want us to continue. We must do it, we can do it, we will do it in memory of our little girl."

A single tear crept along Stuart Adler's nose, dropping onto his shirt. The pressure began to return to his head and chest, nausea looming in his stomach. He must do right by his little girl, he knew, but why did his wife have to remind him? It was better to exist in this fog than to remember. Each time he remembered, he felt the crushing pain in his chest and head. He kept his eyes closed, searching for the tunnel that would lead back to that foggy place in which he felt nothing, did nothing; he could simply *be.*

But, Jeannie had stirred the pot. In doing so, she'd destroyed all paths leading to that place that was neither heaven nor hell; neither life nor death; neither pleasure nor pain. What was that place, he wondered? He could not name it, but he suspected that it was a resting spot of sorts. Perhaps it was where Limbotryl took patients, rejuvenated them, and sent them back whole—or closer to whole.

What would happen if he gave himself a treatment? He contemplated the possibility, relishing the peacefulness of a vacation from life itself. He frowned then, reminding himself that only addicts, escapists, or extremely ill patients took that path. He did not belong to any of those groups, and that was not the path he sought, not really.

He disciplined himself to recall the recent visits with Ann-Marie. Her words had always been few, but there had been something almost otherworldly about her reticence the past few weeks. It was as if she knew something, or wanted to share something, but held back for some reason. Did she think he wouldn't understand? Did she fear that he'd withdraw the treatments, and that she'd suffer? Was she trying to spare him the knowledge that she was actually dying? Did she think he didn't already know? Aren't we all dying, anyway?

Stu opened his eyes, agreeing to live in this painful moment, and the ones that would unfold, one at a time, to form an hour, a day, a week, a month, a year. It was hell on earth, but it was the price he must pay. There'd be no salvation for him, no matter how forgiving or merciful his minister purported God to be.

His wife still stared at his hand, tracing the veins, and he noticed that it was the only part of him that felt soothed. She looked up, her eyes a pair of question marks, heavy with the burden of what the answer might be. *Why is she so worried?* Stu wondered.

Me. He knew this in his heart.

His wife might boss people with her opinionated bluster, she would even yell, demand, or insist as the situation required. But Jeannie would not cry publicly. She would never express fear, although she'd admitted to grief that felt like a heart attack when Joy died. She was tough, that Jeannie.

Stuart Adler understood that now, his wife worried about the only other person left in her life. Having heard in his voice the desperation that might precede loss, she feared losing him; if not to death, to that foggy place of neither here nor there, neither life nor death. Abandonment was what she feared, he knew— even if his wife of thirty-five years would never admit it. He must reassure her.

Stu covered his wife's hand with his, meeting her gaze with what he hoped was confidence. The effort could be labeled "fake-it-to-make-it." If convincingly executed, if his wife believed him to be restored to action, then the act was not a lie, for then he would believe it, too.

From the Cincinnati Enquirer *newspaper, page one, Metro section Saturday, December 14:*

Hometown Heroes: Julia & Len Hannigan, Co-founders of M.S. Couple's Support Network

When Julia Hannigan was diagnosed with Multiple Sclerosis five years ago, she didn't quit her job or her volunteer activities. In fact, she enlarged them. With her husband, Len, as a team-mate, Julia approached the Multiple Sclerosis Association of Greater Cincinnati about volunteer opportunities.

A few months later, the Hannigans loaded their two children into a double stroller to march in the annual MS walk-a-thon. Inviting extended family to participate, the event became a re-union for both sides of the family, with the Hannigan-Albright contingent representing the largest pack of walkers, and generating more than $25,000 for the local MS council since 1991.

Two years ago, when Julia's symptoms were severe enough to require a wheelchair, Len provided the muscle to push his determined wife across the finish line. That was also the year their children, Patrick and Erin, then ages 6 and 4, biked the event, Erin riding with training wheels.

Julia and Len Hannigan were recently recognized as Volunteers of the Year for 1996, the first time a husband-wife team has been honored. "This couple almost single-handedly launched a weekly support group for couples dealing with the effects of MS," said Lawrence Greeley, Executive Director of the Multiple Sclerosis Association of Greater Cincinnati. "There couldn't be a more deserving couple."

The Hannigans serve as mentors and advisors to hundreds of couples through a weekly support group in Cincinnati, as well as via an Internet website and chat room. The website was funded by a grant, authored by Julia and Len Hannigan, from the National Multiple Sclerosis Foundation. Mr. Greeley added, "The chat room has offered practical information and support to thousands of people who have MS, and to their families. This couple's willingness to share their time and creative energy, both locally and beyond, is an inspiring legacy. They exemplify the nature of a hometown hero."

From the Cincinnati Enquirer *newspaper, page six, Metro section* *December 14*

OBITUARIES

TRAVIS, Ann-Marie (nee Lynch), beloved wife of Robert Travis, devoted mother of Ashley, Will, and Chad, loving daughter of Harold and Janet Lynch; dear sister of Mary Beth (Jared) Sperry, Harold, Jr., (Missy), Ellen (Joseph) Steinbeck, Maggie (Eric) Wurtz, and David "Chip" (Lisa) Travis. Also survived by seventeen nieces and nephews. Preceded in death by her grandparents, Edward and Loretta Lynch and Carl and Elsie Bromberg. Friday, December 13, age 35. Family will receive friends Tuesday, December 17, from 9:30-11:00 AM, at the Burns and Beckman Funeral Home. Graveside service immediately following. In lieu of flowers, memorials may be made to the charity of one's choice.

10:00 AM

For many people, reading the obituaries was nothing more than an exercise in current events, tracking tragedies in order to send condolence cards to friends and neighbors. Others read them while consciously or unconsciously gauging their own mortality, looking at details such as age, gender, marital status, survivors, and cause of death, the latter often inferred by the beneficiary of memorial contributions.

Julia Hannigan compared the glowing Hometown Hero spot with the sparsely detailed, rather impersonal obituary notice. Was it only because the woman was Julia's age that she felt connected? Was it because the woman had children? Or, was it only the emptiness of the death notice that struck a chord of sympathy?

Snuggled beneath a down comforter on this glaringly bright Sunday morning, Julia recited a prayer for the dead woman, a petition for eternal rest. Above all, Julia prayed with gratitude for the life she had been given, the one she shared with Len, Patrick, and Erin. Even without Limbotryl's grace, her life was filled with meaningful blessings. She counted each one, some more basic than others, falling into an easy slumber as she contemplated blessing number fifty.

Julia would never have guessed at the common bond she shared with the woman featured so starkly, so impersonally, in the obituary notice; or how easily that woman's fate might have been her own.

11:00 AM

The procession of ivory poinsettias formed an aura of silvery green, the dark foliage reflecting verdant hues onto the pale blossoms. In an alcove off the cobblestone path, a pair of men sat at either end of a carved wooden bench. They stared straight ahead, rather than at one another. While their lips moved, as if conversing, no words could be discerned above the swish and gurgle of a burbling stream that snaked through the Krohn Conservatory. Not even an experienced gossip would be able to eavesdrop. The meeting place was private by design, as the men intended.

The older man, in his late sixties, could have passed for fifty-something: distinguished, tall with broad shoulders and a narrow waist, wavy silver-white hair neatly brushed away from his face. He might have been a well-preserved Hollywood actor.

The other man, younger by a decade, was not handsome in the traditional sense. Casual observers took him for ordinary. Yet, just beyond that moment of casual observation, at the point of personal contact, the flash of his smile, the laugh-lines that creased around piercing blue eyes, and the resonant timber of his voice conspired to startle men and women alike. New acquaintances reconsidered their first impression of this bland-looking man, jolted from preconceptions by the man's magnetic field of charm. Then, clarity prevailed: he was no ordinary guy.

And the men's conversation was not ordinary, either.

The Magi had come to deliver the news: he was at the end of his supply of the potion Judge Nathan Warden wanted so badly—needed so desperately. Because they were men, they would strategize. Men were problem-solvers.

"How much is there, exactly?" asked the judge.

"If I could trust my supply, about a month. But I can't trust it. It's tainted."

"How do you know?"

The pause was substantial, as with seconds that pass like hours when one is suffering. How much should he tell? Could one tell a truth of such magnitude to a judge who was sworn to uphold the law? Was a judge professionally mandated to report such a gut-wrenching truth?

Without answers to his questions, and despite great personal risk, the Magi approached this critical angle of attack, fearing but willing to endure the possible death spiral that would put an end to it all: the subterfuge, the lawlessness, the guilt, the self-flagellation he called penance. Suddenly, revealing the truth, at the risk of ending it all, seemed a liberating opportunity. He might rest then, for others would be charged with the responsibility of punishing him. His own burden would thus be eased. He ignored the image of the little girl wearing a pink tutu, who shook her head vigorously; admonishing him for such flawed reasoning. He dismissed the image, believing that he'd sort out any flaws in his reasoning later.

Still looking straight ahead, the Magi answered the question forthrightly. "It killed a woman."

"Good God," the judge whispered, awed at the notion that it might have been him.

"I'll see what I can do to locate an alternate source, but it may take a while." The Magi paused for one last moment of consideration before taking the leap. "There's a way to get it from overseas, through the Internet."

Nate Warden nodded his head thoughtfully.

The Magi turned to face the judge, cracking a wry smile. "You wouldn't be able to give me a legal opinion on the risk of doing that, would you?"

Judge Warden met the other man's glance, a smile playing about his lips. He chuckled quietly, shaking his head at the bizarre irony. The healer, his medicine man, queried *him*, the beneficiary of the treatment, for legal advice about an illegal scheme to continue the only treatment that allowed the beneficiary to retain his sworn position of law and order.

"How the hell did you ever get into this business?" the judge asked quietly, averting his glance.

The Magi turned away, too. Was the question rhetorical, he

wondered? He debated the wisdom of a response. Before he knew what he'd decided, he heard himself begin.

"I was pretty idealistic during anesthesia residency. I'd save people from the dreaded pain of surgery, I'd save them from the terrible nausea of anesthetics, and I'd find a way to manage intractable pain . . . . I was going to do it all, and I had a plan that might have bent rules, but never broke them. I was a rules man, and played by them within a few shades of gray, without exception—until my daughter got sick.

"Funny how you can talk yourself into deeper and deeper shades of gray when it's your little girl who needs something." The Magi broke off, pressure building in his neck and throat. This wasn't about his daughter, he reminded himself. Today, the issue was medicine for Nate Warden, not Joy, who would cheer her daddy on. "When sickness hits you right between the eyes, or straight through the heart, the rules seem more flexible. That's what I told myself, anyway."

The men were silent, each considering private thoughts of family, the ties that bind, and bondage itself. If Nate Warden recognized himself as a similar rules man, he kept his counsel.

The Magi continued. "You know, I never thought I'd have to worry about my own child getting sick. The rules of my game were, work hard, play hard, play fair, follow the rules, and the good life will come my way. But the comfort of the rules was yanked away after Joy became sick. It took me to my knees, as if the gods had whipped the rug of a good life from beneath my feet."

The memory of events within this journey swirled in slow motion, as if a waking dream. The Magi wondered if he could actually tell it, all of it, to this man named Judge John Warden.

✦

"Hugh is a biochemical engineer, Dad. He knows what he's talking about."

"He isn't a medical doctor. He doesn't know a thing about how it affects people."

"Listen, Steven has MS, too. He tried it, but he wouldn't tell us how he got the drug. Dad, it helped him."

"Just because it helped one person doesn't mean it'll help anyone else. There are risks associated with anesthesia! And how do you know your friend didn't experience a placebo effect?"

"What are you two arguing about? I can hear you from the front yard!"

"Mom, there are these two guys in the support group. They've been talking about the role of sleep in healing, brainwaves, neurotransmitters, and a bunch of stuff I can't begin to understand about brain chemistry. Anyway, they've found a drug—an anesthesia drug—that stimulates R.E.M. sleep. That's the sleep stage where healing occurs, and these guys have been successful easing symptoms, MS symptoms."

"For one person, one time."

"Still! It's something you could help with, Dad."

"No, I couldn't."

"We're talking about Limbotryl, I guess?"

"Yes. How did you know, Mom?"

"Just a lucky guess," she answered dryly. "It's the only anesthesia drug I know of that stimulates R.E.M. sleep." She turned to her husband. "Imagine that. We could help the whole damned support group."

"No, we can't. It's not available at the local pharmacy. It's for anesthesia use only, and you know it, Jeannie."

"But Dad, what if there are people who want to be part of a research study? Some of these people are desperate. I'm not desperate now, but I'd like to think that down the road . . . well, who knows what the drug might do. What if it could throw me into remission? What if—"

"No. I'm not a researcher. If you want, we'll talk to someone at the University. We'll find out if anyone is working on this elsewhere, or if N.I.H. has any protocol for MS. You can participate in something like that, when the time comes."

"Maybe the time is now, Stuart. Before Joy gets to the point that she feels desperate."

"What are you asking? You want me to steal the drug from work? I could go to jail for that. I'd lose my license. Is that what you want?"

"Stuart, you know as well as I do that there are ways to get that *medication from there to here, and no one would be the wiser. What do you do with medication—narcotic medication—that isn't used during surgery? You throw it down the drain. Not you personally, I know, I know. But that's where it winds up. Are you telling me that you can't think of a way to put that wasted medicine to better use?"*

"You mean," Joy asked, incredulous, "the hospital just pitches the medicines that aren't used? That's such a waste!"

"Yes," her mother agreed. "It is a waste. Now, you let your father and me discuss this. We'll have a little brainstorming session while you get some dinner."

✦

"At first, I held my ground. I wasn't a thief, not even in the nature of Robin Hood. My wife was furious, and my daughter devastated."

"But you changed your mind."

"Not for a long time. I worked the professional network, going back to everyone Jeannie and I had contacted when Joy was first diagnosed. I asked them about research protocols, and even tested the water with one fellow who seemed open to what he called un-fundable research. He seemed excited about the possibility of Limbotryl, but the guy seemed too out-of-bounds for me to trust with Joy."

Nate Warden nodded formally. "I'd do anything to help myself, as you know. But it's different with our children. We must be scrupulously careful, when it comes to unorthodox treatments for a child."

"That's what I thought," Stuart Adler murmured, frowning, and sighing simultaneously. "Of course, Joy wasn't a child at that point. Legally, she was an adult, early twenties, and thought she knew everything." *Her mother's daughter, on that count,* Stu thought. "She became worse very quickly, which isn't typical of MS symptoms. They usually progress over a period of years. So, my wife, being of a stubborn, entrepreneurial nature, contacted the men in Joy's support group.

"These men weren't happy that Joy had divulged their experiment. The group discussions are confidential, and Joy took a lot of criticism—which she deserved for breaking the group's rule—in the next several sessions. I think she stuck it out because she knew her mother's tenacity for getting what she wants.

"If the one man didn't die, I might never have become involved. But he died of something viral, and Jeannie and Joy went to the visitation. Lo and behold, there was one of my partners, brother of the deceased."

Nate whistled, filling in the blanks.

"Right," agreed Stu, heartily. "You can imagine what happened next. Jeannie swore my partner to secrecy, because of my objections, and they conspired to use this sad occasion synchronistically—that was one of Joy's favorite words—to promote quality of life. My colleague diverted the drug, and he and my wife created a network to deliver it to people in the support group who wanted to test its effects."

"How did he avoid detection?"

"Usually, he'd just mark the drug record as if he'd administered the entire amount during surgery. Then, he'd swap syringes. The replacement syringe was marked as Limbotryl, but it contained saline. As long as he ejected the contents, it looked like an empty Limbotryl syringe. Quite a trick, leaving just enough fluid to give the appearance that medication had been inside the syringe."

"And he's still doing this?"

"No. He's practicing somewhere else. Had an offer too good to pass up."

"Leaving you. But what made you *do* it?"

"My daughter, my wife, my conscience, I don't really know if it was any single person or thing that made me risk it. It's that, together, they were the waves that pound a rock to sand. I questioned whether or not I was right, or just righteous. I questioned what kind of a father refuses his sick child medicine that might help, and wouldn't hurt anyone else. I don't know . . ."

✦

"What are you giving her?" he demanded angrily.

"Don't shout at me. It's not going to hurt her. Get out!"

"I won't get out. Give me that syringe! Now!"

"Dad, leave! You get out, now!"

"Joy, I don't expect you to understand this, but your mother does. I can't believe you're doing this, Jeannie. It's wrong. It's illegal. I'd do anything for Joy—anything—within the law. Give me that!"

He strode purposefully to the bedside, grabbed his wife's wrist with a brutal wrench, and pried at the fingers that surrounded the syringe with a death grip.

"Get away from me!" Jeannie shouted, shoving her husband to the bed. "This isn't your place. You want no part of this? Then get the hell out of here!"

Stuart Adler pushed away from the bed, blood rushing to his head with the force of a tidal wave, furious. He'd take that damned needle if he had to wrestle it away.

"Daddy, don't! Daddy, don't!" The shouts from the bed, tearful pleas instead of orders, rose shrilly, desperately. Joy struggled to leave the bed, to protect her mother, but most of all, to protect the contents of that syringe. Her body would not cooperate, and the sheets and covers conspired to trap her. Boom! She thudded to the floor.

"Jesus Christ, Stuart! Look what you've done!"

Joy lay huddled in a shroud of linens, moaning tearfully. Her mother slapped the syringe on the bedside table, bending quickly to tend her child. She cooed soothing words, stroking her daughter's head, cradling her shoulders. "I'll help you back into bed, Joy. There, there. Easy now. Here, let me untangle these covers. There, there."

Stu stared, momentarily frozen in place. The syringe, now out of his wife's clench, spurred him to grab it forcefully. In a swift motion, without presentiment, he plunged the fluid into the wastebasket. There. Mission accomplished. He turned to cap the syringe, his eyes meeting the accusatory glare of his wife, whose nonverbal venom speared him like poisoned darts.

Joy would not look at him. She whimpered softly, "How could he? How could he?"

"There, there," her mother shushed, straightening the sheets and comforter with a snap and fluff before tucking them around her daughter's shoulders. "There's more where that came from. We'll try again, later. There, there."

"Jeannie—" Stu began.

"Shut up and get out!" she hissed, eyes glowering with fury.

"Joy," he tried again. "I'm s—"

His daughter opened her eyes, glistening with resentful disappointment, but she did not speak, merely whimpered.

"Out!" his wife commanded.

He left. He left the room, and then he left the house. He did not return until days later, coaxed home by a call from Joy, who announced that she was well. Very well. And that she and her mother agreed: it was time for her father to return home.

✦

"So, that's when you started?"

"No. But I stayed out of the way."

"When did your rock of determination get dashed to sand?"

"Several months later, when my partner was on vacation for three weeks. It doesn't happen very often, getting three weeks vacation in a row. But he had first choice in the vacation rotation, and the lucky devil got three consecutive weeks."

"Didn't he make sure there was enough medication? For your daughter, I mean?"

"He thought he did. In fact, he and my wife believed there was plenty for even a couple of the folks in Joy's support group. But Joy took a turn for the worse. It was a terrible time."

✦

"Please, Stuart. Do something! She's on the edge. Please."

Neither he nor Jeannie had slept the previous night. Even the narcotics hadn't softened Joy's cries. She'd choked on the mucus that trickled to the back of her throat, and vomited twice. If she could be medicated ad-

equately, she might avoid the secondary pneumonia associated with aspi-
rated fluids. If she could be medicated adequately, she might rest, she
might stop crying, and that would stop the mucus from accumulating
near her windpipe. These days, she had little strength to clear the viscous
saliva from her throat.

"I'll try."

"Thank you, Stuart! I'll tell Joy. It'll give her a reason to hold on."

*What have I agreed to? How am I going to do this? What if it doesn't
work?*

+

Sweat beaded his upper lip as he unpacked first one box, and then
another, searching for the elixir that would breathe life into his daughter.
He was clear about one thing: he was doing this for Joy, and no one else.
No matter what.

His lab coat pocket bulged slightly, stashed with syringes he'd filled
with saline and marked, "Limbotryl." Taking one of the syringes, he held
it up to the fluorescent light, comparing the coloring of the saline with that
of the Limbotryl that he'd exchange. They were the same. He tapped the
barrel of each syringe, grateful that Limbotryl was such a thin liquid.
What might he have substituted, had Limbotryl been viscous? Corn syrup?
No, that would have had too distinctively sweet an odor, and the pharmacy techs might have noticed.

He located first one, then a second, a third, and a fourth syringe,
all nearly full. They must have been for very short surgeries. Or, remainder for longer procedures. Ah, a local standby case offered tremendous bounty. His heart pounded beneath his scrubs, his ears tuned
attentively for approaching footsteps, his fingers cold with anxious fear,
no longer nimble or dexterous. How did Ron do this, day in and day
out?

The syringes burned in his lab coat pocket, reminding him of his
choice. At this crisis of conscience, Stu recalled the alternative: to sacrifice
his daughter on the altar of his pride, his professional oath, and a set of
laws that have little to do with humanity. He would not let his daughter
die, just because he lacked the courage to do what a stranger did for Joy.

He'd DO it. He'd RISK it. He'd go to hell and back, but he would choose what he now believed was the higher road, rather than the legal path.

The act would cost him sweat, fear, anxious tension, and guilt. All day, he would wear the pallor of gray nervousness. He'd feel the eye of God vacillating between mercy and condemnation, the syringes an emblem of sealed fate, or perhaps a sold soul.

✦

"I have it."

"Good."

"No, Daddy."

"What do you mean, 'No'?" her mother demanded irritably.

"Just no."

"Joy, the hard part is over. I was able to get what you need, and no one will be the wiser. I think we can get through these next few days, and then Ron will be back."

"No, Daddy. No Mother. I mean it." A moan escaped, and she clenched her jaw with stubborn determination. "Please, just give me more Demerol and leave me alone."

"Joy! Your father brought you what you need. Why are you refusing this?"

Joy opened her eyes, focusing on her father's ashen visage of perplexed relief. She winced a brief smile, or tried to. Her facial muscles were less cooperative these days. "I know how tough this was for you, Daddy."

"It's all right, Joy. I want to help."

"Not this way, Daddy. I know how much you love me. To do this."

"Stuart, just give her the injection! She'll be glad for it tomorrow."

"No! I said NO, mother!" A fit of spasms wracked the young woman's frail limbs, triggered by the intense emotion and effort expended to prevent her father from administering the elixir of wellness, a miracle drug that promoted health, albeit temporary.

"Why? You've taken this for months and months? Why not now?"

"Mom, it's my choice, to take or not take the medicine. It's Ron's choice to offer the medicine. This is not Dad's choice. I can't imagine what it's cost him to do it. Can't you understand that, Mom?"

"Don't be silly! Your father chose to do this for you, and he chose it freely."

"No. Ron will be back soon."

"Really, Joy," her father pleaded with sincerity. *"I really want you to have the medicine. Let me give it to you. Please."*

"No, Daddy. Thank you, but no." Joy closed her eyes, and willed herself to be still, to feign sleep, or at least to rest.

✦

"You *never* gave her the medicine?"

"No."

"And your wife didn't give it to her, with or without consent?"

"No. That was the hardest part. She hates to feel helpless, but that's what she was left with."

"You must have been relieved, in a way. You didn't have to follow through with something you didn't believe was right."

"Not at all," Stu denied firmly. "I'd committed to it before I even stole the first syringe. I certainly was not relieved. If anything, I was angry. I'd taken certain risks, and for nothing. At least, that's what I thought for a while."

"What happened then? Your partner came back and gave your daughter the injections?"

"No."

Stu paused, the pressure building in his chest and throat, again. It wasn't the elephant pressure of a heart attack, but the constricting pressure of regrets that he hadn't been willing to help his daughter until too late. "My daughter died," he stated plainly. "She committed suicide."

"Oh, God! I'm sorry," Nate apologized. "I didn't know. I thought she'd died of her illness."

"It's all right, there's no way you could've known." Silence, silence, and more silence. Then, Stu asked, "Have you ever lost a child?"

Nate Warden shook his head, unable to look this still-grieving father in the eye. It wasn't the same, he knew, to lose a child to death, or to lose a child by banishing him from your life. Temporarily or otherwise. He was thinking of Dan, of course.

"Joy left a note, one she'd written sometime before. She couldn't write at all, at the end. She forgave me for refusing to steal the drug when she first asked. She said she knew I loved her, and that she was proud of me for being an honorable man." Stu's voice cracked, unapologetically.

He went on, collecting his composure with a stern "ahem!" from the throat. "She said she was proud of her mother, too, and that both of us were honorable to our ideals. She called us 'authentic.' And she planted the seed that just because relief came too late for her, it wasn't too late for others.

"That became the kernel of hope for me. Hope for redemption. It didn't germinate overnight, and it was a few months before I became as involved in the treatments as Ron. But we had the perfect source of referral: a support group for people with chronic pain or conditions. And we had the perfect point of intervention: Jeannie's home health agency. It seemed serendipitous, as if we had no choice at all."

Nate Warden sighed. "Your daughter had courage. She was tough. It's astounding, to me, that she could have refused the drug. I certainly can't. Won't. You know," he stated softly, "I've always thought of suicide as an act of cowardice, not courage. But I can't help but think that a girl who was tough enough to refuse to be an accomplice to the devil—and that's what she thought she'd be, if she let you give her the medicine—must be courageous to a fault."

The judge looked the Magi in the eye, then. "And how about us, Medicine Man? What now?"

Stuart Adler had no answers.

Chapter Twenty–Nine

CHRISTMAS

Saturday, December 21
7:15 PM

"Quite honestly, I don't care to fly at all," the woman stated bluntly. "I'd certainly never allow my husband to fly as a hobby!"

John Williams shrugged and smiled, refusing the bait. Just as well, for the woman's husband swallowed the jig whole, protesting that one was safer in the air than on the interstate. John observed the couple amiably, yet distantly, as if he were invisible. He would not be drawn into the argument, and he would not defend his leisure pursuit.

Jeannie and Stu Adler approached, cocktails in hand. "Merry Christmas, John," Stu greeted.

"Merry Christmas," he returned, saluting the couple with his goblet.

"I couldn't help overhearing. Are you recruiting a flying buddy?" Jeannie asked brightly.

"Not really," John responded.

"Jeannie," the first woman interrupted. "If Stu were to ask to take up flying, would you allow it? Rick, here, is dying to play Icarus. I simply won't hear of it."

"Well, Suzette, it's more likely that *I* would take up flying than Stu, and neither of us needs a note from mother for permission." Jeannie winked to ease any sting of the reproof. "But I *would* increase the life insurance coverage."

"What's the toughest part about learning to fly?" Suzette's husband asked.

"Right now, it's practicing stalls under the hood—that's a device that fits over your head and lets you view the instrument panel, but nothing else."

"That's to train you to fly in bad weather, right?"

"Well, these little planes aren't designed to fly in bad weather, but at least instrument training can get you through clouds or fog."

"But why practice stalls?" the man persisted, as Suzette rolled her eyes.

"Experience," John acknowledged. "You'd better know what to do if the engine goes out."

"Richard, don't even think about it," Suzette insisted.

"So, you shut off the plane?" Jeannie asked.

"Not exactly," John responded, noticing that Jeannie and Stu were particularly attentive. "You can practice stalls with the engine on or pulled back to very low power. But with the training I'm doing, it's a matter of pushing the plane past its comfort zone, putting it at an unusually steep pitch. Each plane is a little different, but the engine will stall at a specific angle—it's called the critical angle of attack—and you have to learn how to recover so that the plane doesn't go into a spiral."

"Good lord!" Suzette sputtered. "Don't tell us any more, John. You'll convince me that you have a death wish."

Jeannie nodded. "That's an interesting exercise in discipline, John. You take the plane beyond what it's intended to endure, and you create a situation in which the rules of physics and gravity are challenged. Then, you systematically regain control in a way that allows you to land the plane safely, unscathed. And neither the plane nor the pilot is any worse for it, right?"

John frowned, suddenly not certain they were talking about flight training. "If it's done correctly, that's right."

"It's so much simpler to drive a car!" lamented Suzette.

"Yes, it is," agreed Jeannie. "But there are advantages to flying. You get further in a short time, if you fly. There's less traffic in the air than on the interstate. You have more options in the air, if only because there's a third dimension in which to maneuver. Isn't that right, John?"

Is this a trick question? John wondered, darting a guarded glance at Stu, who quickly averted his gaze in response. John read the avoidance as an indication that Stu understood his wife's question, the message beyond the words.

"Well, perhaps I'm wrong," Jeannie stated softly. "I don't know much about flying."

"No, you're right," John asserted swiftly. "But you have to know what the limitations are—whether for the aircraft or the pilot—and how far you can push the envelope and still recover safely. If you don't operate within the guidelines, you may not arrive at your destination in one piece. It's a matter of safety."

"Yet," Jeannie pressed, "you test the boundaries of safety in order to learn how to recover. Recovery is crucial."

"Life and death sort of crucial," snorted Suzette.

Jeannie ignored the remark, commenting, "I imagine that a pilot who learns how to recover from stalls becomes a better pilot."

"Yes, better prepared for the unexpected."

"Then, that pilot's passengers are safer because of it," Jeannie surmised.

"Yes."

"Yes," Jeannie repeated. "And I find it interesting that airplanes can only move forward. Isn't that something? A jumbo jet, powerful as it is, can't back up without being pushed by ground crew. It can only move forward. I suppose that's why there's no need for rearview mirrors."

"Yes," John agreed, increasingly uncomfortable with the secondary conversation.

"It's a bit like life," Jeannie added, an edge to her voice. "In life, as with aircraft, there is only forward momentum. There's no looking back."

John sustained eye contact, saying nothing. Jeannie Adler challenged him to blink, and John Williams refused.

Suzette and her husband exchanged a puzzled glance, turning quickly to greet new arrivals, perhaps relieved for the interruption. As they were swallowed by the gaggle of tuxedoed men and silk-sheathed women, Jeannie broke the silence. "We wanted to tell you, first: Stu intends to submit his resignation from the group. It's time for us to retire."

Wednesday, December 25
7:30 PM

Nancy Williams slouched in the overstuffed chair next to her mother's bed, tired, bone-weary, and depressed this Christmas night. Glancing at her mother, Nancy noted the shallow, regular breaths that indicated sleep. She envied her mother's slumber. Plagued by daytime sleepiness, it had been weeks since she'd felt the blissful, deep, restorative sleep that renews energy. And those dreams of her father, well . . . .

Sandy appeared at the doorway holding a small gift, wrapped in red and gold striped paper, and topped with an elegant hand-tied bow of gold satin ribbon.

"You should open this," Sandy stated quietly. "The card is underneath."

Nancy looked away and sighed, closing her eyes. She didn't want John's gift. She did not want his sentiments, either.

Sandy crossed the room to their mother's bedside, smoothing the covers, and lightly kissing her mother's cool cheek. Turning to face Nancy, Sandy paused, as if gathering her courage and her words.

"What?" asked Nancy sharply. "Just say it. There's nothing you can say that will make this Christmas any sadder. You think I should just crank up the Christmas spirit, open John's gift, and then call him with gushing praise and apologies."

"No, I'm wrong," Sandy said. "I shouldn't be telling you what you should or shouldn't do. It's your gift, your decision."

Nancy remained slouched in the chair, but her eyes widened at Sandy's comment. This was the first time her sister had back-tracked from pushy entreaties to reconcile, to accept and re-spond to John's many letters and calls.

For the millionth time, Nancy wondered what John was do-ing today. He had no close family, although he may have gone to Christmas dinner at Mac's, or even a cousin's home. John had lived with them after his mother died, but they weren't a close family to begin with, and John had seen them only a couple times a year since college. His contact had dwindled further when his aunt and uncle died, and ceased to exist at all once the Cavanaughs warmly welcomed him into their family.

No, John probably hadn't been with them for Christmas din-ner. Maybe he *was* with Mac and Dan Franklin and their twins. Twins. Babies. Nancy sighed again, considering her response to Sandy.

If she agreed with Sandy, there might be hurt feelings about what, as sisters, one could say to the other. If she disagreed with Sandy, she would have to *do* something. Like read John's letters. Or think about talking with him. Would that constitute flying the plane?

Damn John, damn Stu Adler and his secret medicine, damn Mom for giving up the only thing that would allow her to live somewhat normally, Nancy mourned. She called forth the silent complaint in search of a spark of anger. It was only when she felt angry that she had any energy at all. Yet, there was no flint, no rock, no crystal, no sunlight to refract into a flame. A heavy, gray shroud pinned her to the depths of her mother's chair; she could not move. *Like sitting in Mama's lap, her overtired child . . .*

Nancy blinked, and then met Sandy's eyes. "Thank you for saying that." She paused, adding, "I don't feel like I can *do* any-thing, Sandy. This has been the most depressing time of my life. It's even worse than when Dad was dying."

Sandy nodded in agreement. "It's totally different now."

There was an intersection of the sisters' thoughts, as each contemplated what life would be like without their mother. Given their recent estrangement, each anticipated a dark, monstrous sort of loneliness, and like grief, it weighed heavily. Both women wondered if they would ever feel joyous or lighthearted again.

"I'm going to Tom's for a bit. Mom will be fine for the night." Sandy set the package inside their mother's closet, and faced her sister squarely. "You know where it is, if and when you want it."

Nancy nodded silently. She wanted to say something: To explain the importance of not pressuring her to return to John, and the intense need simply to *be* with her mother. But how could she explain a willingness to sacrifice, or to put on indefinite hold, the sort of relationship that she knew her older sister wished for in her own life? In the next moment, born of unplanned inspiration, Nancy surprised her sister with a gift that might have pained someone else.

"Guess who's going to have a baby, Aunt Sandy?"

7:45 PM

"St. Louis is a lot like Cincinnati," John commented. "Both are Midwestern river cities, not too big, but large enough to have great restaurants and excellent theatre."

"Of course, it's the theatre that brought you to St. Louis, and don't act as if that isn't the godawful truth. Still, I'll take what I can get from this prodigal cousin."

"You're letting him off too easy, Mary Claire. Make him spell out the distinctions or I'll go back to Chicago."

John chuckled, comfortable with the repartee of this theatre assembly. He couldn't have dreamed that he'd spend this Christmas with a cousin he hadn't seen in several years. The near decade had been kind to Mary Claire. Her sprite-like humor and contagious laughter—even when sharing some of the more painful memories of childhood—inspired John's confidence that he still had a place in the family that raised him; at least he did with Mary Claire.

"Aw shucks, Chuck! Maybe we should just fillet and grill this cousin of mine until he's as high-minded as you are about this town." Mary Claire shrieked with laughter as she waved the carving implements overhead. "Pour us s'more wine, Chuck, or you'll be the next one on my carving block! Maybe we'll re-enact 'Little Shop of—'whaaaa! Put me down, you certifiable Neanderthal!"

Chuck tossed Mary Claire over his shoulder with a caveman grunt, twirling the jean-clad pixie through the dining room to the two-story foyer, swooping to and fro beneath the oversize kissing ball of mistletoe.

"I don't wanna' grow up! Always wanna' be a kid!" Mary Claire sang gleefully, still clutching the carving tools, her arms spread in flight, her belly planted firmly on Chuck's broad shoulder.

In a swift, un-choreographed motion, Chuck flipped Mary Claire from her perch to recline in his arms, her back arched in a deep dip. Improvising her part fluidly, Mary Claire stretched one arm toward the floor, the other across her forehead, releasing the carving tools that fell to the floor in a clatter. She'd stopped singing. Perhaps she'd reconsidered her decision not to grow up . . . .

"Get over it, you two!" shouted a tall, bronze-haired goddess. "We don't want to scare away your long lost cousin, Mary Claire. At least feed him Christmas dinner!" The woman winked as she took John's arm. "Hope you didn't come looking for Father Christmas and 'God bless us, everyone!' Not at *this* cousin's house, anyway."

"Somehow, I figured that Mary Claire's would be a welcome break from tradition," John assured. "It's exactly what I needed this year."

"Yeah," agreed the goddess. "Exactly what you'll get, whether you want it or not."

"Did she tell you I met up with her at the Cincinnati production of 'A Christmas Carol'?"

"Um hmm. Must have been fun to watch your cousin staring back at you from the stage, and reading her smart ass bio in the playbill."

"Mary Claire's always been full of surprises. She was my favorite cousin, really. You know how fun it is to watch someone else stir the pot—hilariously—and no one was spared. She must have been a foundling, abandoned on the doorstep, because the rest of her family had no sense of humor."

"Why didn't you keep in touch with her? I mean, you don't have to answer that, but it seems like you two would have hooked up more than once in a blue moon."

John sighed. "Even if I tried to explain, it would just be excuses. There's no good reason for it. We just went separate ways, all of us. I was too busy studying to take a break, even if a dose of Mary Claire would've been therapeutic. Then, I sort of gravitated into my wife's family and just stayed put. I felt rooted enough, too comfortable to strike out and find the cousin-siblings I grew up with."

The goddess remained expressionless.

"See, I told you it would just be excuses." He smiled, then sipped his wine.

The goddess turned her gaze to the host couple, the handsome prince kissing Sleeping Beauty. The moment radiated gentle passion: magical, spellbinding, silent. And time stood still.

"She's an angel, and she'll always count you as family."

John looked sharply at the goddess-woman, whose gaze left the couple to meet his stare. Had she really said that? She said nothing, now, but glided away elegantly, slow as syrup.

A burst of country-western style "Jingle Bells" suddenly blared from the stereo. "Ride 'em, Cowboy!" whooped Mary Claire, now riding piggyback on heigh-ho-Silver-Chuck. "Let's round up these cowpokes for some beans 'n grits!"

John lifted his glass in salute, catching his cousin's eye. The contagion of her merriment sparked, within him, a youthful sense of immortality. With Mary Claire, he was untouchable, indestructible, and fearless. As well, there was something about Mary Claire that reminded him of Nancy. Or perhaps it was more a reminder of the way he used to feel, during their early years, whenever he was with her. He glanced at his watch, wondering not about the time, but about what Nancy was doing this Christmas night, six hours away, an hour ahead of St. Louis.

Chapter Thirty

Fatal Error

Friday, January 2
4:00 PM

"That emergency aortic aneurysm has been canceled," Hannah Gilbert called to the young nurse setting up the operating room. "You can float back to Recovery."

"All right," the nurse sighed. "I'll take care of this stuff first."

"Check with Margery and see if she needs you for anything else. We're nearly finished with shift change, and most of the afternoon patients are back in Same Day. Recovery may not need you. If Margery gives you the okay, you can leave. Just have her sign for your overtime."

"Okay." The nurse sighed again, appearing weary of having to set up a room, only to tear it down again.

Hannah Gilbert nodded abruptly, and left the room.

The young nurse smiled, once the OR Supervisor was gone, thrilled for this opportunity, grateful to be a floater between the Recovery Room and the OR. She always volunteered to be a floater on days that Dr. Lytle had block time. He typically had semi-emergent surgical add-ons at the end of his schedule. Surgery cancellations, such as the aortic aneurysm, represented a first class opportunity to serve herself from the sweet smorgasbord of the drug tray.

Typically, the Limbotryl could be drawn up in one syringe, and saline could be drawn up in another, with the saline being pushed into the original bottle to give the appearance of a full, untouched vial. She'd also treat herself to some Fentanyl and Versed. Maybe she'd take a hit of Fentanyl a while from now, in the restroom, after she'd collected her weekend stash. She'd have to work quickly, though. The anesthetist hadn't arrived yet, and the young nurse prayed that the cancellation had already been conveyed. The key was to be in the room *alone*.

With anticipatory anxiety, the young woman lifted a vial to the light, confirming that it was the drug of choice. Next, she pulled a syringe from her gown pocket, inserted it through the rubber stopper, and drew up a full syringe of the drug. She then withdrew the syringe from the vial and capped the needle, returning it to the deep pocket of her OR gown. *Sweet success!*

She reached for another vial, and raised it to the light. From the corner of her eye, she noticed the orb of the camera trained on her profile. *No worries,* she thought, *as long as the drug count is consistent, I'm home free!* In a moment of cavalier audacity, fueled by the ease with which she'd pocketed such riches, the young nurse tossed her blond head, and smiled coyly, sassily, at the eye that recorded her theft.

Don't get overconfident, a silent voice cautioned.

Willing herself to ignore an anxious rush of adrenaline, the nurse drew another empty syringe from her pocket, and proceeded to fill it. She repeated this twice, nervous energy causing her hands to tremble and perspiration to bead across her upper lip and beneath her arms. Suddenly, a bizarre combination of heat and cold, almost feverish in intensity, tingled within her body. It was at this point that her actions became more hurried than accurate.

Although the evidence would be long since destroyed, if anyone ever suspected her of drug diversion, the young nurse did not know that this would also represent her final error. And that it was this type of mistake, confusing a paralytic for harmless saline, which had rippled to affect another woman with the same lethality.

9:00 PM

The moan of the bass sax withered and died, replaced by the plucky jazz guitar, artfully tooled by the young blond's favorite artist, Eric Clapton. The melody was bright, yet the words of grief were as melancholy as the mournful wail of the sax. The words and music enveloped her, embraced her in a warm blanket of borrowed emotion, compliments of the beat of the drum, the lament of the sax, the spunk of the guitar, and the elixir of the drug.

Without the music, without the drugs, she felt as little as the dead. *My souls is what's dead, my shabby little life is what's dead . . . .*

She'd never had a child, but the loss of the artist's child, bravely sung, mirrored the loss of her soul. She wondered, then, whether she felt more like the disconsolate mother, or a motherless child.

And then, she felt the pain. *So, I must be alive,* she thought.

Her eyes opened to slits, just enough to see the tapered treat that promised bliss, and she reached laconically for her pleasure wand. She moved slowly, deliberately, so as not to break the spell, and to preserve the sanctity of *feeling something.*

The cap removed, she guided the tip of the needle—glinting, a candle flame against the backdrop of blazing hearth logs—and gently punctured a vein in her left arm. Pushhh, and the liquid eased through the barrel, beyond the hollow needle, pulsing within her veins. The syringe dropped from her hand. She watched it bounce with a ping, and roll across the slate toward the blazing fire.

She imagined herself being discovered by someone handsome, courageous, with the will to take her from this drab little life. He would enter the room forcefully, observing her slow-motion recline, while flames from the fireplace licked the air warmly, creating a dance of light and shadow across the pale, diaphanous nightgown, her body limp, her hair draped shroud-like across her face and shoulders, not at all the vestal virgin, requiring a knightly, godlike rescue, nonetheless.

But where was the bliss? The ecstasy she'd expected eluded her, like the teasing lover who ducks a kiss. She'd be patient. Ahhhhhh, here it comes.

And when it happened, not as she'd expected, but in all its frightening horror, claustrophobic tightness, and smothering heat, Clapton's voice reassured her . . . *"Yes, I know, there'll be no more . . . tears in heaven."*

Chapter Thirty–One

THE PUZZLE EXAMINED

Tuesday, January 6
8:10 AM

Dr. Simon Mercer, Assistant Hamilton County Coroner and Professor of Pathology at the University of Cincinnati College of Medicine, was a star-performer in the theatre of forensic medicine. As a creative pathologist-detective, and a prolific author of medical forensics articles, he'd earned the nickname "Quincy," after a television hero of the same profession.

Today, Dr. Mercer envied Quincy's luxury of wrapping up mysterious deaths within that magical hour of prime time television. Within the past twenty-four hours, two nurses had been found dead, the causes yet to be determined, but both possibly overdoses by injection. The bodies awaited autopsy and toxicology studies in the cool chambers of the Coroner's refrigerator.

One of the nurses worked at St. Catherine's Hospital, the other at Mount Vernon, a small women's hospital on Cincinnati's "Pill Hill." They may have been acquainted, and the police investigation would delve into any relationship between the women and their deaths. Dr. Mercer considered the eerily similar scenarios: single white female nurse leaves shift, returns home, and fails to report for work the following day. Colleagues become irritated, then concerned. Police are called when repeated attempts to contact the nurse fail; landlord refuses to allow access unless police authorize it. Police then find nurse, dead, with no evidence of physical injury, but drug paraphernalia strewn next to the body. He wondered, *Was this simply a matter of two unrelated drug overdoses?*

Dr. Mercer exhaled noisily, and tapped in the seven-digit number for Inspector Morrison of the Cincinnati Police Department's Homicide Division.

"Morrison here," snapped the voice on the other end of the phone.

"Yes, I heard you called about—"

"We got a report on the nurses who were brought in yesterday," Morrison interrupted, pausing then to answer a protracted question from another officer.

"And, what?" Mercer asked, his annoyance rising in direct proportion to the time he spent waiting for Morrison to give the details.

"Sorry," Morrison said, unapologetically. "There are several people who reported that Casey Blanchard and Barbara Parks were friends. They were seen in the lobby of St. Catherine's after change of shift, and apparently they were big partiers in Mount Adams on weekends. We haven't identified any other commonalities yet, but wanted you to check for something else—Limbotryl."

"You think they were using a surgical anesthetic?" It was more of a statement of incredulity than a question, as Mercer was well acquainted with the drugs of choice of medical professionals. "I can check it out, but it's unlikely that they would've killed themselves with it. More likely, it'll be Sufentanil or one of the big-gun narcotics."

"We have reason to believe that someone at St. Catherine's is tampering with Sufentanil, Fentanyl, Demerol, all of them. Limbotryl, too, for some reason," Morrison explained. "PDU has been working with the anesthesia folks over there but it's not a tidy picture. It's possible that someone laced the narcotic with a lethal paralyzing agent."

Mercer's interest was piqued by this whiff of a hot trail. These deaths were not the routine blood and gore street shootings of the Coroner's Office, but puzzles to analyze and solve. A boyish eagerness animated his otherwise monotone voice as he grabbed a mechanical pencil, spat a series of rapid-fire questions, and scribbled a jangle of semi-legible notes onto a stray envelope.

"I'll call you with my findings. Autopsies are on for today," Mercer said brusquely. He clicked the phone into the cradle before Morrison could respond.

It would be a busy day, and he'd have to reschedule four meetings. Although an associate pathologist had been assigned to perform the autopsies, Mercer could easily arrange to do them himself. In view of the potentially high-profile nature of the cases, especially with the reputations of two hospitals and their nurses at stake, Dr. Mercer would insist on performing the post-mortems personally.

10:00 AM

It was only a hunch, based on a well-placed tip from Inspector Morrison in Homicide. Barbara Westover felt grateful that the Security Director was free, and that he'd offered to review the videotape with her, STAT, even without an explanation. "Wait a sec," she commanded. "Back that up."

Dave Johnson hit the pause button, scanning in reverse. He'd seen it, too.

"There," she announced. They stared at the frozen image, which smiled directly at them from the screen.

Dave frowned, the "aha" congealing into a formulation that included partial information of who, what, where, when, why, and how. He mentally kicked himself for failing to review, in fast-forward, every frame of tape. He had been so committed to his war room, so reassured by the computerized drug record, that he'd overlooked this obvious resource for evidence.

"She knew she was being taped, and it didn't bother her," Barbara murmured. "Why?"

Dave continued to stare at the screen, answering, "Because she knew that the tape wouldn't be viewed unless there was a problem reconciling the narcotics count. Clever girl. We haven't reviewed tapes in months. Why did you ask to see this today?"

The PDU officer tapped a pen on the table, considering this question. She shrugged. "Just a tip," she replied, as if it didn't matter in the least. She raised her pen and met Dave's stern visage. "There's no log of personnel who access the satellite pharmacy?"

"Yes, by badge swipe."

"In your office, you have a printout of which people were on each shift, right?"

"Yes," Dave acknowledged.

"Let's review the tape for each day this woman was working."

"I'll do that with the group here, first." Dave crossed his arms as he reconsidered this plan. "Then again, perhaps if we review the tapes first and find a pattern, we'll have more to tell them—show them—when we convene."

"Exactly," Barbara agreed, her mouth giving a mild twitch that might have been a smile, had the stakes not been so high. "I've gotta go. Thanks for letting me see this."

"No problem," Dave responded. "I'll call you when I find out who it is."

Barbara Westover smiled slightly and waved behind her as she exited the Security office. She knew who it was. She could have told Dave Johnson who it was; but to buy time for this investigation, she didn't.

10:15 AM

Dave Johnson would not make the same mistake twice: including one of the PDU cops without notifying others in the group. The members, including John Williams, Hannah Gilbert, and Doug Howard, would convene in fifteen minutes for a quarterly review of pharmaceutical security measures in the OR and Recovery areas.

However, fifteen minutes was not enough time for the Security Director to preview last week's tapes. He had almost taped over them, a cost-saving attempt that would have prevented him from accessing any recording of this coy nurse's pattern of activity. *Which one is she,* he wondered silently, glancing at the list of nursing staff for the Recovery and Surgical OR areas.

"Dave, I can't attend the meeting." It was Hannah Gilbert, the Perioperative Nursing Supervisor, looking tense—possibly frightened—as she stood in the doorway to the Security offices. "One of my nurses was found dead at home. A young nurse. I'll catch up with you later," she announced firmly, dashing from the doorway.

Dave picked up the phone and called the Vice President of Nursing Services, his questions answered a few moments later. He crossed to the file cabinets that indexed employee identification, flipping through the first several files within the B-section.

"BINGO!" he shouted, startling his secretary, who was just walking in the door.

"What?" Katie asked, her hand flying to her heart at this unusual greeting.

"A piece of the picture," he said softly, ignoring his secretary's ire, frowning at the duplicate photo of the one that appeared on the employee's ID badge. "Cancel my 7:30 meeting with Dr. Williams and Doug Howard," he stated firmly.

Strolling to the war room area of his offices, Dave searched for the name on the board. Yellow string identified the person as a nurse. Because this nurse was a floater, the strings crossed from the Recovery Room to the Surgery area. Therefore, the circle of access was wider for this nurse than the others.

Taking the cap from a dry erase marker, Dave circled the name in red. He had his man. And John Williams had been right: it was a woman, a young woman. This nurse, who had smiled wittingly at Johnson and Westover from the videotape, was now dead.

12:00 noon

John Williams was just winding up lunch in the doctors' dining room when a wave of buzzing, like a symphony of cicadas, swirled throughout the room. Placing his tray on the conveyor that led to the belly of the kitchen, he noted the intensity of the tone; it bore the notes of personal grief and shock, more than just nasty, hospital-soap-opera gossip. The physician dining room insulated docs from the other hospital staff, and as he exited to the main cafeteria, he saw Mac, nodding and shaking her head amidst a group of shower-capped OR nurses.

"What's the news?" he asked Mac, as she turned from the group, which continued to emote a complex combination of excitement, shock, and grief.

"One of the Recovery Room nurses was found dead in her apartment. She didn't show up for work Saturday, and her landlord wouldn't let anyone into her apartment until yesterday. I guess the police were called and they found her. Someone thinks she may have had a heart condition, but it could've been anything. She was pretty young, only twenty-seven."

"Who was it?" John asked, hoping it wasn't anyone he knew.

"Casey Blanchard. I never worked with her much," Mac replied.

"I think I know who you mean. She used to work in the Cardiac Cath Lab and SICU." John paused, more out of a sense that he *should*, as a gesture of respect for the deceased, rather than any bereavement. He then changed the subject, unwilling to commit to any conversation about death.

12:00 Noon

"Thank you for adjusting your schedules," Dave Johnson began. "Hannah Gilbert won't be joining us, and we'll reschedule our quarterly meeting for next week, if that will work for both of you."

John exchanged a look with Doug. What was this meeting about, if not to accommodate Hannah's schedule?

"I can make that," Doug agreed.

"I'm post call, but that's okay if we meet early," John offered, scribbling rapidly in his electronic organizer.

"Settled, then," Dave asserted. "For now, I'd like to talk with you about the situation that caused this meeting to be rescheduled. Casey Blanchard."

John looked up as he heard the name. "What about her?" he queried. "She's the one who was found dead yesterday," he added, fairly certain that Dave would know this.

"Yes," Dave replied, "and she floated between Surgery and Recovery that Friday of the Code Blue that stumped us so many months ago." He paused for effect. "And this past Friday."

Doug and John shared a second glance.

"So did a bunch of other nurses," Doug argued.

"But you think Casey Blanchard *stole* the narcotic and overdosed," John stated. Then, the larger potential flashed into awareness. "No," he said slowly, softly. "She floated between areas, unlike the other nurses. You think she took what she *thought* was narcotic, and either drew up the wrong drug, or took a syringe that had been tampered with." If that were the case, John decided, Casey Blanchard was one unlucky girl. No one would have been able to resuscitate her.

Dave did not respond to the suppositions as he flipped through a computer printout, a two-inch accordion of pages. John had no idea what information those pages contained, and he waited impatiently for Dave to speak, noting that the Security Director's expression and posture remained intent, but unexcited, almost reptilian. Regardless of the emotional climate, whether hot, cold, or moderate, Dave's countenance rarely veered from center. Even a break of sorts failed to elicit animation.

"Well, which do you think it is?" John pressed.

"Could be either, at this point," Dave said, remaining noncommittal. "There's no evidence to back one hypothesis or another. Neither one explains much, other than how she might have died."

For all three men, this was unsatisfactory. If a Recovery nurse was stealing narcotics, she was probably taking it from the Recovery supply, not from one of the anesthesia drug kits. Or, were they missing some other link, a loophole to be identified and repaired in the hospital's pharmaceutical security plan?

"Cincinnati Police will follow up," Dave stated simply. "I'll keep you posted."

He did not mention the strange video of the nurse smiling at the camera in the satellite pharmacy.

12:30 PM

Barbara Westover tapped the frame of her keyboard, concentrating on the jumble of strands in her head, not even seeing the words on the screen before her. What the hell was going on at St. Catherine's? Or, what now? It seemed there was always something to investigate, regardless of the institution, its policies, or security measures. Inevitably, someone would push past the boundaries. Perhaps that was due to what the human factor afforded: temptation and free will. In the field of drug diversion investigation, the forbidden fruit would always lure someone to the table, and Barbara Westover would always have a job.

But what if Morrison was right? What if the two nurses didn't overdose, but died because they mistook a lethal paralytic for narcotic?

Barbara Westover shook her head slowly, reminding herself that Morrison read way too much pulp police fiction. Where did he get these ideas, these conspiracy theories?

There was nothing to do until the toxicology results came back and the autopsies were completed. It might take a couple of weeks. In the meantime, what next?

✦

There were many missing pieces, or at least unexplained pieces, in the puzzle that represented the links between Julia Hannigan, Ann-Marie Travis, and Casey Blanchard, among others. In the end, Casey Blanchard's death precluded answering all of the questions. And for a while, her friends and family celebrated her lively good humor, the image of the girl who had the world by the tail, never dreaming that the illusion of confidence was fueled by drug abuse; and never comprehending that what lay beneath the surface of beauty, talent, and intelligence was a vast emptiness of spirit. It might have been treatable. If only they had known.

Over time, what was pieced together was a theory, one that would never be proven. Casey Blanchard was stealing narcotics, and as she became more dependent, she became careless. She was believed to have caused the near-death of the young woman whom John Williams resuscitated. By hurriedly drawing up a syringe of what she thought was Limbotryl, getting the paralytic Succinylcholine instead, she had eventually confused the syringe intended for herself with the one that was to be administered to the young woman in post-op Recovery. That same desperate rush to obtain the drug, some for now, and some for later, had ultimately resulted in her death.

But, there was someone who *did* understand the link, the common denominator between those who had died, and the ones who'd been spared. Guilt gnawed at his gut, stirred him from sleep, and nearly drove him from his mission. It was his sense of duty that kept him from fleeing: duty to Judge Nate Warden, Kathy Martin, Julia Hannigan, and the memory of a little girl in a pink tutu. And, because of the man's refusal to accept forgiveness, perhaps there was also duty to his soul, perpetual penance in place of redemption.

This man knew, beyond a shadow of a doubt, that Casey Blanchard had been the one who'd mistakenly drawn up the Succinylcholine in the syringes labeled Limbotryl. She may have intended them for herself, and possibly left them with the other unused surgical medications, when she was unable to conceal them. They were part of what he'd been able to retrieve from the workroom: what he'd provided to Ann-Marie, and almost to Julia, to jump-start the healing process that Limbotryl provided.

If only FDA approval weren't such a convoluted process, he complained silently. This powerful drug forged a path of quality living, for people with chronic, debilitating diseases or conditions. He had no time for clinical trials and FDA hoops. Neither did the people he served and treated. And that was the operative difference: they were *people,* not just patients.

He knew that Limbotryl might have made all the difference in the world to the little girl in the pink tutu, the daughter who became too exhausted by the battle of life to choose it. If only he could spare one parent, one spouse, one child that type of pain . . . .

But that thought became eclipsed by the realization that his form of help unwittingly caused the premature death of a woman who was *someone else's* daughter. The tolling bell of guilt, proclaiming his role in Ann-Marie's death and her family's bereavement, would not be silenced. And the quieter voice, which encouraged him to remember those who could still be helped, failed to mitigate the pressure of his conscience.

As for Barbara Westover, Dave Johnson, Doug Howard, Hannah Gilbert, John Williams, and others who had questions, they were left with the vague, dissatisfied suspicion that one small puzzle piece would reveal the entire picture; and thus answer all of their questions.

Yet, in real life, there was seldom the opportunity to know *all of it.* There might be brief glimpses into the lives, thoughts, and feelings of others, but that yielded only partial understanding of what constituted the wholeness of a given person. Given the filter or lens through which others are viewed, one might see the snapshot, but never the whole picture.

Chapter Thirty–Two

SOUL SEARCHING

Tuesday, January 13
6:15 PM

Nancy didn't believe in angels. And she wasn't ready to accept that there were no coincidences in life. In addition to repetitive dreams of the flight with her father, she found it daunting to repeatedly stumble onto newspaper articles and television features that challenged her ideas about marriage. Then, her brief contact with a respected colleague conspired with the media, seemingly to force Nancy's reconsideration. Instruction and inspiration came unbidden.

It began with extensive press coverage of the President's marriage, and his wife's position of loyalty. Nancy's last out-of-town trip had included two nights away. During those quiet evenings, she'd happened to flip to two nationally broadcast news magazines, and one local talk show. All three featured alternatives to quitting a marriage. Next, the Cincinnati paper offered an Ann Landers column and a Lifestyles article on the same issue. The latter headlined four couples in the midst of divorce proceedings. They'd become involved in Family Court-sponsored mediation and counseling, with the surprising outcome of a decision to work out their issues and remain married.

It was the quote that struck a nerve for Nancy. "When we were in our twenties, we lived together before getting married.

We were so terrified of divorce. We believed that living together would help us decide if we were really meant to be together. Now we figure that a good marriage has less to do with finding that perfect soul mate, and more to do with negotiating the marriage path, knowing that there'll be some good times and bad, and some give and take."

While this concept of sustaining an imperfect marriage nibbled at the edge of consciousness for days, Nancy resisted it intentionally. Her marriage was not merely imperfect; her family had been betrayed, she believed, and that was quite different.

However, when a fellow pilot, Anne McCauley, challenged Nancy's views in an uncharacteristic moment of self-disclosure, Nancy heard the call to attention. A few years older than Nancy, Anne exuded well-grounded common sense; her stability and rationality inspired confidence. Other female pilots and flight attendants sought Anne's perspective for both personal and professional problems. She never gave advice, but always listened carefully, and responded with insightful observations rooted in good judgment. Nancy respected Anne because she cut to the chase, and she didn't permit anyone to waste her time with muddled thinking. The people who valued Anne's wisdom were intent on problem solving, rather than game playing. Still, because of her directness, Anne was not universally admired.

It was a surprise to Nancy, when she learned that Anne and her husband had been separated for nearly a year, until recently. From outward appearances, Anne lived a charmed life: the husband and two school age children, the beautiful home in an affluent Montgomery neighborhood, a nanny who'd been with them since the youngest child was born, altogether a well-ordered life.

When Nancy commented to that effect, Anne smiled sardonically and said, "Scratch the surface of any couple's life together, and you'll see what real life is all about. It's that way for everybody. When I realized that's the way it is, I understood that the difference between those who make it and those who don't is gritty determination to accept the facts of life and marriage. The ones who survive *work* on what they have."

"You sound awfully certain about that," Nancy said skeptically. "I'm not so sure that all marriages are salvageable. Aren't there certain situations in which it would be better to just end it? Aren't there some situations that are hopeless?"

Anne remained silent for a moment, and then turned it back to Nancy to specify such a hopeless situation. Nancy quickly suggested spousal abuse, and Anne readily agreed that such a situation might be hopeless.

"But, that isn't what most divorces are about, Nancy," she added.

"What about a fundamental disagreement about what you'll do for the sake of your family?" Nancy asked.

"Be more specific," Anne volleyed.

Less certain that she wanted to go down this path, Nancy continued to hedge. "Well, like a decision that has to be made that might affect the health of a family member."

Anne looked Nancy squarely in the eye. "I have no idea what you're thinking about, Nancy." The words meant, say what you mean, don't waste time with guessing games.

It was at this point that Nancy took a chance. "John and I are having a serious disagreement about my mom's treatment. I want Mom to do something to the left of orthodox because it might prolong her life, and it'll improve the quality of the time she has left. John won't go along with it."

Anne blinked. "You know, Nancy, there have been about a hundred times that Greg and I have disagreed about something related to our children. I don't think we've ever had a disagreement about our parents, unless it had to do with how to divide ourselves among the family during the holidays."

"Well, this is more than just a matter of choosing who we'll eat dinner with on Christmas," Nancy stated bluntly.

"But it's not necessary for you to put your marriage on the line for something that isn't even your decision. Only your mother can decide if she wants that unorthodox treatment. It's *her* decision."

"Yes, but what if John's response to it makes my mom feel as if she can't continue it—I mean, she *was* doing this for a while."

Anne nodded resolutely, "It doesn't take the decision from your mother. It's still hers to make."

"But John's opinion matters to my mother. If he refuses to support her decision, doesn't that strike you as less than loyal to family?"

Anne shrugged. "Your mother doesn't answer to John, and doesn't need his approval to take whatever treatment she believes will help. If she asked John for his opinion, and if he gave it honestly, then he's not disloyal. I don't understand the issue, Nancy."

It hit like lightning, the flash of insight. *She* was being disloyal—to John! The idea came as swiftly as the resistance that followed. Thoughts tumbled and swirled in her head, leaving Nancy too dazed to sort them. Stunned by the bullet of accusation regarding *her* lapse of loyalty, Nancy failed to realize she'd spoken aloud.

Anne's expression softened, from that of the analytic debater to that of the compassionate confessor. "How do you think you've been disloyal to John?" she asked gently.

Nancy shook her head, startled to think that Anne might have read her mind, then realizing that she'd spoken the words unconsciously. "I-I-I can't explain it," Nancy faltered. "I'm just thinking aloud. I don't even know what I just said."

Anne nodded silently, as if she recognized the painful ah-ha of acknowledging one's part in a marital problem.

"The hardest part of getting through this with Greg was letting go of the idea that he just needed to see things my way." Anne paused, smiling as she added, "It's *still* hard."

With that parting comment, Anne McCauley slammed her locker shut, saluting rather than waving good-bye, and banged through the door, wheeled luggage in tow.

How lucky she is, Nancy thought, to have all her baggage behind her. Or did she? To hear Anne tell it, marriage was a spiraling carousel, and the challenges never ceased. Was that what Anne meant? Perplexed confusion reigned in that moment, and Nancy sprinted through the door to ask Anne for clarification.

But she was gone.

Wisdom of circumstance prevailed, as Anne's abrupt departure left Nancy in a muddle of thoughts and questions. Although tempted to judge Anne harshly for leaving without adequate explanation, Nancy knew that anything *else* might prevent or dissuade her from struggling with this unsettled issue. Surely, it was better to survive a tussle with her own beliefs, than to borrow those of someone else.

Friday, January 16
1:00 PM

"Nancy," Diane Cavanaugh called in a high-pitched whisper.

"I'm right here, Mom," Nancy answered, coming into the bedroom with a pile of towels, still warm from the dryer. "I'll cover you with these."

The cold was the worst part of this, Diane decided. *If only I could be warm again . . . .* Icicles of chilly air stabbed her, as Nancy gently folded back the covers of the bed, retrieving the towels that had lost their warmth, and covering her mother with the freshly heated ones. Diane shivered at the contrast. Her bones were cold as steel pipes buried in the Arctic, but her flesh was hot as sunburn. *Such a strange sensation . . . .*

It was worse during the day, when Diane refused most medication. She wanted a sense of *time* throughout the day. She hated to be essentially unconscious twenty-four hours a day. It was better to sacrifice the pain relief, to endure the cold, and thus preserve a sense of rhythm in what had become her life.

Although it hurt to move, the nurses insisted that Diane shift position in bed frequently, so that her skin did not break down: bedsore prevention. Many days, they moved Diane themselves, using a combination of small and large decorative bed pillows to fashion a variety of well-supported, fairly comfortable recumbent positions. They massaged her limbs gently with warmed essence of lavender to soothe her spirits.

The cold abated minimally, as the warmth soaked slowly

through her thin, vein-scrawled arms and into the sinewy strands of muscle tissue. Yet, the blankets and warm towels could not touch the chill of her bones. *Glacier bones . . . those that never feel the sun's warmth.* Truly, the only thing that penetrated these bones was the narcotic cocktail. *But not now. No drugs now, please.*

Diane opened her eyes to mere slits, watching as Nancy smoothed the comforter across the bed, then stooped to grab the cooled towels from the chair, intending to return them to the dryer for the next round of warmth. The cling of Nancy's turtleneck revealed the swell of life within, yet Diane noted her daughter's growing belly with dispassion. Surprised by the absence of joy regarding this miracle, Diane struggled to understand *why?* She'd expected to feel jubilant, if and when Nancy ever became pregnant. Now that she was, and now that it was evident, Diane was puzzled that she should feel so little—nothing bad, but nothing good, either—at the prospect of another grandchild.

But she was still too cold, too exhausted, to give it more thought. *That* was the problem with the pain medicine, Diane knew. She had to give up *thinking*. It required too much concentration. Whenever she tried, she'd fall into a dreamless sleep, but it wasn't really sleep at all. It was a choice of *being* in the moment, or *contemplating* a situation. But Diane could not do both. Not these days. So, she chose *being* with Nancy, her expectant child, who did not notice her mother's narrowed, watchful eyes.

Picking up a dust cloth that lay abandoned on the windowsill, Nancy wiped the ledge, then lowered and closed the blinds, running the cloth along the curved strips of vinyl. She turned away to wipe the tall chest that stood in the far corner of the bedroom. Head-on or from the back, Nancy appeared no different than ever. In profile, however, the gentle swell of her tummy shared the secret of a new life on the way. At sixteen weeks gestation, Nancy had regained her energy. She claimed to enjoy better sleep at night, and fully active days.

Diane smiled softly as the long man's shirt fluttered with each of Nancy's movements, the sensuous, Madonna-like curve fully revealed by the clingy knit turtleneck beneath. It was this image that Diane sustained throughout the day, and into her dreams that night.

Tuesday, January 20
3:45 PM

"John, do you have a minute?"

"Sure, Stu. I'm on my way out, too."

"Good, good. I just wanted to thank you for what you've started over at the University. It's a good research project for multi-specialty collaboration."

John Williams smiled at the notion of collaboration among the specialists. "Hate to tell you, Stu, but it's more like a turf battle than a multi-specialty collaboration. When research dollars and first-author credit are what drive you up the academic ladder of success, there isn't a lot of friendly collaboration. But the Barrett Center has some genius negotiators, and they know how to move the process along, despite the personalities."

"Glad to hear it. I'm not cut out for that academic medicine rigmarole." Stuart Adler paused at the breezeway adjoining the parking garage. "John, I wanted to talk with you about my retirement."

"Okay. You caught a lot of us by surprise with that announcement," John acknowledged.

"It's the best thing for me, for us. We're moving to a small farmhouse between here and Indianapolis. It's got a great pond, lots of woods beyond the fields, and about eighty acres that we'll lease for planting."

"So Jeannie is retiring, too?"

"No," Stu shook his head slowly. "But one of her experienced nurses will manage the staff for our Cincinnati patients. Jeannie can always commute the hour to check up on things. And she wants to expand services to Lawrenceburg, Batesville, and the rural community just outside Indy."

John considered this news with unease. Was Stu planning to

contact Ron Albers, who lived a discreet but commutable distance? Then, a flash of memory struck, and John recalled the one-sided phone conversation he'd overheard in the changing room last summer. *They must be working together.* "What about the people you two were helping, um, informally?"

"We're re-grouping about that project." Stu looked away as he spoke the words. "Getting this medication to the people out there who need it is crucial, John. We're working out supply issues, within the law. Shades of gray and God willing, of course.

"But what you're doing will help us—patients, doctors, all of us—in the long run, John. I didn't want to tackle that monster bureaucracy. Anyway, Jeannie and I just want you to know how grateful we are that you're doing it." Stu turned to meet his partner's stare.

John foundered for words, unprepared for this conversation. "I don't know what to say. I'm glad I can do something helpful. I just wish it were in time for my mother-in-law."

"Diane's a great lady," Stu stated with admiration. "Her family is her treasure and her legacy. I need to remember to tell her that."

"You still visit?"

"Not professionally. I just enjoy touching base once in a while. How is she this week?"

It was John's turn to look away, but he guarded against any expression of shame. "I haven't seen her this week." *Or last week, the week before, or the week before that,* he chided. "Sandy left me a message that she has good days and bad days. Diane refuses to go to Hospice."

"Yes, it's hard to take, but some people truly need to be at home, to die peacefully. I'm sure it's hard on Sandy and Nancy."

"Yeah, it is."

Silence lingered a moment beyond comfort. John fumbled with his keys, then extended a hand to his partner. "Well, thanks Stu. I'll see you tomorrow; T-minus three days and counting?"

"Absolutely!" Stu agreed heartily, shaking hands firmly, returning John's gesture as if it were an absolution. "No more of these early mornings, overnight calls, meetings, or personnel is-sues for me."

"Later, then."

Too many words remained unspoken; so many things were left unsaid, as was often the way of men—and women. The men brushed through the doors to the parking garage, and were greeted by a blast of Arctic air that froze their lungs, but not their hearts.

Wednesday, January 28
2:30 PM

What was it that made her reconsider? Wasn't this the only position she could take? Obviously not, for Nancy entertained second thoughts, self-doubt, and—could it *be?* —reconciliation.

Perhaps the source of this dissonance was the short, dreary days of January. Or, was it the snowball effect of hormonally driven vulnerability, common to pregnant women? It certainly didn't help matters that a barrage of people conspired to revise her perceptions of life, promises, and marriage. Possibly, it was Nancy's growing sense that she had already lost her mother. Probably, the rare winter beauty of the day rekindled memories of a year ago—*that long ago?* —of the day that she and John had skied to the Madeira Kroger after a blizzard. Against the bright azure sky, daz-zling diamonds of ice had glittered from snow-burdened trees. The effect had been magical, romantic, like a fairyland. *Which of these devils is trying to change my mind, or my heart?* Nancy wondered.

Most likely, her reconsideration was born of *all* of it.

Loneliness gnawed at her heart, despite the companionable wiggle of the melon-size creature nestled beneath her sweatshirt. What Nancy now called loneliness had begun as a mere twinge of . . . *something,* an odd mélange of guilt and regret? But for whom was she lonely? Certainly, it couldn't be her husband; she didn't exactly *miss* him. However, in an anticipatory manner, she missed her mother, and cried easily, aware that tonight, tomorrow, some-day soon, her mother would let go.

Sandy had been traveling for a fortnight, and was due home this evening. She'd be good company, better than the friendly strangers who'd been hired to attend her mother.

Until then, when Sandy returned, what? Restless, Nancy stared at the phone for nearly twenty minutes, debating. She felt compelled to call, but wondered what response she might receive. Why should he take her call? *Would* he take the call? And really, *why should she even call?*

Taking the cordless phone in hand, she walked from her mother's bedside to the guest bedroom. For the past two weeks, this was where she'd stayed, since her mother wasn't speaking and couldn't forbid it. And Sandy was out-of-town, not in a position to know about it. Had her mother asked, Nancy would have complied and returned to her furnished apartment. But that hadn't happened. Nancy harbored a small hope that this gesture of defiance, staying at her mother's home, would make her mother speak. But that hadn't happened, either.

Walking to the closet, Nancy opened the door, and reached for the box of letters on the lower shelf. The unopened Christmas gift, which Sandy had initially stowed in their mother's closet, was now next to the letterbox. She closed the closet door, not wanting to look at the gift.

Why did she miss John? The sensation had crept up silently, stealthily, startling her once she acknowledged its presence. As the twinges of that lonely, guilty, regretful sorrow grew to the point that she could not deny what it was, Nancy attempted to emblazon the cool ember of anger toward John. She failed.

All she could conjure was sadness, borne of the sense that her family had crumbled. She wanted to feel excitement about the birth of her baby, but found herself wondering if God might spare her mother for the soul of this unborn, and unknown child. Certainly, she didn't know this wriggly creature the way she knew her mother.

How can I even think such a thing! Guilt clenched her heart as the thought became conscious, especially when the baby stirred vigorously, perhaps in protest. *How can I ever be a decent mother, entertaining thoughts of barter: my child's life for that of my mother?* She felt disgusted with herself, certain that she didn't deserve the life growing within, offering a prayer of repentance for the thought and gratitude for the child.

Sprawling on the bed, Nancy lifted the lid from the box, and opened the top letter. The envelopes were undated, but the letters were. She unfolded the stiff stationery, which smelled like home: the same scent that had greeted her each time she'd entered the house after a long trip. Strangely, she'd never noticed that smell day-to-day. It was only in leaving for days at a time that she'd return and notice the familiar fragrance of *their* house.

And now, that which had offered homecoming comfort bore the unmistakable stench of reproach. She believed that, somehow, she deserved it; she must withstand it.

This letter was dated two weeks previous, perhaps the most recent from John, one of many stashed inside the floral photo box. But Sandy had been gone for the duration; no one else had intercepted and stowed such mail. Had John simply stopped writing?

Setting the letter on the bed, unread, Nancy proceeded to open all of the envelopes, fifteen—no sixteen—of them. She arranged each letter by date, just as her orderly husband would have done, and began with the first. It was dated November fifth, and essentially requested a meeting to talk. She then opened the second letter.

November 8
Dear Nancy,

I'm sorry about last week at your mom's dinner. I know you feel strongly about getting your mother all the treatment she needs, and I want you to know that I won't stand in the way of her taking the treatments. I've met a woman who has taken these treatments for other reasons. Having seen her at a point that made her want to die, specifically with the help of Dr. Kevorkian, I can't do something that will take away the one thing that allows her to live. She has two young children, and she needs this treatment to function.

Maybe you think I'm cruel to have come to this conclusion based on someone other than your mother. Maybe you think I'm cold or disloyal. I don't feel that way at all, but I can understand how you might perceive me that way.

Nancy, family is the most important thing to me, and you and your family are all I've got in this world. For that reason, as well, I won't interfere with your mother's treatment. If anyone deserves the respite from her illness, it's your mother. I hope she reconsiders her decision. She wrote me a note, indicating that she intended to stop treatment. If it helps her, if she's willing to take any risks, she should do it.

I still believe that it's something I can't participate in directly, but I won't stop it. There are a lot of people who need it. The medicine isn't exactly stolen, but I still struggle with knowing that it's being provided illegally. I'll live with that struggle, but I don't want this situation to jeopardize our marriage.

Please call me. We need to talk this out, in person. Please come home. If you'd rather meet somewhere else, that's fine. You can let me know when you call.

Love,
John

The letter didn't move her, but Nancy noticed that she felt warmer toward John—until the last two paragraphs. She couldn't exactly pinpoint what it was about those closing words that struck an irritable chord. Setting the letter aside, she picked up the next one.

November 9
Dear Nancy,
I know you're flying until the tenth, but I wanted to write as soon as possible. It might be better if you have time to think about what I have to say, and then I'd like to talk with you. . . .

Nancy skimmed the letter. Homesick sentiment blossomed in

the presence of John's familiar scrawl. He'd outlined the same general beliefs as in the earlier letter, and repeated the request to meet.

A sudden lurch by the baby, as if startled from sleep, forced the explosion of thought—no, a reminder—that John didn't even know of this baby's existence! Sandy had sworn not to tell John, not that Nancy had cared so much. Sandy had been firm: this was Nancy's news to share, and Sandy hoped that no one else would take that from her sister. Nancy understood this as a dare to speak with John. However, she misunderstood the subtext of Sandy's message. This was much more than an entreaty to get the couple speaking. But Nancy hadn't understood that at the time.

She sighed heavily, acknowledging her mulishness, as well as Sandy's insistent, persistent patience. Now, it occurred to Nancy that her stubbornness had been a burden for Sandy, and probably for their mother as well.

The fourth and fifth letters were dated mid-November, and Nancy wondered if they contained more of the same, a repetition of John's earlier notes.

They did not, and they were not. In these letters, John shared an inspiration he'd had about a project with the Barrett Cancer Center, as well as the UC Anesthesia Department and the UC Neurology Department's Sleep Clinic. Nancy's attention became riveted on the details, of which there were few. He'd asked to negotiate a joint grant-writing collaboration, initially regarded with skepticism and bad humor. Politics ruled the course of grant application, and interdepartmental cooperation was not part of the system's culture or code. Competition was the name of the game there, John wrote, and it was only when he'd approached the multi-hospital, managed care leadership that he'd found his foot in the door. The players hadn't come to the table willingly. They rapidly faulted John for claiming this could work, when he'd never applied for a grant, nor managed a research project.

Nancy read on, intrigued that he would push such a strategy. *Why not keep it within St. Catherine's?*

John's next letter answered that question. St. Catherine's

didn't have the research resources or the academic hot shots needed to win grant money. *Win* was the operative word, apparently, as this was a contest for big bucks from the National Institutes of Health.

Nancy reread the letters, understanding that her husband had taken the ball and run with it—on his own court, one that allowed him to pursue the possibility of treatment for many people, within an entirely legal, ethical, morally correct framework. It was a plodding process that wouldn't help her mother, but it might broaden the circle of beneficiaries. Stu Adler had been content to soothe his grief on a small scale, stretching neither his imagination, nor his circle of influence, as John now struggled to do.

A flicker of pride kindled appreciation of this man who was willing to *struggle* for people like her mother, if not her specifically. Nancy marveled at his perseverance, not only in the face of that Goliath proposal, but despite *her* stubborn refusal to communicate—and still, he sent letters: updates about committee progress, people at work, and always, always, always a request to meet, to talk, to work things out, for her to come home.

At that, irritation crept back into the equation, but she found herself going back to the parts of the letters that inspired admiration, even affection. Then, she became annoyed with herself. Why did she seek anything positive about her husband? She could justify her actions, her decision to leave their marriage, if she sustained feelings of anger, hurt, and betrayal.

Why am I reading these letters, anyway? Nancy intuited that she sought a reason to reconnect. As she permitted introspection, forcing herself to read all but the last of the sixteen letters, she grudgingly admitted gratitude that this child's father was a man of moral courage and commitment.

And then, she cringed, perceiving the apparent lack of her own. She could've at least agreed to see him; she could've at least agreed to verbally duke it out. But she didn't, she hadn't. It was easier that way, for her. *No,* she corrected silently, *there is nothing easy about any of this.*

Impulsively, Nancy reached for the phone, amazed that she

had trouble recalling the number, nodding approval when it flashed in memory, once again.

The line rang, and rang, and rang. Perhaps John was early out that day. If so, his cell phone would be turned off and stashed in his locker. Clicking off, Nancy rapidly dialed home. *Home.* She could scarcely call it that anymore.

The phone rang twice before the answering machine picked up, John's voice greeting her on tape. With a stab of fear, Nancy clicked off the phone. What would she say to him, anyway? Really, why would he even want to talk with her? She'd rebuffed him for so long, wouldn't she deserve the same treatment? The pile of letters, the last one sent just two weeks ago, suggested that she was mistaken, that John would not refuse her call.

But she couldn't force herself to redial. She felt hopeless, having gone beyond the point of return. She could not face him.

Nancy set down the phone and stretched out on the bed, settling one of the pillows beneath her belly, another supporting her right leg. She piled two sham-covered pillows behind her neck and back, and wiggled into a comfortable position on her left side. The baby wriggled in turn, mirroring Nancy's effort to find a comfortable position. Taking the letters in hand, she opened the most recent one, anticipating the return of homesickness as she read John's scrawl, the comforting scent of *home* rising from the page, at once tantalizing and unapproachable; but only because of her own choices.

5:40 PM

John Williams glanced through the mail piled on the kitchen table. He'd just returned from a tense meeting with various department directors at St. Catherine's, and looked forward to a frozen dinner and a beer tonight. After which he'd return to his reading and proposal writing.

Such was his leisure, for he'd never envisioned the monumental commitment this project would demand. The toughest part was being the outsider, and dealing with other physicians who sought less to collaborate than to stake out the best territory in the grant process. God knew the gladness he shared with Stu Adler, that he hadn't followed the rocky, avalanche-prone path of academic medicine. God also knew that John Williams was not cut from such leathery hide as academic physicians.

Across the room, the flashing indicator on the answering machine announced one message. Tapping the play button, John saw the caller's number flash on the small screen: Diane Cavanaugh's number. His heart leaped, for he knew that Sandy was still out-of-town. *Could Nancy be calling?* Surely Diane wasn't calling anyone these days.

He flushed with momentary embarrassment that he hadn't seen Diane in months. He'd spoken with her once on the phone, after Nancy had moved out of her mother's condo. *If not Sandy or Diane, could it be Nancy?*

In the single second that these thoughts crossed through con- sciousness, his heart incurred another bruise. The only sound that played from the machine was its own beep, signaling that the caller had left no message.

Chapter Thirty-Three

RITES OF PASSAGE

Friday, February 6
5:45 PM

"We'll go right now," Mary Claire insisted. "You're not going to play Cowardly Lion anymore." She slapped a black suede Stetson over a red angora ski cap, the latter for warmth, the former for effect.

"I just want to enjoy a nice dinner out, Mary Claire. Don't wreck it for me."

"No dinner until you introduce me. No buts about it."

"But I'm buying," John attempted, hearing the voice of his now-dead aunt in Mary Claire's declaration, *no buts about it.*

"Of course you are, but I won't be a first rate dinner companion, what with missing Chuck all these weeks in Chicago, and *now* being refused an introduction. Come on, I'll do all the talking. Just let me meet this woman!"

"She may not feel up to company. We should call first."

"Bullshit. We'll leave if she doesn't want company. You just want to see who else is there."

John smiled and sighed, startled both that Mary Claire read him so accurately, and that it didn't hurt when she called his game. Perhaps it would be easier to fulfill the obligation, which is what it felt like, if spunky Mary Claire went along for the ride. He wondered if Diane would be up for such a ride. Fifteen minutes with Mary Claire was like taking a spin on The Beast, that wild and wooly roller coaster at King's Island.

"We're outta' here Doc!"

The Empress Mary Claire ruled, and the evening visit reigned memorable. Diane was alert, even sociable, enjoying a good day, and a better evening. Nancy was flying a trip, a small miracle for which John Williams was grateful; one challenge was enough for an evening.

Sandy and her Thanksgiving boyfriend, Tom, played off Mary Claire's vivacious, contagious humor. It had been too many weeks since Diane had laughed, a blessing that required a prayer of gratitude, and nearly everyone in the room responded silently within those moments of grace.

John Williams might have offered a similar prayer, were he a praying man. Beyond the memorized prayers of childhood, he did not pray, and certainly did not know how to start a conversation with God.

Yet, that night, he'd walked through fire without being consumed. It was the beginning of several points of contact, brief encounters with a soul soon departing, often with Mary Claire in tow; but eventually alone, on the strength of love, unconditional love.

That was the real gift Mary Claire presented.

Wednesday, February 25
4:00 PM

"Okay. Whenever you're ready."

John Williams nodded. It had been months since he'd practiced stall recoveries, a long while since Bob Burke had recommended a break from IFR training. John had flown a bit during the fall, "for the fun of it," as prescribed by his instructor. But this clear, February day, he was under the hood, ready for a round of stall-recoveries.

Pulling back the yoke a hair, John watched the altimeter needle and attitude indicator vibrate and inch upward. Sustaining firm pressure, he anticipated the increased vibration in the yoke, which would soon shudder. He visualized mentally how the scene would unfold: he'd hold tightly to the yoke, pull back to raise the nose of the aircraft gradually, steadily, and keep his eyes glued to the instrument panel, watchful that the wings remained level at all times. Then, when the stall horn shrieked, he'd gently slide the shuddering yoke forward to correct the pitch of the plane, again keeping the wings level, his eyes on the panel. He would not imagine the ground below. He would not picture the plane vis-à-vis the ground at the stall point, suspended in momentary limbo. He'd complete the prescribed method of stall recovery, which would silence the horn and calm the shuddering protest, as the plane receded from the critical angle of attack. He'd done this before, successfully. He'd do it again, fearlessly, for he'd climbed taller mountains and walked through hotter fires in real life. Real Life.

And thus it happened, just as imagined.

"Nice," Bob Burke commented mildly. "Very nice."

"Let's try it, again," John insisted.

6:00 PM

"I'm glad you came, John," Diane rasped, barely audible. "Mary Claire?"

John chuckled good-naturedly. "Nope, just me, today. I was over at the airport and thought I'd stop by."

Diane nodded and closed her eyes. "That's okay."

John had seen this before, with Mary Claire. At first, such lulls had precipitated anxiety. His pulse would race, his heart would pound, and his thoughts would flit every which way, all a jumble. He'd labor for what to say or do, and he'd fight the impulse to flee quickly.

But Mary Claire would just grab his hand and take over. She'd describe the ice-crusted trees, or she'd explain the complexities of the character she was to play next, or she'd read passages from the thin volumes of inspiration on Diane's bedside table. Once,

Mary Claire even talked about her mother. Sometimes, she just sat quietly and hummed gentle hymns, the melody familiar, the words long lost to her cousin. Mary Claire's spontaneous a cappella rendering of southern spirituals and sacred lullabies soothed all present, wrapping them in a tranquil serenity that John did not think possible, given the ominous threat of death.

It would not have been his way, to sing softly in the presence of others, but Mary Claire's unselfconscious presence allowed him to feel comfort, *comfortable,* in the company of a beloved woman, now dying.

John found a path that allowed him to *be* with Diane. He conveyed updates about the research proposal, which sparked her interest and fueled her fight against medication-induced somnolence. In detail, he'd share the whos, whats, and whys of the project. Yet, Diane persisted in asking, "When?" That, he could not answer. "Soon, I hope."

This visit, John also shared his successful flight, confidence of the conqueror warming him to expansiveness. Diane's eyes fluttered open as he detailed the initial stall-recovery. John discerned his mother-in-law's intent effort to stay with the story, and embellished in the style of a practiced raconteur. The role was not familiar to John, but its effect compelled him to continue, to tell the story deeply, descriptively, emotionally.

"What an accomplishment!" Diane whispered in excitement. "I'm thrilled for you."

"Thanks." It felt amazingly invigorating to share the milestone, thus marking the event. John believed, at that sustained moment of contact, that he'd never known Diane better. As well, he'd learned something about himself.

Diane closed her eyes now, unable to resist the pull of the narcotics, surrendering to that netherworld of semi-consciousness. Her lips remained parted, the hint of a satisfied smile playing at the corners.

John recognized her exhaustion, yet opted to stay until the evening nurse arrived. Borrowing from Mary Claire's repertoire, he reached for one of the volumes of inspirational essays, this one actually a collection of autobiographical stories. Settling back in the chair, extending his legs to a tapestry footstool near the bed, John allowed the book to fall open randomly. The story was titled, "Beyond Fear."

Taking a deep breath, he read the first line. "Leap, and the net will appear."

Saturday, February 28
1:15 AM

Nancy felt like an eavesdropper. Her father and a serious, saintly looking man, dressed in a full-length, brown robe and sandals, strolled through a fragrant labyrinth of vibrantly flowering shrubs. The saint spoke intently, but too softly for Nancy to hear.

Then, her father stopped and placed both hands on the older man's arm. The bearded and balding man swung around, apparently surprised by the touch. "What?" he asked.

"So, you're saying that it's like purgatory, a place to wait and learn, until it's time to take action, when ready."

The saint frowned, perplexed. That was not at all what he'd tried to convey. How could he make it clear? "Actually, it's more like limbo, neither of heaven nor earth. And it's not a wayside resting place, where one waits for insight or readiness."

He paused, then, concentrating on each word, determined to speak precisely. "In terms of time, which is so different from what you're used to, it's like a flash of light—over in a second. And this limbo-like space between thought and action is where choice, or intention, takes place. You have to be very brave to go there. The key is to remember that you're *never* there alone."

✦

She could see the coastline, in the dream. It was time to descend for final approach. Yet, she struggled to recall *how* to fly an approach. It seemed so long since she'd done one. Years?

Her father was no longer on the plane. She was alone, except for the special cargo nestled safely in the hold.

It was up to her, it seemed, though she knew perfectly well there were two pilots in the cockpit. Why, then, was it *she* who had to land this plane safely? In good weather or bad, with or without instruments, she must fly the plane—*but, why me?*

Even in the face of questions that lacked answers, she must take the active, an aviation term that indicated a commitment to either take off or enter the final approach. It was a scary prospect, landing this plane, seemingly having forgotten all that she might have been taught about shooting an approach.

This was a moment of truth, a time for faith. She must have faith in herself, but more importantly, faith in God. With a breath of determination, Nancy twisted the handle and pulled open the cockpit door. With a gasp of shock, Nancy stepped through the doorway.

There was no one at the controls. The pilots were nowhere to be seen. A glance at the panel indicated that the autopilot was engaged, and that the aircraft was descending at the steady rate of five hundred feet a minute.

By the grace of God, it was now up to her. She climbed into the left seat, not her usual spot in such an aircraft, for the First Officer always sat to the right of the Captain. Placing the headset over her ears, Nancy rechecked the instrument panel, noting the plane's altitude, attitude, pitch, fuel, speed, and distance from target. Puffing into the microphone of the headset, the whisper of breath in her ears confirming that it worked, Nancy gripped the yoke with her left hand, and turned off the autopilot, continuing the steady descent toward earth. Straight ahead, parallel lights marked the runway. Although she did not know exactly where she'd be landing, the path was clearly marked.

Announcing her intent to land, with airport in sight, Nancy heard the echo of her father's jubilant glee, "By George, dear God, I think she's *finally* got it!"

Chapter Thirty-Four

AN INCOMPLETE CIRCLE

Wednesday, March 19
11:50 AM

Rain drizzled to form a veil of privacy for the mourners, gathered in a huddle of black overcoats, umbrellas shielding them from heaven's tears. Cued by the words and motions of the priest, the group shifted collectively to free right hand from pocket, and in synchrony, each then touched forehead, heart, left shoulder and right. Afterward, the group slowly dispersed.

Within moments, there were only two women left. They embraced as if about to collapse. As the one to the left turned in profile, the man beneath the ancient pin oak lost his breath in a gasp that approximated pain. She was pregnant, probably several months along.

John Williams felt sick with regret, and fought mentally about leaving without approaching Nancy, now round with child. *Why didn't she tell me?* he wondered, puzzled that she hadn't offered him at least that consideration.

Their separation had not been so much bitter as it had been complete. When Nancy left, she had dropped out of his life as completely as if she'd died. Although, truthfully, John had felt as if it was *he* who had died.

A recurrent dream swirled in memory, as John contemplated the scene before him, from beneath the bud-stubbed pin oak tree. His sixth grade teacher, a nun, visited on those nights that he dreamed. In comfort, the nun placed her arm around him and said, "You know, John, this isn't all your fault." Then, he became the young boy whose mother had died. He answered the nun, "I know. God has another plan for Nancy." To which the nun replied, "Perhaps he has another plan for you." That was it, the whole dream, until a few nights ago.

At the time, he'd felt himself leave the heavy, unconscious sleep. His eyes had remained closed, but he'd felt alert, as if he could wake for the day. Intuition told him that it was nowhere near morning. In anticipatory consciousness, he saw his mother moving toward him in slow motion, her full-skirted, yellow and white striped dress floating in the meadow breeze; a broad, proud smile creasing gentle laugh lines around her mouth and eyes.

John felt completely peaceful as she passed from the waving pasture grasses; through the bricks and mortar of the house, her footsteps silent as she crossed the plank floor to have a seat on his bed, just as she'd done when he was a child, part of their bedtime ritual of prayers and a review of the day. Her presence did not frighten him. His only fear was that this vision would end. It was a wonderful dream, and he wasn't ready to awaken. He felt compelled to be still, to barely breathe, so that his mother wouldn't disappear.

She did not speak. She merely conveyed, with great intensity, her love for him and her maternal pride. John did not speak, either. He commanded himself to be silent, to go with it, to prolong it, not to spoil this visit with words. It was as if they were able to communicate only feelings. He nestled within the peaceful sensation of perfect love, such that cannot be of this world.

He did not want this interlude to end; he was spellbound, transfixed, by the mystical power of this spiritual encounter. Warm tears welled in his eyes before overflowing their banks, silently tracing the curve of his cheeks, dripping into his ears and onto his pillow. Still, he was not sad, and he willed himself to stay with the vision, to lap up the love conveyed as brightly as the sun.

Was he expected to do something, or say something? He

waited, unsure of his role in this edge of consciousness drama. In the chilly bluster that represented his life, here-and-now, conviction rooted deep in his soul: Whatever this dream or vision was, however it might be defined, he needed *it* as much as he needed to breathe. It was as close to spiritual conversion as John Williams had ever experienced. He believed—discerned—that something was expected of him, *but what?* The peacefulness of the moment was almost feeding him, nourishing him in preparation for some sort of marathon, or perhaps an endurance test. The specifics were not revealed. *Just stay.* If his mother remained close, he would come to know what he must do, and she would somehow provide him the capacity to *do* whatever "it" was.

Gradually, he emerged into a wakefulness that could not sustain the image of his mother's presence. He awakened with an acute sense of loss, as if he were twelve-years-old again and had just lost his mother. Aware that the event was significant, if not aware of its meaning, John glanced at the red glow of the alarm clock digits. Perhaps linking this phenomenal dream with the time would somehow preserve its impact, or impart its implication. The clock read 1:13 AM.

Fitful tossing amidst the sea of sheets and blankets stole the next four hours, as he tried to reclaim the joyful peace of his mother's visit. With great distraction throughout the next day, he pondered the meaning of her call.

Two days later, with a night in between that was disappointing because it was dreamless, John spotted a photograph of Diane Cavanaugh, smiling from the newspaper's obituary section. *Diane.* A pang of sadness became an ache of grief in his chest.

He set down the newspaper, and found himself in the unfamiliar pose of the prayerful, a student again at Madonna of the Hills. Reverting to his parochial training, John quietly prayed for the repose of Diane's soul. *Eternal rest grant unto her, oh Lord . . . .*

John wrapped up the prayer, surprised that he could even recall the words, so long had it been since he'd recited them. Gently, he folded back the newspaper and read every line of the obituary honoring his mother-in-law. "Preceded in death by her husband, James "Iron Ace" Cavanaugh. Survived by two sons, James (Annie) of Denver, CO, and Steven (Elizabeth) of Washington, DC, two daughters, Nancy (John) Williams and Sandy Cavanaugh, both of Cincinnati, and five grandchildren."

Astonished to see that Nancy had linked him to her loss, publicly recognizing him as her husband, John reread the section. Perhaps Sandy had helped prepare the obituary, and was now paying the price for reminding Nancy of John's place in her life. Not normally superstitious, John wondered if this was a sign, a directional arrow to proceed down this path once more: to try, at least, to gain Nancy's attention, if not her affection.

And five grandchildren, he mused. Was one of Nancy's sisters-in-law expecting a third child? Surely Diane or Sandy would have mentioned it, for babies were front-page news in the Cavanaugh family.

The sharp *brrrrrng!* of the telephone jarred him from his reverie at the kitchen table, and he dropped the newspaper to answer the insistent ring. It was Sandy.

"I just saw the article about your mom. I'm really sorry, Sandy," John said softly, at a loss to know what else to say, treading the safe path of traditional, simple condolences.

In a flash, he recalled how many people had repeated those words when his mother had died, and how empty the words had felt. It had been the emotion heard in a wavering voice, or the painfully puffy, bloodshot eyes that had conveyed genuine sympathy to a twelve-year-old boy. He wished he could fathom words that might have comforted him then, so that he could offer them to Sandy, now. *What would Mary Claire say?*

"Thanks," Sandy responded steadily. She paused, and John paused, allowing an uncomfortable moment to pass. "Listen, John, the reason I'm calling is to let you know that I hope you'll come for the service, and to come to the clubhouse near Mom's condo afterward. If she's in town, maybe Mary Claire could come, too. She was such good company for Mom. Ha! She's good company for all of us. Anyway, I know it's tough to get away from work, but if you *can* get away . . ."

John closed his eyes, touched by Sandy's wish to include him, as well as her willingness to give him an out. He risked exposure to fresh grief—as well as to Nancy—in a public milieu, and fear raised its talons within the viscera of his gut. He hated funerals and wakes. Still, he didn't want to hurt Sandy, and he wanted to honor Diane. He would've preferred to do so privately, not necessarily at a funeral home, a church, or a cemetery. What could he say to Sandy? *Perhaps Mary Claire will go with me . . .*

John heard himself saying that he was glad to be included, but voiced concern that his presence might not be universally appreciated. He acknowledged cowardice, as if he were asking for a note of excusal.

But Sandy, for whatever reason, chose to hear it differently, more as a need to have an invitation, or to have her reiterate the request. And she did so, willingly.

"John," she stated firmly, "You're still a member of our family. Mom was part of your family; I'm part of your family. Nancy is part of your family, too, although she isn't acting that way. I'm not saying that you and Nancy need to pretend or play games for appearance-sake. You don't have to say or do anything. But I wouldn't feel this was complete, somehow, unless you were there, too. I can't explain it." She laughed, as if flustered to be rattling on.

John laughed sympathetically, wanting to agree to everything she asked so as not to inflict another hurt.

"I'll come, Sandy. But I'll probably stay in the background. I don't feel right sitting up front with immediate family, given what's going on between Nancy and me."

"I understand," Sandy said, generously. "I know this is a big thing to ask, John, but I'll feel better just knowing that you're somewhere in the crowd. Remember, Mom believed you were another son, and regardless of what's happened between you and Nancy, I know first-hand that Mom would want you to come, if you can." Sandy's last reference was intended to give him breathing room, and a means of saving face if—in the end—he simply couldn't make himself participate in the death ritual known as a funeral.

"I'll come, Sandy. I've already promised. My partners would expect me to take off for this. It's tomorrow, right?"

"Um-hmm." She paused, then added, "I'm sorry you had to find out about it from the newspaper, John. I'd hoped that Nancy . . . well, anyway. I decided that if she didn't call you by this morning, I'd call you, myself."

"Thanks, I appreciate it. And I'm really sorry. About everything."

"Me, too. But it isn't just for you to be sorry about, John."

"Thanks."

There was another lengthy pause, and John wondered if he'd be out of line to share the committee's progress on obtaining NIH funding to study Limbotryl. He took a chance, counting on Sandy's forgiving nature. "Maybe in a couple of weeks, we could talk about the NIH grant proposal? It's coming along a lot better, now that one of the UC docs is heading it and I'm more of a gopher and cheerleader."

He could see Sandy's smile on the other end through her warm words. "That's great, John. There are so many people this might help. I'd like to think that they wouldn't have to jump through hoops to get what they need."

There was more he wanted to ask, but he couldn't bring himself to form the words. "Well, I guess I'll see you tomorrow."

"I'll see you tomorrow," Sandy echoed. Then she answered the unasked question. "Nancy is doing okay with this. We've had a few months to be with Mom, and we've had a chance to get ourselves ready. You know, mentally. Emotionally. We'll be fine tomorrow. It'll just make everything complete, kind of like a family reunion, if you're there." After another brief pause, she added, "I don't know why I feel like I have to keep saying that."

"It's okay."

"Well, I'm heading out to pick up Jim and Annie from the airport."

"I'll let you go, then. Thanks for calling, Sandy."

John clicked off the phone and set it across the table, then straightened the jumbled newspaper so that he could see Diane's photograph clearly. Once again, he read the words that summed up her life too simply. A life was never that simple, and it was always much more than the jobs you had, the clubs you belonged to, or the family left behind. The value of a newspaper's column inch, always measured in dollars and cents, had little to do with the value of the man or woman whose life was reduced to mere words, a short resume, featured on the obituary page.

It occurred to him that he could have asked Sandy about the fifth grandchild. Well, he'd find out tomorrow.

Closing the newspaper, he stretched across the table for the phone and tapped in the number for the doc in charge of assigning tomorrow's cases. Explaining that he'd be in for a while, but that he'd be leaving at ten o'clock for Diane's funeral, John found himself contemplating some way to avoid the church service. It was clear that Sandy didn't expect him to attend the visitation tonight. Thank goodness. Maybe he could just go straight to the cemetery. He could be a little more anonymous there. It seemed a reasonable alternative to the oppressive incense and chant of the church service. And he would still honor his promise to Sandy. He might even gather the courage to come to the lunch afterward.

The phone interrupted, but John ignored it, allowing the caller to be identified by way of a message. It was Mary Claire, and John quickly clicked on the phone.

"I'm sorry, John," she said, her voice thick, her nose stuffy.

"Thanks. Me, too."

"I thought you might like some company tonight, at the visitation. I could go with you."

"Oh, God, Mary Claire. You don't have to do that."

"I want to. I loved Diane. And I love Sandy, too. You're my family, and I want to be with you for this. Unless you don't want me to come."

"No! It's not that," John interjected.

"What is it, then?"

"I don't know. I was just planning to go to the funeral, not the visitation."

"I see."

The pause extended for days, it seemed. One of the pair erred on the side of compassion, not wanting to push the other during this time of fresh grief; the other erred on the side of reticence, not knowing how to explain without seeming callous.

"Well, would it bother you—or do you think it would bother Sandy and Tom—if I went tonight, to the visitation?" Nancy's name was left unmentioned, but understood.

"No. They've practically adopted you, Mary Claire. They'd want you to be there. Sandy said that you were good for Diane, good for all of us."

The compliment unleashed a torrent of tears, snuffles, and choked back sobs. The silence returned and endured, but John remained calm, unperturbed. It occurred to him that perhaps Mary Claire's affection for Diane, several weeks new but deeply felt, required a ritual of closure to heal the wound of grief. What did it say about Mary Claire, that she connected so quickly, so deeply, with others? What did it say about him, that perhaps he didn't?

Mary Claire inhaled briskly, her voice stiff with determination. "It's okay, John. Some of us like this funereal drama. I should get a life, eh?"

John said nothing.

"Listen, if you want, I could go with you tomorrow?"

"That would be great, Mary Claire."

"Okay. Chuck's gone again, another show in Chicago, so I'm back to public transportation."

"I'll pick you up."

"Okay. Thanks."

"How about ten o'clock?"

"Fine." She snuffled noisily, yet kept her voice steady.

"I'll see you then, Mary Claire."

"Okay. And just in case you wondered, because we never get around to this sentimental shit, I love you, cousin."

John heard the click before he could respond. *I love you, too, Mary Claire.*

That had been yesterday.

Today, back in the gloomy whisper of a steady March rain, the gentle tumble of thunder intoned grief. John brooded over the news that the fifth grandchild was *his,* as in *his and Nancy's child.* He hadn't noticed anything different about Nancy from the back of the church, sheltered within the mob of mourners. Mary Claire must not have noticed either, for even at a time of such sorrow— or confusion—she'd have pointed out the obvious, the truth. Thank goodness she wasn't here to see this; that she'd let him take her home after the funeral Mass.

John tried to squelch the anger he felt at being left out of this momentous event, for he didn't want to approach Nancy angrily or accusingly. He reached for the joy he'd experienced at the first glimpse of Nancy's curved belly. Still, accusatory thoughts plagued every attempt to remain open, positive. If Nancy wouldn't tell him, why the hell didn't Sandy? Why didn't Diane tell him? Had Nancy instructed them to keep it a secret? Would either Sandy or Diane agree to that?

In the next moment, from out of nowhere, a brilliant flash of remembrance struck with the voltage of lightning. The dream in which his mother had visited was a prophecy and an assignment. Within that second of enlightenment, some questions were settled, and others spurred on, in turn. *Is this what she was telling me to do? To go to my wife? To go to my child?*

With resolve born of a need to heed his mother's call, John Williams ventured from the sanctuary of the oak tree and walked toward Nancy and Sandy Cavanaugh, relieved that Mary Claire was not a witness. It would be best to handle this alone.

Yet, he clearly discerned that he was not alone in this pursuit. With heartfelt intention, he framed a prayer to God—or perhaps more of a bargain with God: *Please, God, help me get my wife back; help me get Nancy back. Give me this child to love, and I'll remember You every day.* And he committed to a gentle fight for their marriage. It would be a long journey, and with a second flash of insight, John knew that *this* was the endurance course that his mother's visit was intended to fuel.

Confident that he was on the right path, though uncertain of Nancy's receptiveness, John picked up the pace of his stride, his soggy socks and leather shoes squishing with chilly rain. He watched Nancy and Sandy closely as he approached, alert for any signal of inhospitality, but resolved to persist, convinced that *this* was what he must do. It was expected of him. *It's the right thing to do,* he told himself. *I should've done it months ago, instead of letting Nancy think that I didn't love her enough to fight—face-to-face—for our marriage.*

Sandy saw him coming first. With a cautious smile of greeting to her brother-in-law, and a quick squeeze of her sister's elbow, Sandy turned to face John fearlessly. "I was hoping you'd be here," she said gently.

Nancy darted a glance of inquiry at her sister, then faced her husband with an air of stubborn determination. She nodded, not trusting herself to speak. This was not the occasion for reconciliation, to Nancy's way of thinking. She felt too raw, too bruised, to endure whatever John brought to the table today. Still, she felt a prick of wonder, as if her mother had somehow orchestrated this rendezvous, pestering Nancy from beyond the grave to deal with John and her marriage. Awkwardly, she looked away, embarrassed by the thought.

"I'll let you two talk," Sandy stated firmly. With a quick peck of Nancy's cheek and a friendly pat of her brother-in-law's arm, Sandy walked away, the fading squish-squash of her steps highlighting not only the Williamses' physical proximity, but also their emotional distance.

Nancy looked her husband in the eye, attempting a steady posture of challenge that failed to match her feelings inside: *Come closer, fight for me if you love me.* And also, *Don't get too close.* A third voice attempted harmony, whispering insistently, *Fly the plane, fly the plane, fly the plane.*

This was his moment, John knew. He began earnestly. "Nancy, I'm sorry, about a lot of things. I screwed up. I'm sorry about your mom, and I'm sorry about letting you down. I'm sorry that I didn't help your mom the way you wanted me to, and even more sorry that I didn't visit her very often, at least not until recently. I wish

I would've done things differently, especially with you, with *us*." He paused to catch his breath and to gauge her response, which was non-committal, but told the tale of an internal struggle.

Glancing down, seeking respite from the intensity of her startling blue eyes, John gathered his thoughts before trying, again. "I'm really sorry that, as a result of what I did and didn't do, I missed out on the news about the baby."

By risking vulnerability, John's openhearted confession was like the summer sun on a frozen mountain stream, cracking the ice, freeing the water from its wintertime prison. When he looked up at Nancy, who still did not speak, her eyes were pooled with tears that broke free, cascading silently down her fair cheeks.

Shaking a strand of dark hair from her face, Nancy failed the effort to speak, her lips taut, mouth open in a tormented slash, vocal cords paralyzed. She wanted to voice her own apology, but the risk of uttering words that might unleash the dam of emotions rendered her silent. Her father's voice called, *Fly the plane! Fly the plane!*

Taking an intuitive chance, John approached slowly, his own eyes filling in response to Nancy's mute pain. Praying that she would permit it, he gently folded his arms around her, acutely aware of the firm swell of her belly against his. He implored God to sustain this moment of union to eternity.

An unapologetic sob of gratitude breached his lips. John acquiesced, and even embraced the loss of control, emotionally in sync with his wife at this critical angle of attack, within this moment of reunification. Surely they would survive, the rift could be mended, for Nancy had not pushed him away; she hadn't run, so there was hope.

In turn, Nancy shuddered quiet sobs, surprised, even pleased that this man, her husband, could permit himself the loss of composure, the loss of perfect control.

As they embraced beneath a black umbrella, suspended in a moment that seemed well beyond ordinary life, the two—soon to be three—sustained an intimate interlude of personal surrender.

Relief swelled in Nancy's heart, as this emotional release included *both* of them for the first time. Yet, she felt confused as well. To compensate, she attempted to revive her defenses. Although the embrace reminded her of all the goodness in their marriage, forfeited when she'd slammed the door in John's face months ago, the prevailing issues hadn't been settled. She would not simply melt in his arms at his bidding: all forgive and forget. *No! Fly the plane! Fly the plane, dammit!*

Quickly sensing his wife's resistance, John tried again, determined to do what he must, aware that the brief thaw was a reprieve, not an absolution.

"Nancy, I know that this is a hard time for you, and that I can't expect you to run back just because *I'm* sorry about what's happened. Still, I'd like to try and work things out, to be together. I want to stay married to you, and I want us to live together. I want to be a part of your life, of our baby's life."

Nancy glanced up, startled at his reference to the baby as "ours." In the distance of the five months they'd been separated, Nancy had come to think of the baby as *hers*. A stab of indignation furrowed her brow; that John should feel free to claim the baby, too. Especially when his sole act of relationship with the baby had occurred five-and-a-half months ago, at conception. What had he done since then?

With a twinge of guilt, Nancy recalled the numerous letters John had sent, the phone calls she'd spurned; so furious was she at his refusal to support her mother's treatment, she'd ignored his every effort to reconcile. Now, she tried to convince herself that he'd earned her animosity. But she struggled with the notion, leaning toward the command of the dreams, the insistent pleas of her father—*Fly the plane! Fly the plane!*—and the wish of her heart to be with John, once again. She attempted to speak, but John interrupted, compelled to explain further, his voice at once urgent and earnest.

"I know this is going to sound weird, but I had a dream—actually one that kept coming back, and another one that was so *real*, it felt like it actually happened."

Nancy squinted her eyes, curious as to what was coming next, wondering if they had shared similar dreams.

"My mother actually sat on my bed—our bed—and even though she didn't say a word, I had this feeling that she wanted me to *do* something important, something difficult. Nancy, I think she wanted me to come for you. It was as if she was giving me the strength to *fight* to get you back in my life. You know how I've always said that I would never *pursue* a relationship? Well, I think my mother was trying to tell me that, maybe sometimes, it's necessary to take a risk and go after what I want. Or maybe that I owe it to both of us to go after what we've had for a lot of years. But not to just wait on the sidelines for someone else to make the moves."

Nancy found her voice, albeit hoarse. "When did you have this dream?"

"A few nights ago."

Nancy debated the wisdom of sharing her father's commentary from beyond, as well as her mother's words shortly before she died. She hesitated, fearing her husband's ridicule, as he approached life from a scientific, "prove it to me" perspective. She took a chance. After all, he'd already shared a dream that had provoked him to action.

"The night Mom died, she was more alert than usual. She refused to take any pain medicine, and kept saying that people were calling for her, that she had to take care of something. I thought she was seeing or hearing things, at first, that maybe she was hallucinating or disoriented. But she kept going on about the pretty lady who just smiled at her, but who wanted Mom to *do* something."

Nancy took a breath before continuing. "John, when I asked Mom if she recognized the lady, she said that she'd never met the woman, but that she'd seen her before. She couldn't remember the lady's name. Mom was really agitated—so frustrated that she actually cried. The nurse gave Mom some medication—a sedative, I think—and she cried herself to sleep. When she woke up, Mom said she remembered where she'd seen the woman: in a photo we keep on the shelves of the study. Your mother, John."

John backed away, slightly breathless, as if he'd been sucker punched. He could scarcely believe it. Had he never experienced the powerful encounter with his mother, had it not occurred so recently, he would have felt free to dismiss Nancy's story as Irish superstition. Not now.

"Nancy, when was the last time your mother mentioned the lady who looked like my mother?"

"Actually, it was several hours before she died, John."

"This may seem like a strange question, but what time was that?"

"I know exactly when it was because Sandy was looking through the photo albums we've worked on, and I was rewriting one of Mom's family stories from earlier this winter. We were trying to stay awake, since Mom had been so upset. She became agitated and started in about the lady, again. She couldn't let go of it, and it was impossible to comfort her."

John persisted. "But *when* was that?"

"It was 1:13 in the morning."

Epilogue

Next to the mound of earth, beneath a funeral canopy, vivid gold, violet, and white crocuses formed a Celtic cross in the earth. Encircled by orange-faced daffodils, the miniature memorial garden, so lovingly established, so well tended, was indeed lovely this March. It was a spot of sunshine that held forth the promise of new life, amidst the cold drizzle and grief-filled gloom.

Two drenched figures conversed animatedly for nearly an hour. A trio of spirits, one man and two women, witnessed the pair and smiled, as if recalling the days when the now-grown couple were children who needed reminders to come in from the rain, or to get a slicker to keep from getting soaked. The women spirits shared the same thought: those two were likely to catch pneumonia if they didn't get out of this chilly rain! The male spirit wondered why they didn't follow the post-funeral Irish tradition of gathering at the VFW hall, or at home, working the jaw over a couple pints of ale, or throwing some darts for diversion. They could at least go to a coffee shop.

But perhaps they couldn't talk privately, there. The male spirit turned to his mate. *Maybe they're having a marital chat, as you liked to call our arguments. It just isn't good manners to air your dirty laundry in public.*

Shhhh! hushed the female spirit beside him. *We'll miss something.*

The couple had stopped talking. *They're just looking at one another,* mused the second female spirit, who wore a full-skirted, yellow and white striped dress. *They're like teenagers having their first fight, wondering what to say to one another.*

The celestial voyeurs watched as the man gently touched the

woman's belly, resting his palm at the crest of the swell. The woman covered the man's hand with hers, then moved it from her life-filled tummy, clasping his bare fingers between suede gloves that covered her own. It was unclear if the woman did so because she didn't want the man to touch where the child was growing, or if she was simply trying to warm the man's hands, ready to leave for dry ground. The spirits turned toward the light above, both for reassurance, and to renew their petition.

What does the couple's future hold, the spirits questioned? Perhaps they'd fight it out successfully; perhaps they'd struggle for a while and give up in the end. Because the spirits shared a deeply felt connection with the troubled couple, they petitioned for the former possibility.

The spirit spouses recalled how they had weathered and endured the conflicts and struggles that come up in a forty-two year marriage. They smiled at the memory of his jokes about how it gets easier after forty-three years of marriage, or whatever was one year beyond the number of anniversaries they'd already celebrated. But that had always been a joke; one that he'd pointed toward himself, as in *he* was easier to live with after forty-three years.

The other female spirit, the one in the yellow and white dress, discerned another Truth. There was a lot of similarity between tending a garden and tending a marriage. What was right for a marigold wasn't right for a rose, or a hibiscus, or a mound of impatiens. Each partner was a gardener in the marriage. As such, each was required to understand the needs of whatever was being tended, whether plant or person. Just as important to remember, there were essential ingredients to growing a lush garden: nutrient rich, well-drained soil, water, sunlight—not too much, not too little—a hand to pull the encroaching weed, and a system of defense to ward off pests that threaten what had been sown.

Silently pleased with this philosophical muse, the celestial trio considered the marital equivalents of gardening, their thoughts intersecting rapidly, vigorously. In marriage, love was an action verb, not merely a feeling. It was the backbreaking tilling and amending of the soil. Romance might be an ingredient, though not an essential, they agreed—more like the decorative pieces one might find in a garden: nice accents, but of no consequence to the health of the flora and fauna. Critical ingredients, such as kindness and consideration, as well as the expressions of "Thank you," "I'm sorry," and "I love you," represented the rich compost of a well-tended marriage garden.

The three then turned their thoughts and gazes toward earth. The recently arrived spirit searched for an indication that their intentions had been heard, but the more established spirits knew that it was too soon. Below, the couple crossed slowly toward a stone path lined with sunbursts of daffodils. They rounded a trio of budding dogwood trees, still deep in conversation and unaware of their advocates nearby. Finally, they disappeared behind a stand of evergreens.

Relieved to have placed their words of petition within the care of the light, aware that only time, grace, and willingness would lead the couple to divine these principles of marital gardening, the three spirits stretched their arms toward their children in silent benediction, a salute of good luck, a prayer that their garden would flourish.

Printed in the United States
821100001B